The Last Caesar

www.transworldbooks.co.uk

THE LAST CAESAR

Henry Venmore-Rowland

BANTAM PRESS

LONDON · TORONTO · SYDNEY · AUCKLAND · JOHANNESBURG

TRANSWORLD PUBLISHERS
61–63 Uxbridge Road, London W5 5SA
A Random House Group Company
www.transworldbooks.co.uk

First published in Great Britain
in 2012 by Bantam Press
an imprint of Transworld Publishers

Copyright © Henry Venmore-Rowland 2012

Henry Venmore-Rowland has asserted his right under the Copyright, Designs
and Patents Act 1988 to be identified as the author of this work.

A CIP catalogue record for this book
is available from the British Library.

ISBNs 9780593068519 (cased)
9780593068526 (tpb)

Addresses for Random House Group Ltd companies outside the UK
can be found at: www.randomhouse.co.uk
The Random House Group Ltd Reg. No. 954009

The Random House Group Limited supports the Forest Stewardship
Council (FSC®), the leading international forest-certification organization.
Our books carrying the FSC label are printed on FSC®-certified paper.
FSC is the only forest-certification scheme endorsed by the leading
environmental organizations, including Greenpeace. Our paper
procurement-policy can be found at www.randomhouse.co.uk/environment.

Typeset in 11½/14¾pt Plantin Light by
Kestrel Data, Exeter, Devon.
Printed and bound by
CPI Group (UK) Ltd, Croydon, CR0 4YY.

2 4 6 8 10 9 7 5 3 1

To Simon and Peter, fishers of books and men.

To my parents, for their patience and advice.

To Edward, for reminding me how a story should begin.

To Flurry, for braving the snows and driving
me to Peter's door.

To all those at Transworld who made this
book become a reality.

HIBERNIA

BRITANNIA

Mona
(Anglesey)

GERMANIA
INFERIOR

Glevum
(Gloucester)

Camulodunum
(Colchester)

Colonia
(Cologne)

Isca Dumnoniorum
(Exeter)

Londinium
(London)

BELGICA

Bonna
(Bonn)

Argentorate
(Strasbourg)

LUGDUNENSIS

Vindonissa
(Windisch)

Oceanus
Atlanticus

AQUITANIA

Vesontio
(Besançon)

Lugdunum
(Lyons)

Vienne

Tolosa
(Toulouse)

Massilia
(Marseilles)

Narbo Martius
(Narbonne)

Forum Julii
(Fréjus)

TARRACONENSIS

Ercavica
(nr Santaver)

Tarraco
(Tarragona)

LUSITANIA

Toletum
(Toledo)

Saguntum
(Sagunto)

BAETICA

Corduba
(Córdoba)

N

0   miles   400

0   km   400

Dramatis Personae

Agricola, Gnaeus Julius*	Caecina Severus's best friend
Albanos	A rebel commander
Aulus	Caecina Severus's son
Bormo	A rebel commander
Carnunnos	A rebel commader
Capito, Fonteius*	The governer of Lower Germania
Domitia*	Julius Agricola's wife
Flaccus, Hordeonius*	A senator
Galba, Servius Sulpicius*	The governor of Hipsania Tarraconensis
Lugubrix	A merchant
Martialis	A rebel commander
Martianus, Icelus*	Servius Sulpicius Galba's freedman
Otho, Marcus Salvius*	The governor of Lusitania
Rufus, Verginius*	The governor of Upper Germania
Sabinus, Nymphidius*	The praetonian prefect
Salonina*	Caecina Severus's wife
Severus, Aulus Caecina* (later Aulus Caecina Alienus)	The quaestor of Hisptania Baetica
Tacitus, Cornelius	The governor of Hispania Baetica, father of the historian

Totavalas	A Hibernian slave
Tuscus, Gaius	The camp prefect of the Fourth Legion
Valens, Fabius⋆	A legate from Lower Germania
Vindex, Julius⋆	The governor of Gallia Lugdunensis
Vindex, Quintus	Julius Vindex's eldest son
Vindex, Sextus	Julius Vindex's son
Vinius, Titus⋆	Servius Sulpicius Galba's associate
Vitellius, Aulus⋆	A senator, and close friend of Titus Vinius
Vocula, Dillius⋆	A legate from Upper Germania

⋆Historical character

I

The battle was lost before it had begun. Any fool could see that. We were just a thin red line, two legions hemmed in by dense forest on either side, our retreat blocked, and that British witch Boudicca's horde surging over the field to meet our battle line. Every man launched his javelins at the sea of Celts, smeared and striped with woad all over their ugly faces, and the first wave of their attack faltered. They died in their thousands, but they had thousands to spare. We were two legions against perhaps a hundred thousand. We would have been three legions, but that fool of a legate Cerialis had tried to relieve the town of Camulodunum with only half of the Ninth Legion. They were massacred. We had at most ten thousand footsore, weary men, and it seemed like half of Britannia had come to send us to Hades. The Celts were so assured of victory that their women had arranged the baggage train into a crescent and clambered up to watch the massacre, as if in a barbaric theatre.

I was barely into my twenties, and here I was commanding a few detachments of my legion, the Twentieth Valeria Victrix. I stood about ten paces behind my men, a little way up the gentle slope to have a better view of the battle. The first waves of the enemy had been cut to ribbons by volley after volley of wicked spears that bent on impact. But those men we had killed were the young and foolish ones who wanted to make a name for themselves by being the first into the fray, and hoped perhaps to break our line. Now the older, wiser men were coming forward, and stopped just short of us. The grim blue faces stared at us for what seemed like an age, then the enemy began beating sword on shield. It started slow and menacing, with no noise but a steady *thump, thump, thump.* The beat got faster and faster, until it became an almighty clatter as tens of thousands of swords struck leather-bound shields. Finally the clashing was drowned out by a yell, a wild cry to the heavens as they began their charge. My men stood still, a solid line on which the Britons would break themselves. Or so we hoped.

While the Celtic roar was still ringing in my ears they charged us, and the maelstrom of battle took over. The first screams of pain pierced the air, as iron tore through flesh and shield bosses were punched into faces. We were holding them! Thank the gods I had found this narrow defile, or else we would have been surrounded by now, and I would have died in some cold, wet, far-flung province of the empire only invaded at the whim of the Emperor Claudius. As it was, the Britons could only assault our troops in a battle line no longer than our own. The whistles blasted shrilly for the ranks to rotate, letting fresh men replace those at the front, and the Britons found themselves facing a new set of foes.

But our thin line could only take so much. Soon my men began to edge back up the slope towards me. I took off my helmet and started to shout encouragement to the tiring men, but I felt so helpless. All I could do was watch as we began to crumble. It was the same along the rest of the line. Even General Paulinus and his staff had edged ever backwards towards the forest at our rear. Suddenly I was aware of galloping hooves behind me, and I turned to see a young staff officer, his face ash-white, who called to me from his mount.

'General Paulinus is about to sound the retreat, sir. He says be ready to break off and run for the cover of the woods.'

And then came one of the most extraordinary moments in my life. I am not a pious man; I believe that the gods have little regard for the affairs of men. Rome has flourished and thrived for over eight hundred years, so we must have done something to please them. But what does one man mean to a god? We must seem like insects scratching a living out of the earth, our lives over in a fraction of a moment. So when we are confronted by these life-changing moments, whether orchestrated by gods or Fate or just the sheer randomness of our existence, we should grasp them with both hands. We only have one life. We must make it count.

The young aide rammed his heels into the horse's flanks, so that the terrified beast reared up and flung its rider out of the saddle and sent him crashing to the ground. Now, I would not call myself a coward, but it was painfully clear that our men were flagging under the weight of the Britons' onslaught, and it was only a matter of time before the enemy opened up a breach in the line and flooded through to begin the rout. As it was, our two flanks had been pressed back, and the centre risked being encircled at any moment. The instinct for self-preservation took over, and I grabbed the dangling reins and hoisted myself into the saddle. I had a beautiful wife and a baby boy back home, a son who had never seen his father. Thoughts of them were running through my head as I prepared to ride for my life to the cover of the trees, when the stupid nag took fright, and instead charged full tilt towards our beleaguered centre. The horse scattered our rearmost ranks, and the momentum of the charge carried me straight through.

Cursing with rage, I found myself in the front rank, confronted with a churning mass of half-naked barbarians. I shouted at the legionaries to bring a shield forward and to form a wedge.

Drawing my sword, I knew that I had to get off the infernal beast before it sent me careering into the heart of the enemy horde. Not to mention the fact that I was a prime target for anyone who had a spear to hand. I slipped out of the saddle. Mercifully the horse was still between us and the Britons, giving me vital time to grab the spare shield. I slid my left arm through the cords and put myself at the front of the wedge.

Now the only hope for men formed up in a *cuneus*, a pig's head or wedge, is to press forward at all costs. You have to keep scything through the enemy ranks or you lose momentum; grind to a halt, flounder, and then it is your turn to be cut to ribbons. By this time some lucky Briton had mounted my horse and was riding it back to the encampment, screaming his good luck. That left about a five-pace gap between me and the sea of woad.

Suddenly the horns blew for the advance. Old Paulinus must have seen the wedge forming up behind me, and was taking a huge gamble by throwing the full weight of the army behind it. With fear surging through my limbs, we strode towards the enemy. The first Briton charged me head on. I let him get so close that I could see his bloodshot eyes, then rammed my shield boss in his face. There was a sickening crack as his jaw broke, and he went down like a felled ox. Just keep going forward, I thought, someone behind will finish him off. As I stepped over the sprawled Celt, I looked to see where the next attack would come from.

You might think that the head of the wedge is the most dangerous place to be, and you'd be right. But once you're there, you just have to hope that the two men behind you have your flanks covered, and look straight ahead. If the men behind are useless, then you're dead. But I didn't choose the men behind me, so all I could do was look to my front and pray those two knew their business.

They did. The next man I faced came at me from my right

and jabbed at me with his spear. I took the blow on my shield, but exposed my left flank. Out of the corner of my eye I spotted another lunging for my open side, when the legionary behind scythed his sword downwards – there was a spurt of blood, and my attacker had lost his sword arm. There was no time to shout my thanks, as I skewered the man who had first attacked me, and we kept going forward. I lost count of how many times those two saved my life, and my arms grew weary from striking, parrying, bashing and stabbing as we marched inexorably forward. After what seemed a lifetime, the seething mass in front of me appeared to thin. To my delight, I saw hundreds of those vile Celts at the rear scrambling to get past their wagons and away from the battle.

I learned later that day that the battered wings of our army had seen the centre charge headlong into the enemy and had taken heart. The whole army formed up in the wedge that we had created, like an arrowhead punching through the entire enemy horde. Soon what had appeared to be a certain defeat for us became a rout of the Britons, as those wagons, the grisly British theatre, were turned into a barricade, trapping them.

When at last there was empty ground between us and the wagons and the immediate danger was over, I turned to thank the two men who had followed me into the bowels of Boudicca's army. One, a small grimy man, smiled awkwardly and said that he had reached the space behind me just a few minutes ago, replacing the original man who had fallen to a spear thrust. The other, however, had been with me from the start. There was little time for thanks, as the battle was not yet over. Quickly I asked his name.

'Legionary Gaius Tadius, sir. Second century, third cohort of the Fourteenth.'

'Well then, Gaius Tadius, I owe you my life.'

'No, sir,' he said. 'It was an honour to follow you.' And by the gods I swear that he was blushing like an eager little boy who'd just met his hero.

'Caecina! Caecina!' someone called out. I recognized the voice.

'You took your time,' I shouted back.

The two legionaries saluted the rider; the broad purple stripe on his cloak denoted the rank of tribune, which I also held. My friend and companion, Julius Agricola, was on the general staff.

'You infantry boys have done bloody well,' he hooted. 'Now the cavalry can do what they're damn well paid to do. The general is grateful to you, Caecina.'

Just as the first cavalrymen raced past to sweep the Celts from the battlefield, Agricola struck his chest with his fist and saluted. The brave, bloody, breathless men followed his lead. I'm not ashamed to admit it: there were tears in my eyes as I returned their salute.

I, Aulus Caecina Alienus, write this brief history of what truly happened eight hundred and twenty years after the founding of Rome. It was a time of schemers, plotters, traitors and warriors, the time of the last of the Caesars. And as I write these memoirs here in Rome, those times may be upon us all over again. It is a strange sensation, addressing posterity directly, but something I shall have to get used to if I am to tell my story. I suppose I ought to explain why I am writing this account: in the first place, the gods alone know what garbled rendering his imperial majesty's minions will make of it. No doubt they will ensure he gets all the credit. Though I can't promise to be entirely objective: there are precious few alive, just a few years on, who really knew the men in this story. There will be those who say that I do this out of vanity; of course I do, and this is just another way of ensuring that people will remember me, and remember me favourably, when I'm gone. But it's not all about vanity . . . The truth has to be recorded, and you'll surely forgive an old soldier the odd embellishment or two?

As I say, this history is not all about me, more my perspective on (and role in) the astonishing events that led us from one imperial dynasty to another, with a few rebellions along the way. So I shall not bore you with too many tedious details about my past, or the empire's, as the one is not important, and the other irrelevant. One thing I should perhaps explain is why my name changes during this work of history. I was born Aulus Caecina Severus, and that is how people knew me until recently. However, in special circumstances men can acquire a new cognomen, like Scipio Africanus, or even Tiberius Caesar. You will come to understand why I became Alienus, 'the stranger', but not yet. I have started this history with a brief account of my part in that terrible battle where we ended Boudicca's rebellion. Though you may find it hard to believe, I do this not out of pride, but because I can think of no better way to give you an idea of the man I used to be: young, idealistic, and with fresh laurels of victory, but nevertheless a man subject to the whims of Fate, for want of a better word. Fate threw me into the thick of that ghoulish army, and Fate kept me unharmed throughout that day. Well, that and a few good sword arms. I like to think that this is the story of a good man, buffeted by events out of his control, trying to survive each day as it comes. And if by doing so I occasionally covered myself in glory, so much the better.

At the time of Nero's reign I was a young senator of Rome, an officer and, to some extent, a gentleman. More specifically, I was the new quaestor of Hispania Baetica. To put it simply, my role was to administer and oversee the finances of my province, assisting the propraetor, who in my case was one Cornelius Tacitus. It is viewed as the first step on the political ladder, as well as a chance to fill your purse before returning to Rome. The joy of a quaestorship is that if you can find an ambitious clerk, you can spend the year as idly as you like, and all the while the grubby clerk will pilfer a profit for you. For a small commission, of course.

After serving in the legions for a few years I fancied a spell in an exotic province doing not very much, and doing it very well. I shipped out from Ostia on a frosty January morning, leaving my wife Salonina and our son Aulus to themselves in Rome while I enjoyed the fruits of others' labour; which was the done thing, I hasten to add. No man had ever left his province poorer than when he arrived. A young senator with a career to make must have funds. I had no qualms about leaving my family behind. One of my ancestors famously gave a speech to the Senate on this very subject, lecturing them against taking their wives to the provinces, lest they distract the husband from his duties. Salonina was pretty in a graceful, delicate way, and highly distracting when she wanted to be. But I ought to admit that I'd married her for her father's money, never having set eyes on her; the grubby tradesman was delighted to have found a noble suitor for his daughter, and the family coffers desperately needed a refill. My great-grandfather had managed to pick the wrong side in the civil war, and the Divine Julius confiscated everything my noble ancestor hadn't been able to cart with him to his exile in Greece with Cicero, so I had a duty to my family to marry for money, not for love. Salonina's beauty had been a welcome bonus.

Our first years of marriage had been difficult, I'll admit. She was little more than a slip of a girl, and soon afterwards I was posted to Britannia for two years, which was more like three once you count the time it takes to get to Britannia and back, and that I was needed to stay a little longer as we made sure Boudicca's rebellion was well and truly over. I left her a spoiled girl and came back to a young woman with a two-year-old son, and he brought us closer together. We were phenomenally lucky. Most if not all marriages in Rome are for money or power. Love doesn't enter into it. But being a mother changed her as much as going to war had changed me. We grew into each other, if you see what I mean. But I still subscribe to my ancestor's belief that a wife in the provinces is at best a distraction and at worst a dangerous hindrance. Furthermore, it was Salonina's appetite for spending that made a year in the provinces a matter of some urgency!

After a thoroughly unpleasant voyage, I took up my duties in earnest, and set out to do as little hard work as I could get away with. The first task was to find a villa that would suit my needs. Obviously the propraetor had first pick, but I found a lovely place on the lower slopes of the hills overlooking the province's chief city, Corduba. Of course it had all the creature comforts – private baths, stables and so on – but the best thing of all was the spectacular setting of the place. Hispania seems quite a dusty country to me, but Corduba itself sat in a rich floodplain, and looking south from my chamber I could see the river Baetis snaking its way through the valley, giving its name to the province. From my vantage point the whole expanse of the plain seemed to stretch out for miles, which is appropriate because it did, about sixty of them, until the far southern mountains merged with the sky in a hazy blur. Having found my modest abode for the next year, I went about employing the clever clerk I was telling you about, to make sure my funds, and to a lesser extent those of the province, were in good order. I had a slave sent into town to find the best clerks in all of Corduba, and had him bring me the second-best man they had on their books.

The next day, he duly arrived for his interview with me. He was a small and greasy individual, whom the slave announced as Melander. Unsurprisingly, he looked a little overawed.

'So, they tell me you're the second-best clerk in the province . . .' The man winced, proving I'd been right to ask for him. There's nothing an able man hates more than being called second-best. Going straight to the point, I asked, 'How would you like to be the second-best clerk, but also the richest?' He looked puzzled at that. 'You do have a voice, I suppose?'

'Yes, my lord. I can't think how to thank you enough.' He knelt down in gratitude and subservience, just how I like my staff.

'Get up off the floor, man, and "sir" will do, I'm only a quaestor.'

Rising up, he asked the all-important question: 'How exactly am I to be of service, sir?'

I beamed, thinking that the interview was going better than I could have hoped. Lying back on my couch, I reeled off his orders.

'You will be my right arm in governing this juicy little province. You shall be in charge of all the accounts, making sure that all my financial duties are carried out and that I return to Rome a good deal richer. You follow me?' The man nodded. 'Good. In return, I shall allow you a commission of ten per cent on all the profits I make, so it will be in your interests to make me as wealthy as possible.'

I got up and strode towards the clerk, and stood close enough to see the filthy blackheads on his nose.

'But at the same time,' I continued, 'don't make this so obvious that I can get prosecuted.' Suddenly, my hand shot out and I grabbed him by the balls; he emitted a piggish squeal. 'And if I even suspect that you are cutting me short, or, the gods forbid, betraying me, I will tear off these slimy balls of yours, make you eat them, and then impale you on a very sharp stake. Do I make myself clear?'

Tears streamed down his face, as he whimpered and nodded. I let go, and he gasped in relief.

'Now we understand each other. Give me a list of what you need and I shall give you an office here, in my home. You may leave now, Melander.'

Dismissed, my new clerk hurried out of my study as fast as his legs could carry him.

★

Those first couple of months were the laziest and among the most enjoyable of my life. Yes, it was still winter, but winter in Hispania is better than, say, summer in Britannia, godforsaken place that it is. My time serving as a tribune had been cold and hard, and I was determined to enjoy the luxuries of my province to the full. The horses, for one thing, are the very best in the world, with men coming from all over the empire to seek Baetica's yearly stock of horseflesh. I pride myself on my knowledge of all things horse, so I was able to lean on one of the merchants to sell some of his finest stock at a cut-down price in return for my forgetting to charge him tax that year. Thus I came to be the proud owner of two mares and a stallion, the best of the best.

Naming your horse is always a tricky business, especially for a military man, since the common soldiers take a pride not only in their general but in their general's possessions too, so a good general needs a horse that his troops can be proud of. Bucephalus I thought a touch arrogant, since I was nearing Alexander's age but with very little to show for it. Then I remembered that the stallion had a white sock on one of its hind legs, so what better name than Achilles? The horse dealer I bought him from insisted that he had been fully trained as a warhorse: to kick, rear and bite in battle. However, I earnestly hoped that I wouldn't have to test the beast on the battlefield for a long time yet.

But the next few days proved that the whimsical nature of the gods can shake up the fates of men beyond belief. There was I, enjoying milking my province, when the peaceful tenor of my existence was swiftly shattered. If you had told me then that those next few months would stir up the most chaotic war in our city's history, I would have given you a look of pity and dispatched you to the establishment where we send our foaming, twitching lunatics! But I shall endeavour to spare you these little annotations of mine; the events are far more interesting.

I had taken Achilles for a ride along the river to get some fresh air into my lungs. I headed home, slipped down, handed the reins to one of the slaves and made my way indoors. On entering the atrium, I stopped in my tracks.

'Giving your duties your full attention I see, Severus!'

The voice emanated from a stocky, grey-haired man who was lying on a recliner, drinking my wine – and from my golden cup, if you please. I was about to ask what he thought he was doing, a stranger in my house. Then I realized that there were few men in the province, if any, who would address me in that manner, put two and two together and replied: 'But of course, Governor, I've just come from my inspection of the tax houses in Corduba.'

This didn't seem to satisfy the man, who looked me up and down. 'You don't seem dressed for an official inspection.'

This was true. I was wearing a simple tunic that was some-what dusty from the ride. Not wanting to lose face in front of my superior, I tried to think of some excuse.

'Well, sir, it was actually a surprise inspection. I wanted to see the works, and not just what they wanted me to see.'

The man chuckled. 'Don't worry, man, interrogation over. You've passed.'

'Passed, sir?' I asked.

'You and I both know that you've just been out for a ride on that splendid stallion of yours, the one the whole province has been talking about. You forget that I've been a quaestor myself and know exactly how much, or I should say how little, the role requires if you have a reliable deputy.'

I had been standing bolt upright, but the governor's affable response took a great deal of the tension out of the conversation, and I was about to take a seat myself and ask the nature of his visit, when he beat me to it.

'I expect you're wondering why I've called on you, despite the fact that you haven't done the courtesy of acquainting yourself with your governor in the weeks that you've been here. And don't give me any excuses; that's not why I'm here. I'm here because we have been summoned to Tarraco post haste.'

I was a little surprised. 'May I ask why, sir?'

'I'll tell you as much as I know,' the governor promised, 'but be warned: it's precious little. We have both been summoned by no less a person than Servius Sulpicius Galba, for "a meeting of the highest importance". Now you know as much as I do.'

'Immediately, sir?' I enquired.

'Immediately. I shall encroach upon your hospitality no longer, and will see you tomorrow morning when we set off for the north.'

Governor Tacitus began to make his way out, and then I remembered to ask, 'Why do you think he wants us?'

He turned to look at me. 'We'll speak about it tomorrow. It's dangerous to gossip. You never know who's listening.'

Dawn made her lazy way over the eastern horizon as my slaves prepared me for the journey. I had no clue whatsoever why Galba should want to see both Tacitus and me, and at such short notice. Questions were brimming inside my head. Why the urgency, and what would the governor of Hispania Tarraconensis, an ex-consul, no less, want with me, a humble quaestor? I was dressed in my riding tunic, but with my old military cloak to keep me warm for the next few days. It was clear from the slaves' faces that they were glad their master was to be away for a while, as they hoped to relax a bit during my absence. (I would have my steward let me know who had worked hard and who hadn't once I had returned, so that didn't bother me.) I made my way to the courtyard, while a slave carried my stuffed saddlebags behind me. Tacitus was already there on a shabby gelding, and one of the stable boys held a similarly dishevelled nag by the reins.

'I'm sure you've ridden better,' the governor explained, 'but we'll travel much quicker by changing horses every twenty miles or so than taking any of your precious beasts all the way, only to have them wheezing before we've even got as far as the next valley! Saddle up, Severus.' With that he walked his horse out of the yard and headed for the track leading towards the city.

I had my slave help me into the saddle, fastened the saddlebags, took a last look at my home, then dug my heels into my horse's flanks and set off in pursuit. After a few minutes I caught up with Tacitus.

'No lictors, sir?' I asked.

Without even looking at me, he said, 'No need. This part of Hispania has been peaceful for as long as there's been an empire. It's cheaper too.'

This puzzled me. 'I thought that all our expenses could be charged to the province?'

That brought a sharp look from the older man. 'Unlike you, quaestor, I don't seek to cheat our emperor in any way, shape or form. I only take what is necessary.'

If that's how you think then you're a sentimental old fool, I thought to myself. It must have showed, for he continued to tick me off. 'I know that must make me seem an old-fashioned relic to you, but in my day public office was a chance to serve and not to help oneself.'

There was little point in arguing with my superior, especially since he held the moral high ground. 'Yes, sir,' I said.

Tacitus must have realized that he was having little effect on me, since he took a more kindly tone. 'I'm sorry, Severus, it's not you so much as the world today that I have a quarrel with. As you're my only company for the next few days, you're going to have to put up with my ranting as best you can.'

'Which road are we taking to get to Tarraco, sir?' I asked.

'Not the coastal route. It's too long and Galba wants us as soon as possible, it seems. We ride all day to Toletum, tomorrow a hundred miles to Ercavica, another hundred to Saguntum, and the final stretch to Tarraco is about a hundred and thirty miles. Think you're up to it?'

Time for a bit of judicious insolence, I thought. 'With respect, sir, I was campaigning with the legions not so long ago. Surely I should be asking you?'

Tacitus threw back his head and laughed raucously. 'So you're not a complete arse-licker after all! Well then, let's see who's smarting the most in a few days' time. Try and keep up . . .'

And with that he was off, and I gave my steed a sharp kick and set off after him.

II

I'm not going to even attempt to describe the sheer beauty of Hispania. I had the next four days to drink it in: the delving valleys, the rocky outcrops and vast plains. I'd spent much of my youth shut up within the walls of our family villas in Italia, and before my time with the legions I'd not had much chance to explore. However, the land where I'd served was so different to the dusty vastness of Hispania, there was little to prepare me for the marvellous sights this land has to offer. Regretfully I must turn to more important things, first because the greenness of the Baetican fields and the expanse of the central plateau bear no relation to my story, and more importantly because I'm starting to sound like those insufferable bards who muse about the bounty of Mother Earth, in the vain hope that one of their betters will like what he hears and toss them a coin or two.

I take it you remember that Tacitus had promised to tell me more about the reason for our journey while we were on the road, but whenever I broached the subject he looked sullen and said that his explanation could wait. It was only on the last day of our journey that he let on anything at all. Weary and saddle-sore, we had reached the Via Augusta and were greatly looking forward to the comfortable beds that awaited us in Galba's villa, which could not fail to be ten times better than those we had rented on our way north. But, on the other hand, Galba was renowned as one of the richest men in the world, and at the same time one of the most miserly. Knowing him, he had probably taken clumps of feathers from the bedding in his guestrooms and put them into new pillowcases to save buying more pillows than was absolutely necessary! I was just thinking about the last time I had seen Galba when Tacitus spoke.

'I suppose the time has come to tell you what this meeting is all about.' Tacitus paused, obviously uncomfortable about the impending conversation. 'The truth is,' he continued, 'I don't exactly know myself!'

'Then why in Hades did you pretend you knew?' I asked, bemused.

'I said that I don't know for sure, but I can guess.'

Irritable after the day's long ride, I indulged in a spot of sarcasm. 'So what does your highly trained guesswork tell you?'

'It tells me, you arrogant pup, that this meeting will decide the future of the empire.'

I must have looked a sight. I was thunderstruck. How had he come to that conclusion?

'And no,' he continued, 'it's not some wild stab in the dark. To anyone who's actually watched this empire of ours over the last few years, it's only logical.'

'Why should it be about the future of the empire?'

'Let's see: we have an emperor who tarts himself up like a poet and performs to the mob, and makes a mockery of the Olympic Games by entering the chariot races, nearly killing himself in the process. What about the Great Fire, and all those rumours that not only did the foul man enjoy watching it destroy almost half the city but also that he probably started it, just to see what it would do? The man's a monster!'

'But how do you jump from an unbalanced emperor straight

to a Galban conspiracy, if that's what you're implying?' I countered.

'Because, simpleton, all the attempts to oust Nero have been based in Rome, and involved trying to bribe the Praetorian Guard to help out. Here in the provinces a conspiracy is much harder for the emperor's spies to discover.'

'That's a bit far-fetched, isn't it?'

'Is it? Look at Domitius Corbulo. An excellent general, he proved it in Germania and Armenia; his only mistake was to be popular with the people. Once his son-in-law was found to have been plotting against Nero, Corbulo was ordered to commit suicide. The point is that there are precious few men who could challenge Nero, even if they wanted to. Galba is one of them. Now I don't want to talk about this matter again; it's treacherous, and what's more it's dangerous.'

I nodded, and we resumed our ride to Tarraco.

Galba's villa was not difficult to find. I say villa, though palace is probably a better word. What normally happens when senators are assigned provinces is they commandeer whatever villa takes their fancy. But since Hispania is one of Rome's oldest provinces, it has a villa that was specially built in the reign of Augustus for the governor and all his successors. My only regret was that my first sight of it had not been in daylight, since we arrived in Tarraco some time after sunset. Our horses were not nearly as tired as we were, yet we still plodded through the city streets, weaving our way towards Galba's palace, or what we assumed was Galba's palace, since it was by far the biggest building in all of Tarraco.

Imagine our surprise, then, when we were politely informed by the janitor that though Galba did indeed own the palace, he was renting it out to some merchant for six months, and that we could find the governor at another address, which for some reason he was reluctant to give. After a few threats and then an explanation of who we were, the slave hurriedly directed us towards the merchants' quarter. After another half an hour's ride, we were both stunned to find that the governor of Hispania Tarraconensis was living in a building that I would have guessed belonged to some jumped-up grain merchant, not to one of the most important men in the empire.

After knocking on the door, we were ushered in quickly and taken through the courtyard to the stables, where we were told our host would meet us. No sooner had we dismounted and started walking, very bow-legged I might add, towards the villa itself than an elderly man in a simple blue tunic called out to us from the doorway. A crooked nose protruded from a great domed skull that had long since lost the hair that had once adorned it. Even if I didn't recognize him from his nose alone there was the most fantastic chin. It jutted out so far that I found myself thinking, not for the first time, that if pressed you could use the man's face as a nutcracker. My boyish thoughts were interrupted.

'My friends, thank you so very much for coming.'

Tacitus was understandably grumpy, considering our four-hundred-mile trek. 'We couldn't really ignore your summons, could we?'

Galba chuckled to himself. 'No, I suppose you couldn't.'

I piped up, 'Might I ask why I have been summoned, sir?'

The old man gave a knowing smile and said, 'All will be revealed tomorrow. Until then, I can offer you some refreshments, and a bed of course.'

He clapped his hand on my back and escorted us both inside. Well, I say escorted, but the old man suffered badly from gout and could only limp as we walked on ahead. He walked so slowly that out of politeness Tacitus and I paused halfway down the hall and waited for him to catch up. Other men were milling around inside the building, looking just as clueless as we were as to why a rich man like Galba was living in a place like this, and, more importantly, why he had brought us all here. After a round of introductions, it seemed that the governor of each Hispanian province was there, as well as some more, unfamiliar, faces. But the hour was late, and the road had been long. Tacitus and I asked to be shown to our beds, and we quickly settled down for the night.

As we had gone to bed with none of our questions answered, you might expect me to have lain awake all night puzzling over the whole situation. However, you'd be wrong. Bear in mind that I'd been riding for four days solid with a man about as forth-coming as an unpaid whore, and hadn't slept in a half-decent bed since leaving my own back in Corduba. I slept like a log, only to have a slave come in to wake me, saying that breakfast was served and the council would be meeting in an hour. It did little good. The next thing I knew, Tacitus was bellowing at me to get up, as everyone was waiting. At that I leapt out of bed, threw on my smartest gear and hurried down the corridor on my irate companion's trail. Somewhat out of breath, I made it to the triclinium, where all the couches had been pushed against the walls to make way for a large, round table.

'And now that the youngest of us has seen fit to grace us with his presence, we can begin.'

My cheeks must have been crimson as I took my seat opposite Galba.

'As I was saying, no doubt you wish to know why you are here, both in Tarraco and more specifically not in my grander residence. If I may, I shall answer the second question first. As some of you may know, in these days where glorious deeds on the battlefield are more likely to see you executed than rewarded, I have diverted my energies to a rather more grubby profession: making money.'

A chuckle went round the table. This was quite an under-statement; even I knew that Galba could have matched Croesus for wealth and, more amazingly, the triumvir Crassus for avarice!

'Therefore,' Galba continued, 'as I inherited this rather grand villa here in Tarraco, letting out the palace and residing here is both highly profitable and useful. Useful because, and I wish to make this perfectly clear, nothing that is said here today is to be mentioned to anyone without my express permission.'

We all professed earnest agreement at this, though still agog to hear exactly what was so secret. Then Galba pointed upwards, and we noticed a deep red rose hanging from the ceiling; anything said *sub rosa* is of the utmost secrecy, everyone knows that.

'You are all men of honour, and I trust you to keep the matter secret. Now for the more important question: why each one of you is here. For the benefit of those who arrived late last night, I shall make the introductions. On my right is Cornelius Tacitus, governor of Hispania Baetica, and his quaestor, Caecina Severus. Then Salvius Otho, governor of Lusitania, and on my left, my freedman Icelus Martianus, who will be taking the minutes of this meeting. I'm afraid Titus Vinius, the commander of the legion in Tarraco, can't be with us. However, he knows my mind on this matter, so we can do without him for the time being. To put this bluntly, we are here to discuss the future of the empire, and to consider what must be done to stop the emperor from undermining our position as the dominant power in this world of ours.'

I had been forewarned to an extent by Tacitus, but we were still quite surprised, though my reaction was nothing compared to that of Otho. However, I did notice that Martianus seemed perfectly happy to hear Galba openly talk of treason.

Galba resumed: 'The time has come, gentlemen, for a change of emperor.'

Otho composed himself quickly and stood up, and Galba motioned for him to speak. 'Begging your pardon, sir, but with respect, you are not a Caesar, and as such cannot hope to succeed Caesar.'

'You assume I wish to succeed Caesar,' Galba replied. 'You are mistaken. I wish to replace him.'

It had been said, and Otho, too stunned to speak, sat down again. I was less worried by Galba's blatant treason and more interested in how he proposed to achieve his aim.

'I have been persuaded that an older, wiser head is needed to restore stability to the empire. If I were the same age as you, Otho, I could not hope to succeed. Corbulo was not an ambitious man, yet he died simply for his success in the field. I am confident that the people and the Senate will recognize that, due to my age, I cannot hope to have a lengthy reign, but will instead herald the transition to a new system of government. I am not such a fool as to try and turn back time by restoring the Republic, but nor am I in favour of this dynastical monarchy that we suffer under today. Would Claudius, Caligula and Nero have reached even the lowest public office had it not been for their birth?

'Before I continue, my main question is whether I have your support, passive or active. Titus Vinius and Icelus Martianus here are with me, but if I wish to mount a challenge to Nero's rule, I cannot march on Rome leaving a fractious Hispania behind me. Tacitus?'

My governor hesitated before he spoke, choosing his words carefully. 'I am not a supporter of Nero by any stretch of the imagination, but on the other hand I will not recognize your authority unless it is sanctioned by the Senate. Therefore I want no part in this, if you please. Nevertheless I will keep my province secure, not least because it is my duty.'

'Thank you, Tacitus. To put your mind at rest, I do not propose to become a tyrant the instant I leave this city, but to head a council such as this to propose and ratify our course of action over coming months. Severus?'

'I'm with you, sir. But why do I matter? I'm not a governor.'

'Patience, Severus. I'll explain later. Otho?'

'In principle, sir, yes. First I'd like to know how you propose to bring about the end of the Caesar dynasty.'

'It's very simple. Julius Vindex has been made governor of his home province in Gaul. He is just as disillusioned as the rest of us with Nero's reign, and is this very moment preparing a rebellion, proposing my name as . . . an alternative to Nero.'

This was all so sudden. A plot to overthrow the emperor, one that had support from those appointed by Nero himself.

'At this point, Tacitus, I would ask you to leave this council. The fewer people who know my plans the better. My informers tell me that Nero has already sent messengers to demand that I fall on my sword, much like Corbulo. I hope you'll forgive me?'

Tacitus slowly stood up, upper lip as stiff as you like, and replied that he was not at all offended, and praised Galba's good sense. 'Might I ask,' he ventured, 'whether you require me or my quaestor to remain here for much longer?'

'You are free to stay for as long or as short a time as you like, Tacitus. At any rate, you will need to meet various members of my staff if you are to help look after Hispania for us. But I do require young Severus to perform a task or two for the cause, so there will be little need to wait around for your travelling companion.'

I stiffened at that. I knew that he was one of the most powerful men in the empire, but I didn't much take to his assumption that I would do his bidding like a mere slave, especially as I still had no clue what plans Galba had in store for me.

Once Tacitus had left, Galba cleared his throat and resumed: 'Now, to answer your question rather more fully, Otho, I ought to explain how Vindex, and others, can help us topple Nero. The plan is not to assassinate the emperor, but to put him under enough pressure to convince him that he must commit suicide. We have one legion here in Hispania, and Vinius will start recruiting for a second this very week. Vindex is to raise what troops he can in Gaul, see off any trouble, and wait for our two legions in Transalpine Gaul. There we shall join him, and begin our march on Rome. And before you all say that a few rebel legions can't hope to take on Rome, I have one unique advantage: the loyalty of Nymphidius Sabinus.'

That was an advantage indeed. I should explain at this point the exact relevance of Sabinus and how he was in an admirable position to help Galba. You may or may not know that the previous conspiracy to overthrow Nero, only three years before, had led to one of the bloodiest purges since the proscriptions under Mark Antony and Octavian, as Augustus was known then. But more importantly, since Piso's failed conspiracy involved so many men of authority, there were a lot of jobs that needed filling, and any amount of ambitious lowlife ready to plug the gaps. One of these men was Sabinus, the illegitimate child of an imperial freedwoman, by all accounts, and a nasty piece of work. I realize that as yet I have not revealed how well qualified I am to judge the ambition and ruthlessness of others, but all I can say is, be patient.

This Sabinus was an ambitious little turd, and managed to get himself appointed as the new praetorian prefect. That is to say that he was in command of the Praetorian Guards, and chiefly responsible for the emperor's safety. Hence we were unsurprisingly sceptical when Galba claimed to have his loyalty.

'It seems Sabinus is motivated only by power and money. I am sure that his price will be astronomical, but that is no worry for me. His task is to exaggerate the danger of our coup and to convince the emperor to stand aside, or kill himself. Then we shall usher in a new era of peace and prosperity for Rome.'

With that rather optimistic statement, Galba resumed his seat. Once again Otho wanted to speak, and reminded us all that something rather important had been overlooked.

'As I see it, Hispania and Gaul will be yours to command, sir. But surely all the other provinces will want their say once Nero has gone. What about all the legions on the Rhine and the Danube? And what makes you so sure that Sabinus can convince Nero to do the honourable thing? I know Nero better than most; he's capricious, fiercely stubborn when the mood takes him and, most important of all, the bastard's a coward. I don't think that any man could convince Nero to kill himself.'

'You forget, Otho, that Sabinus is uniquely placed to decide whether the emperor lives or dies. This is why he will not be praetorian prefect for long once I have become emperor.'

I admired the subtlety of the man; not only had he made it perfectly clear that Nero was doomed, but at the same time implied that if Nero's nerve failed him, Sabinus would be on hand to do the job himself. Though I couldn't help but notice that he had said nothing to answer Otho's first question. How would the legions in Germania and Dacia react? But now Galba turned his gaze towards me. Up till now, much like Martianus, I had kept my ears open and my mouth shut. But, it was obvious that Martianus, unlike me, was privy to Galba's plans, and had probably helped make them. As this plot unfolded, I was eager and yet apprehensive to learn my role in it.

'I feel it is time to let the youngest of us know exactly what he is doing here. Severus, you have two tasks to perform, if you are willing. One is a lot more difficult than the other. Will you hear them?'

I had to tread carefully; I didn't want to seem too keen to betray my emperor. If a man lets on that he has ambition, especially at an early stage in his career, then he has no chance of ever being trusted again. But if you want to rise up the ranks, or the cursus honorum as we call it, you can either take the slow and often fruitless route through the Senate, or win glory on the battlefield. Both Tacitus and Galba had drawn our attention to poor old Corbulo. Military prowess brought death under Nero's rule. So I had to grasp this opportunity with both hands, avoid looking too ambitious but seem eager enough to be reckoned a useful man by my future emperor. I have seen many circuses in my time, and I imagine you will have too. I felt like the poor man walking the tightrope. This was the start of my momentous journey; beneath me lay political oblivion and perhaps death, but ahead of me was the glittering prize of glory and honour, not to mention wealth, wine and women. The trick is to stay on the rope, they say. Sounds easy enough, doesn't it?

'How can I be of service, sir?' I asked warily.

'First, you will have to go on another long journey, to Massilia. I believe you are acquainted with Julius Agricola?'

'We served together under General Paulinus, sir.'

'So I gather. Your task is to convince Agricola to join the cause. The more active a part he can play the better, but at the very least I want him to prepare the ground for our march on Rome. The Agricola family,' Galba addressed this to Otho, who was looking somewhat confused, 'are very well established in Transalpine Gaul, and I'm sure young Agricola will be able to convince his neighbours to be . . . amenable to my marching through their lands.'

He continued to give me my orders. 'Then you are to find Vindex and serve as my representative, pointing him in the direction that most benefits me, and not himself. You will also serve as his military adviser.'

This provoked some outrage from Otho. He seemed rather prone to these little fits of anger, as many others would find out to their cost later.

'Sir, I really must protest! How can you possibly justify sending this youth to advise a governor of Rome on military affairs? I'll wager this is the first time he's left Italia, let alone been near a military camp.'

This was actually far from the truth, but I was wise enough, just, to see that it wouldn't do to pick an argument with a man that Galba trusted enough to bring to this council. Especially as he outranked me. Instead I put on a dignified but hurt look, as I saw that Galba was also getting a tad irritated with Otho's frequent outbursts.

'What campaigns have you been on, Otho?' Galba asked politely.

Otho had the grace to look a little sheepish. 'None yet.'

'I will tell you exactly why Severus deserves this position, on the condition that you don't question my judgement again.' Galba didn't wait for Otho's acceptance, but launched straight in. 'I have talked to Suetonius Paulinus, and he assures me that had it not been for Severus here, he and three legions would be feeding the crows in Britannia! Not only did he choose the battlefield that saw Boudicca defeated, but when the line began to buckle, he grabbed a horse, saddled up and went to plug the gap single-handed.'

I won't say it wasn't highly enjoyable to watch Otho cower before Galba's tirade, because it was, and all the more so since what Galba said wasn't strictly true. You know how I came to be at the head of that bloody counter-attack, and though I killed a great many more Britons than most on that day, it was certainly not out of choice. Still, I was more than happy for Galba to believe the story, and for him to reprimand Otho with it. However, for modesty's sake I kept my eyes downward and my mouth shut.

Otho hastily changed the subject. 'Am I to take it, then, that Vindex is rebelling purely because he would rather have you as his emperor? I've met the man before and he doesn't seem the self-sacrificing sort.'

'It seems that he is making this rebellion more out of spite towards Nero than any loyalty to me. But he serves our purpose,' Galba replied.

'And when you say rebellion, sir, what exactly do you mean?' I asked.

'Good question, and a difficult one to answer. The rebellion has to be large enough to ratchet up the pressure on Nero, and convince the Senate that my campaign is serious. Not that I have anything to do with the affair, officially or otherwise. You understand?'

We both nodded.

The old man looked straight into my eyes. 'But you must ensure that Vindex does not get carried away. I don't want other legions to get involved, especially those in Germania. I have held command there in the past, but that was many years ago. If, for some reason, Vindex engages Roman legions, you must do your utmost to get his opponents on our side. Thus, if Vindex should lose, it will not matter so long as the Rhine legions don't oppose me. Is that clear?'

'Perfectly, sir. When do I leave?'

'Tomorrow. I know you've been in the saddle for a few days so I'll put you on a boat to Massilia, then you can rest easy for a bit. I shall discuss more of the details with you over the course of today. Well, I think that is all that needs to be said at the moment. General Vinius will have a new legion ready for action in a few weeks' time, and with any luck we should be on the road to Rome by May at the very latest. Any questions, either of you?' He paused, looking from Otho to me and back to Otho again.

'None? Then I shall talk to you individually at some point soon, but in the meantime I'd recommend a trip to the baths in town. The best in all Hispania, they say. I have some other matters to attend to, but do feel free to make yourselves at home. Thank you, gentlemen.'

Galba took an age to rise from his chair, and the two of us stood out of respect. The silent Martianus took the old man by the elbow to help him up, and I couldn't help but notice how Galba patted his freedman affectionately on the arm. The pair shuffled slowly out of the room, leaving me alone with Otho. It seemed he didn't wish to stay either, but turned to me and said,

'Those baths sound rather enticing. I shall probably make my way down after a little more breakfast. Will you join me?'

I was surprised, given his seemingly low opinion of me earlier, but I said I'd be delighted, and watched as he swaggered off in his dandyish way. I was left alone to ponder over what had probably been the most important meeting of my life. Until now, there had been little that I could look forward to in my career. My family had fallen from grace in a spectacular fashion, and such is Roman politics that it could often take a couple of centuries of graft and honest toil to make up for it. It had become clear that to rise under Nero was a death-wish. But now the opportunity to gain favour with the future emperor, if all went according to plan, had just fallen into my lap.

By now you may have gathered that on my list of priorities in life, I had placed myself very near the top. I am sure that I am not alone in this. Most of the Senate would have done as I did, given the chance. But that is my point. The chance. Every man in Rome, whether noble or not, has the same goal in life: to surpass the achievements of his ancestors. For some this means getting rich. For a nobleman like me, there is one golden, glittering prize above all the others: the consulship. That is the dream of every senator in Rome, the pinnacle of the cursus honorum. My enemies say that I am ambitious, as though that were a criticism!

Now that my days are running out, I have no qualms about telling the truth in these memoirs of mine. You must believe me when I say that the man who writes these words is not the same man who sat at the table with Galba and the rest of them. I have always said to my detractors that at every turn I acted for the good of the empire. That night in Hispania I honestly believed it, and in good time you will see when things began to change. After that revelation, I'm going to rest my aching fingers and take some wine with me to bed. Unless the emperor's killers reach me first, I shall resume my narrative tomorrow . . .

III

I'm still here – though I must say I'm getting very twitchy, reaching for the dagger under my pillow every time I hear a sound outside my chamber's door. But if the difference between a knife in my neck or not is a few hours' sleep, it's not an unreasonable price to pay.

That day at Galba's villa was the first time that I had met Otho. You may have deduced that we had no great liking for each other. His reason for disliking me was that I, a nobody in his eyes, had been singled out for an important task. My only grudge was that he had a grudge against me. Nonetheless I did decide to follow him to the baths, after I'd stopped off at the kitchens en route. You'll remember that instead of a hearty breakfast I'd had Governor Tacitus shaking me, like an eager boy urging on his pony by thrashing around with the reins. So after I'd grabbed a hunk of cheese and some bread for the morning meal, I made my way into town at a jog, and soon caught up with Otho.

It was easy to tell who he was from behind; I'd recognize that swagger of his anywhere, not to mention the fact that he wears a wig, which had slipped ever so slightly askew since leaving

Galba's lodgings. I fell into step alongside him, and he gave a cursory nod to acknowledge my presence but continued his silent walk. The baths were by far the biggest building in all Tarraco, saving Galba's villa, which you would think odd, considering the town has several temples and a basilica as well, but obviously some previous governor had prized cleanliness over godliness. Not a word passed between us as we went through the imposing doorway and into the atrium. A couple of attendants escorted us to the apodyterium so that we could disrobe. As we took off our togas, I noticed that Otho had quite an imposing physique that hadn't been diminished by the soft provincial life. One of the slaves motioned to take Otho's clothes, but a muscular arm shot out and grabbed him by the wrist.

'What's your name?'

'Fero, master.'

'You keep your filthy hands to yourself, you hear?'

'Master?' the slave asked nervously.

'How else is a bath slave going to buy his freedom except by going through the pockets of his betters? If I come back and find something missing, I'll know that Fero is responsible.'

'You can trust me, master.'

Otho snorted. 'Come on, Severus, I need a bath.'

By the time I had finished undressing and similarly keeping an eye on which slave took my belongings, walked through the cold room with its plunge pool and entered the next room, Otho had been rubbed down with oil and lay face down on a slab, a slave scraping the dirt from his back. I snapped my fingers at an idle slave and he hastened over, a jug of oil in his hand. I clambered up on to my own slab, wincing as my more tender parts came into contact with the cold stone.

Otho propped himself up on his elbows so that he could look down that long nose of his, his eyes boring into mine.

'Galba trusts you a lot, doesn't he?'

There wasn't much that I could say to this, so I shrugged and said, 'I suppose so.'

'How old are you again?'

'I've just turned twenty-nine.' I winced as the slave found a knotted muscle.

'Really?' Otho looked genuinely surprised. 'I'm sorry for what I said back at the council. You look a lot younger.'

'Is that good or bad?'

'I don't know. Depends on how you want to take it. It makes me think, though; I was about your age when Nero sent me out to the shithole that is Lusitania.' His tone was understandably bitter.

'You've been here that long?' I said, trying to sound sympathetic but at the same time wondering where this conversation was going. The slave began to scrape the dirty oil off my back.

'Nearly ten years.'

'If you don't mind my asking, what had you done?'

Otho looked pretty incensed at that. 'Done! When has "done" got anything to do with Nero?'

'There must have been some reason.'

'Oh, there was a reason all right. The emperor wanted my wife. We'd been good friends for a while, Nero and I. Turns out he was just being friendly with me so that he could get close to Poppaea. One day I'm summoned before Nero, and he has the balls to demand that I divorce her.'

'Why didn't you?' I asked.

'Because, you heartless little sod, I loved her. But the ambitious bitch divorced me instead and married Nero. Just to show how magnanimous he was, he announced that he would spare me, "because of our past friendship", so instead he exiled me to Lusitania, never to return. That's enough.' The last remark was to the slave. He slowly raised his torso from the slab and I distinctly heard two cracks from his spine.

'Take my advice, Severus: don't get any older, it aches. Now, how about a good sweat?' He took off his wig and handed it to the slave. 'Gentle with it, it probably costs more than you do.'

We made our way, the balding Otho and I, to the steam room. The beautiful mosaic showed a scene of the gods that stretched all across the room, centred around the piping hot bath that stood directly above the building's furnace. I took care not to step on any images of the gods, like the crippled Vulcan at his anvil, or Venus with a lover, in case I angered them. The floor was slippery, what with all the steam and the thousands of feet that had worn the mosaic smooth over the years. There was silence between us for a few minutes as we slowly cooked.

'Yes, Galba's a clever one for letting me in on his little plan. I'm the last man in the world to betray him to Nero. Why does he want you so much, I wonder.'

I was beginning to understand at last. Playing the innocent, I replied: 'I can only suppose it's because I know Agricola and General Paulinus well.'

'So an old man, a widower without any children, plucks a young man from provincial obscurity to enlist his help in winning the empire for himself,' he said, spelling it out. 'You can't be such a fool that you can't guess his next move?'

As a matter of fact I had, but I didn't want to let Otho know that I had any brains. No sense in letting a potential rival know what you're thinking.

'No, sir.'

He obviously didn't believe me.

'No one's that thick. He's thinking of the succession, and I want to make it perfectly clear that that successor is going to be me, and not a quaestor who had a lucky break years ago in a province that no one gives a damn about. Understand?'

I nodded, and all of a sudden he became a lot more amiable. We chatted of this and that, simple things like the weather, the condition of the roads in Hispania, matters so mundane that it struck me that Otho had deigned to speak to me to make his ambitions plain and to put a halt to mine, not because he had wanted to strike up a friendship. It was when I noticed beads of sweat trickling past Otho's ever-receding hairline that I said I needed a cold bath to finish with.

Otho followed me back to the first bathroom, the frigidarium. I stood at the edge of the pool, ready to jump in, but Otho put an arm on my shoulder.

'I'm going back to Galba's villa. We understand each other, don't we, Severus?'

'I understand you completely, sir.'

'I knew you would,' he said, then left me to reclaim his wig and his clothes.

I dived into the plunge pool. The cold water enveloped me in an icy embrace, and I kicked hard to get to the surface. When I'm with the army I try to do an hour of exercises at dawn to keep in shape. When I was a civilian a few lengths in the frigidarium were enough to keep me fresh for the rest of the day, but not so much that I tired myself out.

Half an hour later I was walking through the town, more conscious of the stench of the street after leaving the perfumed oils and cleansing steam of the baths. I was mulling over what Otho had rather bluntly said in the bathhouse, quietly excited that a man as senior as he thought 'a lowly quaestor' a potential rival as Galba's successor! Things were definitely on the up. So it was in a joyful mood that I made my meandering way back up to Galba's villa, hoping that his cooks would be on form as I turned my thoughts to lunch.

Unfortunately, no sooner had the whiff of the kitchens stopped me in my tracks than an arm shot out from nowhere and tugged at my sleeve. I whipped round to see who had so unceremoniously got my attention, and was about to ask him what he meant by it when I recognized the man as Galba's freedman, Martianus. Before I had the chance to demand why he had snuck up on me like that, he explained that Galba wished to see me at once.

'It is most urgent, sir, and it is the governor's express wish that you come now, and alone.'

With his piece said, he beckoned me to follow him inside. By now I was getting somewhat tetchy, not having had a chance to relax all day. And if you think I was overly complaining, since I'd just had a spell at the baths, let me tell you that I don't regard being grilled by Otho as an entirely relaxing experience. Nevertheless I followed Martianus through the little passageways until we came to what I supposed was Galba's study. Martianus opened the door and stepped aside so that I might go in, then closed the door behind me.

Galba was sitting at a rather shabby-looking desk. His head was bent low over the vellum he was writing on, but he did not look up from his work and said nothing. There was an awkward silence. I coughed a bit to let Galba know that I had arrived. Since he was over seventy I supposed his hearing was a bit off. Still looking down at his work, he quietly said, 'Imagine, Severus, that for some reason I had held a highly secret meeting concerning the emperor this morning. Now suppose I was told that the contents of the meeting were openly discussed not two hours after this hypothetical meeting. What should my reaction be?'

The offhand manner in which he said this unnerved me far more than the fact that he had informants in the town who had reported my conversation with Otho before I had even returned to the villa. Knowing that Galba would be livid come what may, I decided to be as honest and contrite as possible.

'You should be furious, sir.'

'AND SO I AM!' I was so amazed that the old man had such lungpower that I took a step back. He lowered his voice to a conversational level, obviously not wanting to be heard outside the room. Now he looked up at me, his face purple with rage. 'You have the temerity to discuss my plans for all the world to hear, and in the bathhouse of all places! Have you gone completely mad, or have you less brains than a prattling whore?'

I stood my ground, very thankful that I could honestly say, 'If you would consult your informant again, sir, you would know that I never made any reference to what was discussed this morning.'

It was Galba's turn to be taken aback. 'You mean to say that it was Otho who blabbed, and not you?'

Allowing myself a small smile, I replied, 'I shouldn't like to accuse my superior of any such thing, sir.'

'By Jupiter! A soldier and a politician?'

'I've always enjoyed being both, sir.'

'All in good time, Severus, all in good time. But first I need to reach Rome before I can become your patron. I had meant to send you back with Tacitus, but you've convinced me. As you suggest, I will talk to my man again.'

He looked me up and down with his tired eyes. 'Your father would be proud of the man you've become.'

I readied myself for the familiar speech.

'He was a good man, your father. One of the best I've ever known. He saved my life out in Africa, and when he lay dying in that desolate, miserable place, I promised him that I would look after you and your mother.'

'And I will never forget your generosity, sir. Without you the debtors would have taken our lands, our slaves, everything we had.'

Galba modestly shrugged. 'You know full well I have more money than most men in the empire. I know people call me a miserly old man behind my back, but I like to know that from time to time my wealth can do something useful; and keeping a comrade's family, one of the oldest in Rome, from begging in the streets is useful. It wasn't just to repay a debt to your father, I was also investing in you. This is your chance to prove that your father's sacrifice and my money were not wasted.'

'I should thank you as well, sir, for not telling the council about your kindness towards my family. I wouldn't want anyone to think I owed my position to nepotism.'

'You mean Otho in particular, eh? He's a surly brute, but I wasn't telling any lies when I said that you are the best man for the task. I know how close you and young Agricola are, and while your bravery may have gone unnoticed in Lusitania, it was noticed where it mattered. Anyway, I didn't call you in here to discuss the past. It is the future that matters now. You need your orders for the coming months.'

At this the old man fumbled around inside the drawers of his desk, and drew out a slightly faded map of Gaul. 'Right; you will take ship for Massilia tomorrow morning, and all being well you should be with your friend Agricola in a matter of days. Once you have sounded him out about our plans, not too thoroughly mind you, you will need to head to Lugdunum as fast as possible to be at Vindex's side.'

'I trust that I shall have some funds to speed my way, for post-horses and the like, sir?'

'Of course. I'll give you some money before you leave tomorrow, and considering the cause, I won't ask for the money back.'

This was some trust indeed from Galba, the biggest cheapskate in the empire.

'Vindex,' he resumed, 'will require some careful handling. His family is from one of the most powerful tribes in Gaul, one that has only recently embraced Roman ways, so you may find him somewhat rough around the edges. But after your service in Britannia I'm sure you'll survive.'

At this point he paused, seemingly a little uncomfortable about the conversation. 'As I said this morning, whether Vindex succeeds is not of great importance to me. What is important is to see what the reaction is to my proclamation as an alternative to Nero.'

'May I be blunt, sir?'

'Go on.' He looked at me enquiringly.

'Would you rather Vindex failed or succeeded?'

'Ah. Good question.' Galba leaned back in his chair, his square chin resting on his chest. There was quite a lengthy silence, as the would-be emperor considered his words carefully.

'Should Vindex's rebellion go as planned, I am fairly confident that he will keep his promise to me, and I shall have the support of Hispania and Gaul. But I do not want him antagonizing the legions on the Rhine. If they decide to nominate their own candidate, we could be thrown back into the days of bloody civil war. I hope that my achievements and old age will be enough to convince the more ambitious men to back down. However, should Vindex be beaten, I will need you to plead my case with the commanders in Germania. I don't even need their outright support, just their tacit agreement. You can even make some small hints concerning my gratitude to make your task a little easier, but no promises that I will be unlikely to keep. Understand?'

I nodded my agreement. 'May I ask what Governor Vindex expects my role to be?'

'I have told him that you will be my liaison man, and that your military judgement is to be trusted in all matters. I should hope that my recommendation will ensure your place on his staff. If all goes well, then you shouldn't have to be with him all that long, as I will be able to start my march on Rome once he has been successful. Then you can join us en route. I shall also give you a letter of introduction, just so that you can prove your identity to him. I think that's all. Any questions?'

'Just one request, sir. I have some belongings back in Corduba which I should like to be sent on to Rome, if I'm not to return to Hispania. Might I also ask that my warhorse be brought here to Tarraco, so that I can ride him at your side as we make for Rome?'

He chuckled at that. 'You seem to think of everything, Severus. I hope Vindex recognizes your talents. Of course, I shall have your horse brought to my stables, ready for the march. And if that is all, I would recommend that you enjoy the luxuries of Tarraco while you can. Life on a campaign doesn't offer many comforts. I shall see you off tomorrow morning.'

With an effort, Galba raised himself from his chair and took my hand in his. 'Good luck, Severus. With a man like Vindex, you will have to be at your charming best, but serve me well and you might be at the start of a golden career. Now go and have some lunch!'

I smiled, and saluted the kindly old man. 'Hail Caesar!'

Galba smiled back. 'With any luck.'

I was almost out of the door when Galba called after me: 'Oh, Severus! What's the name of this horse you want me to send for?'

Turning back to face my future emperor, I replied, 'Achilles, sir.'

He raised his eyebrows at that, then buried his face in the palm of his good hand, muttering, 'Gods, the arrogance of youth . . .'

It was the next day that taught me to hate travelling by sea. I had travelled from Ostia all the way to Hispania by boat, but the waters had been as calm as you like, and it had been all plain sailing, if you'll forgive the expression. By comparison my journey to Massilia was much shorter, but infinitely more unpleasant. I often found myself clinging to the side of the ship, my prayers to Neptune stopped only by my occasional offering of vomit over the side.

Anyhow, my prayers must have been heard as by some miracle we made it to Massilia unscathed. I had a notion where my good friend Julius Agricola lived, as I had visited his estate once or twice since our days in Britannia, but I had only ever approached it from my own estate in Italia, to the east, and not from the southern coast. It's damnably tricky country to travel in, as Hannibal would no doubt have told you. The place is a veritable maze of rocky gorges and mountain passes, but as Agricola was a rich noble his estate was in the more profitable and flatter land, nearer to the coast. And as he was one of the most notable inhabitants of the region, it didn't take me too long to find someone who knew the way and could point me in the right direction.

Perhaps at this juncture I ought to tell you a bit more about my friend Gnaeus Julius Agricola. You could say we were boyhood companions, for our parents had been close, but since he took charge of his estate in Gaul and I had mine on the other side of the Alps, it wasn't all that often that we'd see each other. Nonetheless, we were the same age, and climbed the first rung on the military ladder together. I should explain that for those nobles with a political or military career in mind, a spell as a tribune was the obligatory first step once you'd reached manhood. That is unless you were the puny sort who couldn't face it, like mighty Cicero, who had to make his way into the Senate through his not inconsiderable prowess as a lawyer. But I digress. Using family connections we managed to get postings to the same province, Britannia. I was assigned to the Twentieth Legion, the Valeria Victrix, who were billeted at Glevum or Isca Dumnoniorum, depending on the circumstances, while Julius drew the Ninth Hispana. I have enjoyed teasing Julius about this over the years, as it was the Ninth that had been almost annihilated by Boudicca in an ambush. Not that that was Julius's fault, since he'd been snapped up by General Paulinus to be on his staff, but because of the legate's blunder, that idiot Cerialis.

Unfortunately I didn't have such exalted connections as my friend Julius; I had to learn the art of soldiery on the battlefield and not in the governor's mess tent. I was lucky to learn quickly, otherwise I would no doubt have been skewered by a British spear years ago. I say this not out of bravado but to make sure that, after reading my account of my accidental heroism at the Battle of Watling Street, you don't take me for a poor soldier, or worse, a coward. You must understand that when you see over a hundred thousand barbarians painted blue from head to toe, desperate to use your various limbs as ornaments for their pestilent little huts, and your own troops are on the point of buckling and being massacred, I challenge any man with common sense not to have done the dishonourable thing and run. But, to cut a long story short, we both survived our time in Britannia and returned home, Julius with the reputation of a competent staff officer with a head for logistics, and me with that of a homicidally brave man with a talent for leading men in war.

So it was with a happy heart that I made my way over a ridge and saw the Agricola estate sprawling before me. Of course it was far less grand than Galba's official residence, and more spartan than my own estate in Vicetia, but Julius had never had quite the same taste for the comforts of life. He was like a Cato of old, even if he got a comfortable staff role while I had to rough it with the legions.

I urged on my weary nag, paid for by Galba, thank you very much, and my mind began to turn to thoughts of enjoying my old comrade's hospitality. The ancient stone walls were the same as ever, cut from the same murky rock that abounds in this part of Gaul. And as ever the gate was barred. Julius hadn't broken the habit since his days with the legions of keeping the entrance to his camp shut at all times. Thankfully it was a warm spring day, and I hadn't travelled all that far from Massilia to get there, so I was in no great rush to get inside. I called up so that I might be let in. Silence.

I called again; still no answer. I began to feel a mite uneasy.

Even the laziest janitor would have stirred himself by now. My horse was impatient, and pawed at the ground with a front hoof, obviously itching to get me off his back and attack some hay. The long silence was unnerving me, and I was wondering what on earth could have happened in this, one of the most loyal parts of the empire.

At last, a voice floated over the walls and made its way down to me.

'What do you want?' it called.

The voice was weak and cracked, and I supposed it belonged to old Petros the janitor.

'Is that you, Petros?' I shouted. 'I want to come in, you old fool!'

'You'll have to give me your name first, sir. I'm afraid my eyes aren't what they used to be.'

'It's me, Caecina Severus. I'm here to see your master.'

Well, that was fairly obvious, but I remembered that Petros had been a bit slow on the uptake, and needed chivvying along if you wanted him to do anything before your own hair started to turn grey.

'Master Caecina! My master will be pleased,' the slave cried out. I was all ready for the doors to swing open, at long last, but Petros had yet another obstacle for me. 'But first you'll have to give me the password.'

'Password! What do you mean, password?'

'I don't know how else to explain it, Master Caecina. I need the correct password. I'm afraid my master is extra cautious these days.'

Fuming by this stage, I bawled out, 'How in the name of Hades will I know a password that's been made since my last visit?'

'The master has prepared a clue for his loyal friends. Would you like me to tell you?'

'No, I thought I'd just rot here until I look as decrepit as you, Petros. Of course I do!'

'I am sorry, Master Caecina. Orders are orders. The clue is: Who was Penelope's chief suitor while Odysseus was away from Ithaca?'

That did it. Julius knew I detested Homer. I had put up with enough nonsense from this slave, and demanded he open the door or I would have the skin flayed from his scrawny hide. Amazingly, I heard the bolt screech as it was drawn back, and the doors slowly began to open. Red-faced, I rode in, dismounted, and cast my eyes around the courtyard looking for the impudent slave. 'Petros! Come out here, I'm going to crush your spine!'

A strong, baritone voice boomed down to me from above. 'I would ask you to reconsider, Caecina. Useless as a eunuch in the bedchamber he may be, but I'm rather fond of him.'

There, standing on the gatehouse parapet, was Gnaeus Julius Agricola, my comrade and oldest of friends. I was speechless.

'You can shut your gaping mouth, Caecina, it's only me.'

'But . . . I thought . . .' I stammered.

He let out a roaring laugh, and wiped tears from his eyes. 'I've wanted to play that trick on you for years!'

My friend started pouring me a cup of wine as I sat down, at long last within the villa itself. 'So tell me, what is the newly appointed quaestor of Hispania Baetica doing at my humble abode, just a few months into his posting?'

'Long story or short story?'

'The shorter the better.'

My friend had never been one for mincing his words, so I leapt straight in. 'How would you react if Nero's reign came to an end in a matter of months?'

Julius had been taking a swig of his wine, but suddenly spluttered and sprayed a fair amount on to my tunic. He looked at me, dumbstruck, his bushy eyebrows threatening to meet his hairline.

'So you'd be happy then?' I asked mischievously, wiping the worst of the wine off my front.

First looking over his shoulder to see if there was anyone in earshot, he said, 'How do you think you're going to get rid of Nero all on your own?'

I laughed at that. 'Come on, Julius, think. How could I hope to overthrow Nero by myself? You make it sound as though it's my plan.'

'Who sent you then, and what does all this have to do with me?'

'It's simple. All you have to do is make sure that if the future emperor comes through this part of Gaul, he is well received.'

He looked suspicious. 'That depends on who he is.'

'Galba.'

'Galba? But he's ancient!'

'Precisely,' I said. 'It's because he's so old that he hopes the people will see that he's no tyrant, and will accept him as their next emperor. Until he chooses a successor, that is . . .' I gave him a slight wink at that.

I realize that from the above conversation you might think my friend was surprisingly slow on the uptake for a future general of Rome. In his defence, you don't have to be cunning to lead the legions, but you do need to be honest, brave and dependable. My friend Julius had those qualities by the bucketload. Nonetheless I did find it very amusing to watch the implications of what I'd just said sink in. He would never be a good conspirator, Julius, but you would be hard pressed to find a more loyal friend.

'So it seems that after enduring your presence all these years it might actually do me some good!'

'If the gods are willing . . .'

My companion grinned, showing a full set of gleaming teeth. I made a mental note to try his rustic lifestyle one day; he was looking very trim, even though we'd left the army several years beforehand.

'So how long will I have the pleasure of your company for?'

'Not long,' I replied. 'I have to be heading north soon.'

'Why north? Surely you're bound for Rome? I've heard rumours of trouble brewing up there.'

'Like a rebellion?' I enquired, looking as innocent as I could.

'Maybe. Julius Vindex up at Lugdunum isn't best pleased with Nero, from what I hear . . . Oh I see! You're going to talk to Vindex, aren't you?'

I said nothing but instead slowly clapped my hands, applauding my friend's dazzling intellect, and I got the rest of the wine in my face for my troubles. We laughed, and Julius got up to fetch another pitcher of wine, as well as a cloth for my face. We whiled away the hours in soldiers' gossip, catching up on each other's news. I was sorry to hear that his mother was away at her estate in Italia, as I would have liked to see her again, even if she had called me a feckless idiot from time to time. Our fathers had been good friends and neighbours in Rome. However, my father had died of a fever when I was five, and Julius's father was put to death by Caligula the very year Julius was born. Our bereaved mothers took comfort from each other's company, and consequently Julius and I saw each other almost every day, and later shared the same tutor. Yes, I had no better friend in the world than Julius.

'There is something important that I want to ask you, Caecina,' he said.

'Oh? So important that you've left it until we've polished off two pitchers of your wine?'

'Have you thought at all about who your son might marry?'

'I haven't, actually. He's only eight, but I suppose I'll have to think about a betrothal soon.' I had an idea where this was going, but I didn't want to make a guess and hideously embarrass my friend if I was wrong.

'Caecina, we've been friends a long time now, and I wondered if you might consider . . . well, Domitia and I thought it would be nice if . . .'

'Where is Domitia, by the way?' I slurred.

'Oh, she's been visiting a friend. We're meeting her in town tomorrow. But that's not what I wanted to say. What I wanted to suggest was . . .'

'Julia?' I guessed.

Julius didn't say anything, but just nodded. This was a very important moment, as Julius was suggesting that we tie our families together in an alliance. My son and his daughter, betrothed. Julius was not just my oldest friend, but he had one of the finest military minds Rome has ever seen. As I sit here writing these memoirs, he is about to launch an invasion of the wild north of Britannia, for almost no other reason than that he can. Some marriages, like mine, are for money. Some are made for politics, bringing two dynasties together, or merely as political bargaining counters. We both knew each of us would be great in his own way. Julius had no interest in politics; at heart he was still the same boy with the treasured toy soldiers that we had both played with. But a good general could also be a great politician, and Galba had dangled the prospect of a glittering career in front of me. What could we not achieve together?

I let the awkward silence hang a little longer, before breaking into an inane grin and saying, 'I couldn't think of a better match!'

'You agree?' Julius seemed surprised. 'Wouldn't you like to run it by Salonina first?'

'Of course I agree. It's a fantastic idea, and Salonina will think so too. Come on, let's have another drink!'

After much drinking, some singing and more drinking, I eventually reminded Julius that I had been travelling for near on a week, and needed to go to bed. He led me to one of the guestrooms; well, I say led, we had both had far too much wine by this stage and he was in need of a steady arm himself. Anyway, we made it to my room, he wished me good night, and said that I was free to help myself to breakfast when I eventually rose, or lunch if I preferred. Gratefully, I slumped down upon the bed, clothes and all, and drifted off to sleep.

IV

After days of non-stop travelling, a bed under Julius's roof was a very welcome change. Bear in mind that Galba had not been putting us up in his palatial seat, but in some grubby merchant's house in the city. To have a goosefeather pillow was utter luxury, and I was understandably reluctant to leave my cosy room the next morning. I also had a vicious hangover.

I can still remember a light knock, two tremors that reverberated around my skull, and a slave letting me know that breakfast was served. Grabbing the nearest thing to hand, a small pot I think, I groaned at the slave to let me die in peace and flung the thing at the door, which was a mistake. The shattering of the pot and the shards hitting the floor sounded like a galley dashing itself upon the rocks. Next thing I knew, a wave of cold water washed over me. Coughing, spluttering and drenched, I was ready to strangle whoever had doused me, but I found myself looking up at Julius. He was holding a still-dripping pitcher and beaming widely.

Slowly getting to my feet, I spoke very quietly, for obvious reasons. 'You do realize that these are my only clothes?'

Julius chuckled. 'I'm sure I can find you something half decent. Come and have some breakfast.'

Not amused, I squeezed the worst of the water out of my clothes and followed him towards the kitchens. I ought to explain that though any self-respecting gentleman would not dream of entertaining and feeding his guests in the kitchens, Julius was the rustic sort, and seeing as how I was a close friend, he knew I didn't need to go through the rigmarole of proper etiquette between the host and his guest. So I sat myself down at the table and helped myself while Julius went to see what clothes he could find.

Not feeling particularly hungry (the life of the legions does a good job in training your stomach not to need too much food, which is just as well), I took a hunk of bread and some fruit, and ate my fill, stopping only when I'd watered my insides as well as my outsides had been wetted. Glancing over the rim of the cup, I saw Julius come in, holding a dirty bundle.

'What in Hades' name is that?'

'This is the only thing that will fit you. It's your fault for outgrowing me!' He dropped the edges of the bundle and out spilled the crumpled folds of a working smock, the sort of thing the grubby slaves who work the land wear. I was at least a head taller than my friend, but I wasn't going to give up that quickly.

'You're sure there's nothing . . . well, cleaner?'

'Unless you want me to have a sort through Mother's dresses, this is the best that my humble home has to offer you.' And with that he flung the dirty thing towards me. I made an effort to catch it, but forgot that I was still holding almost a cupful of water, and got the smock wet too.

Laughing, Julius said, 'If you want to come to town with no clothes on, by all means. Though I think the good ladies of Forum Julii might be offended, if they looked hard enough!'

I did not deem that last remark worthy of a comeback, and silently carried on with my breakfast.

'Touched a nerve, have we? You'll live,' Julius smirked. 'If you feel up to a trip into town, you can put the kit on and it'll dry off on our way. I need to restock on food anyway, and now I have a big lump to feed we'll have to take the cart. We'll give you ten minutes, then we need to leave, otherwise we'll miss all the best goods at the market.'

The cart trundled over the cobbles towards the little market town at a modest pace. As it was market day, all the world and his carthorse were off to the forum to buy, sell or barter. While one of his household slaves kept a hold of the reins, Julius couldn't help looking over his shoulder at me as I fiddled with the dirty smock that he had forced upon me. Smirking, he'd then look back to the road again. Meanwhile I was having my first proper look at this little outpost of civilization that he had decided to live in. Of course this part of Gaul had been relatively civilized for centuries. Massilia, one of the biggest ports in the area, had been an ally of Rome back in Hannibal's time, and the Greek colony's influence still had some visible traces. But still, this was Gaul, beyond the Alps, and I had difficulty in understanding why Julius spent so much time here.

Of course the most sensible politicians had vacated Rome, as the emperor's paranoid imagination could create plots out of thin air. Abroad was anti-social, but safe. But while I had managed to secure sunny Baetica, Julius had a perverse liking for the wild lands. He had revelled in the cold, wet lands of Britannia, and had always leapt at the chance to go exploring the godforsaken island. He had also chosen to serve his quaestorship in Asia, and though he had all the culture and luxury of the Aegean coast to wallow in, instead he spent most of his time campaigning up in the mountains against pockets of rebels. You see how my friend had always been the one to find adventure where there was none, while I sought to make my time away from Italia as comfortable as possible? And yet it was I who found myself embroiled in circumstances

so extraordinary that they helped turn me from the hero of
Britannia into a man despised by society.

But I am getting too far ahead. My friend brought the cart
to a halt near the shrine to his namesake, the Divine Julius who
had brought wealth to the old Greek port by linking it with his
road to Hispania. Domitia was waiting for us there. She was a
gorgeous woman, Domitia. Blue eyes so deep you could drown
in them, luscious blonde hair, and a face that was brightened
by an infectious smile which spread even wider when she saw
me.

'Caecina, what are you doing here?'

'And hello to you too,' I said, jumping down from the cart. I
spread my arms wide. 'Come here.'

She stepped into my warm embrace. She and Julius had been
married for six years now, and in that time she had become like
a sister to me. That smile beamed at me. You would never know
it from her demeanour, but the couple had lost a son the year
Julia was born. They masked that sadness well, and a happier
couple I have never seen.

'So why are you here?' she asked.

'Call it a surprise visit.'

'I talked to Caecina about Julia last night,' Julius said.

'And?'

'And I think it's a wonderful idea, Domitia,' I began. 'But
don't get too excited; the wedding won't happen for another ten
years, and who knows if you'll be worthy enough to marry into
my family.'

Domitia looked questioningly at her husband.

'He's only teasing, darling. Caecina looks set to have a shining
career ahead of him, all being well.'

'Then who's to say we won't have changed our minds either?
Julius is running for praetor this year,' Domitia countered.

'Praetor, eh, Julius? You might outrank me; what a horrifying
thought!'

He playfully cuffed me round the head. Then he took Domitia's arm in his and led the way.

We spent a pleasant half-hour or so pottering around the market place. Julius made a show of examining everything before he bought it: was the bread crusty enough, how ripe was the fruit, that sort of thing. Eventually we had loaded up the cart and were getting ready to head back to the villa when a clatter of hoofbeats, too fast to be another merchant's cart arriving in town, made me turn to see why someone was in such a hurry. The rider, dirty and unkempt as though he had spent long in the saddle, urged on his horse and manoeuvred it through the crowd towards the centre of the forum.

'People of Gaul!' he shouted. The hubbub started to die down. The traders on the stalls stopped bawling their prices.

'People of Gaul!' the rider cried again. A hush descended around the market, as everyone turned to see what the commotion was. The rider waited until there was enough quiet, and began:

'My fellow Gauls, I come from Gaius Julius Vindex, a Gaul as much as any of you, whose family goes all the way back to the days before Vercingetorix. Days when Gauls governed themselves, days when the Romans did not dare send their legions beyond the Alps, days when the Gauls were free. Too long we have lived under the tyrant Nero, a man as evil and corrupt as he is debauched. Who has not heard the stories of how often he tried to kill his own mother, or of how it was he who set fire to Rome? I look into this crowd, and I can see brave men who would gladly take up arms to rid us of this tyrant, and would join the noble Vindex in his struggle to end our oppression. If anyone here wishes to serve his country, bring what food and arms you can to Lugdunum, and we shall show these Romans what we Gauls can do.'

★

I must admit this rider seemed very sure of himself, urging on this mob of smelly townspeople to war, parading himself and his horse around as he did so, while I had not yet appreciated the momentousness of what he was actually saying. And then it dawned on me. Quickly, I muscled my way through the crowd, trying to get close to this messenger from Vindex. He was busy telling the people to spread the word, and was about to ride off again when I caught a hold of his ankle.

'Get your hand off me!' Thankfully he wasn't armed, and just squirmed in the saddle trying to get free of my firm grip. Those around started to back away, not wanting to get caught up in a brawl. Again he kicked, and I almost lost hold of him.

'Unhand me, you dirty peasant, I have to get to the next town at once.'

'I'm a Roman officer, and this is important. Was that your own speech or were you given it by someone else?' It was too late. At the words 'Roman officer', his eyes had bulged, and with a final wriggle he managed to strike his horse's flank and I let go, having no wish to get caught in the way of a galloping rider. The man headed back out of the town as quickly as he could, while I was left standing there, taking in the situation. I looked round for my friend, and spotted him a few feet away.

'Julius, we need to leave now!' I bawled, gesturing to the cart. Silently, he nodded assent, and dived off into the crowd to find Domitia. I barged through the crowd, jumped up on to the cart and took the reins. As I lashed the beast into life, the cart began its trundle to the other side of the forum, where I stopped to let Julius and Domitia clamber aboard with all their baggage, and gave the carthorse another stinging blow. We shot off along the rickety road back into the countryside, and across the small plain between the hills where Julius had his home.

Thoughts were teeming in my head. The rebellion had started. And without me! Obviously this man Vindex must have had good reason to start the uprising without waiting for the man Galba was sending him, but what could it be? Had he heard something that I hadn't? The poor horse was flagging, not used to pulling such weight at such speed, but we were soon approaching Julius's villa, and I shouted at the first slave I saw, 'Have my horse ready in five minutes, or your backside will be whipped raw!' He duly scuttled into the stables, while I brought the cart to a halt and jumped down.

Julius did the same, and called out for my baggage to be brought to the yard, and a few days' food. Taking his arm in mine, the old soldier's grip, I looked into Julius's face and saw that the grim, determined look he had acquired in Britannia had returned.

'You'd better keep that rag,' he said, looking at my borrowed clothes. 'You've a rebellion to manage, and you can't stop to change. Good luck, Caecina.'

'Thank you, Julius. I'd hoped to stay longer but I'm a busy man, you see.' He smiled at that. I heard the stable door creak open, and turned to see the slave leading out my refreshed post-horse. Julius gave me a leg-up, and I looked down at my friend for probably the last time in a long while. Petros came out from the villa, clutching my travelling clothes, a small bundle of what I assumed was food, and the little purse that Galba had given me. Once these were safely stowed away in my saddlebags, I was about to start the next stage of my journey when I felt another hand on the reins.

'Lugdunum is two days' ride, if you change horses. Head north-west until you find the Rhone, then north, and you will eventually reach the city. Good luck, Caecina. This is what comes of being Galba's favourite, is it?'

'Just you make sure you help him as he comes through. I'll write when I can!' I dug my heels in, and flew out of the court-yard and on with my journey.

★

I followed Julius's directions and wound my way through the foothills of the Alps, going fairly easy on my nag as it had to take me as far as the Massilia–Lugdunum road, and then to the next place where I could change horses. I had two days to ponder what might have happened to convince Vindex to start without me, and whether this idea of a Gallic uprising was his or that of the messenger back in Forum Julii. It wasn't that I overly minded that he had started without me, but the fact that he had done so on his own initiative. I had gathered from Galba that this so-called uprising was just meant to put the frighteners on Nero and not really achieve anything, and furthermore that Vindex was taking his orders directly from Galba. Wouldn't it have made sense to wait for Galba's man to arrive before taking such drastic steps? I supposed that the Gaul wanted to claim as much credit for himself as he could, to prove to Galba that he could do a good job without some intermediary telling him what to do.

I'm not one to panic unduly, so it was in a less agitated state of mind that I came at last upon the Rhone road. The light was beginning to fade and the river was a dark mass of blue a few miles off, stretching north towards my destination. The setting sun was directly in front of me, its orange glow dimming as it slowly sank behind the peaks of the far mountains. The horse deserved a breather, so I dismounted, leading it down the poor excuse for a road and making my way into the valley. A small village nestled at the foot of the hills that levelled out towards the river, and as I snaked my way down the slope the buildings began to grow in number. Soon I saw what looked like a tavern, one of the biggest houses in the village and adjacent to the road leading towards the Rhone. The nearer I got the louder I heard some rather tuneless singing, though I didn't even try to understand the words. My labouring mare was in as much need of a night's rest as I was, and by the time we reached the inn she was ready to drop.

A stable-hand seemed to appear from nowhere, and offered to take my horse while I went in search of the landlord. I grabbed the contents of my saddlebags and followed the sounds of Gallic drinking songs. Opening the tavern door I was hit by a wave of noxious fumes. The place stank of cheap wine, and the customers even more so. Bow-legged, I made my way to what I assumed was the bar and asked to see the landlord, wanting supper, shelter and stabling for one night. The rather portly innkeeper looked askance at my filthy attire, but I gave a small jingle of my purse and put to rest any doubts he might have had over whether I could pay.

Once I had found an empty table and was brought my food, a fine repast of scrawny chicken, decidedly rotten vegetables and a flagon of astoundingly pungent wine, I asked whether there had been any news of a rebellion.

'A rebellion, in these parts! Why should we want to rebel?' the large man asked.

'So you've heard nothing about a Gallic uprising at Lug-dunum?'

'I didn't say that. There have been rumours of course, all free Gauls who hate Roman oppression and the like, but mostways they all fell on deaf ears round here.'

'Why's that?'

'Where have you been hiding yourself? As though my business would survive without that great Roman road over by the river! Most parts of Gaul wouldn't have been civilized had it not been for the Romans. Of course, some of the younger ones have had their heads turned, wanting to win a name for themselves wielding pitchforks and the like. But not for me, thank you very much.'

So much for Gallic nationalism, I thought.

'How many do you think will join?'

'Couldn't say,' the barman replied. 'There's been a steady

trickle of people heading north, but as far as I've heard it's only a few people in this area who've been joining. All Gaul's been summoned, so they say. Seems like not all that many are willing to walk miles to join Governor Vindex.'

I thanked him for the information and gave him one of Galba's coins for his troubles, making sure that I kept the purse well within my bundle of clothes. (You never know who might want to deprive a simple traveller of his purse.) Wearily I trudged up the stairs behind the landlord. The boards groaned beneath the man's weight, and his cumbersome frame made it difficult to squeeze past another of his clients who was trying to make the journey downwards. Eventually, after a great deal of huffing and puffing (not from me, I hasten to add), we made it to what I assumed was his cheapest room. I swear I saw a rodent's tail disappear into the darkness beneath the rather rickety-looking bed. The innkeeper gave me his candle and bade me good night. Too tired to care about the dinginess of my quarters, I flopped on to the bed, only to hear an ominous crack from one of the bedboards. Gingerly, I rolled on to my side.

Deprived of his guiding light, my host must have missed his footing, as I heard several bounces and a crash at the foot of the stairs, followed by a stream of Gallic curses. Allowing myself a small chuckle, as any more strenuous laughter would probably have been too great a strain for my fragile bed, I blew out the candle and waited for that sweet sleep.

V

On a new horse, I made excellent time on the road to Lugdunum. Despite an awful night's sleep, the prospect of managing a rebellion, albeit a small one, kept me fully awake and excited. Having got up relatively early and paid for a better beast than the nag I'd acquired on landing in Gaul, I'd turned on to the Rhone road and was heading north at a great pace. What surprised me was the sheer number of armed men I saw heading the same way. Well, I say armed, but it was mostly young boys with rusty hoes, though there was the occasional more seasoned man among them, a few even carrying ancient shields and swords. So the messengers had managed to drum up at least some support, but I decided to reserve judgement until I reached Lugdunum.

The landscape was slowly changing. While the Alps remained on my right, the mountains to the west began to level out and the river followed a more winding path. I passed other small villages like the one I had stopped at. The stream of men kept up, and occasionally I slowed to ask them where they were headed.

'To Lugdunum,' they replied. 'To end Roman tyranny!'

I was stunned. I knew Rome had ruled Gaul for less than a century, but I had not expected there to be widespread support for a full-scale rebellion. Was Galba aware of what forces he had unleashed here? I didn't think so. I had inferred that this was to be only a sideshow. How would these young farmers react if they found out that they were nothing more than a distraction? I dreaded to think about it.

It was mid-afternoon, and about twenty miles from Lugdunum, when I came upon a town called Vienne. What surprised me was the old fort at the top of a spur that jutted out towards the river: it was full to the brim with soldiers. All manner of tents – large, small, white, coloured – were pitched all over the hill, and I could make out the little pinpricks of men swarming everywhere. I dived off the main road and headed into the town. The place was a-buzz with activity, the people all busy making preparations. The steady clink of blacksmiths' hammers echoed around the streets, and armed men strode about carrying weapons, food and other supplies. What were they all doing here, and not at Lugdunum?

I was getting some strange looks, a horseman in a slave's working gear, but most were too busy with other things to take much notice of me. At a bend in the river I found the stone bridge that led to the west bank and up to the town's garrison. Deciding that it would be worth finding out exactly what was going on, I gave a tug at the reins and urged my horse towards the small fort at the top of the spur. Given how many armed men I had seen, I was surprised that I hadn't as yet been challenged.

With the main town behind me, I trotted up a track that led me among the myriad of scattered tents. I was sure by now that this was no Roman force, as it was far too slapdash for any self-respecting commander to put up with. Men sat around, chatting, drinking, gambling, barely giving me a glance as the horse picked its way through the confusion. The wooden palisade of the hill fort came closer and closer, and I spotted some strange banners flying over the gateway. The largest of them bore the emblem of a blue boar on a white background, and fluttered proudly in the wind.

Inside the fort I expected to find some legionaries, or at least some form of armed guard. Instead I saw what looked like some clerks and a quartermaster. I asked them where the commanding officer was, and they pointed towards the grandest tent I had seen yet. This was the first Roman thing I had spotted in the entire town, other than the fort, of course. A deep military red, it stood at a height of over two men, and was wide enough to accommodate a general and his staff. I shouted at the man I had assumed to be the quartermaster to look after the horse, swung out of the saddle and strode over towards the tent.

I walked straight in, as there was no guard to stop me, and found a few men poring over a large map on a battered wooden table. They didn't notice me at first, but the tallest of them, a great bear of a man with a brush of unkempt brown hair and wearing a sword at his side, looked up from the map and spotted me, standing impatiently.

'Who are you?' he asked.

'A damn good question! How is it that I've strolled into an officer's tent and haven't yet been challenged?'

I was furious. I had seen what I had to assume was a military force in this town, and was beginning to assume the worst. However, I kept my voice low, though the temptation to bawl at these men was huge.

'How dare you speak to me like that! I am in command here, and you have the effrontery, you grubby little peasant, to take that superior tone. I should call the guard,' the man shouted.

I gave a mock bow. 'By all means, commander.'

His face turning puce, he bawled: 'Guards! Arrest this man.'

No one came.

I stood there, unyielding, almost thankful I was wearing these shabby clothes, as it gave me the opportunity to judge the situation for myself. I was quivering with rage at the incompetence of the man. The few men with him looked hopefully towards the entrance to the tent, then, seeing that no one was coming, slowly backed towards the large man.

'There's no one out there. No guards. If I'd been a half-decent assassin, I could have ended this cock-eyed rebellion before it had even begun. I assume you are Governor Vindex?'

The governor looked thoroughly annoyed, and simply nodded.

'And who are these mutes cowering behind you?' I asked, nodding at the pale, skinny men who were edging ever closer to Vindex.

'These are my sons,' Vindex growled. 'And they have far more right to be here than you.'

I couldn't help but smirk at that assertion. 'I wouldn't be so sure about that. My name is Aulus Caecina Severus, quaestor of Hispania Baetica, formerly tribune with the Twentieth Valeria Victrix, and your military adviser.' Vindex's eyes boggled at that.

'Prove it. You don't look much of a soldier.'

In two quick steps I was beside the man. In the blink of an eye I drew his sword from his scabbard and had it at his throat. The young men behind looked aghast.

'Looks can be deceiving, Governor.'

I lowered the sword and retreated a few paces. Turning round, I poked my head through the flap of the tent and beckoned to the Gaul who was tending to my horse. 'Open up the saddlebags and bring me the letter inside.'

When the man handed me the letter of introduction from Galba, I put it into Vindex's hands myself and gave him back his sword. I enjoyed watching him struggling to read Galba's ornate Latin script. After an awkward silence he rolled it up, then had the good grace, just, to look a little sheepish.

'You took your time coming here,' he said.

This surly brute didn't seem to be taking to me all that well, which was not surprising given that I'd just held a sword to his neck, but if I was to be his chief military adviser it would be best not to come across as a spineless little toady. 'To be frank, just over a week ago I was enjoying myself in the deep south of Hispania and had never heard of Julius Vindex. I left Tarraco five days ago, only to find that you've started without me. As the man that Governor Galba hand-picked to assist you, *I* don't need to make any apologies.'

Again, silence.

'So,' I continued, 'would you mind explaining why you are here in Vienne and not at Lugdunum?'

Vindex muttered something quietly in Gallic to his sons, and they started to head out, looking quite relieved to be spared the rest of the conversation.

'I sent out riders in secret to all corners of Gaul a week ago, to tell all they could find to come to Lugdunum,' the man said. 'After three days one of my staff came running into my townhouse, pale as a sheet, and stammered that an army at least ten thousand strong was marching towards the city. You see, I hadn't told anyone in Lugdunum that I was leading this rebellion and expected them to be on side. Anyway, that evening I made a speech to the city, announcing my plans to give all the Gauls a part to play in overthrowing Nero.'

At this point, the now downcast man flumped into a small chair, which strained to support his immense frame.

'The trouble is, I'm not exactly a local. My tribe is the Aquitani, over in the south-west. I hadn't realized how pro-Nero the city was. It seems that when there was that great fire in Rome, the city levied over two million sesterces as a gift to help repair the damage. The very next year, a fire broke out in Lugdunum and Nero repaid every coin he had received from them, returning the debt when it was most needed. The emperor could do no wrong in their eyes, despite all the rumours we've heard.

'So the crowd didn't react as I had hoped. They were sullen and silent. I encouraged them to join me, and to march out to join their brothers outside the city. My sons and I led the way through the streets, and most of the crowd were following. When I ordered the city guard to open the gates, about thirty of us led the way on to the bridge, over to the water meadows where the army was gathering. Suddenly I heard the creaking of the city gates closing behind us, and a huge cheer went up from the crowd. Some of the men with us ran back to the gates, hammering on them and begging to be let back in. My sons and I left them and joined the army outside.'

I shook my head in disbelief. Galba had trusted this man to head a rebellion? It was incredible, and reminded me how little there was to separate farce from tragedy. 'How many men do you have altogether?'

'I don't know. We tried to besiege Lugdunum with the men we had, but we didn't have any siege equipment. As I'd told all the riders to send everyone to Lugdunum, I decided to blockade the town and send all newcomers here to Vienne. Remember, it's a long walk here from some parts of the country.'

'What about an armoury?' I asked.

'There are sets of armour and weapons for about two hundred men in the town's armoury, and we've got the blacksmiths in town working all hours to make as many swords and spears as they humanly can. Most of our recruits have only got farming tools really. Some have their ancestors' swords and shields from the days of the Roman conquest, but they're hardly in good condition.'

It was my turn to drop dejectedly into a chair. 'Let me make sure I've got the facts right. You started a rebellion without knowing if your own provincial capital supported it, you've blockaded that town, split your forces, you don't know how many men you have, they're poorly equipped, in need of food probably, and under the impression that they have come to liberate Gaul not from Nero but from "Roman tyranny". Well, that's just perfect.'

'How was I to get an army without making promises?' he retorted.

My blood was beginning to boil now. I fair screamed at him, 'You didn't need an army! What did you think this was, a chance to conquer Gaul for yourself? This is a sideshow, you fool. All Galba needs is for Nero to believe that he is threatened and that nobody supports him. We are doing this *for* Rome, not against Rome. Somehow I've got to convince your so-called army that this is not some heroic uprising to throw us out of Gaul, but a distraction to help another man overthrow Nero.'

Vindex mumbled something about what I thought he should do.

'I would suggest that you take no more decisions without consulting me first. But it's no good bickering over what's been done; how to fix the mess should be our chief concern. What we need most of all is a good intelligence officer. Someone who can keep an ear out among your "army" and find out what the general mood is around the country, and, most importantly, ascertain how the legions on the Rhine will react. Traders are generally the best, they have good reason to travel about.'

'I know one who might do. Lugubrix, he's a grain merchant, one of the chief suppliers for the legions in Upper Germania. He's also the man I'm trusting to supply our troops,' Vindex suggested.

'Once we know how many there are!' I found it amusing to see how quickly the arrival of someone with authority had cowed Vindex's rather overbearing manner. Having heard Galba's opinion, I had feared that this man was going to see me as an overgrown errand boy. Now it seemed he recognized that my advice would be useful to him. 'Can you take me to this man Lugubrix?'

'Of course. I asked him to meet me in the basilica, which I've requisitioned as my new headquarters. We only came up to the fort to see what there was. This tent was the best thing we found, plus some more supplies. I've had the quartermaster draw up an inventory, which he'll bring once it's finished.'

He got up, giving his poor seat a respite. 'Shall I take you to Lugubrix now?'

It was only on our way down to the town that I got a chance to observe my new commander properly. We picked our way through the various campsites, I on foot for once, and leading my horse with the reins in my right hand, while Vindex walked silently on my left. Despite his imposing figure and somewhat accented Latin, there were still tell-tale signs of a barbarian trying to be more Roman than the Romans. While his hair was an unruly mass of thick, brown curls – as though a bird had almost finished making an enormous nest, decided it wasn't quite right and mangled it in disgust – he was beardless, and wore a toga. Lacking an aquiline nose, he seemed content to carry his own protuberance as high as possible, to give himself that lordly look. Though I remembered Galba telling me that Vindex was an aristocrat, after the Gallic fashion, the man seemed horribly uncomfortable in his own skin. You must bear in mind, reader, that while Roman citizenship and ethnicity have no explicit link, in social terms it is nigh impossible for a 'barbarian' (and I use the word in its technical sense) to be accepted into high society. Thus even the noblest and most gifted of men were held back, only able to look upon the heights from the foothills they occupied.

Because of this, many foreign nobles would pay through the nose to give their sons a proper Roman education. And when I say Roman, of course I mean Greek. Naturally, since the days of Augustus, emphasis has veered back to this side of the Adriatic, but one can't ignore the Greek masters completely. Even I was forced to learn endless chunks of Homeric prose, the oratory of Demosthenes and the drama of Sophocles. Thankfully my mother spared me the perils of philosophy, otherwise my education would have been cut short by a slitting of my own wrists within a week. I suspect that Vindex may not have been so forgiving towards his own sons, hoping that with each generation they would move away from their tribal roots and closer to Rome.

Anyway, I digress. Vindex must certainly have had some sort of grievance against Nero that convinced him to risk his neck and make a stir in Gaul for Galba, in full knowledge that his Gallic origins would ensure that he could not make massive gains, even with an emperor's patronage. What it was I couldn't guess, and didn't particularly need to. I had a task in hand, and would fulfil it to the best of my ability.

When we crossed the bridge over the Rhone and headed into Vienne proper, once again my eyes were met with scenes of hurried activity, in stark contrast to the atmosphere on the looming hill where the fort stood. Vindex even received a few bows from those we passed in the street, his chest swelling with pride on each occasion. What I did notice was that Vindex as yet had not smiled once in the hour or so that I had known him. Despite the obvious respect he commanded in the town, he seemed at pains never to show any outward signs of satisfaction, a trait I thought rather odd. Dismissing this, I continued my little survey of the town. There was a rank smell of urine wafting its way towards us, and I surmised that the tanners were working non-stop to kit out Vindex's valiant freedom fighters with leather jerkins and the like. The area seemed readily defensible, what with the fort and the general lie of the land, which consisted of a series of interlocking spurs jutting out towards the river. However, I did not expect an attack to be made on Vienne any time soon. Nero's nearest legion was the First Italica, stationed near Mediolanum, hundreds of miles away.

We turned a corner, and were confronted with the looming presence of the basilica. Probably the most impressive building in the town, it was also the legal and administrative centre, so a normally busy place was now heaving with people. Tradesmen looking after their shops, small boys running errands for their masters, lawyers discoursing with one another, but precious few men who looked like soldiers. Vindex led the way inside, once I had given my horse to a runner, and we headed for the apse. Like half a dome jutting out at the end of the building, this was the area normally reserved for the senior magistrates, and I suppose that Vindex as praetor for this region had more right than any man to make use of it. A small wooden dais filled the space, where the magistrates would sit and give judgement, but now it had no chairs on it, just an empty table.

'This way,' Vindex grunted. Heading for the colonnade in the northern end of the building, we left most of the hustle and bustle behind us. I know that it sounds such a ridiculous stereotype, that we went into the shadows to find the spy, but here the cliché ends. You know how one expects spies to be small, ferrety creatures with shifty eyes set too close together, and possibly some crooked teeth thrown in? Well, Lugubrix was as different from that description as you could possibly imagine. The man waiting for us looked a few years the right side of fifty but had a few inches on me, and a similar sort of build: lean and sinewy. However, he also suffered from two afflictions that would hamper even the consummate spy's desire for anonymity: he was missing his left hand, and had the most violent shock of ginger hair that I had ever seen. I shall let you decide which was the greater affliction.

'Senator, this is my trusted friend Lugubrix. Lugubrix, this is the man sent from Hispania to help out with the campaign. I'll leave you to it then. Oh, Senator, I will arrange for you to be billeted in the house next to mine, and your horse can be stabled there.' Patting his friend's shoulder, Vindex then made his way back outside.

I watched him leave.

'There goes our glorious leader,' Lugubrix commented.

I was surprised. His Latin was almost perfect, and I told him so. He smiled at that. 'My mother was one of the Roman colonists who came to Lugdunum, but she married a Gaul and was thrown out by her family. We lived with my father's people this side of the Rhine, but I was taught both languages. Useful for trade . . . and other things.'

'And what do you make of the governor?' I asked.

'Honestly?'

'As honest as a man of your trade can be!'

He gave a little chuckle. 'Well, he tries to be Roman, I'll give him that. That's one of the reasons he left so abruptly, I should think. Normally we chat in our native language, but as I assume you only speak Latin he didn't want to be shown up. I mean, you can understand why. He's even trying to learn Greek! And he reads as much of their work, translated into Latin of course, as he can lay his hands on. I think he forgets that the people he's trying to impress are in Rome, and not here.

'I was in Lugdunum when he tried to win over possibly the most pro-Nero town in all Gaul! He has these grand ideas of a pan-Gallic movement, and imagines that Galba might make him a client ruler of the whole of Gaul, not just this province. You should have heard his speech!'

'Good stuff?' I asked.

'See what you think, I remembered some of the best of it. He gassed for about ten minutes on the evils of Nero, all those old stories about killing his mother Agrippina and acting in the theatre for the plebs. Then: "Does anyone think it fitting that such a person is both a Caesar and our emperor? These are sacred titles that must not be abused. They were held by Augustus and by Claudius, whereas this fellow might most properly be termed Thyestes, Oedipus, Alcmaeon or Orestes; for these are the characters that he represents on the stage and it is these titles that he has assumed in place of the others.

Therefore rise now against him; succour yourselves and succour the Romans; liberate the entire world!"'

'Gods, has the man no common sense at all?'

'That's my job.' The reply came as quick as one of Jupiter's bolts. I was beginning to warm to this man far more than his master. Well, I say master. Employer would be nearer the mark.

'I notice that he didn't stay to talk about your job,' I said, 'so I'm guessing that makes me his chief of intelligence, on top of everything else. So, to be blunt, why should I use you and why should I trust you?'

'In essence, because my contacts are wide-ranging and reliable. I run a family business, chiefly in grain, that stretches all over Gaul. My brother-in-law is based at Narbo, so he keeps me informed of what is happening in Hispania and overseas. We have farms about a day south of here, not far from the passes into Cisalpine Gaul, and that way we keep in touch with the news from Italia. Finally, I manage the grain run up the Rhine, from Rhaetia all the way to the Ocean.'

'Sounds like a thriving business. Why give it up to help us?' I asked, a little puzzled.

'You remember I mentioned my father, the Gaul?' I nodded. 'He was a great friend of Vindex's father, and when my father died, the family was good to my mother and me. They even gave me a bit of an education, and enough capital to start my own business. I'm just glad that I now have a chance to repay the debt.'

The man didn't come across as a liar, but as an honest man wanting to do his bit. In fact I sympathized with him. At least my benefactor was a man worthy of service and respect. This man owed his allegiance to a fool. I held out my hand and he took it, smiling.

'I shall need payment, of course,' Lugubrix said.

'Of course, but I'd take that up with Vindex. I only arrived today, and I reckon he wouldn't take it well if I was already handing out vast sums of money in his name.'

We headed outside, keeping our voices down for obvious reasons. The spring sun was straining to reach the part of town where the basilica stood, as one of the great spurs kept this quarter of Vienne in the shade.

'I need you to get to work right away. I don't particularly mind how you do it, just get me regular and detailed reports. First, I want to know what the general reaction to this rebellion has been around Gaul. You can leave out the far north-west, but everywhere else I need to gauge how popular this uprising is. Second, get your contacts to fill you in on all the news from Hispania. I know that Galba is going to recruit a new legion, but I need to know when, and anything else you can discover. Similarly, there's a legion in northern Italia that could be sent, so let me know if they so much as move a mile. Most importantly, I need to know everything I can about the Rhine legions. Numbers, morale, condition, officers, the lot. It is of the utmost importance that they don't become involved in Gaul, but we need to be prepared. Is that clear, Lugubrix?'

'Perfectly. One question though.'

'Which is . . . ?' I paused.

'May I ask your name? Vindex mentioned that you were a senator, and that you were previously in Hispania, and I can't imagine there are many senators there who aren't office-holders.'

Lugubrix was very shrewd, I thought to myself. I didn't want to disclose my name to him, since the fewer men who knew I was helping in a plot to overthrow Nero, the better. However, though I had only just met him, I felt instinctively that I could trust this man. After all, if you can't trust your own spies, who can you trust?

'All right,' I conceded. 'But only on the understanding that you never tell another soul. My name is Caecina Severus. We might as well choose a password while we're about it. How about Vicetia?'

'Vicetia?' Lugubrix did not recognize the name.

'My home town.'

He nodded assent.

'Can I ask you something?' I said.

'If it's about my hand, I had an argument with a man about a deal, a few years back. I lost my hand, he lost more.' Drawing his finger across his neck, he gave a grim smile. Turning, he called over his shoulder: 'I'll report back when I can.'

VI

I spent a week in that town, a week sorting out the Vindex rebellion, as it came to be known. It seems that in his correspondence with Galba, Vindex had somewhat over-estimated his abilities. He was a dreamer not a planner, merely babbling on about the marvellous ideas he had. For instance, at one time he wanted to go on a grand tour of all Gaul, so that he could directly engage with the people and stir them all into open revolt. The next day he suggested minting new coins with Galba's head on them, and after that, the most incredible notion of the lot, to march at the head of his so-called army to the Rhine, and ask the legions one by one to join in the rebellion.

It took careful handling and endless patience to manage Vindex. It would be fair to say that his enthusiasm rivalled his lack of organizational prowess. It fell to me to run pretty much the entire campaign for him, a considerable step up from my previous military role. Julius Agricola would have loved this sort of work. As a member of General Paulinus's staff, the to-ing and fro-ing would have been second nature to him, liaising with various sections of the command, logistics, intelligence and of course the legions themselves. Though my time as a tribune had been similar, it was on a much smaller scale, within the confines of one legion, where I had a more military function. But then again, Julius would probably not have enjoyed this campaign. He liked the chain of command and smooth workings of the Roman war machine.

This was not the Roman war machine.

For a start, Vindex had been so eager to get started that he didn't think before sending out rallying cries of Gallic rebellion, so it would not go down all that well with the recruits to have them square-bashing and kitted out in the armour of the legions. Even the slightest whiff of Roman involvement would cause severe ructions; many would go home before a sword had been lifted, tarnishing the credibility of the movement beyond repair. I took great pains to ensure that my identity did not leak out.

'But I want people to know I have a Roman senator with military experience at my side!' Vindex complained when I raised the issue.

'And how well do you think that will look with these men of yours who want to "throw off the chains of Roman tyranny", as you delicately put it? If they thought for a moment that a Roman officer was helping to run the campaign, you would have a mutiny on your hands. Secondly, do you really think that I want my name shouted around Gaul, and then the entire empire, as a traitor, who had turned on Nero a few months into his first magistracy? I rather like my head where it is, so I'll trouble you not to breathe a word of my existence to anyone.' Then an idea struck me: 'If you must address me in front of other people, you had better use a false name. Perhaps I could be a nephew of yours? I'm certainly tall enough to be mistaken for a Gaul.'

The ruse worked well. If I was to manage the campaign, I could hardly conduct all our meetings in secret, given everything that needed doing. As yet I was the only Roman who had joined with Vindex, the rest being chiefly made up of country boys seeking to emulate the glorious deeds of their ancestors in an otherwise peaceable age. Plus my status as a close relation of the governor would go a long way to explaining why I had such access to him and such influence within the campaign.

One of the first things I did was try to establish how many men we had in Vienne, and how many were keeping watch on Lugdunum. It was especially hard to count those who were with us in Vienne, partly because many of them had billeted themselves in the town, and also because there was no proper command system or any military units, so in the end we had to give a general order: anyone of military age, from seventeen to forty-five, and able to fight was summoned to the hill with the fort at its summit. There they were divided into groups of one hundred and counted. This was tricky at times, for there were a surprising number of men who had difficulty in counting as far as a hundred, so we had to make a rough estimate. We reached an astounding total: twenty thousand in Vienne alone, plus the ten thousand at Lugdunum. This may not seem so massive, given the size of Gaul, but when you bear in mind that Vindex had sent out messengers only just over a week ago, it was a staggering achievement. Whereas I had ridden flat out, changing horses, from Forum Julii, most of our would-be recruits would have travelled slowly on foot, and from different directions, so to have thirty thousand within a week was more than any realistic man would have dared to hope for.

Governor Vindex, however, was not a realistic man. Though I tried to explain to him that thirty thousand men at this early stage was phenomenal, he honestly expected all Gaul to rise up and fight with him. He was buoyant when I promised to take care of training the recruits. Then his brow furrowed. 'But we don't have enough weapons to go round.'

I smiled. 'You don't need weapons for what I've got in store for them.'

Before a legionary claps eyes on his first gladius, he is given a sack and told to fill it with rocks. Our legions have conquered most of the world not through numbers but through discipline and efficiency. Roman soldiers are expected to be able to march thirty miles every day in full armour, and still have enough energy left to build a fortified camp for the night, or even fight. Having detailed a party to collect stones and rocks from the river, I split the recruits into two divisions: two legions under me, and another two under Quintus, Vindex's eldest son. Thankfully he had not inherited his father's complacency, and had a shrewd enough brain for me to have few worries about giving him command of two legions. Of course it pleased his father no end. Quintus was to march his men due east for fifteen miles, no matter what the terrain, and I due west, then about turn and back to Vienne. Of course a crack legion would have done it in a day, but I wanted the Gauls to make up for their lack of battle experience with immense stamina.

There were many grumbles when the news was sprung on the men the night before, but I told them that they could either do as they were told or be dragged before Vindex to explain why they weren't pulling their weight. No one wanted to disappoint their precious governor and leader, so both Quintus and I left with a full complement the next morning. I was determined to show that the march could be done, so I arranged to march with the men, with my own sack of rocks, making sure that Quintus did the same. If men are to have any respect for their officers, those officers have to match their men for courage and commitment. I realize that this may sound rather old-school military discipline, but I have often found that a bit of sweat now and again can make the rigours of command less of an ordeal. Imagine how an ordinary legionary would react if he was given a particularly dangerous mission by an officer whose greatest physical strain was mounting his mighty stallion for a parade now and again, before returning to his comfortable quarters for a gourmet dinner!

I had been wary of using Roman military groupings, such as

legions and cohorts, but the tactical superiority they afforded outweighed any mutterings from the ranks about how free Gauls shouldn't march in maniples. Getting ten thousand untrained men to march in step was a task for a centurion, not an ex-tribune like me, so I dispensed with that task and had my legions assemble at dawn on the western hill, while Quintus's troops were on the eastern side of the river. The youngest stood at the front and the more senior recruits formed the rearguard. It was not a particularly impressive sight, two groups of five thousand men in various states of attire. Many hadn't bothered to cover their top halves, while some of the older and wiser heads had kept a small barrier of material between their skin and the straps of their heavy-laden sacks. Silently I prayed that they would be even half as fit as a legion should be.

'Forward . . . march!' I bellowed, and we trundled off.

I took my place at the head of the marching column, swinging the sack on to my back at the last possible moment, and then strode purposefully away into the orange glow of the rising sun. Phoebus and his fiery chariot would drive directly over our heads as we headed up into the western hills whose slopes caught the waters that would trickle down into the Rhone. Little farmsteads dotted the landscape, and I felt for their owners as twenty thousand feet tramped over the fields. Though I had said that we would be marching due west, I tried to make sure that we took the route that caused as little damage as possible, keeping to small roads and tracks as and when we could. I was wary of stretching the two legions into a marching column that too much resembled a piece of string, as that would only encourage the less fit among my men to drop out when the army went round a bend. Instead a shorter, wider column made its way through the valleys and up into the hills.

I did hope that we wouldn't lose too many on the first leg of the march, but I was prepared in case anyone waited in the long grass for our eventual return and spared themselves several hours of painful exercise. After three hours I decided to drop back a bit and see how the older ones were doing. Telling the front ranks to keep the pace up or face a flogging, I marked time, waiting for the rear to catch up. The ranks walked on past, a little ragged but still resembling a military machine. I was pleasantly surprised to see the older men were bearing up well. Most had sacrificed good posture for comfort, their backs helping to prop up the heavy sacks, forcing their heads to stare at the ground about three yards ahead of them. Many of them didn't notice me, while of those who did, some managed a brief smile before returning to the monotony of the march. Thankfully, a few years' soft living hadn't knocked me badly out of shape, so I was able to quicken my pace and resume my position at the head of the column.

Come midday, with the sun beating down mercilessly, some of the men began to suffer. But it was not the older men. While they were indeed a bit hotter with the extra layer of clothing, the young bucks who had deemed a top layer unnecessary were starting to rue their mistake. Not only was their skin burning, but the cloth straps of their sacks were wearing great sores on their chests and shoulders. I managed to catch a few sneaking some rocks out of their packs, and had them jog in front of me for an hour, then put them in the front rank. Others tried grabbing dock leaves, of which there were plenty at the side of the track, and packed several beneath the skin-burning straps. At last, some had showed proper initiative! I took their names as potentials for promotion.

I decided it was time for a pause as we reached the brow of an especially tricky slope, and gave the order to halt. The men dropped to the ground, some of them gasping, so shattered that they did not care one bit about falling flat on the rough edges of the stones that they had been carrying all these miles. By my reckoning we had done about fifteen miles, perhaps a fraction less than what a legion would have done in the same time, but I doubted that we would make it back to Vienne before dark.

A small brook trickled down the hill that we had reached, and I reckoned that an hour would be enough time for all the men to have a drink and a breather. More importantly, I needed the water for another reason. We'd brought along a couple of packhorses, who carried a few sacks of blue dye as well as some brushes and bowls. Mixing some water with the dye, we splashed a streak of blue on the left forearm of every man who had made it that far.

We slowed the rate down on the way back, and I won't bother to describe the tedious return journey. This time I spent most of the march at the rear, giving stragglers encouragement or a kick, depending on my mood or the man in particular. Eventually, a long time after dark, we made it back to Vienne. I immediately had a count-up. Of the ten thousand or so who had set off with me that morning, there were about eight hundred who hadn't received the splash of dye. These men were told to leave the town and return home. Tired, moaning, the veterans of the march wandered off to their lodgings, whether in tents on the hill or in the town.

Heading back into town towards my own bed, I met young Quintus coming down from the hill that had the town's theatre carved into its side.

'How many?' I called up to him.

He shook his head. 'Fourteen hundred or thereabouts. I can't believe it. Did we really have to send them all home?'

'Quintus, thankfully you've never seen how deadly the legions can be. These men are never going to fight like legionaries, so the best we can do is make them as fit as we possibly can.'

He still looked fairly downhearted, so I ruffled his thick, tousled hair and said, 'Keep your chin up. Officers have to set an example to the men. Who knows? You could become a great commander.'

He looked up, his eyes shining. 'Do you really think so?'

'I'm sure of it. Now, off to your father and make your report. Tell him I sent eight hundred men packing, and I shall see him at the third hour in the basilica tomorrow.'

'Good night, sir.'

I smiled. 'You don't need to call me sir now. I'm meant to be your cousin, remember? You're supposed to call me Gnaeus.'

'Sorry . . . Gnaeus,' he apologized.

'That's all right. Now off with you, I need to sleep just as much as anyone else in this army of your father's.' He nodded, and disappeared down one of the side streets that led to the back entrance to Vindex's quarters. Though my billet was the villa next door, I was the only occupant and had no one to disturb, so I made for the front door.

I knocked, and heard the tinkle of a chain's links sliding across the floor as someone on the other side grumbled and fumbled for the key. The sound of a stubborn bolt being drawn back was followed by the appearance of two blue eyes in a small window in the solid door, which was closed as quickly as it had been opened. It seemed to be taking the old janitor an age to let me in, and I was reminded of a snatch of Ovid: 'The hours of the night are passing, remove the bolt from the door.' Calling for him to hurry up, I turned my back and leaned on the obstinate door.

Suddenly, I glimpsed a small movement out of the corner of my eye, and in the dark made out a hooded figure in the shadows, peering out from around a street corner about twenty yards away.

'Who's there?' I shouted.

The figure turned and fled, and I started to run after him. The hard slap of leather sandals on the cobbles was unmistakable, but the figure was well hidden beneath the hood and thick folds of a dark cloak. He dived off into another street, and I followed as quickly as I could. Vienne was an absolute maze, with tiny little alleys and passageways forming a giant honeycomb, and when I turned the corner I only just made out the flicker of an outstretched leg heading off down yet another alleyway. If I hadn't been marching with the army all day I might have made a better chase of it, but I was already flagging after only a few minutes' pursuit. Cursing, I slowed to a stop, and bent double to catch my breath.

Having admitted defeat, still wheezing somewhat, I made my slow way back to my billet, and asked the janitor if he had seen anyone, or if there had been people asking for me. He swore that no one had come calling, and returned to his bed by the door. Too tired to worry about it any longer, I decided to follow his example.

VII

Rising at the second hour, I called for a slave to bring some hot water for my shave. You might think it a bit strange, me shaving myself. Nero's wife Poppaea, the woman who used to be married to Otho, had started a fashion in Rome of using some strange concoctions of cream to remove hair. I've heard that they put some weird and wonderful things in the creams: resin, pitch, white wine, ivy gum extract, ass's fat, she-goat's gall, bat's blood and powdered viper. Anyway, it wasn't for me. Most decent men had their own barber, but after serving in the legions I didn't have time for such luxuries, so I had got into the habit of shaving myself.

I had just begun to slide the blade along my cheek when one of Vindex's runners burst into my room. 'Sir! Sir!' he shouted. My hand jerked in surprise, making a searing lash on my cheek. I can still remember the boy's face as he saw me, razor in hand and a slow trickle of blood reaching my neck.

'Have you never learned to knock, you feckless idiot?'

Staring open-mouthed at me, he began to apologize.

'Never mind, what's so urgent that you need to barge into my private chambers?' I asked.

The boy stammered, 'Governor Vindex requests your presence in the basilica immediately, sir. He says he has vital news.'

'Thank you. Now perhaps you'll let me repair the damage?'

Nervously smiling, he nodded and closed the door behind him.

I tended to my wound as best I could, then quickly threw on some clothes and headed out to meet my lord and master. Figuratively speaking. I was walking hurriedly along the street when someone grabbed my arm. I was about to give him an earful when I spotted the shock of ginger hair. Lugubrix started walking me back in the direction that I had come from.

'Bloody man didn't think it would be clever to talk with his own spy somewhere private!' Lugubrix muttered angrily.

Soon we were outside my villa and then approaching the same back entrance that Quintus had used the night before.

'What's the big news?' I asked.

'We'll talk inside.'

We used the small back door to enter the place, only to find the governor waiting for us in the garden. He did not look all that pleased. Testily, he stated, 'I do not take kindly to being given orders by my own staff. Why did you feel the need to tell me publicly to go home, Lugubrix?'

'Precisely because we were in public, Governor. Is there somewhere we can go where we can't be overheard?'

'My study, I suppose.'

He didn't seem to take the hint. 'So shall we . . . ?' I asked, motioning for him to take us inside.

Vindex led us into the villa, and along a corridor or two. Though he had commandeered the place very recently, I was surprised to see several marble busts of Greeks lining the wall. There was even one of Alexander. Sheer vanity.

At last we came to his study, and Vindex took his seat behind a small desk. Though there was another chair in the room, he did not offer us the use of it. My eyes flicked from the chair to

Lugubrix, and he smiled and nodded. I dragged the chair to the side of the room, so that I could watch both men while Lugubrix made his report.

'So, Lugubrix, what is so important that it needs to be said in such secrecy?'

'Only this, sir: the legions are stirring.'

'What?' Vindex sat bolt upright, his eyes bulging.

'The emperor has ordered the First Italica to end your rebellion, and they have broken camp. At this moment they are heading towards the Alpine passes to their west, and will march towards Massilia and then north to meet us.'

'It's not as if this was entirely unexpected, Governor,' I interrupted. 'Did you honestly believe that Nero's favoured legion would just sit tight and leave you alone while you rebel against him?'

Vindex fidgeted. 'Well, no, but I didn't expect it so soon. Severus, do you think that we can take care of one legion?'

'Since we outnumber them by six to one, and given the right location, certainly.'

'Excellent, we can march south and catch them in the mountains,' the governor proclaimed.

'I wouldn't advise that, Governor,' Lugubrix said. 'The Rhine legions are coming too.'

This time Vindex looked truly stunned. 'I . . . I . . . thought you said that they wouldn't support Nero?'

'It seems that Verginius Rufus, the governor of Upper Germania, is a bit of a constitutionalist. He has no love for Nero, despite being appointed by him, but he doesn't think it right to rebel against the emperor, even if it is justified. But that's not the main reason why he is coming. From where he's sitting, it sounds too much like a Gallic rebellion for comfort.'

'What is the condition of the Rhine legions?' I asked.

Lugubrix looked solemn. 'Militarily, as strong as they've ever been. They've been carrying out some raids on the barbarians, and are in good shape. However, since they've all been posted there so long, there is something that could help us.' He paused for a moment, probably for the benefit of Vindex. 'The legions are very independent, each with their own rivalries. Now if we were to convince Rufus that we were a strong and organized force, he would have no choice but to counter us with a strong army of his own. He can't empty a part of the Rhine frontier of troops, so he will have to take detachments from all of the legions. Then we can try and play them off against each other.'

'So what we need is some counter-intelligence.' I was thinking out loud. 'Can you feed them some false information about our numbers?'

The Gaul smiled. 'I've already done that. Apparently we number around a hundred thousand, and with the centurions and arms that we captured at Lugdunum,' here he gave a wink, 'our army has been drilled and armed in the Roman style.'

'Excellent work!'

'What do you mean, excellent?' This was from the governor. 'Now we will have to fight an army of veteran legionaries, and then defeat another legion coming up from the south.'

I was amazed that he still didn't understand. 'May I remind you, sir, that our objective is not to win, but to help Galba? Of course we can't beat the Rhine legions, but we can negotiate with Rufus. Try and convince him to stay out of this altogether. We should march in force to confront his army, and then try and meet him in private. Do you know when and where they are likely to move?'

'Not as yet. It will take time to assemble all the various detachments from the legions stationed further down the Rhine, especially the ones near the ocean, but it shouldn't take the Romans long to get themselves organized,' Lugubrix answered.

'What about Galba? Any news from Hispania?' I enquired. You'll notice that Vindex was doing very little of the talking.

'As far as I know, he's still in the throes of recruiting his new legion. If he is going to declare his intentions, it had better be soon.'

'So what would you suggest, Severus?'

I paused for thought. I can still remember that moment even now. Effectively I was in command of my own commander, and by extension his thirty thousand or so troops. It was a new feeling, the exhilaration of military power, and not an unpleasant one.

'Step up the training,' I recommended. 'In an ideal world, we won't ever have to fight the Rhine legions, but we had better make sure our forces will not be totally unprepared. I would suggest lifting the siege at Lugdunum and bringing the men here. Concentrate our force and see what move Rufus makes. We don't initially have anything to fear from the Italica legion. It will take a while for Rufus to assemble a force from two provinces, and we must use the time Lugubrix has bought us as best we can.'

Vindex tried to argue. 'Why should I break off the siege? It is a rallying point for the Gauls, and I won't abandon it lightly.'

'With respect, sir, it is precisely because of this "freedom of the Gauls" nonsense that Rufus has decided to interfere. What practical use is the siege serving?'

The governor's mouth froze and his eyes drifted upwards, as if he was thinking hard. If it were not such a serious situation, I would have called it comical.

'Very well, Severus. It's in your hands, then.' He stood up to leave. 'But . . . I am still going to lead the army against our enemies, aren't I?'

I gave him a reassuring smile and, winking at Lugubrix, replied: 'Of course you are, sir. We wouldn't dream of depriving you of that privilege.'

He looked much relieved. I think he was beginning to realize that he wasn't in quite as much control of the campaign as he had once thought he was. Composing himself, he stood up and walked purposefully out of the room. Not that I knew what pressing demand he had on his time. Perhaps his daily Homer lesson awaited him?

Lugubrix still stood there, looking as happy as an amorous young man who has just seen his love's parents leaving the house for the weekend.

'Why so smug?' I asked.

'I hadn't quite realized until now who was in charge of this little rebellion. And I'm glad it's someone who values me properly.'

I stood up and proffered my hand. He took it gladly.

'By the way,' I said quietly, still gripping his one hand, 'I was followed to my own door last night by someone who was at great pains not to be seen.' I took a step closer, still clasping his hand but smiling politely. 'And if I find that my own spy has been spying on me, losing a hand will seem as nothing compared to the effects of my rather inventive imagination. Understood?'

I was pleased to see a lack of comprehension in his eyes, so I let go of his hand and rested mine on his shoulder as I led him back into the street.

'Now, I need a constant update on the movements of those Rhine legions, and what Galba is up to. Thank you for your help.'

With that, I left him to his thoughts and headed up towards the basilica. Having found a runner boy, I told him to find Quintus and the other senior officers, and to have them report to me up at the hill fort.

An hour later, we were all assembled in the grand tent where I had first met Vindex. At my right-hand side was Quintus; what he lacked of his father's height and build he made up for with enthusiasm and charm. Next to him was Martialis, a small and furtive character, and one of the cleverest Gauls I had yet come across. Then there was Albanos. He was quiet and surly, but had proven himself a good leader. Bormo was a terrific swordsman.

Young and confident, despite his extraordinary talent he was one of the most level-headed and pragmatic men I could ask for. Carnunnos was the eldest of us. I'd reckoned him to be in his mid-forties, with a mane of greying hair. He was from Vienne itself, but widely travelled. I'd heard whispers that he came from a family that had produced several druids, until we came to Gaul and stamped out the barbaric religion.

I had been allowed to choose these men myself, apart from Albanos. He was from the Aquitani, like Vindex, and had been forced on me. That wasn't to say that he was incompetent or obstructive, but nonetheless I resented having someone foisted upon me.

'I have serious news. The emperor has sent his legion in Italia to meet us.' A small murmur went round the table. 'However, that need not immediately concern us,' I continued. 'What does concern us is the fact that Governor Rufus has decided to fight us, and as you know his legions are much closer.'

Martialis spoke up. 'Well, that's the rebellion over. What hope have we against all those legions?'

'Thank you for that positive assessment, Martialis. I'll tell you exactly why we're not giving up. First, those legions are primarily there to keep the German tribes from spilling over the Rhine and into our lands. Remember Ariovistus and the Helvetii? The Romans stopped them from ransacking Gaul. So, they can't weaken their defences too much in opposing us, otherwise the tribes might break through. Secondly, I am reliably informed that the legions all hate each other; some haven't been paid, and don't particularly support Nero. If they do decide to come for us, we don't have to face them in open battle. We can skirmish, and play them off against each other.'

It was Bormo's turn to interrupt. 'But we've never been trained to fight like skirmishers, let alone in open formations.'

'That is why we are going to concentrate solely on manoeuvres and skirmishes from now on. The Romans won't be able to organize themselves for some time yet, they're spread out over too great a distance. That probably gives us at the very least a fortnight to prepare.'

The men looked grim at that, but there was nothing else to be done. Obviously I didn't want to send untrained men to their deaths. That was why I was so desperate to negotiate with Verginius Rufus, and prevent a massacre of men fighting for a cause that didn't exist. But it was not all bad news.

'I shall draw up training schedules for each of your units, and over the next week there will be a series of war games. Most of our recruits come from this region, so the attackers, with local knowledge, will practise against columns of those who aren't so familiar with the area. And of course we shall alternate between attackers and defenders. Except you, Martialis. If we do have to fight, it will be in the region between here and the Rhine. Go and stay with your friends in the Sequani, and spy out the lie of the land. I want you to find potential sites for ambushes so we can use them.'

For the first time, Albanos spoke. 'How is it that you're the one who's going to train us in how to beat the Romans, when you have no more military experience than the rest of us? I'm from the Aquitani, like your uncle the governor, but I can't say I've ever heard of you!'

Quintus was about to step in, but I wasn't comfortable with having a back-story made up for me by anyone other than myself. Not only did I have to come up with an astoundingly good lie on the spur of the moment, but I had to be convincing. If I failed, either my authority would be undermined or, worse, my cover blown.

'I'm sorry if you are unhappy with me in command, but there is a very simple reason that you may not know so much about me. While you were with our fellow tribesmen, working as a . . . sorry, what was it again?' I asked.

'A carpenter,' he admitted.

'Yes, that was it. Anyway, while you were no doubt ferocious in your attacks on your wooden wares, I was learning my trade with Bo—' I checked myself, remembering that the Celts pronounced the name of the British queen with a different accent to we Romans. 'With Boudicca.'

Silence.

'Quintus's father and mine were keen to have good relations with the chiefs in Britannia in the hope that she would defeat the Romans, and the best way to do that was to send a relation to help the cause. A volunteer was needed. Quintus and his brothers were far too young, so they sent me.' I decided to twist the knife a bit. Sarcasm can be so much fun. 'Until that last battle, I happened to think we were doing rather well, you know, destroying three Roman towns and annihilating almost an entire legion. Now, is there anyone else who fancies my command? I'll happily lay it down if a better man comes forward.'

I looked around the table. Quintus was beaming, and Albanos just stared hard at me, which I took to mean assent. Crisis averted, I thought it might be no bad thing if I started to grow a beard. Disgusting things that they are – even some of the Gauls are coming round to ditching them – covering up my facial features with some barbarian bristles might help me fit in a bit better.

'So, Martialis, you will choose a deputy and send him to me, and he can take your place during the war games while you do the scouting. Quintus's division, your men under the deputy and Albanos's troops will head up into the hills west of here where my lot had their route march, and I will take Carnunnos and Bormo's units to the east. I think that's everything. I'll send you the training instructions by mid-afternoon, meanwhile, return to your units and liaise with the quartermaster to see what equipment you still need. Quintus, you'll stay for a moment, please.'

Most of them gave a respectful nod and started to leave.

Albanos muttered something in Gallic, but my back was turned to him as I was about to continue talking with Quintus. But as soon as the words had been spoken, I saw a shocked reaction from both my friend and young Bormo. They looked at me, expecting a response of some kind. Not having the faintest idea what Albanos had said, I didn't know what to say! The best I could do was: 'That will do, Albanos. Return to your men.'

Sniggering, he left the tent, followed by a staggered Bormo. Quickly, I asked Quintus what had been said.

'He called you a jumped-up little turd! You really don't know any Gallic?'

'Some. After all, it's not too different from Latin. But how in Hades am I expected to know your curse words?' I countered.

Quintus shrugged. Arguing the point would solve nothing. 'Well, now he knows that you speak Latin better than any Gaul, and yet next to no Gallic. I don't know why he should have been so mistrustful of you beforehand though . . .'

Poor Quintus. An excellent companion but somewhat naive.

'I'm sorry to say this, Quintus, but it must be your father's doing. Not only is Albanos from your tribe, but he was very strongly recommended to me by your father, far too strongly. He must be here to keep an eye on me.'

'But why would my father want to spy on you?'

'Because I'm in charge of this rebellion, and your father resents that. I don't know what he wanted to achieve in this campaign, but he's a very small piece on a very large board. I don't mind giving you responsibility, you've got talent, but Albanos is just a spy. I reckon your father didn't tell Albanos the whole truth about the purpose of the campaign, but sowed some seeds of doubt about me instead.'

Quintus was speechless. Eventually, he asked, 'What are you going to do?'

I sighed, and planted my hands on the table. 'What can I do? I have nothing against your father. He means well, but doesn't have the ability or experience to organize this movement. His name gives credibility to the whole revolt. If I took command under the false name, either he would denounce me or Albanos would. I need to stay here, or the gods alone know what would happen when we meet the Rhine legions.' I looked up at my young friend, and reassured him. 'Your father has nothing to fear from me, he's just trying to reassert his authority, that's all. I shall ask him to relieve Albanos of command and send him home, probably.'

'I had better set about looking for his replacement then.'

'Thank you, Quintus.'

'Not at all, Senator.' Quintus gave a playfully elaborate bow, and left.

VIII

After a tedious couple of days sorting out the logistics of a possible march towards the Rhine, I decided to broach the subject of Albanos with Vindex. The exchange did not go well. I was angry that he had effectively put one of his hounds on to me, and told him so. He countered with a complaint that he barely knew me, yet he was meant to entrust the entire campaign to me on the strength of Galba's word.

'Just on Galba's word, isn't that enough?' I retorted. 'Your future emperor tells you that I am trustworthy and more than competent, and you have the balls to question his authority and judgement?'

He mutely shook his head.

'Then call your spy off. He must not know the truth, or do you want me to tell your precious army what you're really up to? A pawn of politics, leading a rabble of Gauls against crack Roman legions for your own personal gain, not to free Gaul from Roman rule.'

He was quivering by this stage, though whether through anger or fear, I don't know.

'You wouldn't dare!'

'I would.' I was lying through my teeth, of course. Galba

needed this rebellion to go ahead, and we couldn't risk the army deserting because Vindex had twisted the truth. 'Tell me, Vindex, what are you hoping to gain from this? Why did you offer to help Galba?'

He paused, and I saw his eyes flick downward as he searched for the right words.

'Because Nero is rotting this empire from the core. Galba is the only man who can offer Rome moral leadership without sinking into tyranny.' I didn't believe him, but Vindex's motives were the least of my worries for now.

'Tell your man that my loyalty is not in question, and that his services are no longer required. I'll find a replacement for him shortly.' And with that I swept out, leaving my master fuming.

For the most part, the war games went surprisingly well. I did not envisage a scenario featuring a pitched battle between the two armies, as the misguided Gauls would be crushed. So I concentrated on another kind of warfare.

It hadn't been completely untrue, what I had said about learning from Boudicca. My service in Britannia had meant that I was indeed experienced in skirmishes and the like, except that it was the Britons who had instigated them and not us. I knew the terror of being caught in an ambush, to be marching along an unerringly straight Roman road only to hear the chilling cry of barbarian horns. It is like a man who walks alone at night through a forest, confident that no one is around, and then hears a twig snap behind him.

Suddenly the crashing din of swords hitting shields echoes all around you, coupled with eerie wailing and chanting. Finally, the enemy appears. Hordes of huge, half-naked tribesmen, covered in a ghastly blue dye, materialize as if out of thin air on either side. You are surrounded, trapped. Men break away and try to run for it. They are quickly cut down. Soon your column is broken into small pieces who group together into tight formations, each man praying to his own god that he will survive the onslaught.

It is calmness that saves you. The experienced men band together quickly, forming a near-impenetrable unit. An ambush depends on speed and surprise, so confronting one with a well-organized wall of men with armour and shields dramatically improves your chances of survival. Then you have to endure wave after wave of attacks; sometimes from just the one side, other times you are completely surrounded.

It was that terror that I wanted these Gauls to evoke in their enemies, but it would be difficult. The legionaries would have been fighting tribesmen on the Rhine frontier most of their professional lives, and would be as inured as any human can be to the fear. However, that would not make them invulnerable. Hannibal acted mercilessly at Lake Trasimene. Arminius destroyed the best part of three legions in the Teutoburg Forest. Boudicca did it to a column of the Ninth Legion, annihilating them completely. It was just a matter of training.

After some hours of searching, I found the perfect place to drill my men in the art of the ambush. A dirt track wound its way up from the valley towards the hills, and straightened out between two fairly even slopes. The crest of the hills that overlooked the track had thick woods that offered excellent cover. At this time of year small buds had started to grow, but nothing more, so the attackers would have to lie down until the last possible moment. Normally an ambush can defeat a body of men that outnumbers it, so the ambushers would all wait on one side for their prey. However, so that as many men as possible could observe, I split my command into four. Half of Bormo's men would face half of Carnunnos's, who would be stationed on both hills, while the other units would watch from the cover of the trees.

The preparations were made. I gave Bormo the simple order to march into the hills and to defend his unit. To have them march uphill for an hour would make the experience more realistic. Obviously we gave the men the sticks that they used for training, but otherwise I wished to make the exercise as lifelike as possible.

Bormo marched at the head of just over two thousand men, a wooden training sword in his grasp. From my vantage point I could see them in the distance, advancing inexorably into our trap. Bormo even had the first few ranks marching in step! I glanced at the boy next to me, who had been entrusted with a cumbersome war horn. It was a huge thing, unwieldy and still covered with traces of old cobwebs. It had been unearthed somewhere in Vindex's villa, and he had demanded that we gave it an airing before starting on the campaign proper. This was to be the signal for the attack, and the young Gaul next to me was fair glowing with pride at being given this responsibility.

The men were much closer now, and I could begin to make out individuals. The back of the column was starting to look a little ragged, as those furthest from their commander took the opportunity to slow their pace as the track climbed uphill. Some of the more alert ones were glancing from side to side, in a somewhat agitated manner. The brilliance of this training was that the men down below knew they were going to be ambushed, but had no idea when. That lingering fear is the closest you can get without being a real soldier marching in enemy territory.

The boy glanced up at me, his brown eyes questioning. I shook my head. Lots of the attacking party were getting fidgety too. It is all very well to know that you're the ones about to attack, but if a few idiots lose their nerve and charge early it gives the enemy vital time to organize themselves. It is a bit of a cliché among us soldiers, but waiting is the hardest part of war.

I waited a little longer. The ambushers and spectators alike lined the slopes, and I lay at the end of the line, furthest from the valley. Waiting for the front ranks to reach the spot in line with me, I whispered to the boy to wet his lips. Bormo was perhaps ten yards below that all-important spot, and that was the moment in which the ancient horn blew.

Perhaps a beat after the horn was sounded, the screams and shouts of the Gauls thundered in my ears, mixed with the deafening crashes of sticks on shields. In an instant the crest of the far slope was lined with a thousand shouting, screaming men. The Gauls on the track froze. I could see the figure of Bormo hurrying back to join his troops, marshalling them into some sort of formation. At various points along the two ridges, junior officers gave the order to charge, and immediately two thousand armed men thundered down the hills towards the terrified ranks of Bormo's men.

At once the rearmost segment of the column broke off from the main party and fled back down the track, while simultaneously Bormo tried to organize his men into two lines to face the separate attacks. The momentum of the charging Gauls meant that any sense of order would have been lost. An ambush has to be lightning fast, and I could see that the remaining Gauls on my hill were awed at the speed of Carnunnos's ambushers. I could see the old man himself surprisingly near the front, sprinting as fast as his ageing legs could carry him. Soon there was an ear-splitting crash, as the two charges hit home. The sheer force of one group's charge took them straight through Bormo's line to the other side.

I nodded to the boy again, and the two short blasts that were the signal to disengage ended the fight almost as soon as it had begun. There was no way of proving how successful the ambush would have been without inflicting casualties, not something that I was over-keen to do to my own men.

Calling for those who had not taken part to follow me, I made my way down to talk to my command. Carnunnos's men looked absurdly pleased with themselves, though some of the older ones were still gasping from the sprint down the hill. Once down on the track, I ordered the assembled men to split, leaving a space about ten yards wide. The rear of Bormo's column was coming back.

Shamefaced, they walked up through the gap between the troops, to a chorus of catcalls and abuse from the men that they had abandoned, though most just pointed and jeered. I had some sympathy for them. Most had never held a sword until a fortnight ago, and now they were facing ambushes. However, they needed to be criticized in front of the rest of the men.

'Would someone please explain to me why you decided to run?'

A voice piped up from somewhere in the middle of the group: 'We were scared!'

'Scared? You're meant to be soldiers, and you ran to save your own miserable skins, despite the fact that this was only a drill! If you are ever ambushed like this again, you do not survive by running. Runners are picked off one by one by the cavalry, who feed on cowards like you.'

None of them dared to look me in the eye; they all shuffled about nervously.

'However, I'm not going to punish you. You have lost the respect of your comrades, which should be punishment enough.' I looked around. 'Bormo!'

'Sir?' he replied, navigating through the ranks of his men.

'You will reorganize these men into their own cohort, so that they can all prove to me that they are not really cowards when we come to face the Romans.'

I paused, turning to look at the others. 'Scary, isn't it?'

They chuckled.

'In Britannia, we did that to a column of the Ninth Legion, the ones who had killed the druids of Mona. Within an hour, we wiped out every last one of them. That is what a well-practised ambush can do. Terror and speed – that combination won *us* the victory, not them with the heavy armour they hide behind, or their famous discipline. We will be lighter, faster, more manoeuvrable. Swarm and surround them, trap them, kill them. We can take any Roman army, and destroy it piece by piece!'

A triumphant cheer went up. I even spotted a few tears from some of them.

The next few days went better than I could have hoped for. Each unit had a turn of ambushing and being the ambusher, and Quintus reported that the training had been just as successful with his troops. Albanos's replacement, Mhorban, had proved himself more than capable, and the men's morale could hardly have been higher. So it was with a merry heart that I decided to hit the tavern.

Quintus, Bormo and Carnunnos accompanied me to a grubby-looking place down by the river. It was approaching dusk, and after several days toiling out in the hills I felt that we were in serious need of some time to wind down, and drink heavily.

It would be pushing it to say that the inn was charming. In fact, it was a downright hovel, but my friends assured me this particular establishment offered the most fun for those on a meagre budget. I kept forgetting that these good men I had come to know over the last couple of weeks were very ordinary and down to earth. Of course, I'm from an old and wealthy family, a senator of Rome. But these men, with the exception of Quintus, were tradesmen. Bormo was an apprentice blacksmith. Carnunnos, from what I'd heard, applied some of the magic his ancestors had practised at fairs and festivals. We had learned not to ask him too much about it; the subject was strictly taboo, even among the Gauls. Anyway, the point is these men enjoyed the simple things of life, and I was more than prepared to join in.

As soon as we entered, I started coughing and spluttering. The smell inside was rank, a mixture of smoke and vomit. Carnunnos gave me a friendly thump on the back.

'Come on, you'll get used to it soon enough. Let's get some beer down you!'

At this stage I should point out that I had only tried beer once, in Britannia, and I hated it. Wine was much more suited to my delicate Roman palate. Unfortunately, the Gauls drank almost lethal amounts of the foul black stuff, good wine being far too expensive for the man in the street. However, if I was to maintain my disguise, I was going to have to go through with this ordeal by ale.

We grabbed ourselves some rickety stools a comfortable distance away from the fire, as smoke was one of the more bearable smells in the place. Soon a barmaid was bringing over some worryingly large tankards. She leaned across to place them on the small table in the centre of our group, and I was ideally situated to run my eye over her finer points, if you follow me. This is history, not some cheap filth you might buy for a few coins in the seedier parts of the forum!

Even if I had wanted to watch her ample frame bulging out of her skimpy serving attire, I couldn't, as a tankard of the vile stuff was placed into my hands, and I was forced to drink heavily. I knew beer was bitter but that didn't stop me spitting out the first gulp, as I felt some solid bits of I-don't-want-to-know-what swilling around my mouth. My friends laughed, after appreciatively necking their own beers in a single go. Another round was ordered as I was told to down the bilge and enjoy it! Deciding to get it over with, I went for it. With my nose too big for the mug, I was only just able to make out the level of liquid dropping as it gushed down my throat, and thankfully I couldn't tilt the mug far back enough to finish it all. My effort was applauded with a resounding cheer, and I made a promise to myself that these men would be treated to a proper Roman drink, as and when circumstances allowed.

The rest of the night was a drunken haze as I was forced to down more and more beer, until at long last I was past caring.

I can vaguely remember attempting to join in with some old Gallic drinking songs, and throwing up in the corner, but it seemed to add to the jollity of it all. Bormo had managed to convince the pretty serving wench to sit on his lap and attend to him more thoroughly. Carnunnos was trying to remember the punchline of a joke that the swaying Quintus would certainly not recall in the morning.

I made my farewells, and, after knocking into a stool or four, staggered out of the inn, hoping that sheer blind luck would take me to my door. A few minutes of zigzagging got me as far as the street corner, and I remember taking a last look back at that grotty little inn before unseen hands grabbed me.

The next thing I knew, a filthy sack was put over my head. I am surprised, given the state I was in, that I can remember at all what happened that night, but I do remember giggling, thinking it was some sort of game. Then the hands spun me around, as if I needed disorientating! Unfortunately the effect was to make me throw up inside the sack, and I heard several shouts of disgust. Then there was a sharp, painful blow to the back of my head, and I collapsed in a heap.

They always say that when you're knocked out, you feel nothing. I can categorically tell you that that is an absolute lie. There may have been a few hours between the blow to my head and coming round, but as you're unconscious you aren't aware that you're not in pain. So it was that when I did come round I was in just as much pain as I had been when I was assaulted. My head felt as if there were a thousand horses trampling inside it, and I groaned.

I heard a chuckle. 'Head hurts, does it?'

My other senses flooded back. The stink of sick, the agony, the cold feel of the stone floor, the voice; I opened my eyes a fraction, only to see the grim features of Albanos staring down at me. His nostrils were arching, probably in complaint at my putrid smell, and yet there was an unmistakable gleam of joy in his eyes.

It can only have been a few hours since I was knocked out. For one thing, I spotted Albanos with an oil lamp, and secondly all the beer I had drunk was still having an effect. If it hadn't, I would have been in much more pain.

'Kind of you to drop by after your drinking session. I hope you won't be too difficult a guest.' There were other laughs, each like a hammer blow inside my head. I tried rolling on to my other side, but that brought my newly formed and tender lump into contact with the floor, and I winced in pain.

'Now, Roman, tell us why you're pretending to fight for the Gauls,' Albanos said.

'I'm not a Roman!' I protested.

'Not a Roman, eh?' He kicked me violently in the ribs; the pain was horrendous. 'Then speak some Gallic.'

I was stumped. Any few words that I had picked up in recent days seemed to vanish as soon as I had thought of them. So I tried a different tack.

'I was never taught to speak in Gallic.'

A smile lit up my tormentor's face, his cold grey eyes narrowed. 'That is painfully obvious.'

Trying to pick myself up, I retorted, 'Because my uncle is a senator, he wanted his family to be brought up Roman.'

I received another kick for my troubles. 'Bollocks. Your so-called uncle was the one who told me to keep an eye on you. I reckon you're a spy.'

I tried a laugh myself, but it sounded feeble. 'Spy! Why do you think I'm a spy?'

At this point his thugs picked me up by my arms and held me up against the wall. Albanos let fly a sharp jab to my gut.

'Why? Because you talk like a Roman.' Then he punched me in the face. 'You look like a Roman. You fight like a Roman. You lie like a Roman.' And every time he said the word 'Roman', he rained yet another blow on my face.

My head rocked, and I felt blood trickle down from my nose, and its warmth in my mouth as his savage strikes had loosened a tooth. He asked me again, 'Why are you pretending to fight for us?'

I spat out the gore-covered tooth, and it hit him square between the eyes. He blinked. Then he took his time, delicately wiping the flecks of my blood from his face.

'Soften him up.'

He gave me a last, contemptuous look. Then he left me in the company of his two thugs.

I put up the best fight I could, but considering I was still fairly drunk and already weak, it wasn't much. They knocked me about for I don't know how long, and thankfully I soon fainted from the pain.

IX

Battered and bruised, I came to after feeling a rough hand slap me about the face.

'Hold him tight.'

I was pinned against the wall, still very groggy. When my eyes finally focused, I saw Albanos's hand clutching a dagger. I tried shouting that I wasn't a spy. He ignored me, and nodded at one of his accomplices. While one of them restrained my right-hand side, the other put all his weight on my left forearm and wrist, leaving only my hand free to wriggle.

Albanos then took my free hand into his own, and brought the wicked little blade closer.

Leering at me, he leaned in so close that I could smell his filthy breath on my face. 'Now you can tell me everything that you have told your Roman friends, or I can slice off your fingers one by one.'

I was shocked, appalled, horrified. The unfairness of it! I hadn't told anyone anything about what I was doing, in fact I was doing my best to prepare the Gauls in case they had to fight proper soldiers, and now I was to be tortured for selling them out.

'Talk to my uncle,' I pleaded. 'Why do you think he called you off, if I wasn't loyal?'

'You tell me.'

'But I'm not a spy! Even if I was, how would I know why he'd send you away if he believed you and not me?'

I was jabbering now, not sure myself if I was making any sense. The filthy Gaul took hold of my smallest finger and rested the blade against its base. He held it there, toying with me. Finally he gave a swift cut, and I felt the cold metal slice through flesh and bone.

I screamed, catching a glimpse of the bloody stump. Seeing the blood pump from the wound had the unfortunate effect of sobering me up, and the pain sharpened dramatically.

At this point you may be thinking how brave I was being, withstanding torture and not revealing my true purpose and identity. As much as I would like to put it down to bravery, it was stupid, blind hope that kept me going. I knew that my story, though improbable, was at least credible, and I clung on to that, praying that this gleeful Gaul would either believe me or give me a quick death.

But hope can only drive you on so far, and I was close to cracking. Whimpering, muttering, cursing, I babbled that I was on his side, and that I'd never tell anyone what I'd done with the Gauls. Which was true in a way; I certainly didn't want to tell anyone that I'd been helping out in a rebellion.

'So you admit that you're a spy, then?' Albanos demanded.

Inwardly, I was raging at the bloody unfairness of it all. I was not a spy, but if I told him his precious Gallic rebellion was just some idealistic drivel dreamed up by Vindex to get him recruits, he'd have gutted me there and then. I didn't have any idea what to say to him that could possibly save my neck.

He sighed. 'How much more of you will I have to cut off before you tell me the truth?' Then he raised the dagger once more to my reddened hand. I screamed at him to let me go.

The door was flung open, and in charged some shouting figures. Albanos looked behind him to see who the arrivals were. I took advantage of this distraction to use the only free limbs I had. My boot flew into that tender patch between his legs. Not the most gentlemanly of moves, but it did the trick. Albanos bellowed like a skewered boar, and crashed to the floor. Abandoning the fiendish dagger, both his hands dropped to cradle his damaged pride.

I received an elbow in the ribs from one of the Gauls, and sank down on to the floor myself, the breath knocked out of me. There was a flash of iron and the offending arm was slashed, spraying me with blood. By now the floor was slippery with the stuff.

Then silence . . . One Gaul was dead, slumped in the corner, a flapping red hole where his throat used to be. To my right, the other was moaning, looking at his damaged arm. Only Albanos seemed relatively unharmed. He writhed on the floor, and then he froze. His breathing was fast and shallow, his chest rising and falling quicker than my own. At that moment I saw why he had frozen. The tip of a sword rested at his throat.

My gaze followed up the blade. It was the short blade of a gladius, and the owner's hand had a large golden ring on the middle finger. I followed the sword arm up, until I saw the grim and determined face of Quintus. Behind him stood Carnunnos, Bormo and two others that I didn't recognize. The latter two sheathed their swords, walked over and offered their shoulders for me to lean on. I shook my head.

Gingerly, I went over to the prone Albanos, slowly bent down towards the floor and picked up the fallen dagger. My torturer's eyes widened into a petrified stare. I smiled at him.

'My, how the tables have turned!' Instinctively, he clenched his left hand into a fist and buried it in the folds of his cloak.

I laughed quietly at that, but stopped quickly, as the sudden movement was too painful for my battered ribs. 'Don't worry, I'm not so petty as to want a finger back in return.'

This time it was Albanos who tried a weak smile, but it didn't stay there for long. With a huge effort, I plunged the dagger into his heaving chest. He made an odd, gulping noise, and then scrabbled futilely to remove my hand that still clutched the knife. The scrabbling slowed and weakened. I looked directly into his eyes, unwavering, waiting to see the life ebb from them. With a last gasp, his eyes rolled and his head slumped to the floor.

Only then did I collapse, and a brief gesture from Quintus sent the two others to my side. Between them they carried me out of that hateful room and into the street. The bright sunlight dazzled me; there had been no natural light in my torture chamber, and it seemed an age since I had last been out in the sun.

Our party hurried through the streets, as if searching for something. Bormo found it, whatever it was, and I was dropped on to a barrel. Groggily I looked around, and was surprised to see that we were in a blacksmith's. I didn't understand. Surely I needed a doctor, not a smith? Then a brazier of coals was set down about a yard away. Horrified, I realized what they were about to do. Before I had time to protest, someone had grabbed a scalding coal with a pair of tongs, another held my arm in position, and then a few moments of white-hot pain. The smell of my own flesh sizzling was fit to make me throw up, and I gagged at the stench. The coal was searing the skin and cauterizing the wound. Immediately afterwards my poor hand was dunked into a bucket of water. Whether from relief at being out of that hellish place or from the intense pain, I have to admit that I fainted again.

I don't remember much of what happened after my ordeal by fire. The body has a wonderful knack of sending you into a long deep sleep after such traumas. It is all part of the healing process. Yet there was one drawback. Normally I

116

don't remember my dreams, but after my time at the mercy of Albanos they came thick and fast. Sometimes it was just him, wielding burning knifes and dagger-shaped coals, other times it was all the Gauls. Martialis, Bormo, Vindex, Carnunnos, Lugubrix, Quintus, all of them, laughing at me for pretending not to be a Roman.

When I opened my eyes at last, I thought I was still dreaming, as I saw Lugubrix sitting in a chair in front of me.

'Welcome to the land of the living,' he said cheerfully.

Groggily, I asked, 'How long was I out for?'

'Nearly two days.'

I tried to sit up, but then several painful twinges warned me not to move too much. I looked at my left hand, and sure enough there was a thick bandage wrapping round my wrist and where my finger should have been.

'The doctor did suggest sewing it back on, but he charged extra for that,' added the spy, grinning.

In response I crooked most of my remaining digits towards my palm, leaving the middle one standing to attention.

'I know, bad joke. Still,' he gave a little wave of his stump, 'it could be worse.'

There was one question I was desperate to ask.

'How by Pluto's arse did you know where to find me?'

'Ah. You remember that charming conversation we had in the governor's house, about what would happen if you discovered I was spying on you?' I was about to reply, but he didn't bother to listen and carried on. 'Well, I hadn't told anyone to follow you, so someone else must have done instead. I simply chose a reliable man and told him to tail you until he found out who was spying on you. I then put the tail on the tail, so to speak. Lucky for you I had come back the day of your little drinking session. My man saw you being bundled into a cart, ran his legs into the ground in following it to that house, and then hared to my quarters to give me the news.

'I had a bit of trouble sobering up your companions, but figured they would be the safest ones to use if Albanos had discovered that you were a Roman, so I couldn't very well choose anyone else. I'm sorry we couldn't get there any earlier, but better than not getting there at all!'

Dumbstruck, I just stared at him.

'By all means thank me.'

I found my voice at last. 'Thank you, I suppose, for disobeying me.'

'To be fair, I only sent a spy to spy on another spy. Any other complaints?'

Shaking my head, 'None.' Then I thought for a bit. 'I don't suppose you know whether Albanos was acting on his own initiative?'

'Well, ideally I would have liked to question him, but your sticking a knife in him made it rather difficult. Can I ask you a question?'

'You can ask,' I said cautiously.

'Why did you kill Albanos? From what I hear he wasn't a threat to you once Quintus and the others arrived.'

I chose my words carefully. 'Revenge. Well, mostly. I know what you're thinking, that it saves me the trouble of explaining to the others why a Roman nobleman is in command. But when you're alone in a cell with men who are determined to torture and kill you . . . it's not like facing death on the battlefield. A chance spear or a stab from some unknown soldier and that's it. When it's someone you know who's going to kill you in cold blood, and you can't defend yourself, the last thing you feel towards the man who threatened you is pity.'

Lugubrix nodded his understanding. 'So you think he was acting alone then?'

'I can't be sure. I mean, if he had been following orders from Vindex he wouldn't have tortured me for information.'

Lugubrix frowned. 'Unless he wasn't told the full truth but

just given orders to extract information from you, and then kill you, depending on what you said.'

I pondered this a while. At length, I asked, 'Would you trust Vindex if you were me?'

'I don't think it likely that Vindex has the brains or the balls to arrange something like this. Yes, he puts on a good show in front of his subjects, but I reckon you know as well as I that most of it is just bravado. But then again, it showed surprising initiative for Albanos to do all this on his own. So on balance I would trust the governor, but only up to a point. I'd watch my back if I were you, just in case.'

This seemed like sound advice.

'So what news do you have now you're back here in Vienne?' I asked.

'Oh,' he said casually, 'just that Galba has officially thrown his hat into the ring.'

'What? Already?'

'His troops in Tarraco have called upon him to make himself emperor, but he prefers the title of Legate of the Senate and People of Rome for the moment.'

'But will he march on Rome?'

'I don't think so; not yet anyway. He's not prepared to abandon the province yet. He has to leave it in good order, with a legally appointed replacement ready to take over. From what I hear, I think he's hoping to be called upon by the Senate rather than having to march on Rome itself. But to be honest I'm not sure if the news has filtered through to Rome yet. It only happened two days ago, and my contacts are closer to Hispania than Rome is. But in the immediate term, there's even bigger news. Verginius Rufus has begun a siege of Vesontio.'

'Wait a minute, that's two hundred miles from Mogontiacum. How did he get there so quickly?'

'You've been unconscious for two days, remember? That's only a week's march for the legions. It's not as though it's news to me, I was waiting to report back once I knew where they were headed.'

'Why Vesontio?'

'It's the capital of the Sequani, and one of the few towns that has openly declared for Vindex. You see, the ordinary troops are livid that the Gauls are rebelling against them. I think Rufus is trying to keep them on a leash, making sure that as little blood as possible is spilt, and at the same time flushing out Vindex's army. Vesontio is a real bastard to take, so they could be there for some time.'

'And how far is it from here?'

'As the crow flies, about a hundred and twenty miles.'

I was amazed. A Roman army was four days' march away, and I wasn't exactly enthusiastic about sending in the Gauls to close ranks with them!

'What's Vindex been doing in my absence, then?'

'Making speeches to the troops mostly, and before you ask, you don't want to hear what he said; it was the usual rousing stuff. He's tried his best to organize the men for a march, but I think he'll need you by his side as soon as you're back on your feet.'

At this point, a man who I assumed to be the doctor entered, and chided my friend for disturbing me. Lugubrix was ushered out, wishing me a speedy recovery, and then the man tut-tutted in the way doctors do, and set about examining my various injuries. My little finger was healing up nicely, he told me, and the skin was making an effort to close over the stump.

The bruises and internal damage would take another day or two to heal properly, despite all the pungent poultices and weird and wonderful ointments that he prescribed. So I had to give orders from my sickbed, though I had visits from my friends to relieve the tedium.

However, this did give me plenty of time to mull over the political situation. Galba had been wise to refuse the title of emperor outright. It seems that even in the days since the fall of the Republic, the image of Cincinnatus's refusal of ultimate power is still very potent. Julius publicly refused the crown, Augustus only reluctantly agreed to become First Citizen, and Claudius definitely did not want to be an emperor. Of course there have been exceptions, but the act of refusing power and taking it only when 'convinced' that it is in Rome's best interests goes down extremely well, with both mob and Senate alike. One should never seem too grasping.

Still, any fool could see that this open declaration by Galba meant that he was putting his name forward to succeed Nero, and his success would depend on two factors: the military and the Senate. To make his accession constitutional, Galba had to be approved by the Senate. The senators' lives under Nero had been uncomfortable at best, many being threatened with trial on a trumped-up charge for gaining a modicum of popularity, or else being politely told to commit suicide.

Yet the legions would also play their part. This was a dangerous precedent that Galba was setting, being declared emperor by his troops, and far from Rome. What would stop other ambitious senators with legions at their command from doing the same? Galba had only one legion to call upon in Hispania, plus another that was composed of raw recruits. The Rhine provinces had seven legions, not counting auxiliaries. But I am getting ahead of myself. Everything shall be told, but in its proper place.

X

The essential thing now was to arrange a private meeting with Verginius Rufus, if it was at all possible. But first of all we had to get to him. As Lugubrix said, it was only about a hundred and twenty miles from Vienne to Vesontio, but there were a seemingly endless number of things to do. Normally the quartermaster's brigade would be sorting this out, but as we had to make do with a few of Vienne's civil servants things were rather more chaotic.

It was obvious that the logistics of moving thirty thousand men was far beyond their capabilities. Food had to be collected and carts found for it. Someone would have to work out how to ration it out between thirty thousand mouths over several days. Each man had to be armed, horses shod, tools collected for constructing camp, tents rolled up, forage gathered – it was a nightmare.

Moreover, the men had to be taught how to construct a defensible camp at the end of each day's marching. Not only was this difficult because in my time in Britannia I had only ever been responsible for one part of the operation, digging the trench, so I had to improvise the rest, but I was still confined to my quarters. I therefore had to relay these orders to Quintus and the others, and hope to the gods that they would manage somehow.

It took another three days before we were ready to move off, and then only as far as Lugdunum. It was only about eighteen miles away, on a proper Roman road, so I expected us to reach the city in no more than half a day. I was fit enough to ride by then, or at least sit in the saddle. An army on the march can do about four miles an hour, so just sitting in the saddle was pretty much all that was required. The troops were lined up on the road leading northwards out of Vienne, and the townspeople came out to see us off.

It was a moving sight; garlands of flowers were flung on to the street by a cheering swarm of Gauls. Mothers tearfully embraced their sons, wives pressed their husbands close, sweethearts and companions, some having met only the night before, whispered fond goodbyes. The governor sat on a resplendent steed draped in red saddlecloths to reinforce his military image, and signalled down to that same young boy who had been entrusted with his precious horn. The general order to advance was sounded, and I was delighted to see that, albeit after a few paces to get started, the army was marching in step!

I watched rank after rank pass by, twenty thousand or so men marching ten abreast. It seemed to take for ever for them all to pass me. At length the carts and various beasts of burden drew alongside, then only the rearguard was yet to come. In case you are wondering why I was staying put while the army moved off, I was simply waiting for the rearmost ranks to pass so that I could tag along behind, to make sure that no one slipped out of the column with a free pack of tools and rations to dispose of.

Finally, the last rank marched by, and I wheeled my horse round to head north. By now Vindex and the vanguard were well out of sight beyond the next bend in the river, behind a spur that jutted out into the valley. But you could still hear them. In fact the sound of twenty thousand men marching in step on a proper road is quite daunting. The consistent, rhythmic tramping could be heard for miles around. Some soppy poets have penned that the earth trembles fit to shake fruit from the trees whenever an army is on the march. Well, that may be true of battles like Gaugamela, where they say there were a million Persians and at least five hundred elephants, but I didn't see a single grape tremble as we moved up the Rhone.

After five hours or so, the pace slowed for a time, then it sped up again. I never actually got to see Lugdunum, as the road to Vesontio branched off from the Rhone about a mile south of the city, which is shrouded on that side by thick woods. Soon I saw why there had been a stumble in the column's march. Thousands of new troops streamed through the trees, but many of these were mounted.

It had troubled me a little that we had no cavalry at Vienne. If you know about Caesar's campaigns in Gaul, you'll know that the Gallic tribes are excellent with horses, hence the use of the Aedui and others as auxiliaries way back in the last days of the Republic. But over the years following our conquest, Gallic society underwent a strong period of Romanization. The tribes began to matter less and less as the Gauls adapted to the *pax romana*. As the tribesmen drifted towards the old towns and new colonies, their way of life changed dramatically. Soon it was only the privileged few, the *equites*, who could afford to buy and look after horses.

So it was with great surprise that I saw a force of about a thousand cavalrymen forming up at the side of the road. At their head I recognized Sextus, Quintus's younger brother. He was only about eighteen, a slender figure but full of boyish enthusiasm.

'Where on earth did all these horses come from?' I called out to him.

'Father sent out messages to all the important families of Gaul, asking for help. We must have the noblest cavalry in the empire!'

I saw what he meant. Among the entire force I made out perhaps two dozen beards. This was partly because these aspiring gentry had aped the Roman fashion for a clean-shaven chin, and also because few looked old enough to have any hopes of growing a beard even if they wanted to.

'What are you doing here at the rear? You should be scouting far in front of the column for ambushes.'

For a moment his face fell. 'Father told me to assemble my men and report to you.'

'Then ride to the van, give the governor my compliments, then start doing what cavalry are meant to do!'

'He also told me to tell you that he has left two thousand men to cover Lugdunum while we head to Vesontio.' Then he dug his heels in and was off, with a thousand thundering horses following.

Several hours later the rearguard and I came upon a camp, of sorts. There were no palisades, no ditches, no watchtowers, no walks, just a collection of tents all massed together in a huddle. The men were tired after a full day's march, and were fit to drop. I was feeling rather delicate as well. A day in the saddle meant some of the aches and pains from Albanos's hospitality had made their return painfully clear, and after dismounting I hobbled bow-legged towards Vindex's tent.

All around me the Gauls were busy attending to their own tents, arguing over who would sleep where. Some had fires going already, others were gambling. Not exactly a highly disciplined force, but surprisingly chirpy at the prospect of taking on the armoured might of the legions. Still, they had volunteered, I suppose.

I was, however, pleased to see that Vindex had taken some of my advice on board, and had posted two sentries at the entrance to his tent. When I approached they asked me what I wanted, for I was still in civilian dress, and I told them who I was. They stepped aside. I then took them to task for allowing me in just because I claimed to be Vindex's nephew. They apologized, and I made my way inside.

Sextus, Quintus and the governor were all there, celebrating with a pitcher of wine. They ushered me in and Quintus poured me a drink.

'What are we celebrating?' I asked.

Vindex seemed to be in his cups already. 'Why, our first day's march of course.'

'And this is reason enough to celebrate?'

'Relax, Severus, or Gnaeus or whoever you are. Have some wine!' The governor made an effort to pour himself another drink, but missed the goblet and spilled some down his fine toga. He swore loudly.

'May I make a suggestion, sir?' I still stood stiffly, as an officer should.

'If you must.'

'Since the army obviously hasn't learned how to set up a proper, fortified camp, Quintus should command the rearguard and I the van, so I can be on hand tomorrow night and oversee the whole thing. Every day brings us nearer to the Romans and they will have their own intelligence, so we need to be able to defend ourselves in case a force has broken off from the siege.

'To that end, I suggest that we should leave the road and cut across country. The rough terrain suits your men far better than it does the cumbersome legions.'

'But I thought that we didn't want to attack the Romans unless absolutely necessary?' Sextus queried.

I was starting to lose my patience. Obviously I had only a few years' experience with the legions, but that was in a guerrilla war. These three were amateurs caught up in the excitement of the campaign, and had no inkling of the dull, practical matters that really win battles.

'We,' I replied tiredly, 'will be expected to use the road. If anything, this route will be tougher but a lot shorter, cutting off the corner so to speak. Staying up in the hills will make it a lot harder to walk into a trap, and easier to spring one. Our men know this land better than any Roman, remember? Now if you don't mind, I need some sleep.' I began to hobble back out.

I heard someone whisper, 'Father!'

'Oh, yes. Er . . . I shall send a surgeon to see to you, Severus,' Vindex mumbled.

'Thank you, Governor.'

The going was slower up in the hills, but that was to be expected. We had turned north-east off the road and set up camp the next day not far from a small town called Geneva. Having this new force of cavalry eased my worries considerably. With such a large scouting force it would be nigh impossible for us to be taken unawares, and they could help us choose the route which offered the greatest strategic advantage.

We tramped over those long lines of hills ever northwards, and ate up the miles. The men were in good spirits, singing old war songs to their old gods. Some were rousing, with a percussive beat ideal for marching; they made you feel absolutely joyous at being a soldier. Others made your heart soar for their beauty. Sometimes I was even glad that I didn't know the words, in case they didn't do the music justice. You may think I'm being overly sentimental, musing about barbarian war chants, but music can lift a man to heights that he had never thought possible. The true beauty of it is that the mightiest, richest man in Rome can be put to shame by a filthy swineherd with a good voice. Music is truly liberating. And while these common little Gauls might dream of the splendid lives we lead, these men from different tribes, with different customs, can come together in song and move you more than any Roman or Greek poet. I may well be biased, having had tedious odes and turgid couplets drummed into me from boyhood by starched and humourless old men, but if you are one of those men who boast of their wealth and influence but have never ventured the far side of the Alps, you are missing out.

Perhaps at this point I should expand a little on the growing attachment that I felt for these very ordinary men. In Britannia, we had contact with the natives of course, but we would mostly keep to our camps and garrisons. This was the first time that I had spent a long period with people who weren't what we would call true Romans, even if many were now citizens within the empire. I had been living among the Gauls for weeks now, and had been treated like one of their own. Despite their thinking that I was a Vindex, a nobleman, I had been treated as an equal by all those I had encountered. Though Vindex himself tried desperately to cover up his Gallic roots, these simple, down-to-earth people were the most welcoming I had ever come across.

Mind you, I was looking forward to returning to the civilized world once Galba rescued me from Vindex and took me with him to Rome. A bath and a shave were my top priorities. Nonetheless, I would miss the simple, open company of the Gauls.

On the evening of the fourth day, we encamped ten miles from Vesontio on a small hillock, far enough away from the city to go unnoticed by the Roman scouts; at least I hoped so. This time the camp was built properly: a long rectangle, defended by a trench, slope and palisade. Men were on sentry and changed guard regularly, with new passwords for each shift. On the outside, it could be mistaken for a Roman fortress, if you overlooked the fact that there were no watchtowers, no uniformed soldiers, just a horde of Gauls inside.

A council was summoned for the following morning. I had made it clear to Vindex that this was not to be a grand council of war, and only those I had chosen should attend. So it was that the governor, Quintus, Lugubrix and I met in Vindex's billowing tent, with two stout men posted outside.

We all sat in a semicircle round a fine table, which had taken some knocks and scrapes over the journey. Vindex was in his element, regaling us with various ideas that had struck him along the march, each more ridiculous and impractical than the last. Thankfully I didn't hear too much of it, as my ears had picked up some muttering from outside. The guards parted and in stepped Martialis, looking very greasy and unkempt.

'Martialis, good to have you back with us. Here, have some food.' I gestured to what Vindex had left untouched at his supper the previous night. There was some cold chicken, fruit and wine left over. Deciding not to stand on ceremony, Martialis pulled up a stool and began to attack the stuff.

We sat in silence, letting the man have some breakfast before he made his report. He hadn't had much good eating during his time here, judging from the manner and speed in which he devoured his meal.

Wiping away some of the grease on his mouth with his sleeve, he looked up at us and asked, 'What do you want to know?'

Lugubrix started. 'How much do the Romans know about our rebellion?'

'Quite a lot,' he answered. 'When the Romans came this way they weren't expecting any resistance, but when they demanded supplies from Vesontio the Sequani absolutely refused, telling them to take it if they wanted to try. That's when the siege began. I stayed with friends of mine in the villages around here. The Romans sent foragers out to commandeer food for the troops, and at the same time collected as much information as they could about the rebellion. Eventually, they found an old couple who mentioned that their two sons had gone away for a while, but had now returned.

'The two men were tortured, and told everything they knew. Apparently, they had both been sent home after a march, but they still knew that we were based out in Vienne. They know how many men we have, how we were training them, our lack of proper armour and weapons, and that we have no cavalry. Everything.'

Quintus was confused. 'How do you know exactly what these two men told the Romans?'

Martialis looked grimly at him. 'They weren't killed. Instead, their arms and feet were cut off, so that they could never harm a Roman soldier.'

There was a dour silence.

'And the siege-works? What do you know about them?' I asked.

'Vesontio is almost impregnable. The whole city fits into a loop in the river. Imagine a river bend so tight that the land at the neck is only three hundred paces across. This neck is blocked by a mountain that stretches all the way to both sides of the river, with a small citadel at the top. The Romans have posted units of men about five hundred strong at the end of each bridge leading to the city, while the main force has dug itself in with a warren of trenches, surrounding a whole side of the mountain.'

At last our glorious leader had a question. 'How many Romans are there?'

'I'd say twenty thousand, perhaps a few more, but around four thousand are watching the bridges.' Strangely, Vindex looked pleased with this information.

'Well, I think that's all, Martialis. Excellent work. I think it's time that you rejoined your men. We shall have a proper council of war in due course,' I said.

Martialis smiled, stood, and then took another handful of chicken before leaving us.

We waited until he was out of earshot, then Vindex rubbed his hands together in glee. 'Only twenty thousand men, what a chance!'

'Only twenty thousand?' I echoed. 'Governor, might I remind you that we are barely touching thirty thousand, and the vast majority of our men have never taken part in anything more dangerous than a tavern brawl!'

He looked sulky at that. 'Then what are we here for if not to fight?'

I simply could not believe the stupidity of the man. I tried to restrain myself. 'To negotiate, Governor. I will attempt to get a message through to Verginius Rufus, and then we can try and convince him to join us. Not a drop of blood will need to be spilt, if things go according to plan. I suggested this meeting to decide the best way of approaching Rufus. As I see it, there are two options: either to sneak into the camp and deliver a written message, or use me to talk to the general face to face.'

Lugubrix spoke up. 'I would suggest, Governor, that given, ahem, Gnaeus's previous experience, it would be foolish not to use his talents.'

'But how do I know that—' Vindex started, but I cut him off angrily.

'That you can trust me? Well, I'm flattered, Governor, but while I may not be your man, I am Galba's man, and I am here to carry out his orders. Those are to avoid bringing the Rhine legions into a conflict, and since you have made it impossible for Rufus to ignore us, we shall have to convince him to join us. Do you honestly think that once I'm in their camp I will betray you? Why should I?'

'To win a reward perhaps?' he suggested.

'I'll get a damn sight bigger reward from Galba if I can pull this off, and so will you. Now, if there are no objections, I shall prepare myself for the mission.'

Furious, I stormed out of the council.

Back in my own tent, I sat down, trembling with rage. What a stupid, bloody fool I had been landed with. Of course it made sense for me to use my position, not to mention my flawless Latin, to masquerade as a Roman officer in order to meet with Rufus. In fact, I had only raised the possibility of a secret message delivered by an intruder to see if Vindex would go for it, and I was bitter to find out that he still did not trust me, after all I'd done for him. I glanced down at the stump of my little finger, a constant reminder of that odious man's lack of faith. Still, my loyalty to Galba overrode any misgivings I had about continuing to serve Vindex.

I had some vellum and ink ready. Any number of things could go wrong that night, and there was one thing I needed to do before I rode off. I wanted to write to my wife. When I left home for those years of fighting in Britannia, she was eighteen and pregnant, irritable and difficult to love. But we were both older and wiser now, and we loved each other for our faults as much as for our qualities. She was a social climber; I was sometimes selfish. She was stubborn; I wasn't the most romantic of men, but still I missed her. How I'd missed her! The way she smiled, flashing her pearl-white teeth, even the way she would wrinkle her nose whenever I cracked my knuckles. I had been away from home for over half a year, and I might never see her again. I grabbed the stylus and began to write.

My dearest Salonina,

I wish I could tell you where I am and the incredible things I've been doing, but I dare not write them for fear of this letter falling into the wrong hands. All I can tell you is that I am risking my life for the empire. If all goes well this campaign will give Rome a fresh start and a new moral leadership, though others seek to do this at the expense of Roman lives. What I am doing tonight might save those very lives, and no other man could do it, even if I wanted to back out of the oath I took to defend Rome.

I have already said too much. I am a soldier, you know that all my affairs are prepared should the worst happen. I know I don't tell you often enough, but I love you with all my heart. If I survive, the first thing I shall do is call you to my side, wherever I am in the world. We have spent too many years apart, Salonina. I know that is my fault, but a senator of Rome must always put his duty first, and I would never want you or our son to be in any danger. If tonight goes well, I may even be back in Rome for the autumn. If not, then I thank the gods for every day that we have had together. Give my love to Aulus, and I pray we will be together soon.

With all my heart,
Caecina

I rolled up the letter and sealed it with candle wax. I did not stamp it with my family ring in case the letter was intercepted; after all, I didn't want all Rome to know that I was with Vindex and his rebels. Quickly and quietly, I made my way to the tent that had been set up a hundred paces or so outside the camp. It would not do to let the men see how I would be dressed in a few minutes' time.

Quintus was waiting for me. So was my 'disguise'.

'That was diplomatic,' he said.

'Don't get me started, Quintus, I'm not in the mood. You can give me a hand instead.' I gestured towards the cumbersome bundle on the ground.

Removing the layers of cloth in between the items, I laid them out on Quintus's bed. First I had to remove my tunic and replace it with the double-padded tunic that formed the bottom layer. Next came the heavy metal breastplate. Quintus held it up while I threaded my right arm through, and then I held the other aloft while my friend secured all the fastenings down my left side. On went the stiff leather sandals, the burnished iron greaves, and I was almost ready.

To gain an audience with Rufus, it was vital that I was equipped like a Roman tribune, so I had to don a narrow red sash over my hips and a deep red cloak over my shoulders. That left just my helmet and a sword.

Whoever had been charged with cleaning and polishing my

gear had done a fantastic job. When we had found the armour in the old barracks at Vienne, it had seemed a shabby and dingy collection. Now it shone. The cheek pieces of the helmet moved freely, and were inlaid with swirling patterns of brass. The sweeping curve of the neck-guard had lost its old scratches, and a new plume of crimson horsehair stood erect, from the brow backwards towards the neck. I walked over to the last item I needed and pulled the sword from its ornate scabbard. This was one of the new styles of gladius, produced in vast numbers in the fortress town of Mogontiacum. The leaf-shaped blade narrowed a small distance from the hilt, then broadened, finally tapering to a wicked point. This was to help stop the blade from sticking fast in your enemy's flesh. The wooden pommel was large to counterbalance the weight of the hard iron blade, with no fancy decorations. It was a simple, ruthless tool for slaughter, and not some parade-ground bauble.

Sheathing the sword, I looked up at my friend.

'Almost ready.' I tied my sword belt securely, and Quintus passed me the helmet. I had forgotten how heavy the uniform was. The legionaries had it worse though; as infantry, their body armour weighed considerably more than mine, while staff officers needed speed and manoeuvrability.

My horse was waiting for me directly outside Quintus's tent. If the men saw a Roman officer lingering near their camp, it would result in a headache for Vindex. Swinging up into the saddle, I looked down at the young man who had come to be like a brother to me; a naive younger brother who still needed taking care of, but a brother nonetheless.

'You will deliver that letter for me, won't you?' I asked.

'Of course I will,' he said.

'See you this evening, if the gods are willing!'

Then I dug my heels in, and shot out of the camp and into the open countryside.

XI

Doubts and fears plagued my mind as I galloped through the fields towards Vesontio. My primary concern was how I could be sure that Rufus would agree to meet me alone, and not in front of his subordinates. I was confident enough about gaining entry to the Roman camp, given that I had once been a tribune. But then again, I thought, tribunes are usually aged between eighteen and their early twenties, and I was pushing thirty. I resolved to keep my helmet on for as long as possible, lest they spot the age difference. It did feel good to be clean-shaven at long last though!

But as I say, getting in was the least of my problems. Various scenarios ran through my head as to what might happen once I met with the governor. If he didn't get rid of his staff, I was going to have a decidedly tricky time of it trying to negotiate secret deals in public. And what if I was given the opportunity, but Rufus decided to remain loyal to Nero?

Normally, a Roman citizen cannot be executed, unless convicted on a charge of treason, but it was difficult to imagine an action more treacherous than asking an imperial governor to betray the emperor. I could expect any one of some terrible punishments: beheading, strangling, being thrown from the

Tarpeian rock (an archaic but popular method), live burial or, worst of all, crucifixion. The thought of being strung up and left lingering on a cross for up to three days, with the added attraction of nails hammered through the wrists and ankles, was enough to make me feel queasy. And this from a man who has seen the druids of Mona build a wooden cage in the shape of a man, put people inside, and then set fire to the cage as a sacrifice to their heathen gods.

The ride to the city took me no more than two hours, keeping the winding river to my left, but the fear that clenched at my heart made it feel so much longer. I knew all of Rufus's army would be concentrated around Vesontio and that wearing the tribune's uniform meant that I was safe from attack, but I half expected to be ambushed by my own people, charging down from the menacing hills that loomed above me.

Ahead, I could see smoke spiralling upwards, not just one plume, maybe a dozen. The city was close at hand, and surely Rufus's army nearer still. I rode up the crest of a spur that jutted into the river valley, and then I caught my first glimpse of a Roman city under siege. I remember it so vividly: the stench of a city at war, buildings on fire, and the echoes of a thousand sufferings, punctuated by the occasional crash of artillery. Britannia had been bloody, but this was Roman citizen against Roman citizen, never mind the fact that the city folk were Gauls. But while my heart went out to the people of Vesontio, fighting for a cause that did not really exist, my path lay towards the fortified camp hardly more than a spear's throw from the citadel. I had to put a stop to this madness. There was no use in continuing to fret; I just had to hope that a combination of bravado and balls would see me through. Coming to the heavy wooden gates of the fort, I bellowed to be let in.

'Who's asking?' a voice shouted back.

Time for some brash arrogance, I thought. 'What rank are you, man?'

'Optio,' he called back.

'I am Gnaeus Junius Silvanus,' I said, having invented the name during my ride over, 'tribune and second in command of the First Italica, with a vital message for General Rufus. Now open this bloody door or I'll have you broken to the ranks!'

The optio was quick to try and put right his mistake. 'Yes, sir, sorry, sir.' The gate creaked open. I urged my horse on, keeping an eye out for someone in authority who would know where the general was.

I saw a centurion a few paces ahead, easy to spot because their plumes go across the helmet rather than down it, like mine.

'Centurion, where can I find the general?'

He peered up at me, a quizzical look on his face. 'Which general are you wanting, sir? All the legion commanders should be in camp.'

Impatiently, I answered. 'The governor, General Rufus, of course!'

'The big crimson tent, slap bang in the middle of the compound, sir. Can't miss it.'

I nodded my thanks, and headed off. As he said, it wasn't difficult to find. A man with several legions to call upon can't reside in a shabby tent. However, the guards told me that he was inspecting the artillery, and pointed north towards the city.

It was another ten minutes or so before I actually found the general. He was talking with a squat-looking man at the foot of a powerful onager, so called because its action resembled the kick of a donkey. Thankfully, there was no one else around since they were all too busy with the siege equipment.

'General Rufus, sir?'

I was confident he was the man I was looking for. He wore a fine breastplate with the emblem of a fox engraved upon it, and a red cloak coloured with the very best dyes. He looked to be in his mid-fifties, but nonetheless was tough and lean, with a head of closely cropped grey hair.

'Yes, what do you want?'

'I am a tribune with the First Italica, sir, and I bring an urgent message.'

'Yes, yes,' he said tersely. 'And . . . ?'

I tried to look embarrassed, and made an obvious glance towards the other man.

He understood. 'Please leave us,' said the general, 'and you may start the artillery assault when you're ready.' He turned to me. 'Now we can have some privacy. By the way, haven't you learned to dismount when addressing a senior officer, or don't they teach you manners in the First?'

I was unwilling to dismount as I wanted a quick getaway should the general not take kindly to my proposal. However, I couldn't disobey him; after all, he was not only a general but also an ex-consul.

I slung myself out of the saddle, and looked him in the eye. My voice kept down low, I said: 'I bring a message from Sulpicius Galba, General.'

He froze, his grey eyes widening. 'You come from Galba?'

'Directly from Hispania, sir.'

'Then you're not from the First at all?' he asked.

'No, sir, I needed to speak with you in private.'

He chuckled at that, and my feverish heart began to settle. He didn't seem as though he was about to call his guards and lock me up.

'It would make things a lot easier, General,' I said tentatively, 'if I knew where you stood in terms of the political situation.'

It was his turn to look nervous now, and he glanced over his shoulder to make sure that no one could overhear our conversation.

'It's not that I disapprove of Galba, but the constitutional matter worries me. Nero, for all his faults, is a Caesar, and Galba is not. I could not support anyone who simply wishes to snatch the purple for their own ends.'

'Nor do I,' I hastened to add.

'However,' Rufus continued, 'I will not leave Roman citizens unprotected from a Gallic insurrection.'

'But it's not a rebellion! Vindex simply got carried away. He wants to see the back of Nero, and the idea was to show the people of Rome that there is significant support for . . . an alternative. There is no question of civil war, unless you want there to be.'

He blanched at that. Rome does not have a good history when it comes to civil wars, and it seemed that Verginius Rufus was not the type of man to start one willingly.

I continued, 'Though I am in Galba's confidence, would you be willing to meet with Governor Vindex tonight and discuss the matter?'

'He's here?'

'And his army with him.'

He seemed to mull this over for a while. 'Where?'

'There's a small village five miles south-west of here, near the river. In one of the fields near by there's an old oak. There, at midnight, and you can bring one man you can trust, to meet Vindex and myself.'

I put out my hand. 'Agreed?'

He took it. 'Agreed.'

It rained heavily that night. Actually, that was an understatement. Imagine, if you will, a set of Olympian baths up in the heavens, with the gods relaxing and talking of heady, divine matters. Now imagine the floor falling out of these baths, and you might be able to understand what it was like. Despite standing under the protecting boughs of the old oak when the heavens opened, we were drenched to the skin in a matter of minutes.

I held a torch aloft, which stayed alight in the downpour only because the rags had been soaked in oil.

Using my free hand I pulled the hood of my travelling cloak further over my head. Vindex had not taken the same precaution. He was a sorry sight. He had donned his finest gear for the occasion, only to have his military image somewhat spoiled. His brush-like hair was matted, though some clumps were still bearing up against the deluge. His leather breastplate was completely sodden, but nonetheless he sat bolt upright in the saddle, not complaining for a moment.

'Do you think he will come?' he asked.

'I think he's unlikely to miss a meeting that will determine the future of Rome just because of a spot of rain.'

As if to undermine my point, one of Jupiter's thunderbolts flashed through the sky. For a split second, I thought that I saw two horsemen coming down the crest of a hill to the east of us. Then they were gone. There was a crash of thunder, and our skittish horses tried to turn and gallop away, but we managed to keep them under control.

The sound of hoofbeats drumming into the sodden earth could just be heard over the lashing of the rain, and in the dark I could make out two shrouded figures on horseback. They reined in a few paces ahead of us, and the leading one pulled his hood back a fraction, enough so that we could see his face without him getting drenched like Vindex. The other man did the same. He had a large, hawk-like nose that cast a shadow over his face, and he stayed behind his general.

'This is Fabius Valens,' the general began, 'legate of the First Germanica. He is here as a representative of Lower Germania. Now, I hope what you have to say is worth that horrendous ride.'

I decided to get straight to the point. 'I take it your presence here means that you would rather Nero was no longer emperor.'

'Yes, he's tarnished Rome's image almost beyond repair. But I will not support a coup. It has to be constitutional, or my legions will stay loyal to him. I want no part in the sordid plots of an ambitious man.'

'That is precisely why it must be Galba and no one else,' I reassured him. 'Galba is an old man, he couldn't last more than another five years, and he has no sons to pass the purple on to. That is why he is still in Hispania, waiting for the Senate to ratify him and cast out that perfumed fool. Do you know what happened in Tarraco only this month?'

'What?' asked the general.

'His troops saluted him as emperor, and he refused the title. He renounced any desire to force a ruler upon Rome's citizens. Instead, he's calling himself "Legate of the Senate and People of Rome". Now he's just waiting to see if he is called upon by that same Senate and people to serve.'

Rufus seemed to be nodding his approval, and then he turned in the saddle to face Vindex.

'May I ask, Governor, did Galba approach you, or was it the other way around?'

Vindex, sopping wet, made an effort to look dignified. 'I wrote to Galba early this year suggesting that he put himself forward as an alternative to Nero, and that I would back him to the hilt.'

Inside, I was elated. Vindex may have been a proud, stubborn fool, but at least his motives were honest, and this information seemed to impress Rufus no end. Valens I was not so sure about.

I can't begin to describe the tension there was that night. Four men, two of whom were almost mute spectators, were making history beneath a sodden oak tree in a wild corner of Gaul. Of course, Rufus was a self-professed constitutionalist, and his fears and wariness of any man bold enough to want to take the empire from the Caesar dynasty had to be allayed. But I did not foresee any other obstacles, at least not yet.

'So, what is the incentive for betraying my emperor?' Rufus enquired, offhand as you like.

'Other than the wellbeing of the empire, of course?' I responded.

'Of course,' he added hastily.

'Strictly speaking, I do not have the authority to make any specific promises. However, if you decide to help us, you will have gained a very powerful friend in Rome. What more could a man want who has already been consul and held one of the most prestigious commands?'

'I hadn't really considered.'

'Well, I should be reporting to Galba at some point soon, so this is the time to make any demands . . .' Perhaps not the right word, I thought. 'Or rather, suggestions.'

I left the offer hanging there, and Rufus took his time. After all, it isn't every day that you are asked to name your price for a comparatively simple favour, except perhaps in the moral sense.

At length Rufus made his 'suggestion'. 'I have always wanted to see the East. I reckon that, as one of Rome's more senior generals, command on the Parthian frontier might be a . . . a fitting role.'

I grinned. 'Parthia it is, or at least I shall recommend as much to Galba when I see him.'

'When will that be?'

This question came from Vindex, whose head had whipped round at the allusion to my leaving for Hispania.

'When the matter of Vesontio is settled, I think the governor here will manage perfectly well without me, won't you, sir?' The sarcasm was almost imperceptible, and thankfully over the heads of the other two, but I saw Vindex's nostrils flare at that, as though there were a foul stench under his nose.

I continued. 'I would suggest that you, General, break off the siege, and try to convince the men that Galba will smile upon the legions that helped him to oust Nero. At the very least try and secure some sort of agreement for non-intervention.

142

Meanwhile, the governor's army will relieve Vesontio once you have gone, and retain the rebellion's credibility.'

'I take it that you intend to make a career in politics, young man?'

'Only once we have an emperor worthy of Rome,' I answered.

'So if I were to ask you which comes first, loyalty to Galba or to yourself, you expect me to believe that you'd choose Galba?'

'I didn't beg and scrape for this job, if that's what you mean, sir. Galba actually sent for me and asked me to serve before I'd even heard that there was a conspiracy.'

I could just make out his eyes narrowing, as if he was trying to see through me and detect whether or not I was telling the truth. Evidently he must have decided that I was fairly trustworthy, for he nudged his horse forward and put out his hand. I jerked my head in Vindex's direction. Rufus was quick to realize the snub that he had just given, and hastily turned in the saddle to shake Vindex's hand, while I gave my aching arm a rest by switching the torch to my right hand, at the same time making it impossible for Rufus to shake my hand next. I hoped to placate Vindex in this way, since I had rather dominated the negotiations, while he had sat stiffly in the rain.

'I shall speak to my officers first, and then the legions an hour after dawn. We will probably head north, back to the Rhine.'

'Does that mean that we can get out of this bloody rain and back to camp, then?' asked Valens.

Wearily, the general replied, 'Yes, Valens, it does. Gentlemen, I hope we shall meet again when all the politics is over. Until then . . .' and they wheeled away, leaving the sodden Vindex and me alone again beneath the sheltering tree.

Saying nothing, Vindex gave a tug at his reins and began the journey back to our own camp. We plodded onwards into the darkness, as the torch's flame began to flag, flicker and die. I cast the remaining stump aside, and guided my horse directly alongside the governor's. From what I could make out, he looked very sullen, with a scowl fixed on his face.

I could have left well alone, but instead tried to coax some conversation from him.

'The negotiations went well, I thought,' I began.

Nothing.

'And Rufus seemed a decent man.'

That sparked him into life. 'Oh yes, you and he were having a pleasant little chat, weren't you? Never mind me, who's actually meant to be in charge of this whole affair. I could have just gone to bed this evening and stayed there, for all my input was worth!'

'That's not fair, Governor; neither of us could have gone on our own, could we? If it had been just me, why would he have even begun to believe that I was telling the truth? I could have been anybody, for all he knew. Having you here showed him how serious and advanced the Galba campaign is. And if I hadn't been there, he would have seen the leader of a Gallic rebellion, and not a leading member of Roman society, as we know you to be. You see, we need each other for this to work.'

Vindex still did not seem content.

'It's because I'm a Gaul, isn't it? If I had been born a full Roman, then I could have been gossiping away with him, and would be trusted. By the gods, I'm a senator of Rome, aren't I? Why shouldn't my fellow senator trust me?'

I sighed. He was naive beyond words.

'That's the way it is, Governor. The Roman Senate are snobs, everyone knows that. Why do you think it's the patricians who have the best positions? In most cases, ancestry and patronage count far higher than talent. Even Cicero found it difficult to become a consul, despite being the best orator the world has ever seen, just because he was a new man.'

'But I'm not trying to be consul! All I want is to lead my army tomorrow, my day of glory. After all, I've stuck my neck out for

Galba, without expecting a great deal in return. The days when the Gauls fought against other tribes and the Romans are long gone, and how else can I win glory for my name and family? As you say, I won't be able to do it in Rome, so that leaves only the battlefield. I raise the first Gallic army since Vercingetorix, only to hear that the Roman army is going to pack up and leave before we reach Vesontio.'

The poor man. He did so want his shot at glory, but politics and my desire to save lives had denied him the chance to prove himself as valiant as his barbaric ancestors. Then it struck me.

'But that is your triumph! Don't you see?'

He looked quizzically at me. 'No.'

'When was the last time you heard of a Roman army that ran away from a barbarian one?' I asked.

There was a lengthy pause as we both racked our brains. Romans had certainly lost against barbarians before – think of Varus's disaster in the Teutoburg Forest – but I couldn't remember a time when we had run away from barbarians without giving battle. Fabius Maximus Cunctator had done it against Hannibal, but that was over two hundred years ago.

'Precisely! You will lead an army of almost thirty thousand Gauls against some of Rome's finest legions, and the Romans retreat in terror back to their strongholds on the Rhine. You will go down in history, I can guarantee it.'

Vindex considered this, and a ghost of a smile appeared momentarily, before he returned to his stock expression of a scowl. Another few minutes of silence followed, before we could just make out the dim glow of the camp fires on the hill ahead. We slowed our horses to a gentle trot, and approached the rather feeble-looking palisade that our army had built.

'Who goes there?' a voice shouted. Well, at least someone on duty was awake, I thought.

'Julius Vindex and his nephew Gnaeus,' the governor called back.

'Governor? Why are you out so late?' the sentry asked.

'Mind your own bloody business and let us in!' I shouted. The gates duly opened and we urged our horses inside. It was raining as hard as ever, and as we dismounted Vindex turned to me and said, 'How about coming to my tent to celebrate? I've got some excellent wine from Tolosa with me.'

I wasn't sure. 'Given that we have to be up in a few hours for the march, don't you think that getting drunk now might not be a good idea?'

'Just one cup? It'll be better than that muck you had in the taverns back in Vienne.'

This was true. I hadn't had any proper wine for weeks, and they say the wine of Tolosa is better than anything produced in Italia.

'All right, just one cup, then,' I said.

A relieved smile broke his usually dour expression, and putting his arm on my back, he guided me towards his grand tent while an attendant took care of the sodden horses.

I was very glad to get out of the rain, and once inside the tent I flung off my sopping cloak. Vindex strode over towards his great table, where two cups of wine stood already poured, and a third empty one was set aside. This was a great deal more efficient and organized than Vindex usually was.

He picked up both the cups and proffered the one which had been standing on my side of the table, and I gratefully took it, indulgently wafting the glorious scent up towards my nose. It did indeed smell wonderful, and the deep red nectar looked splendidly inviting.

Vindex raised his goblet. 'To a glorious day tomorrow.'

We both drank deeply, with Vindex coming up for air first. I carried on until there were just a few dregs at the bottom, and smacked my lips in appreciation. There was a slightly strange aftertaste, but I put that down to the dirtiness of the cups. After all, we had done a lot of travelling, and even the most fastidious of slaves forgets that a long journey will get dust into some of the most inaccessible corners of one's baggage. Vindex looked much more relaxed now, and began to grin widely. He sat down in his ornate chair, watching me closely.

All of a sudden I felt immensely weak and tired. Of course it had been a busy and nerve-racking day, and it was well after midnight by now, but that did not explain why one cup of wine had had such a dramatic effect. My knees began to quiver as I felt the strength drain out of them. All the while Vindex said nothing, but stared at me, with that unnerving smile and a fiendish look in his eyes.

It finally dawned on me, and as I looked at that empty cup my legs gave way completely. A numb sensation was spreading throughout my entire body, and I was certain that I was dying. Still Vindex said nothing. As I felt myself losing consciousness, I had just enough energy to mouth one word at this back-stabbing Gaul. 'Why?' In response he simply raised his cup in mock salute, and then took another drink. Thinking that my last hour had come, I started flailing about on the floor. I don't know what I thought I could achieve, but men who have been poisoned are not likely to be in a rational frame of mind. My limbs were heavy now, and it took every last bit of strength that I had left to move them at all. Then it all went dark, and my spreadeagled body lay motionless on Vindex's floor.

XII

Words cannot describe how happy I was to wake up that morning. I had been convinced that I was about to die in Vindex's tent on some insignificant hill in eastern Gaul. But thank the gods I was alive. Alive but groggy.

Strangely, I came to with the familiar sight of my own tent roof directly above me. Somehow I had gone from the governor's tent to my own, so Vindex had obviously felt no pressing need to kill me. Then why had he drugged me?

I swung my legs across, out of my cot, and placed my still-sandalled feet on the ground. I tried to stand but failed completely, crashing back on to the bed. Whoever had mixed the drugs had done a good job. My thoughts were just as jumbled and flimsy as my limbs were, so all I could do was sit still until I recovered enough to be able to walk around. Finding my sheathed sword beneath the bed, I was not so addled that I wasn't able to put it on, and I attached it securely to my belt. After a huge effort, I raised myself up, clutching at the tent's central pole for support, before my legs gave way again and I collapsed to the floor.

While I tried to get back on my feet by grasping the pole and gingerly levering myself up, I was struck by how quiet it was. There was no noise at all outside my tent; normally a legion's camp pulses with activity – the hammering of smiths, officers shouting, horses whinnying – but there was nothing. There were nearly thirty thousand men inside the camp, and yet it was almost totally silent. I could hear an occasional cawing of the crows, but precious little else. Bracing myself, I had another attempt at getting up, and this time succeeded. Still dizzy, I had to shuffle very slowly towards the tent flap to see what was going on, or rather what wasn't going on.

It was deserted. The whole camp was empty. The palisade and gates still stood, and the tell-tale marks of extinguished fires were dotted all over the place, but all signs of life were gone. I looked up at the sky, and dawn was about to break; I could just make out an orange glow from the eastern horizon.

Then I heard a loud snort behind me, and I whipped round to see my horse, whose reins had been fastened to one of the many stakes that had been scattered round the camp. He was fully saddled and bridled, and ready to be ridden. I was in no fit state to ride, but that couldn't be helped: Vindex had clearly marched off without me, and someone had to make sure that the obnoxious fool didn't do something ridiculously stupid.

After several failed attempts, I managed to mount up, and gingerly prompted the horse to head north-east, to Vesontio. We cantered along at a fair pace, following the army's tracks. A column of tens of thousands of men isn't too difficult to spot, and the ground, sodden from the night before, had been churned into a mass of squelching mud. The swathe of mud was about twenty yards across, and I could see it snaking its way for miles through the hills, leading inexorably towards the besieged town.

Despite how foul I was feeling, I had to reach the army as soon as possible. So I dug my heels in, and the horse flew into a gallop. The change of speed made my innards lurch, forcing me to shift in the saddle and throw up on to the grass below. I don't know how long I rode for. Every jolt was agonizing. My heart pounded, my mouth and lips were dry, except for the bitter aftertaste of vomit that I could not get rid of. Once or twice the stupid horse veered into the squelching mess that the army had made and its front legs got stuck in the ooze, which catapulted me forward out of the saddle.

It was just after the third time that I had fallen into the mud and was trying to heave myself into the saddle yet again that I heard it: away in the distance, the tramp of the army ahead of me. The distant pounding of feet became a series of muffled thuds by the time it reached my ears; I still had a lot of catching up to do. As I made it over the next hill, the marching sound stopped. Obviously they had reached the town. I was praying that Vindex wouldn't do anything stupid, as it was only half an hour after dawn, at the very latest, and Rufus had said that he would address his men an hour after dawn.

I knew that I wasn't far from Vesontio now. I had done the same journey yesterday, but in my delicate state I couldn't be sure that my memory wasn't playing tricks on me. I could just make out the westernmost spur that jutted into the river that almost encircled the town. I was three miles away at the most. With renewed energy, I mounted the sorry excuse for a horse for what I hoped was the last time. Tugging viciously at the reins to encourage it away from the mud, I set off once again. The terrain was as I remembered it. Valley, hill, valley, hill, again and again as I crossed the last range of foothills that separated rural Gaul from the towering Alps. Galloping up the final slope, at last I caught sight of the rearguard. Sextus's cavalry division were milling around on the nearside of a small wood that crowned the top of the hill. I remembered this hill. Beyond it was the valley that rose up steeply towards Vesontio's citadel. I spotted Sextus himself, idly chatting with a small group of horsemen. Tugging the reins to my left I bore down upon him, scattering the men in my way.

He looked in my direction to see what had caused the commotion, and I was just close enough to see him freeze, mouth agape, like a man who has seen a ghost. I reined in close to him, and looked him directly in the eye.

'Where's that backstabbing shit your father?' I said bluntly.

'Er . . . with Quintus,' he replied.

He clearly had not expected me to appear, and had not leaped to his father's defence, so I assumed he had at least known of the plan to drug me.

'And where exactly is that? Tell me quickly, every second counts.'

'My father won't want to see you,' he said nervously.

'I don't bloody care,' I snarled at him, 'what he wants or doesn't want. Unless you tell me where he is, right now, you could be responsible for the deaths of thousands of innocent men. Do you want that, Sextus?'

He pointed towards the woods. 'On the other side, with the infantry.'

Dispensing with the pleasantries, I dug my heels in again and headed straight for the woods. I hadn't ridden through these woods the day before, but from the outside they hadn't looked that dense. But now that I was in the heart of them, my horse was having a lot of difficulty moving through at speed. The ash trees weren't particularly big or sturdy, but the long narrow trunks everywhere made the wood a lot harder to cross. One man on foot would have no problem, but on horseback it was nigh on impossible to go faster than walking pace.

Eventually I came to the edge of the wood, only to be greeted with the sight of thousands of men in pristine ranks, stretching across the fields. Just behind them, in the centre, were two figures. One wore a deep red cloak.

Taking my time, I trotted slowly over towards the pair. Vindex was surveying his troops, and Quintus looked round, nudging his father when he recognized me. Vindex's head snapped round to look at me, and immediately he took a couple of steps back in shock. I pulled up and swung down out of the saddle, still fairly dizzy. I steadied myself, and walked slowly towards the governor. He tried to compose himself, and I was just about to demand what he thought he was playing at, when I heard in the distance, once again, that rhythmic tramping of an army on the march. The citadel and Roman siege-works were hidden behind a gentle rise to the north, but then a shrill blast of trumpets heralded the arrival of the Army of the Rhine. On the brow ahead of us an opposing force of metal-encased legionaries marched towards us, led by a thin line of skirmishers.

While Vindex was staring at the army, I took another couple of steps forward and tapped him on the shoulder. He turned to look at me, and I smashed him in the face. He flung his hands towards his nose and staggered back, blood streaming down his chin.

'What do you think you're doing, you arrogant turd? Through your pride, you've just condemned your army to death,' I shouted at him. 'First you drug me, then you march off and force Rufus to fight a battle for which there was no need. What did you think would happen? A glorious victory, with a bunch of farmers led by someone who's never held military command, against the finest army in the world? You're even more stupid than I thought.'

All the while, Vindex was shouting something in Gallic at Quintus, who stood still. Vindex shouted some more, but Quintus just turned to me and asked: 'What do we do now?'

I was about to order a rebel army into action against a highly trained Roman one, but there was nothing else for it. 'Bring me Bormo, Martialis and the rest. We have to fight, otherwise their cavalry will cut us down in droves.'

The commanders were duly summoned, and all the while rank upon rank of heavily armed infantry appeared to the north. The glow of dawn on their armour made the soldiers difficult to see individually, so it was hard to gauge how many had appeared so far, but from what Rufus had said, there ought to have been around twenty thousand men, minus the cohorts who were guarding the city's bridges. Yet even they would be here soon enough, with a full-scale battle in the offing.

Carnunnos, Sextus, Bormo and the rest were soon assembled, all looking somewhat worried. Sextus in particular was awe-struck by the military machine on the other side of the valley. Vindex was nowhere to be seen.

Martialis was the first to speak. 'I'll bet ten denarii that we win.'

'Anyone here fancy taking Martialis up on that bet?' I looked at each of them in turn. Bormo and Quintus gave a chuckle. Carnunnos showed his contempt with a casual spit.

'Good,' I said. 'Because not only can we win, but we are going to win, so long as each man follows his orders. Is that clear?'

The men nodded at me, looking a little less perturbed than they had done at the start of the conversation. Now I had to decide on tactics. The dilemma was whether to try and win the day, at the risk of throwing away thousands of lives and Galba's hopes for the entire campaign, or to withdraw, to save lives but simultaneously destroy the credibility of the entire movement, leaving Galba isolated in Hispania. We could end Roman lives in a battle that need not take place, or deny Rome a worthy emperor. For a patriotic Roman, neither choice was particularly appetizing.

My decision made, I began to reveal my battle plans. 'As we all know, in the open, we cannot hope to match the legions. So, we shall line up very much as we are now, just in front of this small wood here. No one is to move from their position until ordered. Clear so far?'

Bormo spoke up. 'So we wait for the Romans to come to us, and then we charge down the hill?'

'Not quite. We will wait for them to come to us, and wear themselves out a little on the slope. Their usual strategy is to get within fifty yards, launch a volley of javelins and then charge home. We will take that first volley, and then retreat into the woods. It is vital that the retreat looks disorganized, shambolic even, just like the cowardly militia they think we are. With any luck, they will follow us into the woods, and then we will spring the trap.

'While those thin ash trees may not look like much, the sheer number of them will disrupt their formations. All our archers will wait in the woods and give covering fire while our men re-form. Then, while our archers are pouring volley after volley into their disordered ranks, our men will be able to fight man to man with the Romans.'

'And the cavalry?' asked Martialis.

'They will be waiting behind the woods on our left flank, hidden from the legions. Once most of the enemy are committed to entering the woods, the cavalry will swing round behind them and charge into the melee.'

'I have a question,' said Bormo. 'If we are to withdraw into the woods anyway, why do we have to let the Romans throw a volley of spears at us?'

Carnunnos interrupted, 'Because, idiot, it would look a bit strange if we ran away as soon as they came close; the Romans aren't that ugly!' That provoked a round of nervous laughter from my men. I was thoroughly glad we had at least one older man among us who would not lose his head in a crisis.

'And what of my father?' Sextus queried.

I allowed myself a small smile. 'It has been decided that my uncle's life is too precious to risk in battle, so he will wait at the back of the field while we win the battle for him. I am in command, unless you have any problems with that?'

Given that he was surrounded by men who, I hoped, were more loyal to me than Vindex, it would have taken a brave man to contest my right to command the army. Fortunately, Sextus was not such a brave man, and he mutely nodded his assent.

'That's settled then. Now, each man to his troops. Quintus,

you will command the archers, but be sure to hold fire until the enemy are fully committed to chasing us into the woods. I shall take my place with the infantry. And good luck to you all.'

As the commanders made their separate ways to various parts of the line, it hit me that I had just referred to my fellow countrymen as 'the enemy'. I realize that having been a part of the Vindex campaign all this time I should have been prepared for this, but I had never expected there to be a pitched battle. Strictly speaking, the vast majority of my army were themselves Roman citizens, making this day the beginning of a civil war. Not pleasant thoughts to have running through your head moments before your first command of a full-scale battle, but these misgivings were soon forgotten as the shrill blast of trumpets sounded the Roman advance.

XIII

It is a majestic sight, a Roman field army in those moments before battle is joined. Those great, shimmering columns of men in perfect formations, just as they had practised on the parade ground for hours on end. I remember something the men under Tiberius's command said, when he was a general on the Rhine: his drills were bloodless battles; his battles, bloody drills. Over the centuries, the Roman army has adopted and adapted different formations and tactics to overcome almost every nation they have encountered, and, for a military man like myself, it is a joy to watch them in action.

Except for that day.

You see, having served in the army, I had always watched the legions marching forward in perfect ranks towards a terrified enemy. This was the first time that they had been marching towards me. The assembled army numbered at most two-thirds of our own force, and even with a sound strategy in mind, not only was the outcome of the battle very uncertain, but I don't mind saying that for a moment I was quaking in fear. I snapped out of it soon enough. A good leader should never reveal his fears to the men, but the sight of those legions marching unerringly towards me on that day is forever etched on my memory.

I delayed joining the ranks for a bit, staying further up the slope to keep my good view of the shallow valley, watching to see how the opposing army deployed. By the dress and formation, I judged there to be three regular legions and one legion of auxiliaries in Rufus's force, with no reserve that I could see, and no cavalry, which was a blessing. In the centre of each legion stood the aquilifer, the standard bearer, whose duty it was to carry his legion's eagle: a simple, metal bird that represented the honour and pride of the legion. I have seen men hurl themselves at the enemy to retrieve a lost eagle, for a legion without an eagle loses all respect and honour, despite perhaps a century of dedicated service. The rank and file lived for the legion and their comrades, and once battle was joined it would take a superhuman effort to defeat them. This was what I was hoping to achieve that day, all for a man I had promised to serve after less than a day in his company. I was just glad that, thus far, few people knew that Caecina Severus was in command of a rebel army. I silently prayed to all the gods I could think of to help me in this gamble that I had taken for Galba.

I could tell that our men were getting nervous at the prospect of finally joining battle with the Romans. As the legionaries in the front ranks reached the bottom of the valley and began to march up towards our position, the rearmost ranks of the Gauls began to take a step or two backwards, itching to get under the cover of the woods. The elder soldiers and junior officers growled at them to get back in line, and I had a look to make sure that each commander was setting his men a good example.

Carnunnos stood still, a weathered rock for the younger men to cling to. I could see Martialis weaving about the ranks, making a joke here, a reassuring line there, cursing and cajoling according to the man. Bormo stood a few yards back from his men, limbering up for battle silently. He was the master of the sword-ring, but having nothing but a sword was a severe handicap in the chaos of a battle. As a shield would have impeded his natural speed and style, instead he opted to wield two swords, probably from his own smithy, and trust to his skill and agility. Sextus had rejoined his unit behind the leafy screen of the wood, so that just left Quintus. This was probably the first time that he had been out of his father's shadow, I mused to myself. And what a first time too! To lead the archers is not usually the most prestigious of commands, but given how they fitted into our strategy, Quintus's timing of that first volley would be crucial in deciding the outcome of the battle.

Thankfully there were still no cavalry to be seen, nor the bridge detachments from the city, just these eighteen thousand or so legionaries in front of us, who were marching up the hill as quickly as they had headed down the far slope, still looking fresh and ordered.

Two hundred paces away. Close enough to see individual legs and feet moving beneath the Roman shields. Fortunately I was able to see over the heads of my men, being considerably taller than most. Most generals these days stay on horseback to have the best possible view of the battle unfolding, or more likely in case they have to make a quick getaway. I preferred the old-school way, standing on your own two feet, sharing the danger with your men. I also find that being involved in the fighting yourself means that you have a heightened sense of how the battle's balance is shifting, and then you can take steps accordingly.

One hundred paces away. Up till now, the battlefield had been largely silent, except for the constant chorus of marching feet and clunking armour, for that is the Roman way; silent, grim and efficient, but occasionally treating oneself to a cheer or two. Suddenly, a trickle of men in front of me began to scream and shout, bashing sword upon shield. This trickle rippled through the ranks, and soon it became a flood. Eventually the whole army was roaring, and rhythmically striking their shields. I even found myself shouting with them, even if it was in a different language. Then the Gallic army took up one of those fearsome, haunting war songs. It was all I could do not to cry. Music can do strange things, especially given the right occasion. This glorified militia, howling scorn and contempt upon the greatest military machine in the world, and only me aware of how precarious our position truly was. Since that first day in Vienne, over these past few weeks I had gained a sense of almost kinship with the Gauls. Maybe not kinship, but comradeship certainly. These proud people, who loved the simple things of life, were far better company than many of the noblest men of Italia. That combination of their pride and my sorrow was overwhelming.

We were still shouting and screaming when the enemy came to an abrupt halt. And then, as we saw each legionary reaching for his pilum, our ululating cries began to fail. I can still remember that moment as if it were only seconds ago. Sometimes I wake up shivering and sweating as it recurs in my nightmares. As the last war cries were dying on our lips, the whoosh of thousands of javelins flung towards us was chilling. You see them, like an iron hedge in the sky, hurtling up towards the peak of their trajectory, then the sharp-tipped heads plunge down at you.

It was probably all of six heartbeats between the end of the war cry and the first screams of pain, but it felt like an eternity. They are brutal things, Roman javelins. Not only are they far stronger than the spears made by other nations, but they also have a wicked barbed point to them, and if that passes through your shield, in the heat of battle it is almost impossible to remove, forcing you to fling away your main source of protection. If you are very unlucky, the long narrow shank behind the point can penetrate the shield and carry on to puncture your chest beneath.

I had no shield, not even a breastplate, having forgotten in my drugged state that such things come in useful for a battle, but the man to my right thrust his own shield in front of me, and did his best to huddle with me behind it. We were so close I could smell his reeking breath. The stench of liquor was so strong that I even remember thinking of leaving the relative safety of his shield just to escape the smell. Then a spearhead tore through the shield, the hook gouged a further hole, and the hateful thing whistled between our heads and thumped into the ground. We looked at each other in amazement, before my saviour tried to salvage his shield, then dropped it and the entangled pilum to the ground. As it was designed to do, the spear had bent on impact, making it impossible to throw it back at the Romans, but this was not my plan.

Up and down the line, hundreds fell. I could hear the screams of agony as men were skewered where they stood, some spitted as the spear passed through their shields, their bodies, and still further into the soft earth below. I could already see the men running back for the cover of the woods, and I raised my sword high above, signalling our planned retreat, and the officers urged those who had not decided to run to do so.

As we sprinted for shelter, I glanced back to see the Romans raise their arms in triumph, and then begin their pursuit with a roar. It was working! Though the volley had done much damage, our line was still in good order. We now began a deadly race. Our troops had to reach the safety of Quintus's line of archers quickly enough to allow them at the very least two volleys at the Romans, without any of our men in the way. If we took too long, then Quintus would only have time for one volley before the Romans were upon us, and they would be only slightly outnumbered by an inferior force.

'Run, you bastards, run!' I harangued them, and sprinted as fast as my weakened body would let me. We were racing ahead, and the more cowardly among us had already reached the trees. Then I almost froze in horror, making me trip over my feet and sprawl to the ground. What about the wounded?

I had forgotten that a quick retreat would mean that all those who had been hit in the volley would not be able to match our pace. As I scrabbled to my feet, I saw all those bodies strewn on the hillside, plus several hundred who had survived the attack, but my plan had left them at the mercy of the Romans. The front ranks were closing in on my wounded men. It was inevitable: as the legions tramped over the littered bodies, the dead would be crushed and those still living would be hacked and stabbed by the oncoming legionaries.

Seething at my own stupidity, I was powerless to help them. All I could do was reach the woods in enough time to repay the damage. Surging back into a sprint, I was now one of the last of the Gallic army on that bloody ridge. Fire coursed through my veins as my aching limbs complained at the effort, but I had to get to safety quickly or risk being mown down myself. Another few yards and I was in among the trees. At last I saw the double line of archers ahead of me and barged my way through, only to see the ordered ranks of men behind them. Carnunnos and the rest had done their job well.

The Roman formations fragmented when they hit the woods, as each man had to negotiate his way through the densely packed trees in his cumbersome armour. I heard Quintus shout an order, and then the first volley of arrows was loosed. We had no archers like those in the proper army, but many of our men were hunters and had brought their own bows for the campaign. Over such a short distance, even their poor-quality shafts were able to pierce Roman armour. Men were flung back by the impact of that crashing volley, and I looked along the length of our line and saw that the sacrifice of our wounded was not completely in vain.

Normally when under missile fire, the legions form the *testudo*, making a tortoise-like shell with the front rank holding their shields before them while the rest raise theirs to form a protective roof. However, the exuberance of their charge and the number of trees made this impossible, and we responded by sending shaft after shaft into that mass of men. Soon we were out of arrows, and all we could do was charge the legions while they were still disorientated and out of formation. The Gauls have always been individual fighters, and many were delighted at the chance to face the Romans man to man.

Bormo was one of the first into the enemy. He wielded his dual blades with deadly skill, stabbing at the neck of one man one instant, then slashing at another's hamstring the next. I could sense the Roman line buckling under the weight and ferocity of our attack, and I grabbed the nearest man and shouted in his ear: 'Get to Sextus and tell him to charge. Now!' Then I headed into the fray myself.

I hadn't held a blade in anger since those dark days in Britannia, but that familiar feeling of battle was coming back to me. You stop thinking about tactics, or self-preservation, and instead think about targets. Neck and groin. Those are crucial. A good blow there will kill a man very quickly. Cut, thrust, parry, hack. Sometimes you don't need to think, and it becomes purely instinctive; an almost trance-like state, where your body takes over completely and enemies fall dead at your feet. Such men develop a passion for battle and killing.

Fortunately I am not one of those blood-crazed killers. I put my survival down to two things: strength and speed. While you might think that my height would hamper my swordplay, it does not make me less of a swordsman. Flashy tricks are for the arena, not the battlefield, and a rough shove to the ground followed up by a stab does the job just as well as fine wristwork. But in my case it is coupled with lightning-quick reactions, so it was with confidence that I strode out with my men towards the enemy.

The first legionary I encountered made a feeble attempt to strike me with his shield boss, hoping to knock me over and deliver the killer blow. I easily sidestepped the effort, and swung my blade down towards his outstretched shield arm. Cutting straight to the bone, the stump sprayed my face with blood, and my opponent gave a yelp of pain as his severed forearm and shield crashed to the earth, and the man behind me finished him off.

Out of the corner of my eye, I glimpsed a sword coming at me from the right. Spinning round, I desperately parried the blow. The legionary tried a counter-stroke, but this time I anticipated and blocked it quickly, knocking his sword out of the way before unleashing a powerful stab at his stomach. The thrust met the resistance of his armour, but the strike was strong enough to pierce the woven plates and deliver a fatal wound. As I felt my sword penetrate, I twisted the blade so that it wouldn't stick in the muscular flesh, and with an almighty heave pulled it free.

But I was having more success than most of my men. We were certainly holding our own, but the enemy were beginning to recover from the initial shock of finding a resolute enemy instead of a scrabbling rabble of men on the run. Where was Sextus with the cavalry? We needed them to flank the enemy line and hasten the victory.

My sword arm was beginning to tire with all the hacking and stabbing in the front rank, but I was determined to lead by example, and not to drop to the rear for a breather. A chorus of whistles changed everything. The centurions, prominent because of their red-plumed helmets, were blowing their whistles. Normally this signified a rotation in the ranks, with the front moving to the rear and all the others moving up one spot, so that the enemy were presented with a fresh rank of men every few minutes. But the ranks were retreating!

Thinking it strange, given how evenly matched the exchange had been until then, I was trying to fathom why the legions would retreat. As an idea struck me, I saw that my men were following the fleeing Romans with whoops and shouts of joy. I tried to call them back into line, but I was like a charioteer who had lost hold of the reins. The Gauls sensed victory, and they would let nothing stand in their way.

As the Gallic army left their general and the shelter of the woods and ran back into the open, they saw, too late, the solid Roman formations drawn up in front of them. The first of our men to charge had such momentum that they were unable to stop in time; instead they had no choice but to fling themselves upon that wall of men. Now the Romans had the clear advantage. In the open the ill-disciplined Gauls were no match for the legions, and my rage was made all the worse by my awareness of the irony of it. The Romans had feinted a retreat just as we had done, luring my impetuous troops out of the shelter and back into the killing ground.

Now some Gauls began to run away, genuinely this time, in an effort to save their skins. The cries of my men being butchered by the merciless Roman ranks still haunt me to this day. Except that these cries were soon drowned out by a thundering of hooves, and I looked desperately to the left. Sextus rode at the head of his squadron, his boyish face grinning in delight as they headed straight for the Roman flank.

Orders were barked to the men closest to the new threat, and the files on the legion's right turned to face the cavalry. Ruefully, I stood still and watched, knowing what was about to happen. Sextus had charged too late, meaning that instead of meeting the Roman rear, he faced a solid flank. Waiting until the last possible moment, the legionaries lowered their spears, resting the butts on the blood-spattered ground, and braced themselves for impact. No horse in the world will charge a forest of spears, and most pulled up short. But the horses ridden by Sextus and the reckless boys at the front did not have time to react, and were impaled on those iron barbs. The riders were flung headlong into the middle of the formation, where they would be dispatched unseen by us on the outside. Those Romans who had been too far back to use their javelins at the beginning of the battle flung them now at the cavalry, who had stalled in front of those gleaming spears.

Horses whinnied and shrieked. Men tumbled out of the saddle, impaled on those cold metal shafts. They lay on the grass, twitching. It was pure carnage.

By now most of our army was on the run. I could see the older men were trying to hold back the tide, but the battle was as good as lost. It served no purpose to waste yet more lives. I signalled to the commanders to let the men flee, hoping that the Romans would not give chase. Thank the gods they had no cavalry that day, or they would have butchered the lot of us as we ran. I hoped that the Romans would instead cheer their victory and then set about plundering the bodies. Meekly, we slunk back to the woods, amid the jeering of the victorious legions.

XIV

A crisis. A great big bowel-emptying crisis. That was what I was in. Galba's vaunted army of Gaul had been obliterated, massacred by the Roman legions. Those legions were hardly going to declare their loyalty to Galba, having that day defeated an army supposedly raised in his name. I had failed him utterly. Or rather, Vindex had failed him.

I was still fuming at the arrogant fool for presuming he could lead the army to victory, and now his pride and lust for glory had brought ruin. Striding purposefully through those wretched woods, along with all the other survivors, I tried to work out what to do next. Men hobbled away, clutching at their wounds. Dying men cluttered the paths, a trail of the dead and the dying leading the way out of the woods and away from the slaughter.

A young boy, the downy hair of his first beard stained with blood, writhed in agony. He was bent double on the ground, like an abandoned baby. His hands pressed tightly at his stomach, but I saw some of his entrails leaking out between his fingers. I crouched down, and put my hand on his shoulder. The boy moaned pitifully, but was trying his best not to scream. He turned to look at me, and spoke something in Gallic. I felt so useless, not knowing what he wanted to say. All I could do was shrug my shoulders and look questioningly at him. Gritting his teeth, the boy took a hand away from his open stomach, and there was a sickening squelch as something hit the earth. I didn't dare look down. Tears ran down the boy's face, but still he didn't cry out. His wavering hand reached for my sword hilt. I understood, and stood up. The boy quickly brought his free hand back to the wound, and screwed his eyes shut. Drawing my sword, I gave a swift slash to his neck, and ended his pain. The blood spurted up, all over my chest, and I turned to vomit on the blood-soaked earth.

I was almost mad with rage and revulsion by the time I made it out of those woods and into the open grassland on the reverse slope. I had been betrayed, but that was nothing to the betrayal of the army by the man who had called them to arms with glorious words of rebellion. My thoughts turned to revenge. Two men stood in the long grass just twenty paces away, near where I had first come upon Sextus that morning. Quintus had his back to me, but I could hear him talking to his father. I must have looked like some avenging Fury, the young boy's blood flecked over my face and body, hand still clutching a sword stained with the gore of my fellow countrymen, and all because of that man.

The governor crumpled at the sight of me. He fell to his knees, tears streaming down his face. Some blood had caked around his mouth. A result of my breaking his nose, probably.

'My son, Sextus . . .' he began tremulously.

I cut him off. 'Dead.'

He gave a howl of anguish, but I wasn't in the mood to pity him.

'Dead because of you; and thousands of others, sacrificed for your shot at glory, Governor.' I used his title mockingly. 'What did you think was going to happen today?'

'I thought we could win. I thought a Gaul in revolt would help get rid of Nero and help Galba to the throne. I'm not just a senator of Rome, I am the chieftain of the Aquitani. Galba promised to make me High King of Gaul. High King of a client kingdom of Rome, but my sons and I would rule Gaul. If you were me, what would you have done?'

I was reeling. All this time I had thought Vindex was a simpleton who just wanted his day of triumph, but his ambitions had been far higher. I had been fooled, twice. To be fooled by a man like Vindex hurt, but what hurt more was that Galba had not trusted me enough to tell me the whole truth. Vindex's ambition was yet another reason the old man had been adamant that there should be no battle with the legions, no Gallic rebellion. I had come so close to giving Vindex the victory that he craved, but did not deserve.

'You're a traitor to Rome,' I accused him.

'What has Rome ever done for me?'

'Aside from maintaining your family's lands and titles, and giving you a seat in the Senate? But more importantly, what have you done for Rome? Today I've watched thousands of men die and led an army against my own people to save Rome from a tyrant.'

'Sextus is dead,' he bawled, his eyes red with anguish. 'Don't you think I've been punished enough?'

'Not nearly enough, you coward. You could at least have had a noble death, in battle, like Sextus. But instead you ran here, hoping I'd do all the hard work for you. Well, here's your reward.'

Quick as a whip, I grabbed the dagger from Quintus's belt and flung it towards Vindex. Its point stuck in the muddy ground with a squelch, just in front of the despicable man.

Quintus appealed to me. 'Is this really necessary?'

I didn't look at my friend, but kept my eyes fixed on the governor. 'Either he kills himself with it, or I'll do it for him. Say your goodbyes, Vindex, you have five minutes.'

With that, I walked a respectful distance away and turned my back. I could hear him whimpering to Quintus, and chose not to listen. After a few minutes, the blabbering stopped. There was a brief moment of silence, then a faint gushing sound, and then nothing more but the distant echo of an army in flight. I felt a hand on my shoulder.

'It's done,' Quintus said.

'Good. We need to get moving.' I started to search for a riderless horse.

'Aren't we going to bury him?' my friend asked.

I stopped, and sighed. 'What with? Besides, there are hordes of men who want to loot and take prisoners as slaves. We have to move, now.'

'One minute, then.' Before I had a chance to argue he had run back to his father's body, and grabbed a handful of dirt. He sprinkled it over the corpse, whispering a short prayer. He took two small coins from somewhere, and laid them over Vindex's closed eyelids, before bending over to kiss him on the cheek. Finally, he slipped the large golden family ring from his father's finger, and placed it on his own.

As much as I had despised the man, it didn't feel right not giving him a decent burial, but the events of that day had hardened my soul, and I had to put practicality over sentiment.

As we searched for a couple of horses, walking side by side, Quintus must have sensed that an explanation was needed, but I didn't want to interrogate him so soon after the deaths of his brother and father.

'I am not like my father,' he began.

'I'm glad to hear it,' I said acidly.

'Don't judge him too harshly. He wasn't the man he thought he was. It seems everybody knew that, except him.'

'And yet you knew he planned to drug me and try to take the glory for himself.'

He looked at me fiercely with those tear-stained eyes. 'Actually, he planned to poison you, and tell Galba that you fell in battle. He ordered me to poison your cup, so I gave you a weak sleeping drug instead, and made sure there was a horse tied up near by when we left camp.'

I was taken aback. Quintus and I got on well, but I had no idea that he had been willing to disobey his father to protect me.

'Why?'

'Because we needed you. Why else? Father had nothing to do with Albanos's decision to torture you, though at first he did have him watch you. You saw what Father was like. He was proud and stubborn, and he resented how you took over the whole campaign. I don't know what made him decide to poison you in the end.'

I did. Every time I went off alone, to talk with Rufus or to do anything important, I had noticed Vindex looking increasingly malcontent. The negotiations yesterday must have been the final straw. That explained why there had been an empty third cup, to use in case Vindex decided that his dignity had not been compromised and that he would spare my life. It dawned on me that I didn't deserve a friend like Quintus, who had risked his father's wrath so many times by siding with me, in the interests of the campaign.

'I'm not sure how I can even begin to thank you. It can't have been easy to disobey your father.'

'It wasn't,' Quintus said irritably.

How can you thank a man for saving your life when you have just pressured his father into committing suicide? There is a poignant moment in the *Iliad* when old King Priam goes into the tent of Achilles to beg for the body of his son, after the Greek hero had dragged it behind his chariot round the walls of Troy. Yet somehow each man retains respect for the other. That is the nearest comparison I can think of, a blend of pity, anger, remorse and forgiveness. One day I would thank him properly, but all I could say in that moment was 'Thank you.'

He nodded his acceptance. Any other thoughts were unspoken.

Hoping to avoid the pillaging army, we took a detour to the

west before heading northwards to the city. It was clear that I had to find General Rufus and discover his intentions, let Galba know what had happened, and if possible stay close to the general and update Galba accordingly.

We rounded the woods, and had no choice but to head for the Roman camp on foot. If I remembered rightly, it was only another five minutes' walk beyond the crest of that hill whence the victorious army had come. The wind changed, and began to blow from the east, wafting the stench of death towards us. We were no more than half a mile from the point where Sextus's inglorious charge had crashed into the Roman flank, but the stink was enough to make you retch. It begins as a sickly sweet smell, but then the rank odour of decaying flesh hits you hard. Quintus bent over double, heaving the contents of his stomach on to the hillside. Already the crows had begun to flock from miles around and were circling above us, summoning up the courage to begin their own scavenging, despite the number of men still on the hilltop.

My attention was caught by a group of horsemen a short way up the far slope. Why should that be strange on a battlefield, you may ask, but the only cavalry I had seen that day were our own. It was only a small group, about half a dozen, yet they seemed to be standing in a vague semicircle around one man seated on a splendid grey horse, and with an especially fine plume on the crest of his helmet. It had to be General Rufus.

'Come on,' I urged Quintus. 'You're about to meet a general.'

Quintus looked uncertain, but I ignored his misgivings and began walking at a brisk pace towards the victorious commander.

As we came near enough, I could hear the tone of the conversation, but not the words. It all sounded like light-hearted chatter, the prerogative of those who had just won an easy victory, I thought to myself. One of the staff officers paused in the conversation to look out on to the field, and noticed the two of us approaching.

'What do you want?' he called out, curtly.

'Messenger to see General Rufus.'

'You don't look like couriers.'

I shrugged, and proffered my bloody sword. 'We came across the Gauls and had to fight our way through.'

'And at the same time lost your armour and horses? A likely story!'

'Saturninus, may I be permitted to take part in this conversation?' the general said sarcastically.

'These two men, sir, said they had a message for you. But I think they look more like Gallic fugitives than Roman couriers, don't you, sir?'

'Don't try and think, Saturninus, it doesn't suit you. And what I think is none of your business. I can certainly vouch for one of these men, but I'm not so sure who this other fellow is.'

He looked closely at Quintus, and before I had a chance to say anything, Rufus's face brightened. 'Oh, I remember you now. You must be Vindex's eldest, Quintus. We were introduced at that dinner your father hosted in Lugdunum.'

It took a few seconds and several gasps from his entourage before he realized his mistake. He had just publicly identified my friend as the son of Gaul's, if the not empire's, most wanted man. The careless remark was as good as a death sentence.

All of a sudden there were cries of 'Traitor!' and worse, and the staff officers made to seize Quintus. Reacting quickly, I clasped a hand to Quintus's shoulder, and declared: 'This man is my prisoner!'

'Your prisoner? Then why is he armed?' one of them asked.

'He gave me his word.'

'His word!' another sneered. 'Why would you trust a grubby little Gaul?'

'Because he is a senator of Rome, or at least he will be soon. Vindex is dead, which makes his son here of senatorial rank.'

'Then who are you to take a senator prisoner?' asked the first officer, Saturninus.

'Senator Caecina Severus, formerly of the Twentieth Valeria Victrix, with the thanks of the Senate. And you are . . . ?'

I do love pulling rank sometimes. The young subaltern took a moment to compose himself. 'Tribune Cornelius Saturninus . . .' I glowered at him, '. . . sir.'

'Then, Tribune, you can give me your horse while I have a talk with the general back in his quarters.'

Sheepishly, the young man dismounted and offered me the reins to his horse. I thought it would be pushing it a bit to demand another horse for Quintus, so instead I manoeuvred beside Rufus and said, 'After you, General.'

Rufus nodded courteously, and then turned to one of the aides. 'Send a message to the Legate Valens, asking him to meet me in my quarters as soon as possible. We shall be interrogating the prisoner.'

We trotted back to camp slowly, so that Quintus would not be left flagging behind us. I was about to ask the general something, but he cut me off.

'Not yet, if you please. I would rather we had a private conversation, and not within earshot of half the army.' So we carried on in silence, except when we entered the camp. There were almighty cheers from the men, and their proud general thanked them for their reaction, and congratulated individuals for various acts of valour on the battlefield. Eventually we got past the joyous throng, and at last reached the relative security of Rufus's tent.

You might well think that the heart of a Roman camp is one of the safest places to be, but I was very unsure of my political position. Had Rufus had second thoughts when he returned from the negotiations last night? Would he remain loyal, and turn us over to Nero? I must say, a traitor's death was not an appealing one. Valens was already inside, waiting for us.

'Ah, Valens, you received my message then?'

The legate looked at Rufus with one of those frosty, superior gazes. 'Evidently, sir.'

Rufus ignored the barb, and began to divest himself of his heavy armour. 'Well, what a pickle, eh?'

That was an understatement if ever I heard one.

'First of all,' continued the general, 'I am sorry for your loss, Quintus. I had only met your father briefly, but he seemed a decent enough man, even if we were on opposite sides today. He must have had a great tactical mind; you almost defeated my army this morning.'

Quintus forced himself to smile. 'The credit must go to your fellow senator, General. My father was . . . indisposed during the battle.'

'Congratulations then, Severus! It was some damn fine soldiering, taking all our spears before luring us into the woods. Such a good move, in fact, that I decided to copy it.'

'Glad I could be of help, sir,' was all I could think to say. 'But with respect, might I ask why the army marched this morning?'

'There was damn all I could do to stop them. I had ordered the men on parade to discuss the, ah, unique situation we find ourselves in, when one of the sentries burst in to announce that an army was drawing itself up less than a mile away. Trumpets were sounded, officers rallied their men, and we were off to battle. I couldn't get a word in edgeways, isn't that right, Valens?'

Valens nodded. 'It could be said that the army commanded their general today.'

Rufus stiffened at that. 'I'd be much obliged, Legate, if you didn't make witticisms like that in my presence, and even more if you didn't make them at all.'

'Yes, General.'

'If I might interrupt,' I said, 'we need to discuss the immediate future. As far as I'm concerned, Gaul has lost a small militia force, and that is it. The fact remains that Nero is a dangerous

174

lunatic, and that Galba is more than qualified to do the job. The question, General, is whether you still stand by what you said last night. Do you?'

Rufus took his time before replying, and no wonder. It was a politician's question, though asked in simple, blunt, military terms.

'Speaking for myself, I agree that Nero ought to go, and that Galba is much better placed than most to succeed him, but I don't see my command as a political role. This has to be done constitutionally, or not at all.'

'I would add that it's unlikely that the troops here will support the man whose army they have just defeated,' said Valens.

'That is true,' I conceded. 'But what about the legions which aren't here, the ones further down the Rhine? Could they not be persuaded?'

'I reckon I could probably sway the senior officers, but our governor, Fonteius Capito, I can't speak for. He cares too much about money and his own sordid pleasures to involve himself in politics.'

'Then it is clear what has to be done. The myth of the Gallic rebellion will have to be presented as fact, so that we can dissociate Galba from the shambles of this morning. General, I would recommend making another attempt to address your men later today, and I can guarantee that there will be no army to interrupt you this time.'

That brought a small chuckle from Rufus, but for obvious reasons was a little too macabre for Quintus. It was Quintus now who spoke: 'And what am I to do?'

I gazed sadly at my friend. 'You must return to your family, they will need you now. And then you might take up your father's role in Gaul. I know that you are not yet a senator, but someone needs to replace your father, and I can think of none better. But on reflection I would not live in Lugdunum if I were you. Vienne would be much safer.'

'Well, I think that seems to be everything settled,' Rufus declared. 'And what will the two of you do now?'

'I should like to return to what's left of my family as soon as possible, sir,' said Quintus.

'Of course. And you, Severus?'

'If you don't mind, I should like to stay with the army, sir. I reckon I could be of more use to Galba here than back in my province.'

'I shall have some quarters fitted out for you shortly, then, with a proper uniform to go with it, if you're going to wander round the camp, that is.'

'That would be most kind, General. Thank you.'

With that, Quintus and I made a polite bow, and left the confines of Rufus's tent.

'Right, if I'm to go to Vienne, I'll need a horse!'

'You're going already?' I asked.

'As you said, the region needs a governor, and there's not much I can do here. If you wish to reach me, I'm sure Lugubrix will still be useful. Besides, I need some time alone.'

'Of course.'

Quintus, young and innocent as he was, was not the sort to discuss his feelings openly, but preferred to wrestle with them alone. So I did not pursue the matter, and rested my hand on his shoulder, and he likewise, before we embraced in a tight hug.

'I promise you, Quintus, I will do everything I can to help you and your family. You will be a senator of Rome now. It's the least I can do after everything you've done for me.'

Breaking free, I looked into those boyish eyes of his and said, 'May the gods be with you, Brother.'

He grimaced. 'Not today, Brother. They aren't with me today.'

All the men under Rufus's command paraded right after the evening meal. I had donned the uniform of a tribune once again and stood a short distance to the side of the general's platform, so as to hear him and watch the army's reaction at the same time.

The entire army was in camp that evening. After hearing that Vindex's army had been crushed, the city of Vesontio had surrendered almost immediately, offering up their stores of goods and grain to the legions. All the foragers and various detachments had been recalled to hear what their general had to say. I watched them filing out of the mess tents: some were still scraping the last morsels from their canteens, others were showing off the plunder they had scavenged from the fallen, others still were retelling stories of their brave exploits against the Gallic hordes.

Slowly, the formidable centurions and optios began to direct the men into ranks, as the legions formed up in front of the rostrum. Each legion commander stood at the foot of the podium, facing his own legion. Valens was there, in front of the First Germanica, so called because in its entire history the legion had barely ever left the Rhine frontier. The Twenty-Second Primigenia stood in pristine order next to Valens's legion, and after that came the Fourth Macedonica. A young-looking tribune stood at their head, as I gathered the legate had died in the battle. The remaining space was filled by the smaller detachments of legions from Lower Germania, as well as some auxiliary units. These were Germanic tribesmen who had left their wild lives east of the Rhine and served Rome, in return for food, steady pay, and the chance of Roman citizenship after twenty years of loyal service. Normally these mercenaries served a long way from home, but Rufus had obviously decided that since the enemy were Gauls, and not the empire itself, it would not be too great a risk to use them on the campaign.

Any chattering in the ranks died away the moment Rufus emerged from his quarters. Resplendent in silver armour, and with many medals dangling over his chest, he ascended the steps on to the platform and positioned himself for the speech.

Good generals tend to be good orators, as a lifetime in

the Senate is the ultimate arena for rhetoric. Aside from the law courts, that is. I did not know much of Rufus's military background; for years now, Nero had been appointing nonentities and incompetents to important positions, lest he should be outshone. Look what happened to Corbulo. But a man does not get to be consul by being a useless politician, normally, so I was eager to hear how the general would deal with the problem ahead, playing politics with his own soldiers.

Rufus stood stock still, milking the silent anticipation of tens of thousands of faithful soldiers, all waiting to hear what he had to say. Slowly, he raised his arms high and wide, as though he was trying to encompass each and every one of them in an embrace.

'Soldiers,' he cried, 'the gods smiled upon you this day. An insidious army of foolhardy Gauls dared to challenge the might of the empire, and you, the mightiest of that might, have conquered!'

There were frenzied cheers, and men punched the air in appreciation and agreement.

'Who will forget how the Fourth Legion led the charge into the woods at the first sign of the Gauls' flight? Or how the Twenty-Second stood firm against the enemy's entire cavalry force, and put them to flight? I certainly won't, and I suspect the Gauls won't either!'

The men guffawed at that. It was sycophantic stuff really, but it takes a good leader to judge his troops' mood and speak accordingly, and Rufus was playing them like a harp. Or at least the men directly under his command, for he had failed to mention Valens's legion from the next-door province, or the auxiliaries.

'Once again you have proved that a Roman army with its discipline, courage and skill can triumph over anything that stands in its way. I cannot begin to describe how proud I am to lead you into battle, knowing full well that you will never let me down. Sometimes I think that Rome does not deserve men like you, and those who live safe because of your commitment and duty, far away from our wild borders, will never appreciate you as I do.'

Then he let out a deep, deep sigh, as though deflated by the thought.

'There is a sickness in Rome, my friends, a sickness at its very core. You are in some ways privileged to be here, on this barbarian frontier, because you are spared the knowledge of what Rome has become. Rome is far more than just a city, it is an ideal, something to yearn for and aspire to. Our German friends here, in the auxiliaries, you joined the legions in the hope that one day you might be rewarded with the ultimate prize, that of Roman citizenship, a prize that will be handed down to your descendants until the end of time.

'But now Rome is in grave peril, not from some external threat, for we all know that you would triumph over such an enemy. But this enemy is within Rome. I do not speak of this matter lightly, nor should I, for this sickness has corrupted something that we hold very dear in our hearts. My friends, our emperor, Nero, is destroying Rome.'

There, it had been said. It was plain that most were aghast to hear such things from their general, and muttered furiously to one another, but they were not so aghast that they ignored Rufus as he explained himself. They drank in his every word.

'We have all sworn an oath of loyalty to the emperor; indeed, he personally appointed me to this command after my consulship. But under his guidance, Rome has become a cesspit of moral decay. He flaunts his body in public declamations, chariot races in the Circus, and has even taken part in the Olympic Games, where the proud Greeks are forced to award him first prize in every event in which he competes.'

This was not particularly strong ground. What do the legions care if the emperor has some strange habits, so long as they are paid well and on time?

'And when did he last see you, the most resolute of his armies? Has he ever stirred beyond Rome except for his own amusement? He kills the generals that lead you to victory and to glory, and ignores the troops who keep him safe in his luxurious lifestyle. Meanwhile the Praetorian Guard grow fat, lazy, debauched and rich in Rome, while you endure harsh winters and ferocious enemies, and for what?

'I suggest that it is time for a new emperor, one who respects and values the army. He must have held the highest offices of state, for it would be folly to replace Nero with a man who could not ably serve the empire. The man I have in mind has even held command in this very province, if I remember rightly; a man of dignity, prudence and competence, all the virtues that Nero lacks.'

It was at this point that a voice from the Twenty-Second shouted out: 'We will follow you, General! Rufus for Caesar!' The cry of 'Caesar!' was taken up by those around him, and the refrain spread throughout the whole legion, and into the Fourth, and soon the other units were joining in, even the Germans, who probably did not understand what was going on. I was appalled; this was not meant to be happening! Whether intentionally or not, the requirements that the general had stated applied to both Galba and himself. Both men were ex-consuls, both had held command on the Rhine, though admittedly it had been perhaps twenty years since Galba had served here under Caligula. I looked up to see how Rufus was reacting to this turn of events. Thankfully, he looked just as shocked as I did. He opened and closed his mouth, like a dim-witted fish coming up for crumbs, but then he came to his senses and tried to silence the men.

Shaking his head slowly, he took his time, spelling out his point. 'Men, you honour me, but it is an honour I could never accept. I am a simple soldier, nothing more. Indeed, I am the first of my family to have reached the heights of the Senate; I do not have the gravitas or authority to even contemplate taking the imperial throne. It is not for any of us here to decide, but for the Senate and People of Rome. If a worthy man does step forward we can lend him our support, but we cannot and must not take it upon ourselves to impose the first man we think of on the rest of the empire. However, if you do want a man to follow, I can make a suggestion.'

'Who?' a handful here and there among the army asked.

'A man who has devoted his whole life to public service, a man of noble bearing whose family can trace its roots back to the very beginnings of the Republic: Servius Sulpicius Galba.'

Their reaction, when compared with previous ones, was underwhelming. Yes, some nodded in appreciation, but for the most part the men looked bemused. Why would their general refuse their offer of imperial power and instead praise a man who in comparison meant nothing to them? Yes, Galba was one of the grand old men of the Senate, but had it not been for his convincing discussion in that modest house in Tarraco I'm not sure I wouldn't have agreed with them. But then again, other than their general, who was Rufus? A new man, of ordinary equestrian rank, notable only because he had been elevated to the Senate, and chosen for the command because of this very anonymity.

Rufus was unsure how best to proceed. I think he had been counting on a more tangible reaction. 'But as I say,' he continued, 'such a decision has to be made by the Senate and ratified by the people. We must put aside our own interests, and ably serve whoever sits on the imperial throne. Once again, you have fought like lions, as befits the legions of Rome, and reaped your rewards from the enemy, whom you have littered upon the hillside. Rome is fortunate to have men like you to call upon, so enjoy yourselves tonight; I shall have an extra ration of wine given to every man. You have earned it.'

This brought the loudest cheer of the lot. After all the praise he had given them already, and an acclamation to stand for emperor, the promise of an extra ration of booze is enough to cheer the most sullen soldier. I sometimes wonder if Rome would have the same reputation that she does today without a judicious portion of alcohol.

As the men were dismissed, and wandered off to find the legion quartermasters for their liquid reward, I made to collar the general as he descended from the podium. Halfway down the steps he spotted me, and visibly reddened. He gave a nervous laugh, and commented, 'Not the sort of speech you give every day, is it?'

'I agree. You don't often hear a general denouncing his emperor, in fine Ciceronian style, only to come to a shuddering halt.'

'Well, what else was I to do? How could I know that they would call on me to be emperor?'

I must have looked incredulous. 'You mean it didn't occur to you that the legions would want their own general on the throne, a man who would reward their loyalty generously?'

'Me? Gods, no. As I said, I'm only a new man, I couldn't possibly be emperor. You heard me recommend Galba.' He looked flustered, flapping his hands about in his anxiety to defend himself.

In truth, Rufus did seem the honourable type, and his line of defence was credible. After all, he had turned down his own troops' offer of the throne, I thought, firmly ruling himself out of the running.

'Very well. I shall have to write to Galba and let him know the latest. Might I borrow one of your tribunes to deliver the message?'

'Hmm? Oh yes, by all means. I'll send Saturninus.'

'And might I use your seal on the letter, so that he can use the post-horses to get to Hispania?'

'Certainly. I suppose you'll be needing a tent then, if you're staying with us. I'll have someone sort it all out. Now if you don't mind, I need to get some sleep.' With that, the general wandered off towards his quarters, leaving me alone with my thoughts.

XV

To S. Sulpicius Galba, Legate of the Senate and People of Rome, greetings.

I am sorry to have to inform you of a double loss, both of the army of Gaul and its leader, Julius Vindex. After I had contacted Verginius Rufus and negotiated successfully the Rhine legions' outward neutrality and tacit support, Vindex took it upon himself to engage the legions in battle. I was not in a position to stop him, having been drugged the previous night, but upon my arrival I relieved him of command and led the army into battle. Unfortunately the Romans' superior discipline carried the day, putting our army to flight. Vindex committed suicide shortly afterwards. His son Quintus has returned to the province in order to continue the administration from Vienne for the time being.

I have attached myself to General Rufus, who assures me that he continues to support you. In an address to the troops this evening, he called for a new emperor, only to have his legions declare their support for him. Professing inexperience and his humble background, he refused, and next proposed your name. This did not gain favour with the men, who seemed bemused that he had turned them down.

It would seem then that the loyalty of the Rhine legions to Nero is not strong, but neither could they be said to be greatly enamoured of you. On the face of it, I would judge Rufus's actions as naive but honest, but I cannot be certain. Fabius Valens, the senior officer of the detachments from Lower Germania, suggests that those legions could be swayed, if he and his fellow officers were suitably encouraged and rewarded. I would recommend that you begin your march on Rome as soon as possible, so that these legions and indeed the world are made aware that you are a serious and credible replacement for Nero, forcing all the legions to make their choice. Nero may be popular with the plebs, but the army has been neglected. I believe that this action will push them to side with you.

At the moment my immediate plans are to stay near General Rufus and make sure that his professed loyalty to you is genuine, and await your instructions.

Au. Caecina Severus

Short, and to the point. No unnecessary flattery, just an appraisal of the events, some gentle advice and that was it. As I sat in the privacy and relative comfort of my own tent, I wondered about all the things that I had omitted. An insecure man would have spent valuable parchment detailing the difficulty of getting the Gauls fit for military service, the horrifying ordeal of torture, the stubbornness of Vindex. But the man was dead, and what was done was done. Besides, a gentleman like Galba was sure to write to Quintus on hearing of the death of his father, partly to offer his condolences and also to discuss the management of his province, and Quintus would be honest about my conduct over the past months.

As I had said in the letter, all I could do now was to wait for further instructions, and to keep an eye on General Rufus. I eased back in my chair and reflected on the situation. It was quiet now in the camp, but the atmosphere was volatile. It occurred to me that if Rufus had truly ruled himself out of the running for emperor, then the legions might turn to the other governor on the Rhine, Fonteius Capito. I had heard from Valens that he was drunken, sordid and petty, but that would not make him the worst emperor we'd ever had. Who could say whether or not he would refuse the offer, should the Army of the Rhine call upon him?

The only reason I could not foresee this happening quite yet was the fact that almost half his forces did not know about the situation. Only the troops here, under the command of Valens and others, were aware that there was in effect a potential imperial vacancy. But once those troops returned to their bases further down the Rhine, word would spread, and maybe Galba would have a rival. That was why I had urged Galba to come out of the shadows, march on Rome and ratchet up the pressure on Nero.

Rolling up the letter, I reached for the candle on the far side of the table, and held it at an angle over the dispatch. As the wax splashed on to the vellum, I gave a big yawn and managed to spill some on to my hand. It wasn't painfully hot, but the surprise was enough to make me swear. Young Saturninus, who had been standing silently to attention, let out a snigger. I looked darkly at the youth, and fumbled around for Rufus's seal. The large golden stamp had the imprint of a fox's mask, the Rufus family crest I presumed, and after a few seconds' pressure the waxen duplicate stared up at me. I handed the letter over to the tribune, who saluted and went to find his unlucky mount for the first leg of his journey.

In those next few days, waiting for Galba's reply, I was in an unpleasant state of limbo. Though kitted out as the senior tribune, with a broad purple sash running down from my shoulder to my waist and around it, I did not feel as though I belonged. There was little for the army to do. We had not yet heard whether

Quintus had succeeded in calling off the siege of Lugdunum, though the First Legion were on course to arrive there within the next fortnight, and so General Rufus had decided to stay at Vesontio rather than head northwards to the Rhine. I couldn't very well attend Rufus's meeting with his staff, partly because I was unknown to his officers and my presence would be questioned, and also because there were very few such meetings. The general largely kept to his tent, sending occasionally for individuals as and when he had an idea that merited discussion, while the men enjoyed the inactivity, whiling away their time with drink, gambling and tall tales of past battles.

So it was a welcome distraction when Fabius Valens poked his head round my tent flap on the third day after I had written to Galba.

'Would you care for a talk?'

I said that I would be glad of one, and followed him outside. It was a clear, warm evening in June. The men had finished messing, and in ones and twos were kicking out the camp fires and heading in to sleep. The chorus of crickets had already begun, a ceaseless chirping that bugged me, no pun intended, all through the night. One thing I'll say for Britannia, it's spared that racket.

I decided to forgo the pleasantries. 'Is this a social event, or is there something particular you want to talk about?'

'Politics.'

I said nothing more, wanting to hear what Valens had on his mind. My position was clear.

'What did you discover during the assembly the other day?' he asked.

I shrugged. 'That Rufus is well liked by his legions, that he is a middling orator, and either a brilliant politician or a terrible one.'

'What about the men?'

'Well, what about them?'

'Don't you think their reaction was telling?'

186

'What does that matter? The legions are led by the legates and generals, not by mob rule.'

'True, if the general in question has any backbone, but nowadays backbone is a bit of a rarity among senior officers. You'll see, the ordinary legionaries will be just as important as the generals in deciding who becomes emperor. If not more so.'

I scoffed at that. 'Rubbish! What self-respecting general would allow himself to be dictated to by his own men?'

'Oh, I think given the right circumstances people can do very surprising things. Humour me a while, and have a wander among the tents. I always do that when I want to know what the men are thinking.'

With that he gestured towards the area where the Twenty-Second Legion were billeted. Most of the men had gone to bed now, eight men to a tent, and as we picked a path through the guy ropes and general clutter, we overheard snatches of conversation.

'Why d'you reckon old Rufus backed out then?'

'Perhaps he honestly doesn't want the job.'

'Come off it, Titus, who wouldn't want to be emperor?'

'You heard what he said, he's barely been a senator. You can't get rid of the Caesars and just replace them with a new man.'

'How about Galba, then?

'Can't see how having him in Rome is going to make my life any better. Better to have someone who'll be good to us, even if he isn't as old and grand as Galba.'

As we went along the rows, the words were different but the sentiment was broadly the same.

'Convinced yet?' Valens asked me.

'They're not opposed to Galba outright, they're just thinking about themselves. Not that that is entirely unexpected.'

'It hasn't occurred to you that with a bit of encouragement, these men could be persuaded to support whoever we tell them to, so long as we look after their interests?'

Staring contemptuously at him, I replied with disdain. 'It has occurred to me, but I have not considered it. Understand?'

'So you'll cling to Galba, come what may?' he asked.

'Because he is the best man for the job, and that is the most important consideration of all. Don't you agree?'

Without waiting for his reply, I turned my back on the odious man and returned to my tent. I had now recognized Valens for what he was. I had suspected it, of course. Why else had he accompanied Rufus to those negotiations with Vindex and me that stormy night? Once he had uttered that word, 'circumstances', I marked him down as an opportunist, a man who will ditch his principles when they threaten to harm his career prospects. As I had said, I was Galba's man, through and through. I had pledged my allegiance in the belief that he would make a far better emperor than Nero, and everything I had done since that meeting in Tarraco had been to that end, and not for myself. And if Galba chose to reward me for services rendered, well, that was his affair.

After a week, Rufus decided that the threat of insurrection was over, so he could send his troops their separate ways. The German auxiliaries would march west to join with the First Italica at Lugdunum, to help control the region. The detachments from the lower Rhine legions, Valens included, would march due north, while Rufus himself would take the Fourth and the Twenty-Second north-east, by way of Argentorate, to his headquarters at Mogontiacum.

I would have liked to join the Germans and head back into the heart of Gaul, and to stay with Quintus while awaiting further developments. However, Galba's reply was sure to go directly to wherever Rufus was, so that meant another long march, but this time to the Rhine. It would take about a week for the two legions to reach Argentorate, and then another five days or so to Mogontiacum. I prayed that I would hear from Galba soon, so that I might be spared the boredom of almost a fortnight's march.

We broke camp at dawn the following day, and twenty thousand men spilled from the hilltop in different directions. The Germans retraced the steps Vindex's army had taken before the battle, through and beyond the valley that was now empty of corpses. A large and levelled mound of earth marked the mass grave dug for the remains of my erstwhile comrades.

Valens and the lower Rhine contingent marched through Vesontio and took the northward road, while Rufus's two legions turned eastwards. Our route was not particularly arduous, just long. It would be several days' march through fairly hilly country until we reached Argentorate, and then followed the river north to Mogontiacum. Every day was a torment, and it was all I could do to stop myself from turning in the saddle and scanning the horizon every ten minutes for signs of a messenger. Six interminable days passed, six days of plodding the miles that drew us nearer to the Rhine, hemmed in by the hills that dominated the skyline. At least I was spared having to walk the thirty or so miles every day, and was relatively comfortable on the nag that Rufus had lent me. She was an ageing beast, and nowhere near as splendid as Achilles, who was waiting for me in the stables back in Corduba. Nonetheless I was grateful for a horse at all; it would hardly have befitted my rank to trudge on foot like a common soldier.

It was as we approached Argentorate that the news finally came. Rufus and I were up with the van, and the young tribunes were scurrying around, preparing to oversee the construction of that night's camp. Then behind us came a chorus of whistles and murmurs of appreciation. Both of us turned to find out what was causing the commotion. At first all we could see was a man riding along the road towards us, and leading another horse by the reins. And what a horse. It was built like a proper warhorse: a long, dark mane, a head that was proud and high, and a frame so thick and powerful that, if there were a contest between the beast and a sturdy stable door, you'd have to consider the odds very carefully before placing your bet. It was only when the horseman had cleared the column that I saw the white sock on one of the rear legs. It was Achilles, or else a twin that the messenger had found on his travels!

The young tribune Saturninus, whom I had dispatched to Galba all those days ago, looked a shambles. His once fiery-red cloak was hidden beneath a cake of mud, he was unshaven, and, judging from the way he walked after dismounting, had spent many hard hours in the saddle. Considering the distance he had covered, he could have looked a damned sight worse.

The young man gave a smart salute nevertheless, and with the formalities over he recounted his news. 'General Rufus, sir, have you heard? Nero has been overthrown! I heard it down in Massilia, from another courier,' he gabbled. 'Everyone's talking about it. The Senate . . .'

'Whoah! Slow down, Tribune. What do you mean, the emperor's been overthrown?'

'The Senate declared him a public enemy, sir, they want him gone.'

'Is Nero still alive, then?' the general asked.

'Yes, sir, at least that's what I heard. There are some wild rumours around. Some say that the emperor marched to Ostia with the Praetorian Guard, and was going to sail to his loyal troops in the East. Others say that he disguised himself as a slave and escaped from Rome. I heard a fantastic one in Lugdunum, that he—'

Rufus waved his hand impatiently. 'Spare me the gossip, please.'

'Is there any word from Galba?' I asked.

Saturninus nodded. 'Yes, sir, I have a letter for each of you. Senator Galba was explicit, sir. He said that General Rufus's was to be read immediately, and the message for you could be read at your leisure. But I don't know how useful these will be – word from Rome about Nero had not reached Tarraco when I left.' He dug into the folds of his cloak, where the precious vellum had been stashed away to protect it from the elements, and proffered a letter to Rufus.

The general snatched it up, and broke the seal with his manicured fingernails. I watched his face closely as his eyes devoured the missive. He paused for a moment and stole a glance at me. What had he done that for? I was aching to see my letter from Galba, but the old fox must have had a good reason for making me rein in my curiosity. My imagination was wild with theories. Why was Nero still alive if Nymphidius Sabinus was near at hand? Galba had all but said that the praetorian prefect would kill Nero when the time came. Had the plan gone awry?

'It seems that your lord and master's ears are everywhere. He commiserates with me for the loss of one of my legates during the "unfortunate incident at Vesontio".' He stressed those words. Galba's words, not his. 'Yes, Cotta was one of those poor bastards who died in that cavalry charge on the flank. As the Legate of the Senate and People of Rome, Galba . . .' He paused here, searching for the right word. '. . . *recommends* that I appoint you in his stead, Severus.'

I was taken aback, I can tell you. Me? Command a Roman legion? I was far too young for such a rank. Even the best connected men barely ever became legate before they were approaching forty, and I was still some months away from my thirtieth birthday.

Rufus continued, 'I am happy to recognize Galba's authority in this matter. It would be different if you were incompetent, but you are clearly not. In the circumstances, I would suggest that you make your own way ahead of the column to Mogontiacum, and then you can have a proper introduction to your command, not here on the roadway. You can return that horse to me once the army has caught up.'

'No need, sir,' I grinned. I slung myself out of the saddle, and took both my letter and Achilles' reins from Saturninus's hands.

'You mean to say that this is your horse?'

'Oh, just a little something I picked up in Corduba,' I said. 'Thank you for sparing the horse, Tribune. I'll forgive you for keeping us in suspense for the last few days.'

Rufus looked affronted, and no wonder: his own warhorse was no match for Achilles. He composed himself.

'Severus, you'd better take this.' He rootled around in one of his saddlebags, and handed over what looked like a small wooden cylinder. 'It is my seal, so that you can prove who you are when you arrive at the barracks in Mogontiacum.'

'Thank you, sir, but won't you need it?'

He raised his left hand with the back of it facing me. A large golden ring enclosed his little finger. 'Not when I have this too.'

In the excitement I'd forgotten that no self-respecting Roman would be seen dead without his family ring. I raised my right hand and flashed my own signet ring (normally the ring is worn on the smallest finger of the left hand, but after my encounter with Albanos in Vienne, practicality demanded I break with convention). I smiled meekly, acknowledging my stupid mistake.

'Permission to leave the army, sir?' I asked cheekily.

'Get on with you.'

I mounted my horse, dug my heels in and Achilles sped off down the road. A thought struck me, and I gave a sharp tug on the reins. Achilles reared up at the sudden command to halt, his front legs beating the air. I called back to the general, my new commander: 'I forgot to ask which legion, sir!'

'The Fourth,' came the reply. 'The Macedonica.'

It was only as I rode through the streets of Argentorate that it even occurred to me that I should read Galba's letter; I was that overwhelmed by my sudden promotion. Of course it was a massive step up – I must have been the youngest legate for decades – but the joy had for the moment clouded my judgement. Hadn't Galba promised that I should accompany him to Rome, as client and patron? Command of a legion normally lasted around four years, effectively tying me to my post, which meant that I was to be tethered to the Rhine until I reached the next rung on the political ladder. This was why I had come to Argentorate itself, instead of hurrying northwards to settle in before Rufus and the army arrived. I had to write to my wife.

My beautiful Salonina. I am somewhat ashamed to write that I had not thought of her over the last few months as much as I should have. I had left Rome in the winter of the year before to take up my position in Corduba, only to find myself caught up in a whirlwind. Assuming that I would be returning to Rome soon, I had expected to be reunited with her in a couple of months at the most. Now that my fate for the next few years appeared to be settled, I decided to summon her to my side.

I sleep alone nowadays. Well, practically most days. But still, hardly a night goes by when I do not think about her. My memory brings back images of a waif-like thing, standing with her proud father on the day of our wedding. We were both very young. It is twenty years ago now, that late summer's day in Pompeii. I was nineteen, and she was only a few months past her sixteenth birthday. But my family was in desperate need of ready money, and as the only son it was my duty to add to the coffers with a rich bride's dowry. Our home in Vicetia, lovely as it was, did not have the grandeur or the atmosphere that Salonina's villa did, standing near the golden shores of the bay. The double peaks of Capri could be made out on the horizon, while the lush slopes of Vesuvius were only a few miles away. The place was perfect, the dowry very reasonable, and I was about to be shackled to a slip of a girl whom I had never laid eyes on.

I was prepared for the worst. The rule of thumb is that the larger the dowry, the uglier and older the bride. I was steeling myself for some porcine creature with a limp and a stammer to shuffle into sight, and then I saw her. Sleek tresses of chestnut-brown hair were arranged fashionably around a headdress, discarding the loose style of an unmarried woman. But it was the eyes that caught me. Deep blue eyes that fair sparkled with life. A slight, willowy figure betrayed the fact that she was only on the cusp of womanhood, but she was beautiful nonetheless.

Two years later she bore me a son, just a month or so after I had been posted to Britannia, so I missed many of those precious moments that a father cherishes as long as his memory permits. I left at home a pregnant wife and returned when little Aulus was nearly three years old. Three years in which the boy had never known his father, and had walked and talked while I rode and fought for the empire. I no longer cared what my pompous ancestor said about family in the provinces. It was time to see them again. Maybe if I had followed his advice things would have been different . . .

But before I wrote home, I needed to see what Galba had to say. Still in the saddle, I eagerly tore open the wax seal, stamped with Galba's crest of a wild boar, and pored over the contents.

To Au. Caecina Severus

Let me first congratulate and thank you for all the work that you have carried out in Gaul; considering the circumstances, I could not have wished for a better man to act on my behalf, nor for a better outcome. I hear that you suffered a wound to your hand during the campaign. Such loyalty and dedication is to be highly commended.

I know that you had entertained hopes to ride with me all the way to Rome, but circumstances dictate otherwise. Do not think that I have not valued your service; indeed it is because of your success that I have decided that it would be better for you to remain in Gaul.

As you mentioned in your report, the Rufus situation is a

thorny one. This is why I have ordered him to appoint you legate for the Fourth Legion. If I am to be emperor, I will need trustworthy men in key positions, and I can think of no better candidate to serve as my eyes and ears on the Rhine. Therefore I have arranged for your splendid horse to accompany this letter north, so that you may have him with you in Mogontiacum.

I am sure you are aware that the command of a legion is a lengthy one, so the likelihood of my being alive on your return is not great. You may be sure I shall commend you to my successor, whoever he may be. Furthermore I will try to make sure that Rufus's successor as governor of the province will be sufficiently weak-willed to give you more of a free rein. I am afraid this is all that I shall be able to give you, but I am sure you will agree that your hard-earned reward is more than fair.

Please keep me informed of any major developments, and my thanks once again.

S. Sulpicius Galba

I won't pretend that I wasn't disappointed. After that little chat I'd had with Otho in the baths at Tarraco, I had honestly thought I was in with a decent chance of Galba choosing me as his successor one day. I was even prepared to bet a large sum that Otho himself had convinced the old man to leave me to rot on the Rhine, while he remained close at hand. But I wasn't bitter. Yes, I'd been through some difficult times and deserved my reward, but my ambition was sated. Galba had given me command of my very own legion before I was thirty, a high honour indeed. No man in my position would complain.

Perhaps I had been over-excited during those days in Tarraco. After all, Galba had watched my career with interest over the years, and my mother and I owed everything to him. But it was when Vindex had told me of Galba's promise to make him High King of Gaul that I realized Galba trusted me only up to a point.

In his eyes, I had served my purpose, and now that everything was in place for him to become emperor, he would expect me to dutifully obey his commands. So it was with a fairly contented heart that I continued my search for the way station, to send a letter to my beautiful wife.

XVI

Mogontiacum is a dismal place. It seemed dreary enough on first inspection, but in my merry mood I had decided to reserve judgement until I was properly acquainted with my new posting. But there was no avoiding the fact: the town reeked of tedium. Drusus, the Emperor Tiberius's brother, had chosen this place to construct a large fortress that would guard this stretch of the Rhine.

But that had been decades ago. The small town that had been founded to provide for the legions had grown since then, sprawling along the river bank year after year, until someone decided it was big enough to become the provincial capital. You wouldn't know it was the administrative centre of the province if you happened to be strolling along its gloomy streets. Yes, they were paved, and the city was laid out in a regular fashion, but these facts revealed nothing but the city's youth. Although Mogontiacum was young, it was lacking in vigour.

As I rode through the city, I was met by a sea of miserable faces – a crowd of hairy, smelly plebs were going about their business. Perhaps I am being too harsh; the city was not completely without individuality or culture. They were in the throes of building a brand new theatre. Carts came and went, carrying great loads of stone to the building site. Teams of slaves fetched and carried, while the more skilled hewed at the vast lumps, fashioning them into seats. The cleanest, best-quality stone was reserved for the front rows, where the local nobility would sit. I sat in the saddle and watched for a time as a mason set about one of these blocks with a chisel, cutting an elaborate border around one of its faces.

When asked about the building, the obsequious craftsmen bobbed their heads comically, like apples in a water barrel, and boasted that it would be the largest theatre north of the Alps.

'It should be able to hold twelve thousand men,' I was assured.

'But this place can't have anywhere near twelve thousand citizens, and I don't expect the soldiers will want to spend their wages here!'

'Ah, but you're just thinking about today, sir. This city is only ever going to get bigger. Look over there.' One of them pointed to the northern horizon, where the murky shadows of stone and bricks had begun to eat up the skyline.

'The city keeps growing and growing,' said another. 'Ever since this was made the capital, the Gauls have flocked into the slum quarter. Even a few barbarians have crossed the Rhine to settle here peacefully. All these people need food, clothes, jobs and all the rest of it; the city's flourishing.'

Wanting to be on my way, I asked for directions to the barracks and left them to bask in each other's civic pride. Cantering through the western quarter of the city, I could not fail to notice the influence that the legions had while the place was taking shape. While you would think that all the market stalls, taverns and the like would be close to the harbour, near all the traffic that sailed from the Alps to the sea, the merchants had established themselves much closer to the barracks. Any off-duty legionary could tumble out of the barracks and find himself spoilt for choice in ways to spend his wages. Whorehouses, normally confined to seedy back alleys in the older cities of the empire, stood tall and proud on the streets that led into the heart of Mogontiacum. I even saw patches where rival taverns stood on adjoining plots, so desperate were the proprietors to set up shop close to their main source of trade.

The only respectable building I came across in these shady suburbs of the city was a large shrine. Not to Jupiter, Mars or even a local Gallic god, mark you, but to General Drusus himself. Of course it is right and proper that our past emperors are worshipped as gods, worthy of a seat in the heavens. But Drusus was no emperor. He could have been one, being the brother of Tiberius and, through his mother, Livia, Augustus's stepson. However, he had retained his father's love of the Republic, and I gather that the imperial family were somewhat relieved, privately of course, when he died of wounds when on campaign against the barbarians beyond the river.

But he was not only a Claudian but also the city's founder, and citizens and soldiers alike came to the shrine, praying and sacrificing so that the noble Drusus's spirit might watch over them. I made a mental note to pay a visit once I'd settled in properly. It was only after I had ridden past the shrine that I caught my first glimpse of the fort. So far the trees and build-ings had blocked the view, but now the road sloped up a slight rise that led to a flat-topped hill. The huge stone fortress loomed over the city like an assassin, dagger in hand, standing over his sleeping victim. Looking up at that mighty gatehouse, with its sturdy towers and high battlements, I couldn't help but shudder at the thought of trying to assault it. This, I might add, from a man who has served against some of the most savage tribes known to the empire.

Touching my heels to Achilles' flanks, I hastened on for that last half-mile of my journey, a journey that had in truth begun all those weeks ago when Tacitus had arrived at my quarters back in Corduba. As I came closer and closer to that indomitable wall, I remember thinking that this was my new home.

'Halt! Who goes there?' was the predictable shout from the battlements.

'Senator Severus. I come from Governor Rufus's column,' I shouted back.

For a moment I was worried that he didn't believe me, but then an almighty groaning and creaking announced my right to enter as the solid wooden doors were prised open.

Castrum Mogontiacum, as it ought to be called, is not your typical legionary fort, for the simple reason that it has to accommodate not one legion but two, and some auxiliary units as well. Whereas in some parts of the empire two separate camps would have been built to guard a strategic place, here it made more sense to have a single impregnable stronghold to safeguard one of the province's few bridges over the Rhine. Everything that you would expect to find inside a normal legionary camp was there, but its mirror image lay on the other side of the east–west street that cut the camp in half. The camp was very quiet, but that was only natural as Rufus had nearly emptied the place to put down the Gauls' rebellion. The barracks on my left, with their long rows of whitewashed walls, stood empty, waiting for their occupants to return. The granary on the north side of the street would have been similarly depleted. Grain was hoarded to provide food for the legions while on the march. You see, we had discovered long ago that confiscating it from the locals was rather unpopular, and instead the empire paid vast sums to fill the military granaries and the bellies of her soldiers, which kept the big grain merchants happy.

The few men who were about eyed me interestedly. I surmised that newcomers riding a horse that was worth several years of a legionary's salary were not a regular occurrence. I kept my chin high and trotted on by, pretending not to be affected by their persistent stares. My eyes were fixed on the principia, the central hub of the entire camp. Two impeccably turned out guards stood on either side of a rather shabby wooden door.

Swinging out of the saddle, I made sure that the horse would be attended to before going in.

Unlike outside, the principia was full of activity. It always was, and always will be, even if there are no soldiers. Clerks scuttled busily about clutching armfuls of scrolls, little wax tablets dangling from a leather thong round their wrists, far too busy to notice the stranger who had entered their administrative sanctum, and who can blame them? Rosters need arranging, applications for everything from compassionate leave to permits to trade in camp need approval, grain prices must be tallied, armourers' requisitions need examining, dicta from on high must be relayed. Eventually I managed to stop a clerk by standing in his path, and when he tried to dodge round me I sidestepped and blocked him again.

'Where can I find the camp prefect?' I asked.

The clerk, his head just peeking out over a pile of paperwork which he clasped to his bosom, gave a muffled answer: 'Through the door behind you, but he gave orders not to be disturbed.'

'He will want to see me.'

'In that case,' the clerk said, 'would you mind taking these?'

Without waiting for a reply he heaved his burden into my arms, smiled his thanks and left me to it. I didn't want to kick up a fuss; how was he to know I was the new commander? Instead I turned and gingerly felt for the door with my foot, my sight almost totally blocked by the load of documents. Finding it, I gave the door a prod with my toe, the door screeched open, and I manoeuvred my way into the office.

A sidelong glance revealed that the room was deserted. Unkempt and deserted. Tablets were scattered about the place, over the floor, on the desk – but what caught my eye was a tablet that seemed to be levitating just behind the desk. Even stranger was the fact that it was bobbing up and down rhythmically. I shuffled quietly and crab-like towards it, so as to see where I was going, and dropped the papers on to the desk with a heavy thud.

The tablets went flying as the prefect tumbled from his makeshift bed, the tablet falling off his stomach. Cursing, he got to his feet in an ungainly fashion, bleary-eyed and foul-mouthed.

'What the fuck do you think you're playing at, son? I'll have you broken to the ranks! I'll—'

I raised my hand to silence him. 'Another word, Prefect, and I'll have you on a charge of insubordination, and sleeping on duty.'

'What do you mean? I only take orders from the Legate Cotta and his senatorial tribune.'

'Well, now you only take orders from the Legate Severus and the senatorial tribune. The legate fell in battle.'

'Cotta dead? I don't believe it.'

'Afraid so. I can't say I knew the man, I'm just the messenger. But I'm also his replacement.'

He looked puzzled at that. 'His replacement? But surely those decisions are taken in Rome?'

'By the emperor, yes, I know. However, the Senate has declared Nero a public enemy, and I don't see anyone challenging Galba's authority.'

'You mean Galba appointed you to this command? But why?' The prefect blushed. 'Sorry, sir, it's not like me to question my superiors.'

'That's quite all right . . .'

The man understood why I had paused: 'Tuscus, sir.'

'. . . Tuscus. These are special circumstances. I was serving as a quaestor in Corduba, and Galba sent a letter of recommendation to Rufus once he heard of the vacancy. If you don't believe me, here's the general's seal.'

I reached into the folds of my cloak, took the seal and set it on the desk. I could have told him why Galba had entrusted me with command on the Rhine but I had no desire to publicize my involvement with Vindex, so it was easy to tell from the look on

Tuscus's face that he thought I was just some puppy of Galba's, eager and obedient.

'I realize I'm a little younger than most legates, but I served with some distinction as a tribune under General Paulinus in Britannia.'

'Not *that* Severus? The man who charged Boudicca's army when the legions began to break?'

I smiled modestly. Any doubts that Tuscus had were instantly dismissed, and he threw me as smart a salute as you'll see outside Rome. Prefects are a surly lot, being the bravest and best of centurions and having survived long years of service, and despite their age they are the most dedicated soldiers in the army. Tuscus's salute was high praise indeed.

'Well, sir, what can I do you for?' he asked. His whole demeanour was warm and friendly, almost unrecognizable from that of the grouchy old man whom I'd woken just five minutes ago.

'I'd like to get settled in before the column arrives, quarters sorted, that sort of thing. It's a long time since I've been stationed in a fort; I've rather forgotten what camp life is like.'

Tuscus scratched his head thoughtfully. 'I can get you kit and the like, sir, but quarters will be a bit difficult.'

'Why?'

'We haven't any rooms to spare, and General Cotta's wife, or widow I suppose, uses the same rooms as he did.'

'Ah, that's a bit delicate. Could you put me in one of the junior officers' quarters for the time being? I can move in once Cotta's wife is ready to return to Rome.'

'Thank you, sir, that would make my life a lot easier.'

'I'm not here to make your life easier, Prefect, but these are rather awkward circumstances. Now, I wouldn't want to keep you from your strenuous duties, but perhaps you could show me to the lady's quarters?'

'Of course, sir. You will forgive me about earlier, sir? Just resting my old eyes, you see, sir.'

'Don't worry, man, as it's my first day I'll forgive and forget. So long as you serve me well, of course.'

Tuscus led the way through the camp to the officers' quarters. Despite the mass of troops who were away, there were still enough soldiers about the place to keep the camp functioning. We passed stables, smithies and foul-smelling kitchens until we came to a halt by a hefty-looking door, and the prefect took his leave, no doubt to embark upon the backlog of neglected paperwork. My arrival had really stirred him into action.

I was just gazing up at my future home and noting the second storey, a rarity in any Roman camp, when the door opened, and a wiry figure jumped in surprise.

'I'm sorry, sir, but you frightened me out of my skin.'

There was something I couldn't place about his accent. It was so fast and lilting, and he kept chatting on, sorry for getting in my way, wouldn't I like to come in and so on. What confused me more was that he was very much at ease in Latin, but was clearly no Roman. His pale skin and wiry tangle of black hair was one giveaway, and the other was the tablet that hung around his neck, marking him out as a slave. But this man was not the submissive creature that most slaves are. His demeanour was upright and supremely self-confident. I told him brusquely that I had come to see his mistress; the word Cotta was clearly stamped on his tablet.

That shut him up for a moment. He led me into a small anteroom before knocking gently on the next door.

'Who is it?' a voice called from the room beyond.

'An officer to see you, mistress.'

'Very well, send him in.'

I was shown through into a modest-looking triclinium. The simple whitewashed walls lent a cold and unwelcoming feel to the room, and there was little in the way of furniture. But I was forgetting that this wasn't some fine villa in Rome, but a military base on the banks of the Rhine. A lady reclined on one of the three couches, idly plucking at a bunch of grapes, a look of intense boredom etched on to her face. A few wrinkles betrayed her age, contrasting with the lustrous sheen to her chestnut hair and artful make-up. This was a proud Roman matron and no mistake.

'You can tell that fool Tuscus that I won't take no for an answer.'

'My lady?'

'I mean, is it too much to ask that the army should pay to keep a legate and his wife in the manner to which they are accustomed? It's not as though I'm after a house of our own. Just a few silks and cushions to make this place habitable.'

This was a woman used to giving commands and having them obeyed instantly, and looking into those imperious eyes, I didn't have the courage to break the news right away. I decided to change the subject.

'Surely having your own slaves here makes life tolerable for you, my lady? What about the one outside?'

'Him? He's not for me but for my husband. Ever since Castor died last winter my husband hasn't had a body slave. I decided to buy him a novelty for his birthday.'

'How is he a novelty?'

She looked bemused. 'Why, an educated barbarian of course! Apparently he's from some island beyond Britannia, but he can read and write! Publius will be delighted, he loves surprises . . .'

All this time I had stood still, hands respectfully behind my back. Steeling myself, I decided now was the moment to break the news.

'I should tell you, my lady, that strictly speaking I'm not an officer from this camp.'

'Strictly speaking? You either are or you aren't. Which are you?'

'I've been sent as a replacement, my lady. I come with news from Verginius Rufus's column.'

At once she sat bolt upright, eyes widening. 'From Verginius Rufus?' she echoed.

'Yes. I'm sorry to have to tell you this, but your husband fell in battle against the Gauls.'

'Publius is dead?'

I nodded. She sat there dumbly, staring into the distance. I didn't want to break the silence. At last she looked at me, sniffing heavily, and asked, 'How did he die?'

'I'm sorry, all I know is that he is dead. I am sure that the governor will explain everything as soon as he arrives.'

This was not exactly the time to tell her that I would be obliged if she could move out. The most tactful thing to do would be to leave quietly. I took a few backward steps, and let myself out.

The next few days were filled with tedious bits of bureaucracy. Signing receipts for parade armour, battle dress, quarters, sorting out the details of pay and rations, familiarizing myself with my new office and its clerks, it was a nightmare. Things were made even more complicated by the death of Cotta. Normally there is a simple handover. The contracts, leases and so forth are brought to the chief clerk, who wipes the incumbent's name from them and writes the new man's name on top. Cutting corners if you like, but we didn't conquer the empire by red tape alone. Taking up my new command in the middle of Cotta's regime threw the clerks into turmoil. New forms had to be drawn up for everything, and I tried to be out of the office as much as possible to spare myself the anxieties of my overburdened staff. If ever you think of commanding a legion, hope to the gods that your predecessor is alive and well for the handover.

It had occurred to me that I would be in need of a body slave, and after a respectful period I offered the remainder of Galba's gold in exchange for the dark-haired fellow I had met on my first day in Mogontiacum. After all, he would be of more use to me than to Cotta's wife. He arrived for my inspection one evening, after I had spent the day giving Achilles some exercise and learning a bit more about the surrounding country. I was just easing myself into a chair in my temporary quarters, aching after a long ride, when there was a knock at the door.

'Master?' a voice called.

'Come in.'

The slave entered, leaving the door open.

'Close the door, man,' I told him. 'You're letting in a draught.'

Apologizing, he did as he was told. Then he turned back to me, clasped his hands behind his back and stared fixedly ahead, as though there was something interesting on the wall behind me. I was used to this behaviour, having seen it on parade a thousand times or more. This was the posture of a confident man in the presence of his superior, and it puzzled me that this slave should ooze authority from every pore.

'The lady Cotta tells me that you are a novelty.'

The slave chuckled. 'Depends how you define a novelty, master.'

The cheek of the man startled me. No slave had ever answered back to me before. He must have seen my reaction, as he hastily explained.

'I'm sorry, master, it's just my manner. It is true, I can read and write, but only in Latin. My first master thought that I would fetch a higher price if I was educated. You know, an educated barbarian.'

'Who was your owner?' I asked.

'The legate of the Ninth Legion, master, Petillius Cerialis.'

'That's a coincidence,' I remarked. Cerialis had commanded the Ninth while I was in Britannia with the Twentieth.

'I take it you weren't born a slave, then?'

'No, master, the legate took my mother and me captive when the Ninth defeated the Britons on Mona.'

So that's what Cotta's wife had meant by an island off Britannia. Mona is a savage place, lying off the western coast. As Roman power expanded on the mainland, the legendary Celtic druids had retreated with some of Britannia's finest warriors to Mona. Suetonius Paulinus had sent the Ninth to take the island, partly because the druids were the chief priests of a foul, barbaric religion, but also to break the spirit of the Britons by destroying their last stronghold.

'You can't have been more than a child at the time. So he just picked you at random and had you taught to read and write?'

'No, master, I already knew my letters. Just not in Latin.'

'I thought you said Latin was the only language you'd learned?'

'Since becoming a slave, sir, yes. My native language was the one I'd learned first.'

'The Celtic of the Britons then?'

He shook his head. 'No, sir, my mother and I were exiles from Hibernia.'

The slave's history was getting stranger and stranger. It probably didn't help that he was telling his story back to front. Every time I thought I knew who he was, he revealed another layer. If my new slave really was from Hibernia, that would explain why I hadn't recognized his accent. After my service in Britannia, I had met men from tribes all over the land, but none quite like this one. I doubt that you, reader, will have even heard of Hibernia. I have been further north than most, and still I have only heard tales of that land. It is an island, beyond even Britannia, and its people are even wilder than those who fought with Boudicca. No Roman has ever been there, that's for sure. There are no myths of legendary wealth to draw him there, only a fearsome reputation, befitting a land at the very edge of the world. Even the British druids fear their savage brethren across the sea.

I was sore, and ready for supper in the mess, so I did not

question the slave further. I quickly listed his duties, and pointed to the corner that would be his sleeping place until I moved into my new quarters. Before going off for my meal, I realized that I had forgotten to ask my new slave's name. He replied to my question with something guttural and unpronounceable.

'You must have a slave name that I can pronounce. What does it say here?' I grabbed the tablet from around his neck and brought it close enough to read out the name: Totavalas.

'Not much better, but it'll have to do.'

'Yes, master. Is there anything you want before you go?' Totavalas asked.

'Bring a few pitchers of water here and fill a bath. Then you can get yourself some scraps from the kitchens, but be back in time to attend to me.'

'Of course, master.'

XVII

Rufus and his two legions arrived the next day. I say his legions; in theory, as an appointed proconsul he was more a lieutenant of Nero's, since we were one of the imperial provinces. But Nero never stirred himself beyond Italia except for a change of scene, wanting to try debauchery in foreign styles perhaps. The proconsul, as Galba had done in Tarraco, ran the province and generally left military matters to the normal chain of command. Except when there was a crisis. And a Gallic rebellion counts as a crisis.

Though he rode in at the head of the column, Rufus actually lived in Mogontiacum itself. I suppose it would have looked a bit odd if the triumphant general, in sight of the barracks, had reined in, said 'See you later', swung off the road and gone home. Instead he looked resplendent in his burnished armour, leading the column up the hill towards the fort. I was near the gates when the column was sighted. As the troops came nearer, I thought that it would be best to wait in the principia for Rufus. Better that than awkwardly hovering round the parade ground like a customer by a table where the occupant is deciding whether to call for the bill!

First, I went back to my temporary quarters, where Totavalas was busy polishing my new armour.

'Have you seen a large seal, with a fox's mask on the stamp?' I asked.

'Yes, master.' He put a pile of clothes down, and opened one of the drawers in the small writing table.

'Hold on, why have you been through my private papers?' Not that I had many private papers at that time, but a man's desk is still a man's desk.

'I haven't, master.'

'Then how else would you know where I put the seal?' I said, as though interrogating a small child.

'You asked me last night to remind you that you'd put it there for safe-keeping, master.'

Faintly embarrassed, I just smiled and said, 'You've got an answer for everything, haven't you?'

'Not quite everything . . .' There was that cheek again. I would have to be extra firm during this break-in period, I thought. But I wasn't in the mood to discipline him just then, so I told him to hold his tongue and get on with his work. He bowed his head dutifully and stepped outside.

I sat in the hallway of the principia, turning the seal over and over in my hands, fidgety at waiting for Rufus. Shortly the outside door creaked open, and the man himself came in. From the stiff way that he walked he clearly wasn't the most comfortable man in the saddle. He had only ridden at the pace of a marching army from Vesontio, while I had ridden full pelt the length of Hispania and hadn't suffered too badly. Come to think of it, Tacitus was about thirty years older than I, and he had coped just as well. But then in minor provinces like Baetica the Senate makes the appointment and has little to fear from picking men fit for the job. Rufus was Nero's choice, and in normal circumstances the general would never have been a threat. But these were far from normal circumstances: now Rufus held the fate of the empire in his hands.

'Ah, Severus! All settled in, are you?' Rufus gave a weary smile when he saw me.

'Temporary quarters, sir. The lady Cotta wished to speak with you before she returned to Rome,' I answered, rising to shake Rufus's hand.

'Good, good. Where shall we talk, you and I?'

'My office, sir?' I suggested.

'Yours? Oh I see, Cotta's old one, you mean?'

I nodded patiently.

'Well then, lead the way.'

'First of all, sir, I ought to return this.' I proffered Rufus's seal.

'Ah yes. Any trouble when you arrived?'

I smiled, thinking of Tuscus asleep in his chair. 'No trouble, sir. Shall we?'

As we came to the office, I went in first, then stepped aside to hold the door open for Rufus. He gave a polite nod of thanks, and promptly sat in the chair behind my desk. All right and proper, of course, with him being a proconsul, but it rankled slightly. I mean, strictly speaking it was my chair!

Rufus spoke first. 'I take it you've heard the news then?'

'More than Nero being deposed, you mean?'

The old man eyed me wearily. 'The emperor has committed suicide.'

Nero was dead. Everything had fallen into place, exactly as Galba had planned. But how, exactly? I had to enquire carefully, not wanting Rufus to know that when I had agreed to join Galba, we knew that Nymphidius Sabinus was not above murdering the emperor.

'Suicide? I didn't think Nero had the courage.'

'Nor did any of us. The rumour is he had a slave kill himself

212

first, to show how easy it was. Even then the emperor still needed one of his secretaries to do the deed. But he's gone, that's the main thing.'

'Surely the praetorian prefect would have convinced Nero to stay alive? I mean, he's going to be out of a job now Nero is dead.' I said, pretending innocence.

Rufus looked at me incredulously. 'You mean you don't know?'

'Know what?' I asked, as innocently as I could.

'Nymphidius Sabinus publicly denounced the emperor days ago. He has placed himself at the disposal of the Senate until a successor is appointed.'

Now we came to the crux.

'You mean Galba?' I asked.

'The Senate is considering whether to send a deputation to Hispania and ask Galba if he would succeed Nero, yes.'

'And are the Praetorians happy to serve Galba?'

'It seems so.'

Rufus shifted in his seat uncomfortably. The silence in the room was broken only by the sound of the men outside chatting as they were dismissed from parade.

'Governor, you're not having second thoughts, are you?'

His gaze flicked upwards. 'Wouldn't you?'

I was taken aback. This situation could go very wrong, very quickly.

'Consider the facts,' Rufus continued. 'My men have never served under Galba, he's old, and he's miles away in Hispania. Vesontio has whetted their appetites, and Galba is unlikely to sate them.'

'The legions will do as they are ordered. Don't tell me you are having second thoughts only because of what the common soldiers are thinking!'

'But what would I be without them?'

'I'll tell you what you'll be with them: a tyrant and a traitor. If you let these soldiers acclaim you as emperor, not only will you be defying the sanction of the Senate, but you will start a bloody civil war. Is that what you want?'

Slowly, Rufus rose from his seat. He looked down at me, that once genial face now matching the crimson of his cloak. He spoke very quietly: 'You forget yourself, Severus.'

He made to leave, but before he reached the door he evidently decided to carry on the argument.

'I know you're Galba's man, and you are being very loyal. But Galba does not yet have the full backing of the Senate, or the loyalty of my legions. Until he does, I will take whatever steps I feel are necessary for the good of the empire.'

'The good of the empire is not achieved by pitting legions against each other, Governor.'

All Rufus could say was 'We shall see!' Muttering darkly, he left my office.

It was a long time before I stirred from my seat. This changed things utterly. When I had first met Verginius Rufus all those weeks ago, he had been adamant that everything should be done by the book. He was not like Valens, who clearly revelled in all this subterfuge. The old Rufus was a kindly man with a strong sense of honour and decency, difficult to win over out of his loyalty to the Caesars. But now he was clearly feeling the pressure, and his high morals were beginning to buckle. I didn't believe for one minute that he seriously contemplated challenging Galba and marching south with his army. Instead I reasoned that he was a simple man with a degree of ambition, but hopefully he would have the sense to realize that the imperial purple was beyond his reach.

After all, who was Verginius Rufus? A nonentity, a first-generation senator who had made it to consul simply because he was widely regarded as a harmless, genial old buffer. Nevertheless, he still commanded twenty thousand men, men who would much rather support their governor than an old man in Hispania. The legions further down the Rhine would surely support Rufus too. Fonteius Capito, their governor, was a wasteful degenerate who clung to an amphora of wine harder than a limpet to its rock. No man in his right mind would follow Capito over Rufus. In backing Rufus over their own governor the other legions could hope for great rewards.

That night, as I lay in bed, I wondered what on earth I could do to save the situation. It was clear that the harder I urged Rufus to be reasonable, the less reasonable he became. All I could do was hope the governor would realize his own shortcomings and concede in favour of Galba, and that Valens would realize that it was in his interests to convince the other legions to give Galba their loyalty. Effectively my hopes rested on the humility of an ex-consul, and on the loyalty of an ambitious legate. Hardly comforting thoughts before my first official day of command!

Totavalas woke me at dawn, and I painfully resumed the daily exercises that I had neglected since taking that cushy job in Hispania. I had put on a little weight over the last few months, though the gods know how I had managed to do that, after training an army, enduring torture and fighting in battle. Vindex's wine may have had something to do with it, I suppose. Anyway, I had to get back into shape now that I was with the legions again.

After breakfast old Tuscus the camp prefect was waiting outside to give me a tour of the camp. Normally this wouldn't be necessary, as no self-respecting legate would be unfamiliar with camp life. Mogontiacum was an exception. I have said before that it housed two legions within the same walls, and so its layout was somewhat different from the usual. I won't bore you with all the details; if you're after an in-depth guide to the peculiarities of a two-legion camp then look elsewhere! The most important event of my first day was to meet my command. By this time the men were heading back to their quarters after breakfast to smarten themselves up for the morning parade.

Tuscus was kind enough to stay with me on the parade square while we waited for the cornicia's call. My insides were squirming, but whether that was down to an attack of nerves before addressing my legion for the first time, or my first army breakfast for several years, I don't know. The camp augur was also on hand, looking bleary-eyed and obviously missing his bed.

'Is there anything I ought to know about the legion?' I asked Tuscus.

'It's probably the legion most devoted to the Caesars in the whole empire. Julius recruited it and beat Pompey with it in Macedonia. Hence the name. In the civil wars it was always for Augustus too, never Antony. Then a brief posting in Hispania, and here in Mogontiacum for the last thirty years.'

'And how did they feel about my predecessor, Cotta?'

'How honest would you like me to be, sir?'

'Brutal.'

'Well, sir, General Cotta was never entirely happy here. He fancied himself a bit of an expert on Parthia, and never really got over the fact that he was posted here instead. "Guard duty over a few savages in mud huts" was how he described our job.'

'Not popular, then?'

'Oh, likeable enough in the officers' mess, sir, but he never took much of an interest in the men. Thought it beneath him.'

Fatal error, I thought. That is if you actually care about the success of your command.

The call for parade was blasted shrilly throughout the camp. The men came in groups of eight towards the square, each man with the seven comrades who shared his quarters. Still chatting, they formed up into centuries and cohorts, marshalled by the centurions. Eventually silence fell, only for it to be broken by the barks of the centurions as each century completed the roll call. All were present and correct.

The first-spear centurion, a stout man in his early fifties, approached to accompany me in my first inspection of my legion. I couldn't find anything to fault in the first cohort; every piece of armour was burnished brightly, even the metal hidden beneath the overlapping scales was polished. Here and there the first-spear centurion would offer some commentary. 'Lanius, sir. Good man,' or 'Varro, sir. Good scout,' or whatever skill he had. He made a point of only using the word 'good' for praise; never excellent, or great, just good. But I suppose if you merited praise from the most senior centurion in the legion, there was no higher reward.

By the time we reached the seventh and eighth cohorts, the occasional scabbard strap was broken, or a small scuff was showing on the armour, but all in all it was a very good turnout. Not that I'd expect anything less of a veteran legion. The inspection over, it was time to introduce myself properly to them. I headed back to where Tuscus was standing at the top of the square, then turned to face my command. Over their heads, I could see my new quarters behind the square, and Totavalas at an open window watching the proceedings.

'Men of the Fourth, my name is Aulus Caecina Severus. I served as a tribune with the Twentieth in Britannia under Suetonius Paulinus. So I think it is fair to say I have just as much experience in putting down rebellions as you!' A chuckle went round. Most of them appreciated that Vesontio had been nothing compared to what we went through in defeating Boudicca. I fancy a few of them had recognized my name too. The word would soon spread.

'I am sorry that you have lost the Legate Cotta. He was a man of great talent and wisdom, a man who died in defence of Rome and her values, leading you to your triumph over Vindex and his rabble of ungrateful Gauls. I hear that you were the first on to the battlefield when the news came that the rebels were approaching Vesontio, and that it was your courage and cunning that lured them from skulking in the woods to be slaughtered in the open. You richly deserve your reputation as the finest legion on the Rhine.

'This legion has a proud and noble history. Under the Divine Julius you triumphed over Pompey and his rebel scum in Macedonia. You served under Augustus loyally, even before he was made emperor, and with him you conquered the furthest reaches of Hispania. Truly, there is no legion as loyal to the house of Caesar.' The men raised their spears and cheered. The legion basked in its glorious reputation, and the men lapped up my praise. I raised my arms to silence them. Now came the difficult part.

'But as you know, the house of Caesar is now at an end. Nero, a man who by his vanity, paranoia and wickedness brought shame to the great dynasty, has taken his life. He has purged himself from our world, with no Caesar to follow him. Let me assure you there is no question of letting the Senate rule. The days of a decaying Republic, run by a coterie of corrupt, decadent old men, are over. Instead, Rome needs an emperor who is beyond reproach, a man who will govern with wisdom and generosity, on behalf of the Senate and People of Rome. That is why I ask you today to swear an oath of allegiance to that same Senate and People of Rome, to serve the next emperor with the same loyalty that you gave to the Caesars. Before you decide, I promise you this: whoever becomes our new emperor, I guarantee that he will be a man of irreproachable character, with a name that goes back to the foundation of the Republic. For it would be disrespectful to replace the great Caesar dynasty with some unknown provincial. Second, he will have a long record of military service, so that he can appreciate the vital role that you play in the defence of the empire, and will reward you suitably for your loyalty. I will urge the Senate to heed these demands, and I know that Governor Rufus will do the same.'

With that I gave a curt nod to the augur I'd summoned to administer the oath. The ceremony was short and straight-forward. I should perhaps explain that this was not normally the case; usually they are grand affairs, full of pomp and ritual. But brevity and simplicity was the order of the day. I did not want the men to have too long to think over the matter, and an oath of allegiance to the Senate requires less sycophancy and flummery than an oath to an emperor. I could see there was some uncertainty among the men, but there was no trouble when it came to the swearing of the oath. Thinking that anything I said now would be superfluous, I gave the order to dismiss the parade. A frenzy of murmur and chattering broke out as the legionaries discussed the sudden turn of events, and in turn each cohort dispersed as the men scattered to their morning's duties.

Tuscus was stunned. 'I've never seen anything like it.'

'I don't suppose you have,' I said offhandedly.

'How in Hades did you convince the men to swear allegiance to the Senate when they know that they could get huge rewards from Governor Rufus?'

I gave a modest smile. 'When you study under Domitius Afer, and sit in the Senate with Seneca, you learn a thing or two.'

'Who's Domitius Afer?'

'Only one of the greatest orators of our age, Tuscus.'

The prefect looked sheepish. 'Ah . . . well, not my field, I sup-pose!'

'I suppose not. Now, Tuscus, would you do me one last thing? I'd like to go beneath the principia.'

Tuscus frowned. 'To the treasury, sir?'

'No, not the treasury. The shrine.'

Now the prefect understood. 'Of course, sir.'

★

Tuscus quickly dismissed the augur and gestured for me to lead the way. It was no more than two minutes' walk from the parade ground, but by the time we had reached the door I felt sweat begin to trickle down my arms and legs. It must have been all that heavy armour I was wearing beneath the summer sun. The guards on the door were unblinking, even when they sprang to attention as Tuscus and I drew near. Now it was my turn to follow. Tuscus strode past the various chambers, briefly visited his own office and came out with a bundle of some kind that clattered and jangled as he moved. I was going to ask about the bundle's contents, but the prefect just winked and said, 'You'll see.'

At last we came to the back wall of the building. There on the brick floor was a great trapdoor, so big the old officer needed a hand to lift it. The trapdoor was a brute to raise. I looked down, expecting to see nothing but pitch black, but there was a faint, flickering light that revealed the beginning of a stone staircase. Tuscus went first, a set of keys jingling in his hand as he made his precarious way down the steps.

'Would you close the trapdoor behind us, sir? We can't have some nosy clerk following us.'

'What about a torch?' I asked.

'No need. The torches at the bottom give enough light to see by.'

I was hesitant. I had braved battlefields and torture, but if there is one thing I cannot bear it is confined spaces. Taking a deep breath, I followed Tuscus underground.

I could see the prefect ahead of me, and I could just make out some shapes at the bottom of the tunnel. As I paused, the darkness seemed to crowd about me. The timber props in the tunnel wall seemed so close I could almost make out the curve of the grain. Keeping one hand firmly planted on the wall, I edged carefully down the steps, not trusting myself to look all the way down to the bottom but keeping my gaze fixed straight ahead. Eventually, I made out the two shapes at the bottom to be guards, standing either side of a stout door. Tuscus spun the keys on his finger impatiently.

Pulling myself together, I came down those last few steps as nonchalantly as I could manage, not wanting to lose face in front of the guards. Tuscus busied himself with the keys, muttering as he jiggled them in the lock, obviously having forgotten which key was which. At last the lock clicked, and Tuscus swung the door open.

My eyes were greeted with a sight to make a poor man weep. On my left was the entire wealth of the Fourth Legion, and on my right was that of the Twenty-Second. On each side were hundreds of denarii neatly stacked in identical columns, piled around a solid-looking chest, each protected by a hefty padlock. There was enough gold in those strongboxes to pay an entire legion for three months!

But I wasn't here to look at the gold. Directly ahead there seemed to be a strange collection of weapons propped up against the back wall. The torchlight danced about the chamber, so I had to force myself further into that cramped place to have a better look. Then I understood. Two small alcoves had been carved into the wall, some two paces apart and at about shoulder height. Beneath the right-hand alcove was an assortment of barbarian weaponry, mainly German. The left-hand pile was far more varied. I recognized German spears, and slings from Hispania, their leather darkened and stiff with age. These rested at the foot of a beautiful Celtic shield, painted with swirls of blue and green. I even found a solitary gladius in the mix. These were the weapons of the legion's enemies since the day it was founded, laid to rest beneath the niche in the wall that I had come to see, the home of the legion's eagle.

I bowed my head in respect, and was about to sink to my knees in prayer when Tuscus coughed loudly. The prefect began to unwrap the bundle he had brought down from his office. When the last knot was undone, he pulled away the cloth covering and revealed a new set of weapons. It was mostly a ragtag collection, a rusty conical helmet that the Gauls sometimes use, an old shield boss and a few daggers. But I recognized the pride of the spoils, a pair of finely crafted swords with the tell-tale Celtic swirls etched into the iron. There was a lump in my throat as I remembered when I had last seen them, in the hands of Bormo as he swung and slashed his way into the Roman army at Vesontio.

Tuscus held out the weapons, expecting me to make the offering to the eagle. I just couldn't. I mumbled something about not knowing the proper ritual, and asked him to do it instead. How could I, the legion's new commander, dedicate an offering to my new legion's eagle that was made up of the weapons of my Gallic companions? It would have been blasphemous to the gods, and disrespectful to those brave men who had died for a cause that wasn't of their making. I had meant to say my own prayer to the eagle, but when Tuscus had finished making the offering I told him that I had seen enough and wanted to go back upstairs.

Hurriedly, I led the way out of the room and back up that suffocating tunnel. As Tuscus locked the door, it was as if I was leaving the past few months behind me, buried deep with Bormo's swords.

XVIII

The lady Cotta left the next day, at last abandoning the villa that was going to be my home for the foreseeable future. It was a sumptuous place. Of course not quite as grand as, say, Galba's palace in Tarraco, or even my villa back in Corduba. At least there I'd had a splendid view that stretched for miles across the achingly beautiful plains of Baetica. This view was . . . well, how shall I put it? German.

It was high summer, the month of Augustus, and the climate could hardly be described as pleasant. The mist from the valley moved sluggishly before eventually breaking up under the sun's feeble rays. There were the edges of the great German forest beyond the Rhine. In short, nothing spectacular, but it was home now and I would have to make do. Totavalas had little enough to bring from my temporary quarters, and I decided that it would be safest to leave everything as it was, knowing full well that my wife would soon turn the place upside down and back to front to create the perfect look. You know how women are.

Actually, Cotta's wife had taken several cartloads of furniture with her, so there was little to sort out. Those first days felt very strange, being alone in that big, empty place. Totavalas was thrilled to have the slave quarters all to himself. That would soon change. Soon there would be cooks, cleaning girls, janitors, an ornatrix, slaves for show, a tutor for Aulus, then the house would be teeming. I had a letter from Salonina saying that their little convoy had set off and would be with me very soon. She'd asked her father for some money to finance the journey, and couldn't wait to be with me again. She was also bringing a new tutor along for Aulus, one who could teach him all the subjects now that the specialists in Rome were out of reach. I was sure that Aulus would love growing up with the army, there would be so much for him to do. The soldiers might even take a shine to him; after all, they did to Caligula!

I passed the days waiting for them handling the bureaucracy, taking parades, drinking in the officers' mess, learning everyone's names, that sort of thing. I mean, being stationed on the Rhine isn't the most active posting, not like in Britannia, where three legions barely controlled half the island. The veterans in the legion probably saw Vindex's rebellion as a pleasant diversion from camp life, and wouldn't expect another chance like that for several years. The tribes in Germania are fierce, but not stupid. They know they can never hope to defeat us without great numbers, and for that their tribes would have to unite. Fortunately there was about as much friendship between them as between a mass of rats in a sack.

Things were quiet now, though, so quiet in fact that I decided to head into the town and buy a present for my wife. Jewellery is always a pretty safe bet with Salonina, but apparently I lack taste. So I brought Totavalas with me; these Celts have a fine eye when it comes to precious stones and craftsmanship. I was in full uniform except for a helmet; I like to think I have few vices, but I have to admit that vanity is one of them. Plus, the market-sellers would hardly dare to con a senior Roman officer. I was idly browsing through a collection of amber necklaces when I felt a hand on my arm.

My hand darted down, gripped my sword hilt, and I spun

round, the tip of my sword at my assailant's throat. I was a flick of the wrist away from puncturing the impudent fellow for laying his hand on an army officer, when I saw the shock of ginger hair, and the nervous smile.

'Lugubrix! I might have killed you!'

'You still might, unless you put that sword away,' the Gaul riposted.

'Sorry,' I said, sheathing my sword. 'But what do you expect if you creep up behind me and put your grubby little hand near my nice clean uniform?'

'It is a smart uniform, I'll grant you. Legate of the Fourth Legion, you must be delighted. Makes a change, doesn't it?'

I paused. 'Shall we talk somewhere a bit less public?'

'My thoughts exactly. There's a tavern a couple of streets down, the landlord knows me.'

'Sounds fine. Come on, Totavalas, shopping's over.'

Totavalas made to follow, but Lugubrix put out his hand to stop him. 'Friend of yours?'

'Slave, actually. He's a Celt too, as a matter of fact.'

There was a very brief conversation between my old friend and my new slave. Lugubrix seemed satisfied, and we were on our way.

'So what brings you to this fine town, Lugubrix?' I asked.

'Business.'

'Just business?'

Lugubrix grinned. 'That can wait.'

We wound our way down a couple of back streets towards the river. You could tell this was a shadier part of town just by looking at the cobbles. They were darkened by flecks of dirt and scraps of rubbish that would have been swept up in the middle of town, and each cobble was rough and bumpy, laid at the same time as the smarter town centre but not worn smooth by countless footsteps.

'Is it much further? I don't have a good history with riverside inns.'

'Don't worry, it's just round the corner.'

It was a drab little place, but then I suppose if all you're after is a cheap drink, you aren't particular about where you have it. The mortar was crumbling and grey, the door didn't quite fit in its frame, but I was only going in there for a talk, not a bed. Lugubrix caught the eye of the landlord, then tossed him a coin.

'My usual table free, Bel?'

'Anything for you, Lugubrix,' the landlord said.

'Belenus,' my friend told me, 'owes me a favour or two.'

We were shown to a back room, with a solitary table and a bench on either side.

'A beer for me, and a cup of decent wine for my friend. Make sure we're not disturbed please, Bel.'

Totavalas spoke up. 'Shall I wait outside, master?'

I thought about it for a moment. If he was going to be my body slave, I would have to trust him sooner or later. 'No, you can stay. Just stand by the door and keep quiet.'

'Also,' said Lugubrix, 'have a check through the cracks in the door now and again to make sure no one is eavesdropping. Now, to business.'

'Have you heard from Quintus?' I asked.

Lugubrix looked surprised. 'You don't want to hear the big news first?'

'That can keep for a few minutes. How's Quintus?'

'Emotionally shattered. What do you expect? He's lost almost his entire family.'

'Is he still in Lugdunum?'

'No, Galba has appointed a man called Junius Blaesus to replace Vindex, and when this man Blaesus arrived, Quintus went back to his family with the Aquitani.'

'Are you going to see him any time soon? I'd like you to give him a message.'

'I might see him next month, I suppose. What's the message?'

'If he wants it, I could keep the post of tribune aside for him. My current tribune goes back to Rome at the end of the year.'

'You've grown quite fond of the lad, haven't you?'

'He was a good, loyal friend. It's the least I could do. He'd do a good job too, I mean, he's probably the most experienced man of his age in the entire empire!'

'Very true. I'll pass on the message, I promise.'

'Thank you, Lugubrix. Now, you said you had big news . . .'

'Huge news more like. Fonteius Capito has been killed. By two of his legates, Cornelius Aquinus and Fabius Valens.'

Valens! I thought. What was that ambitious snake up to now?

'Killed? Why?' I asked.

'Valens proclaimed that Capito was planning to march south with his legions and declare himself emperor, and had asked the legates to join him in the conspiracy. Of course, Valens and Aquinus, as loyal servants of the Senate and People of Rome, saw no honourable course open to them except to kill him with their own hands.' Lugubrix clearly had the same low opinion of Valens as I did.

'Valens killed his own commander? That's hardly going to endear him to the legions. They would probably have followed Capito, drunken sot that he was. How did the troops take the news?'

'Somehow, he managed to convince them to swear an oath of allegiance to Galba.'

'Galba!' I said, astonished.

'I know. Valens doesn't exactly strike me as the self-sacrificing type. But it makes a lot more sense when you hear what really happened.'

There was a loud knock, and my eyes darted to the door.

'Your drinks are here, sirs,' a female voice called out.

'Let them in, Totavalas.' The slave cautiously opened the

door and a young serving girl came in, carrying a full tankard of beer, an old goblet and a skin of wine. We said nothing as she set the cups down on the table, and steadily began to pour my wine. I was aching to hear the news, and the stream of crimson liquid seemed to spill almost lazily into the cup. At long last the girl left, and Lugubrix could continue.

'It was Valens and Aquinus who approached Capito, pledging their support if he declared himself emperor. For whatever reason, Capito refused. Maybe he realized he wasn't up to it, or maybe he was afraid to take the risk. So, this leaves Valens and Aquinus with a problem. They have revealed to the governor that they are more interested in personal power than allegiance to Nero or the Senate, and are on the brink of mutiny. Rather than risk Capito reporting their treachery, they murder him, on the pretext that it was Capito and not them who was being disloyal.'

'And the only way to save face in front of the men is to claim you acted in a noble cause,' I surmised, 'by pretending that Capito was the conspirator. Capito is dead, the legates do not lose face, but gain the approval of the next emperor by winning the loyalty of the lower Rhine legions. It's genius.'

'Cold-blooded, ruthless genius, but genius, I grant you,' Lugubrix agreed.

'But how do you know all this while the legions don't?'

The Gaul smiled. 'I'm afraid I make a point of never revealing my source. It would be bad for business. I swear by Toutatis, or Jupiter if you like, that it is the truth.'

I was stunned. I knew Valens was an ambitious bastard, but plotting a conspiracy, murdering your governor and doing a quick about-turn to save your own hide, all in a matter of days, was sheer bloody brilliance. The only good thing to come out of this whole business was that the troops in Lower Germania had now sworn their allegiance to Galba. Nothing could stop him now.

'Lugubrix, there's something I have to do.'

'I understand. The latrines are out the back.'

I chuckled. 'Not that. It's politics. What do you know about our governor, Verginius Rufus?'

'Not a lot. I'd heard he's a strict constitutionalist, that he'd just sit tight and let events pass him by.'

'Well, let's just say he's thinking of stirring himself.'

There was a flash of understanding across Lugubrix's face. 'You'd better hurry, then.'

We both stood up, and I took his arm in mine. 'Thank you, old friend. You will get that message to Quintus, won't you?'

'Right away. And if you ever need to get word to me, give a letter to Belenus and it'll reach me.'

'Won't it be opened?' I asked.

'Not in my network it won't. Go on, I've got some more business to do here.'

'Thank you again.' I picked up my untouched goblet and drained it in one, the wine's sharpness leaving a vinegary taste. I reached inside my tunic and fished out a small bag of coins, taking out a denarius and throwing the bag to the slave.

'Have another drink, Lugubrix,' I said, laying the coin on the table. 'Totavalas, I want you to go back to the market place and buy that amber necklace I was looking at. Get the best price you can, then go back to the villa. I'll be back in an hour at the most.'

Rufus's quarters in the town were more functional than fashionable, I thought to myself as I sat in his atrium while a house slave went and fetched him. Inasmuch as a man can be judged by his house and its contents, there was little to surprise me. There were no gaudy decorations, no expensive souvenirs from campaigns around the world, just a few benches and pot plants surrounding the impluvium, the small pool that caught the rainwater from the square opening in the roof.

I heard the sound of footsteps smacking along the corridor, and sure enough Rufus came into the hall, clad in thick sandals and a luxurious-looking tunic. His face was tired and wrinkled. I almost felt sorry for what I was about to say.

I rose. 'Governor, I'm sorry to have to speak so bluntly, but there is no way that you can be the new emperor.'

Rufus raised his hands as if to calm me down. 'Severus, please . . .'

'I'm sorry, Governor, but I will be heard on this. I have important news from Lower Germania. Fonteius Capito has been murdered by the legates Aquinus and Valens, because he would not countenance their plans to make him emperor. After the murder, the legates claimed it was Capito who was the plotter, not them, and have convinced their legions to swear an oath of allegiance to Galba.'

Rufus stood there, stunned. His eyes narrowed, as though trying to understand the enormity of what I had just said.

'It's over, sir. The legions down the Rhine as well as my own have sworn allegiance to the Senate and to Galba. They cannot follow Capito, and now they will not follow you.'

He still looked confused. 'Capito dead, you say?'

'Yes, sir, dead.'

Rufus told the slave to leave us, and slowly approached me.

'I owe you an apology, Severus.'

Now it was my turn to be confused. 'An apology, Governor?'

'Yes, an apology. Come, sit, sit, sit.' He lowered himself on to the bench and beckoned for me to do the same.

'I was very short with you that day we came back from Vesontio. You were talking common sense, and I was tired, irritable, and dreaming of a golden future. I must admit that when I heard you had convinced the Fourth to swear the oath to the Senate, I stayed in this house sulking for a few days.'

'You mean you've changed your mind, sir?'

'In all honesty, I would like you to believe that I had changed it already, even before I heard the latest news from Rome. There have been . . . developments. It seems Nymphidius Sabinus took it into his head that he could legitimately become emperor, on the strength of his support among the Praetorians, and on a cock and bull story that he was the bastard son of Caligula. I ask you!' Rufus allowed himself a small chuckle. Sabinus's mother had indeed been an imperial slave, but the idea that he was Caligula's son was ludicrous.

'However, the bribes that Galba promised the Praetorians outweighed any personal loyalty they had towards their prefect, and on entering camp a group of them hacked him to death. The next morning, the Praetorians sent a message to the Senate that they were content to have Galba as their emperor. A delegation of senators has been dispatched to sail to Hispania and confer upon Galba the imperial power. They should be landing at Tarraco any day now.'

I was astonished. Despite everything – Vindex's idiocy, the ambition of Rufus, Valens and Sabinus – somehow every stumbling block that Galba had faced had vanished. The gods must have been smiling over the old man that day he first dreamed of being emperor.

'So Capito is dead because he didn't want to be emperor. I suppose I should be thankful that you are the legate of the Fourth and not Valens, otherwise I might have gone the same way!'

I smiled. Well, what can you say to something like that?

'I must say, you are quite a remarkable young man, Severus.'

'Me, sir?'

'Yes, you. Galba thinks very highly of you, why else would he make you a legate before you turn thirty? You can't expect anything else from him, he's already promoted you beyond your station, and you still fight his corner. Who knows, if you'd wanted to, you might have convinced me as Valens tried to convince Capito. And yet you didn't. Why?'

'What reason do I need other than the fact that Galba is

clearly the best man to bring unity and stability to Rome? If you were in my position, wouldn't you do the same?'

Rufus smiled. 'I'd like to think so.'

'If you, or Capito for that matter, had decided to march south with the legions and invade Italia, you wouldn't have been an emperor, you would've been a conqueror. Using the legions entrusted to your command by the emperor and the Senate to start a bloody civil war.'

'Like Julius Caesar, you mean?' Rufus asked.

'Philosophy and ethics were never my best subjects, Governor.'

'I was only teasing. You are right, of course, Severus. I would have been a tyrant, not an emperor.'

'On the bright side, sir, when the historians write of how the Caesar dynasty came to an end, they will say that you defeated Vindex and that you were offered the crown but instead you gave it back to the fatherland.'

Rufus cheered at that. 'Yes, I did, didn't I? Thank you, Severus.'

'If you don't mind, sir, I think I might go back to camp now.'

'Of course. I'm glad we had this little chat. We understand each other, I think.'

We shook hands, and Rufus had the slave escort me out. The man who defeated Vindex, but declined the crown. He had those words etched on to his mausoleum that very year, but he is still alive today, and going strong. A vain man, but a decent one. Dear old Rufus.

I gently strolled up the hill and back into camp. My clerk gave me a small pile of paperwork to look through when I got home. Eventually I came to the front door of my villa. The two men on guard both had the hint of a smile in their expression. I told them to pull themselves together, and went inside.

Still perusing the paperwork, I called out: 'Totavalas, did you get that necklace?'

'He certainly did,' a voice replied.

I looked up. The necklace was right in front of me, nestling just above a pair of shapely breasts. My gaze travelled upwards, to that smooth jaw, those beautiful lips, into her deep blue eyes.

'Hello, husband.'

XIX

I woke up the next morning with her hand on my chest. It was a glorious feeling. Bear in mind that I hadn't slept with a woman since a plump little slave girl back in Corduba. To come home and find that my wife had left the convoy and rode on ahead to be with me, well, we spent the whole night celebrating. That is, after she got over the initial shock of discovering that I was down to nine fingers.

There was a blissful smile on Salonina's face as she lay there sleeping, dreaming of the night before, I hope! Her curls lay strewn across the pillow, and I watched her frame rise and fall with each breath. Gently, I managed to slip out from under her arm without waking her, put on a robe and left the bedroom. I stopped at the door to the spare bedroom, and eased it quietly open. There lay my son, fast asleep after his tiring journey. It was his ninth birthday in two weeks' time, and he had shot up since I'd last seen him. He had darker, straighter hair like mine, but his mother's softer features. He would grow into a handsome lad, but if I had one misgiving, it was that Salonina had spoilt him slightly, and that he hardly knew life outside our estates at Vicetia or the villa in Rome. He was a bit young still for the pleasures of Pompeii. But now was the perfect time for him to come to Germania and begin the change from boy to man.

I heard the rustle of silk behind me, and glanced behind to see Salonina in a blue gown that matched her eyes. 'He's a beautiful boy, Caecina,' she whispered.

'I know, takes after his mother.'

'Eumenes says that he's been working very hard at his Greek these last few weeks. He's even started writing some poems.'

'There will be some very different lessons for him to learn out here, my love.'

'I know that, but we can't have him growing up a little barbarian, can we?'

'I hated Greek, and I turned out all right!'

'And you know I'm very proud of you, but we have to think of society, don't we?'

This was Salonina's only fault. Society. Everything she did had to be squared with what 'society' would think. And her a tradesman's daughter! Still, we all have our foibles.

'I have some other big news,' I began.

'More news?'

'On my way here from Hispania, I stayed with Julius Agricola.'

'How is Julius? And that lovely wife of his . . .'

'Domitia. Julius suggested that their daughter Julia would be a good match for Aulus.'

'Oh.' She paused. 'Well, I suppose she would be.'

'You suppose?' I asked, not liking the tone of her voice.

'Well, the Agricola family are a bit provincial, darling. After all, now that you have such excellent prospects, oughtn't we to be looking a bit higher for our son?' She caught the look on my face, and said hurriedly, 'But I know that Julius is your best friend, so we can hardly object.'

'I think it is an excellent match.'

She paused a moment, looking a trifle crestfallen. 'Then I think so too.'

We stood there a little longer, watching our sleeping son. Then I took Salonina's hand in mine, and drew her towards me.

'What do you think of the villa?' I asked.

'Oh, I think I can make something of it.'

'You'll have to wait for our furniture to arrive first. I spent the last of my ready money on this,' I said, lifting up her necklace.

'And it was very sweet of you.' She kissed me on the cheek. 'Will you come back to bed?'

'I can't, I have to do my exercises, and then some paperwork.'

'You could always do your exercises with me,' she suggested.

'Now that's a thought . . .' and, taking her by the hand, we went back to bed.

Those months were among the happiest of my life. Salonina revelled in being a legate's wife, and the highest lady in Mogontiacum society. Rufus wasn't married, you see, and my fellow legate Dillius Vocula was a first-generation senator, so I socially outranked Vocula and my wife outranked his. She insisted we host dinner parties, attend receptions and so many functions that you'd think being a legate was more a social position than a military one. We must have wined and dined half the province by the time autumn arrived, by which point Salonina had decided who was worth a second invitation and who was not, sifting the social wheat from the chaff. After that she could forge her own intimate circle, and hold court in our triclinium.

With my first pay packet, I bought Aulus a horse for his ninth birthday, and we would go out riding almost every day. Of course we never went too far; my warhorse Achilles wasn't built to do miles and miles of cross-country, and I had duties to attend to back in camp. But I was thrilled that, as the weeks went by, Aulus spent less and less time with his tutor, and more and more in camp with me. He watched as the soldiers drilled

and wrestled, and I even had one of the drill-masters teach him
a little swordplay.

As idyllic as our existence was, trouble was brewing in the
south. Galba had been acclaimed emperor by the delegation of
senators, and instead of joining them on their ship back to Rome
he decided to take the land route with his new Seventh Legion.
Their commander, Titus Vinius, a close friend of Galba (some
would say an intimate friend), had obsequiously given it the
nickname Galbiana. Magnificent subtlety, you'll agree. All was
going well until they reached Gaul.

First, a decree was issued, demanding the execution of all
those who had conspired with Nymphidius Sabinus. Along with
some of Sabinus's creatures, this decree included two prominent
men, Mithridates of Pontus, once a client king in the Bosphorus
but now a resident of Rome; and the consul-designate for
the next year, Cingonius Varro. Now these two deaths were
justified. Perhaps showing a lack of clemency on Galba's part,
but nonetheless justified. However, also condemned to death
was the legate Clodius Macer, whom Galba had persuaded to
help turn the screw on Nero by impounding the grain ships on
their route from Africa to Rome. His crime was to have raised a
second legion in Africa, and this was interpreted as a sign that
Macer too harboured ambitions to wear the purple. Of course
Galba could not countenance even the slightest risk of a rival,
and the list of the dead continued to grow.

News of these grisly events trickled through to us in
Germania, and while one might have overlooked the deaths as
necessary for the stability of the empire, Galba's next moves
were particularly disturbing. He had the governor of Aquitania
executed. His only crime was having dared to ask Galba for
troops to put down the Vindex rebellion, as a loyal governor
should have done. Verginius Rufus begged me to send a letter
to Galba, reiterating his loyalty. I mean, if Galba executed a

governor simply because he had wanted to end a rebellion, what would he do to the man who had come so close to challenging him for the imperial crown? Of course I sent the letter.

An even bigger mistake was Galba's treatment of the various Gallic tribes that had been involved in the Vindex rebellion. The Aedui, Arverni and Sequani had made up most of Vindex's army, and those who did not march with us had contributed what weapons and provisions they could spare. By way of thanks, Galba reduced their annual tribute to Rome, and gave them new lands. Of course these new lands had to come from somewhere, and Galba thought it fitting to take them from the tribes that had stayed loyal and helped the Rhine legions. The men did not respond well to this. It was as though Galba was going out of his way to denigrate and dishonour the Rhine legions which had been so troublesome to him. The one piece of Valens's advice that I did take up was to wander through camp after hours. Aside from the run-of-the-mill conversation, the talk was all of the 'slap in the face' that Galba had given them, and many wondered why Rufus had not gratefully accepted their support.

In an effort to distract them from this barrage of gloomy news, I suggested to my colleague Vocula that we take the men on a route march, so that they might shed any extra weight they had gained after an idle summer. Vocula, a stoic and silent man at the best of times, agreed that it would be good for them to do some hard work at last.

A couple of days before the march, I was sitting at my desk, doing nothing in particular, when there was a knock.

'Come in.'

One of the clerks cleared his throat nervously. 'There's an imperial courier here, sir, who has a message for you and for Governor Rufus.'

'Well, show him in.'

'He said that he was ordered to deliver the governor's message first, and he came to ask you to guide him to the governor's villa.'

'All right. Have a look through these requisition forms and process them while I'm gone.'

The courier was still in his saddle when I came out. He threw me a smart salute, and I gave a quick nod of acceptance.

'Ready, then?' I asked.

The young man looked confused. 'You're not riding, sir?'

'No need. It's a short walk, and I like the exercise. It'll give your horse a break too; the poor beast looks like it could do with it.'

'After you then, sir.'

I waited until we were on the lonely road between the camp and the town, out of earshot of my men, to ask the courier what the message was all about.

'I'm afraid I haven't a clue, sir. I was just given the messages by one of the emperor's freedmen.'

'It wasn't by any chance a thin, effeminate-looking man?'

'How did you know that, sir?'

'Never mind.' Icelus Martianus had retained his influence with Galba, then. There were always rumours that Galba favoured his own sex. After all, he had been widowed fairly early on in his life, and had never remarried. And Icelus Martianus had one of those slender figures and pretty faces that didn't suffer much as he aged.

As I strode down the road and into the town, I wondered what Galba had to say that affected both me and Rufus. The latest reports said that the emperor and his entourage had come as far north as Vienne. Perhaps he was giving us fair warning of an imperial visit? Or maybe Galba had heard how I had stabilized the situation in the province, and that Rufus had given up his designs on the throne? In any case, we had done nothing to merit any punishment, so I was pretty confident that whatever the message was, it contained good news.

Rufus was dozing in a shaded spot in the garden, a half-opened scroll lying on the table next to his chair. The slave who had showed us in gently woke his master.

'Master . . . master!'

The eyes opened in a flash. 'What is it?'

'An imperial courier has a message for you, he's here with the Legate Severus.'

'Oh. Thank you, Aristides, you can leave us now.'

The courier saluted Rufus, and promptly handed over a tightly bound scroll.

'A message from the emperor, sir.'

We both stood there in complete silence as Rufus read the letter. After his eyes had flicked from left to right a few times, his whole demeanour changed from alert and upright to a disheartened slump. Another few minutes passed until he finished the letter.

He looked wearily at the messenger. 'Is he far behind you?'

'A day or two at the most, Governor. He is not a young man any more.'

Rufus smiled grimly. 'That is very true. Well, thank you for the message. I'm sure my slaves will find something in the kitchens for you before you begin your journey back.'

The courier took a step forward and saluted the governor once more. 'Thank you, sir.' Then he turned right round to face me, blocking Rufus's view of me. With his right hand he saluted me, and with the left he held out a folded piece of paper which also bore the imperial seal. Moving as little as possible, I took the note and stuffed it behind my belt, smiling my thanks and appreciation of the man's discretion.

Rufus watched the courier out of the garden, and began to speak only when he was out of sight.

'I take it you haven't heard the news already?'

'Is the emperor coming?' I asked.

'No, not the emperor. Someone else.'

'Who then?'

'My replacement.'

'You mean . . .' I began.

'I mean that Galba has relieved me of my command and summoned me to join him on his march to Rome.'

Rufus looked as dejected as a farmer in a drought. His shoulders seemed to sag beneath a heavy load. The letter fell from his limp fingers and on to his lap.

'The news could be worse, Governor.'

'Could it? Listen to this: "We thank you for your long years of service in Germania, however we require you to give up these duties so that you may join our entourage as we march to Rome." Now what do you make of that?'

I saw his point. This, coupled with the summer's stream of news that Galba had been less than forgiving with his subjects, was ominous. 'When I was with the emperor in Tarraco, he did say that he would create a council that would advise him until he reached Rome.'

Rufus's face brightened for a moment. 'You mean that's why Galba is summoning me?'

'Why else should he do so?'

'Aside from the fact that I command troops who offered me the throne not so long ago?'

'Is there no hint in the letter?'

'Not really, the rest was pretty formulaic stuff. No mention of thanks, no mention of my loyalty, no mention of his plans for me once I arrive, nothing. He's going to kill me, isn't he?'

I could offer Rufus little comfort. The message was ambiguous, cold and curt. If I hadn't heard the news about the poor souls who had decided to oppose Vindex back in the spring, or not declare their loyalty to Galba instantly, then I might have believed my own white lie that Rufus was being called to join Galba's council. But then I remembered something.

'The emperor must have received my letter by now, and I

informed him of your unswerving loyalty, Governor. Galba knows he has nothing to fear from you, and he does not strike me as such a petty man as to have you executed for commanding ambitious men.'

'Thank you, Severus. You've been very diplomatic, but you and I both know that I am right. The emperor wants stability and, flattering and untrue though it may be, he clearly thinks he cannot have it if I am alive.' Rufus stood up slowly, and put his hand on my shoulder.

'I pray you will have a long and glittering career, young Severus. I fear mine is coming to an end. Now, if you'll excuse me, I'd like some time alone.'

'Of course, Governor,' I said.

'Not governor.' He smiled grimly. 'Not any more. That title belongs to Hordeonius Flaccus now.'

Rufus turned to walk back to the house like a condemned man walking to the scaffold, making every step count.

'Senator,' I called. 'You're not going to do anything rash, are you?'

'Don't worry, Severus, I am not ready to see the Elysian Fields quite yet. I will ride to the emperor, and hope your letter was persuasive. I pray we meet again, in this life of course.'

'I am sure we will, Senator.'

'Then that makes one of us.'

The message from Icelus Martianus was short: 'Rufus's replacement is Hordeonius Flaccus, who was among the Senate's embassy to the emperor. My master hopes that you will find this man more malleable, and that you will continue to look after his best interests in Germania. We will send a replacement for Fonteius Capito shortly.'

There was no hint at Rufus's fate, and I attempted to put that thought from my mind. Instead I tried to remember what I could about this man Flaccus. He was old, I remembered that much from seeing him in the Senate house, when his illnesses permitted. A frail, sickly man, the type who looked as though he could be carried off by a gentle gust of wind. Somehow the word malleable seemed inadequate for Flaccus.

His predecessor left the next day, the day that Vocula and I planned to set out for our route march. Rufus was well within his rights to make a farewell speech to the legions, and offer them his thanks as well as an explanation for his recall. But he chose not to. Whether he could not face the ordeal, or he was trying to make my life easier by not agitating my somewhat restless troops, I don't know. I like to think the latter. He left quietly, and began the lonely journey to meet his emperor.

The new governor, Flaccus, was due to arrive that day, and I held off the route march as long as I could. Both legions were on parade in full battle gear, awaiting his arrival and inspection. The afternoon passed, and still the governor did not appear. By early evening, I decided we could not wait any longer, and ordered the general advance. We had only been marching an hour southwards when we came upon a small party of travellers. There were half a dozen men on horseback arranged in a square around a shining white litter, carried by four brawny slaves. As they got nearer I could make out patches of dirt on the litter, dust from the road kicked up over hours of sweaty marching, no doubt. The legions came to a halt, then Vocula and I trotted up to see who was blocking the road.

Seeing two officers approaching, the litter-bearers halted, and gratefully lowered their burden on to the road.

'Why are we stopping?' a voice called out from behind the closed curtains.

'Because you are blocking the path of two imperial legions,' said my colleague.

'Legions? Which legions?' the voice asked.

'The Fourth and the Twenty-Second,' I said.

There was a chuckle, which quickly turned into a racking

cough. Once the spate of coughing had subsided, the voice called out, 'Then let's have a look at them.'

A pale hand drew aside the curtains to reveal a frail, elderly man, clasping a scroll bound by the imperial seal. 'My name is Hordeonius Flaccus, and I am the new governor of this province. Now give me a hand up, will you?'

Galba had exchanged like for like, I thought to myself, as Vocula and I heaved the old man out of his litter. One of the bearers reached inside and brought out a crutch, which Flaccus used to prop up his ailing frame.

'Gout,' Flaccus said. 'Gets worse every year. Now, time to see my legions!'

Nero's custom of appointing mediocrities and weaklings had not died with him, it seemed. But while Rufus's fault of indecision was beneath the surface, Flaccus's weakness was there for all to see. The man was verging on decrepit, and Galba had chosen him to command legions. As I watched him hobble his way towards the column, I thought the situation would have been comical if it had not been for the mood of the men. To them, Rufus had been a good governor, if an unremarkable one, and in their eyes he had been a good candidate to succeed Nero. The news that he had been replaced had spread swiftly through the camp, and though initially disappointed, the men had been curious to see who took over, and eager to offer their support to the new governor. They were sorely disappointed.

I could see on their faces that some of the men knew what was coming. As Vocula, Flaccus and I drew level with the front ranks, already I could hear some frantic muttering. Eventually, the old man paused to rest on his crutch, sweat matting his thin white hair from the exertion of limping a hundred yards.

'Legionaries, my name is Hordeonius Flaccus, and the emperor has appointed me as the new governor of this province,' he began. A low moan escaped some of the least tactful men, and it seemed even Flaccus's old ears picked it up. 'I realize that my soldiering days are long behind me, but I can promise you that I shall govern with fairness and benevolence. I am honoured that the emperor has chosen me for this vital military post, and it will be an honour to command the flower of the Roman army.'

Flaccus glanced at me. 'Where are you off to?'

'A route march beyond the Rhine, sir.'

The old man looked disappointed, and turned to face the legions once more. 'Your legate tells me you are off on a route march. I am sorry that I won't be able to join you. I had hoped to get to know you better over the next few days, but alas,' he gestured with his crutch, 'it is not to be. I will be waiting for you in Mogontiacum.'

Silence. No roaring cheer for their new governor, no general salute, just stunned silence. Flaccus tried to mask his disappointment, and smiled ruefully at Vocula and me.

'All yours, gentlemen. I'll be out of your way in just a moment,' and he began the arduous walk back to his litter. When the slaves had moved it off the road, the army advanced, and Flaccus watched them march by from behind his silken curtains.

Vocula shook his head. 'The men aren't happy. They want a commander they can respect. How can they respect a feeble old man like Flaccus?'

'They won't. We have to make them respect us instead, or else there will be trouble.'

'You're very sure of yourself. How do you know that the men will take to you? You're as much an instant replacement as Flaccus is, and while he's too old for the job you have to admit you're rather young.'

'You think I don't know that?' I said. 'Simply put, it's sink or swim. And I mean to swim.'

XX

We forded the Rhine, and marched into Germania. I should make it clear that the Roman frontier is often perceived as a permanent boundary, and that the army keeps to its borders. It is starting to look that way these days, but not at the time of my story. In those days the legions had spheres of influence, and frontiers were not set in stone, or in water for that matter. There was little that was unusual about the legions crossing the Rhine on an expedition. It reminded the tribes of our presence, familiarized us with the land beyond the river if ever we needed to cross for war, and broke the monotony of camp life.

The forests thickened the further we marched into Germania, and the roads worsened. I did not dare to march more than five days eastward, for fear of provoking the tribes into attacking us. But the men's sullen mood began to diminish the longer we spent away from the fort, where the walls seemed to hem them in; a body of fighting men is not a docile thing. Cage an angry beast for too long, and if one day you open the door the animal will rage unchecked. But let it out from time to time, on a tight leash, and it becomes more manageable.

Our marching songs echoed around those dense forests and chilly plains, and I have to say it felt good to be in the wild once again. Cold and inhospitable they may be, but those barbarian lands offered a sense of adventure and independence. I love to lose myself in new places, and here I was in Germania with a legion under my command. Our scouts were beginning to pick up news that the villages ahead were stirring, arming themselves and hoarding supplies. The next day we spotted German scouts on a far hilltop, clearly trying to guess our purpose in marching through their lands. The men had whetted their appetites for plunder at Vesontio, and were spoiling for another battle. However, picking a fight with the Germans would have been irresponsible of me, and after almost a week on the march it was high time to head back to Mogontiacum.

Turning back did not stop the Germans' interest in us. The tribe in this region were the Chatti, among the fiercest of the land, and they followed us westward as we made our way back to the Rhine. We built a new camp every day, even before we heard that the Germans were on the move. Not only is it good practice, but consider that if a column of ten thousand men marches at least twenty miles a day, only so many can set off at any one time, so inevitably the vanguard will reach the campsite some hours before the rear. These men had to be occupied somehow, and felling trees, digging ditches and building walls, towers and ramparts, all under the watchful eyes of the engineers, was the ideal way to do it.

The Germans left us alone when we came within two days' march of the Rhine. The following night we set up camp about ten miles away from Mogontiacum, on the last day of our expedition. Vocula and I were standing alone on the western ramparts, away from prying eyes and ears.

'This peace and quiet won't last for ever, you know,' Vocula began.

'I know. As soon as we are back in Mogontiacum, the men will get surly again. They were shocked enough when they heard that Rufus had been recalled, but the more ambitious of them hoped that the next governor might be someone they could follow. Flaccus couldn't lead an afternoon stroll, let alone an army. So much depends on who Galba chooses to replace poor old Capito in Lower Germania.'

'And what sort of governor do you want?'

'What do you mean by that?' I asked.

Vocula shrugged. 'I can't make you out. You're the emperor's blue-eyed boy, aren't you? I mean, you're given a legion to command before finishing your year as a quaestor, years ahead of your turn. But on the other hand, there isn't likely to be another German campaign for at least a decade, the frontier is nice and quiet. What ambitious young legate wouldn't want to have his shot at glory? And it's almost certain Galba will die before your few years here are up, and when you return to Rome you will have lost your patron. So I say again, what sort of governor do you want?'

I liked the simple honesty of the man, and I tried to repay it.

'Another Flaccus,' I said.

'Putting the good of Rome ahead of your own, eh?'

'I know it may be hard to believe, but just because I am young that doesn't make me an ambitious plotter, not like some I could mention.'

'Ah, so you've met Fabius Valens then.'

'How did you guess?' I said, with a smile. 'We have met. Both of us are the first from our families to be elevated to the Senate, and he assumed I would be an ambitious little toerag like him. He suggested, a year or so ago, before all the Vindex business began, that we fake an attack by the Germans on a cohort out on patrol, giving us a reason to start a punitive campaign beyond the Rhine.'

'Gods, has the man no conscience at all?'

'I think it died of neglect under Nero. That one great campaign he planned for Parthia wouldn't have involved the legions in this province: the frontier on the Rhine is too important. Valens doesn't want to rot away and miss his chance to further his career. Can you blame him?'

'His frustration I can understand, but not his methods.'

'Ah well, it takes all sorts to make a world.'

We stopped talking for a moment, as the centurion on duty came along the parapet. He saluted us, and carried on.

'Changing the subject, how did you find Corduba?'

I blinked. What did he care for my time in Hispania?

'It's my home town, you see, and I haven't been back since Seneca convinced me to come to Rome, years ago.'

'You mean you were one of Seneca's chosen few?'

He gave a modest smile. 'You might say that. My father was one of his clients, and Seneca was kind enough to give me a lesson or two. He was a good man, until he started scheming at Nero's court.'

'Nero demanded his suicide the year I entered the Senate, so I only heard him speak a few times, but he was magnificent. Old and weak, but he could hold the chamber spellbound still. More of a philosopher and poet than a politician, I grant you, but it was a pleasure to listen to him.'

'I know what you mean. Not exactly a Cicero, but then who is? Come to think of it, our generation doesn't have much to offer in terms of great men. Cicero, Seneca, the house of Caesar, all gone. Galba will be gone soon. Who will take their place?'

'Seneca's pupil?' I teased.

'I hope the noblest families in Rome can produce something better than me, or the empire is doomed!'

Abruptly, we heard the centurion bark out: 'You! Stand to attention when an officer approaches . . . didn't you hear me?'

I could just make out the silhouette of a man leaning against the wall of the gate, not moving a muscle.

'Jupiter's balls! WAKE UP!' The centurion raised his thick

staff and struck the man hard in the stomach. The man doubled over in shock and pain, and soon more men were rushing to the scene.

Vocula and I looked at each other, aghast. Being caught asleep on duty is one of the gravest offences a soldier can commit, and is always punished by death. The words 'wake up' shouted so half the camp could hear started a huge commotion, as men instantly guessed what had happened. Soon there were torches lit and soldiers filling up the space below the parapet.

The centurion dragged the poor wretch towards us with a vice-like grip on the back of his neck.

'Sorry, sirs, but this dozy bastard was asleep on duty.'

'Clean your tongue, Centurion. Now, man, who are you?' Vocula asked.

The young legionary had gone ash white, and stammered with fear. 'Legionary M-m-milo, sir, second century f-f-fifth cohort of the Macedonica.'

Vocula looked at me. 'Your legion, your decision.'

'What have you got to say for yourself, Milo?'

'Please, sir, I couldn't help it. My woman at the camp gave birth about a week before this march, a little baby girl. I've had permission to spend the nights in town to help look after her. We think she's ill, and she's always crying, and I haven't been able to sleep at all. Last night was the third night I've been without sleep. I know I was meant to be keeping a lookout, sir, but I couldn't help it.'

I looked at the boy's face, for he was little more than a boy, perhaps twenty, twenty-one, a worried father with the threat of execution hanging over him. But the army is the army, and discipline is discipline.

'Put him in chains,' I ordered. 'I'll decide what to do with him when we get back to camp.'

The centurion nodded, and motioned to a couple of men

to take hold of the prisoner. Then he set about dispersing the crowd. 'Get a move on, you maggots, show's over. Nothing for you miserable lot to gawp at here.'

As the men headed back to their beds, Vocula and I were left alone once more on the parapet.

'I don't envy you your dilemma,' my colleague said.

I said nothing, but just looked out into the darkness, brooding.

I did not have to make an instant decision, thank the gods. There are any number of offences that can be committed in the army, most of them minor affairs that are dealt with privately, within each century. More serious cases are brought before the legate every week. I had held the most recent hearing a couple of days before, which gave me another five days to decide what to do, Milo another five days in the camp prison, and a sick baby girl five days without a father.

I told Salonina about Milo the day we returned, and I was very surprised by her reaction.

'The poor baby, and the poor mother! Do they know what's going to happen to Milo?'

'I guess Milo's friends will have told the girl by now, so yes, probably.'

'And what are you going to do?'

'What can I do? My hands are tied. He fell asleep on sentry duty, in enemy territory. The punishment is death. How can I be lenient with someone who risks the safety of the legion?'

'You can be compassionate.'

'Compassionate? This is the army, not some Christian prayer meeting!'

'I'm not appealing to your sense of charity, my love, but you're hardly going to endear yourself to the men by executing a terrified father.'

'You think I don't know that?'

She thought for a moment, then smiled at me. 'Your hands may be tied, but mine aren't.'

That same day she went into the town, hired a physician, and went to see Milo's woman and his baby girl. The physician spent a few days with the child, and as Salonina's purse emptied, the baby began to recover. It was a masterstroke. As she was the legate's wife, Salonina's charity would imply that I felt sorry for Milo's predicament. I did, but there was no way that I could grant the man clemency – the law of the legions demanded his death. But Salonina's intervention would show the men that we cared.

The day of the trial came. Milo's century was put on parade, while other men from the legion hung around the edges of the square, waiting to see what would happen. I say it was a trial, but it was a foregone conclusion. The centurion gave his evidence, and poor Milo again offered his excuse. Raised voices could be heard behind us, and everyone looked to see what the commotion was.

A bulging man sat astride a decidedly unimpressed horse. His toga strained to cover his enormous girth and was so covered in sweat that it seemed to cling to his skin. He was waving a letter in the air, and shouting my name.

'Where is the Legate Severus? I must see him.'

Glad to put off sentencing Milo, even if it was only for a few minutes, I approached the globular rider.

'I am Severus, what do you want?'

He leaned down from the saddle, proffering the small scroll. 'My letter of introduction, if you like.'

Yet again this letter carried the imperial seal. What was it now? I broke the seal, and began to read it, silently.

The man before you is Aulus Vitellius. He is the younger son of the ex-consul Lucius Vitellius, and has inherited none of his father's qualities. There is no man I fear less than one who thinks of nothing but food, so I am happy to appoint him as the new governor of Lower Germania. In his gluttony he will milk the province for all it is worth, but he should pose no threat, I think.

Thank you for your letters, Severus. Verginius Rufus has joined me at Massilia, and I have decided to appoint him to my council for the time being. You were right; he seems a remarkably honest man, if a little bumbling. You have done him a great service.

With Flaccus and now Vitellius on the Rhine, you should have no problem in keeping Germania loyal.

The letter was signed 'Galba Augustus Caesar'. So much for the end of the Caesar dynasty.

'Is everything in order, Legate?' Vitellius asked.

Smiling broadly, I replied that everything was indeed in order, and pocketed the letter. The bulbous man looked around and caught sight of Milo, standing alone in front of his century.

'What's going on here?'

'This man awaits sentence for falling asleep at his post.'

'And what is the sentence?'

'Ten of his comrades are chosen by lot, and must beat the man to death with nothing but their hands.'

Vitellius blanched. Then he beckoned me over for a private word. My cheeks burned as the men watched Vitellius summon me as though he were the man in charge here, and not me. It made me look like a naughty boy called to the front of the class.

'Don't you think the punishment a bit steep?'

'Milo fell asleep on sentry duty, Governor, while we were on manoeuvres beyond the Rhine. My hands are tied.'

'Look, I know it's not my place to interfere, but it wouldn't hurt to show some mercy.'

Before I could stop him, Vitellius gave a sharp squeeze with his heels and urged his horse towards Milo's century. He raised his voice so all could hear.

'My name is Aulus Vitellius, the new governor of Lower Germania. I have spoken with your commander, and he has kindly agreed to indulge me and show this man mercy. I do not condone the crime, but then I have no wish to see one Roman killed at the hands of other Romans. So the sentence is commuted. He shall lose all his privileges and be transferred to an auxiliary unit, but he shall live.'

An ear-splitting cheer rent the air, as the entire century waved their spears in a salute to the merciful Vitellius. Even the men who watched from the barracks began to chant Vitellius's name. The huge man smiled meekly, and pulled at his horse's reins, heading back towards me.

'My thanks, Legate.'

I was inwardly seething. I had planned to grant Milo mercy at the last minute, going by the book all this time only for discipline's sake, and then win the support of the legion by my clemency. Now it was Vitellius they cheered, and my heart sank. Not for the wasted opportunity, but because it seemed the men might have found a new candidate for emperor.

'The emperor must hold you in high regard, Governor, to be his first choice for a province in Germania,' I said.

The parade was over, the men were happy, Vitellius and I were alone. He had taken great care that none of the common soldiers were around before dismounting, so as to hide his gouty limp. It was a ridiculous sight, the flabby man hobbling towards me, like a vast ship heaving and lurching in a storm.

'I must admit it was something of a surprise, but then I do have friends in high places.'

'The emperor, you mean?'

'No, Titus Vinius. He's been appointed co-prefect of the Praetorian Guard, or at least he tells me he will be as soon as they reach Rome. They were only a few days' march away when I left.'

'I have heard the name. Wasn't he close to Galba in Hispania?'

'That's it. He commanded the legion there, and raised a new one for the emperor. We're old friends. We support the same chariot team at the races, you see.'

And now Vinius had recommended his friend to Galba as a safe pair of hands for Lower Germania. Such is the way in politics.

'Is there somewhere where I can have a bite to eat? I'm famished after all this riding.'

'My quarters are only a few minutes away, Governor. I can guarantee the food will be better than the muck they serve in the mess.'

His eyes widened with interest. 'Really? Then lead on, lead on.'

'More venison, Governor?' my wife asked.

'Don't mind if I do. I must say, this is really most generous of you. I haven't had a meal like this since leaving Rome.'

I wasn't surprised. Salonina had plied him with almost everything we had in the kitchens. It was beginning to grow dark outside.

'Were there no decent taverns on the road, sir?'

Vitellius blushed. 'Yes, but I had a rather tight budget. I had to sell a few things to finance the journey. Truth be told, I had to rent out my house and send my family to live with my mother.'

'You poor man,' Salonina said, taking me by the arm. 'Miles and miles away from your family.'

'I'll be all right, that is if my cooks are anything like as good as yours, dear lady.'

'Would you like some wine with your meat, sir?' I asked.

'Oh, just a drop. And please don't bother with all that "sir" business. I'm a simple man, please call me Vitellius.'

'Thank you, Vitellius. Would it be rude of me to ask why you took such an interest in Milo back at the camp?'

'Milo?'

'The soldier who was on trial.'

'Ah yes. You didn't mind me intervening, did you?'

I did, but that was not why I asked. 'Not at all, I was just wondering why you showed mercy to a guilty soldier from a legion outside your province.'

'You're too cynical, Severus. Is it not possible that I didn't want to watch a man being beaten to death by his comrades? What other motive could I have?'

Ingratiating yourself with a Rhine legion is never a bad thing, I thought, but I didn't dare say that out loud. After all, this man by his act of seemingly genuine mercy had endeared himself far more to my men than old Flaccus ever would. After reading Galba's letter, I prayed that Vitellius was just a compassionate man, and had no ambitions for Valens to work upon.

'None at all,' I answered. 'It's just a pleasant surprise to find a governor who is merciful for mercy's sake. I suppose that's what comes of having lived under Nero's rule. Rome has missed good men.'

Vitellius beamed at me. 'That is very kind of you. You have nothing to worry about. I am not an ambitious man. Well, I'm keen to pay off my debts and enjoy the lifestyle of a governor, but that's hardly the same thing, is it?'

'I am sure that the emperor will not regret his decision to make you a governor.'

'Thank you, Severus. Actually, would you mind if I called you by your first name?'

'It would be my honour, Vitellius. My friends call me Caecina.'

'Caecina it is, then.' His chair scraped across the flagstones as Vitellius raised himself from the table. 'And now I should be on my way. I thank you once again for your hospitality.'

His pudgy fist reached out for Salonina's hand, and he gave

it a delicate kiss. 'My lady.' Then he stood before me. His arms reached out and he enveloped me in a great bear hug. 'I think we shall be very good friends, eh, Caecina?'

'Yes, very good friends,' I said, feeling awkward.

'Governor, you won't cover many more miles today before you have to stop for the night. Why not stay here instead?'

Vitellius broke off the embrace and stared at my wife, his eyes gleaming. No doubt it was the prospect of a comfortable bed and another hearty meal. Then the gleam disappeared.

'My lady, you are too kind, but I shouldn't abuse your hospitality any longer.'

Seeing that Vitellius was only refusing out of courtesy, I said, 'Please, I insist. What sort of people would we be if we turned out a guest into the night?'

Vitellius didn't take long to change his mind. 'Oh all right, if you insist.'

That night Salonina and I lay in bed, talking.

'Did you enjoy being the hostess tonight?'

'He certainly took a lot of hosting. I've never seen anyone eat so much.'

'It seems that's why Galba chose him to govern such an important province. Anyone who takes that much interest in his stomach can't have any interest left for plotting.'

Salonina looked confused. 'Why would Vitellius be plotting?'

'Because there are tens of thousands of crack troops in Germania who have no loyalty to Galba, and are thinking how much money they could make if they convinced someone to challenge Galba for the throne. That's why.'

She rolled over, her beautiful face a hand's breadth from mine. 'And what would it mean for us?'

'Us? Civil war, marching on Rome, legion fighting against legion. Do you want that?'

'It sounds as though it's coming anyway. Didn't you tell me

that Galba was a stopgap, a short-term solution? Surely every legion is going to want their governor to be the next emperor. And Vitellius has just won the gratitude of your legion.'

I felt her leg slide over mine. She was silken to the touch. Lithely, she sprang up so that she now sat astride me.

'Just imagine. If you wanted to, you could have the emperor of Rome eternally in your debt. The power, the prestige . . .' She began to grind her hips into me. I was her prisoner.

'I can't. Galba has been good to me.'

'Forget Galba. Think of us, think of your son. One day, he could be the most powerful man in Rome.'

'Stop it.' My arms shot out and gripped her thighs tightly.

Her eyes widened. Then she crossed her arms over her magnificent breasts, and said, 'If you aren't man enough to take what you want, then you aren't man enough for me.' She clambered off me and lay on the far side of the bed, with her back to me.

'Salonina . . . I can't.'

'We both know that's not true.'

XXI

Everything was bitterly cold. The Rhine had frozen in places. The chilling winds bit into the skin, so much so that I started wearing a bizarre German piece of clothing that they call trousers, a piece of material that covers each leg right down to the ankles. But I had known this cold before. Nothing could prepare me for the coldness of my wife. Ever since I had told her about the opportunity that I was turning down, she had barely spoken a word to me. After a week I actively looked for things to keep me away from home. Poor Aulus was very confused. After all, we had gone from a loving couple to almost complete strangers in a matter of days.

One particularly cold evening I was sitting in my office going through a large pile of dispatches when someone knocked at my door. I was puzzled. The working day was over, what could this person want?

'Come in.'

Totavalas stumbled in, and quickly closed the door behind him to shut out the cold. His long slave tunic did little to protect his forearms from the chilling German winter, and I let him stamp his feet and warm his hands for a moment before asking him why he had come.

'A message for you, master,' he panted, his cloudy breath swirling up before his face.

'Yes, yes,' I said testily. 'Who from?'

'I don't know, sir.'

'You don't know?'

'Begging your pardon, sir, but I was in the town doing some errands for the mistress and I was passed this note, and told to give it to you straight away.'

'Did you know the man who gave it to you?'

'No, master, but he said he had come from old Bel at the tavern.'

He handed me the grubby note, sealed with a thumbprint of wax, then stood by the small brazier I had in the corner, where a few embers were smouldering.

The message was short. 'This is our man. Reply by the same messenger. Valens.'

I gave a deep sigh. I had been expecting something of the kind from Valens. Vitellius might well be a glutton, but his father had been consul three times, and even made censor, perhaps the greatest honour one can have outside the imperial family. He was down to earth, likeable and, from what I had seen, easily persuaded. But Valens needed my support if he was going to convince Vitellius to rebel against Galba, support I was not inclined to give.

'Totavalas?'

'Yes, master?' The slave looked up from the brazier, his hands still outstretched.

'I take it you know the position I'm in?' I asked wearily.

'If you mean deciding which side you're on, I do, master, I do.'

'What would you do if you were me?'

'I don't think it's my place to say, master.'

'Damn it, man, I'm asking you. What would you do?'

'Well, sir, if I were you, I'd wait and see a bit. I mean, the emperor has been good to you, giving you this legion and all.

But did you ever stop to think that by taking this job, you're still doing him a favour, keeping the troops loyal? I think you underestimate how useful you've been, sir.'

'But Galba is the best man for the job.'

'That he is, sir, that he is. But it strikes me that once a man has been helped on to the throne, he never likes to be reminded that he needed help, which is why I'd say wait and see.'

'You think I should help Vitellius?'

'Ah, civil war is a mighty tragedy. It has plagued my island for as long as we can remember. But I thought you were asking what would be best for you, master?'

'I flatter myself my conscience would stop me risking the lives of hundreds, maybe thousands of men, just for my own petty ambition.'

'Then I'm glad it was you who bought me, master, and not Fabius Valens.'

'Nicely put, Totavalas.' One thing nagged at me. 'How come you understand all this politics, then?'

He grinned. 'It must be in my blood, master.'

'Your blood? You told me you were an exile.'

'So I was, sir. My father was High King of all Hibernia. Then he was murdered, and my mother and I fled to Mona.'

My body slave was barbarian royalty! That would explain the man's confidence, but not why he had adapted to slave life so well.

'I see it this way, master: when you've been on the battlefield, barely out of boyhood and surrounded by Roman swords and spears, you thank the gods for every day that you live afterwards. I'm alive, well looked after, and away from my enemies in Hibernia. Life could be worse.'

I was starting to regret not having had a proper talk with Totavalas before now. Until that day I had always seen him as the 'novelty' I had bought from Cotta's wife. Now it was clear he had a good head on his shoulders, and a fine sense of humour.

Rare qualities in a slave, and a barbarian one at that, but at least I was recognizing them now before I sold him on to someone else.

My choice was simple then. Stay loyal to Galba, or follow Valens's path.

But trouble came the next evening. You'll remember how Galba had punished the Gauls who had stayed loyal to Rome when Vindex raised his rebellion. The new year's taxes were fast approaching and some of these tribes sent a deputation to Mogontiacum to seek redress. There was a fever in town, and our delicate Governor Flaccus had decided to try to escape the fetid air by staying in the campsite. So it was that the delegation came to the legions that they had supported, their arms thrown wide in a gesture of supplication.

Flaccus was very sympathetic, but what could he do? If the emperor has decided something, you can't very well ignore his orders, especially ones as clear and as recent as his were.

'I am very sorry,' Flaccus said, 'but I can't help you. You were loyal to the legions, and provided all the help that could reasonably have been expected of you. But these things happen. It seems the emperor is not very forgiving of his enemies, even if you didn't know you were his enemies at the time.'

The head of the delegation was not satisfied. 'And what about all the families who paid their taxes, dutifully gave your men all the supplies they needed, and as their reward have to pay even higher taxes, in the middle of winter, after a poor harvest? Mothers and fathers are starving so that their children can eat what little corn they have. Have you no conscience, no mercy?'

Flaccus meekly shrugged his shoulders and said, 'There is nothing I can do.'

I coughed loudly.

'Yes, Severus?'

'Perhaps if these gentlemen were to find the quaestor, they

could tell him that it was an extremely poor harvest and ask to default on the tax this year, then pay it back over the next two years.'

'Good idea, Severus. I'll have a word with the quaestor myself, and lean on him a bit.'

I couldn't help but smile. The idea of Flaccus leaning on someone and it actually having an effect was comical. The Gauls talked briefly among themselves and the leader spoke once more.

'That would be helpful, but it doesn't solve our main problem, which is why we should pay extra tax in the first place.'

'As I said, there I cannot help you at all.'

'Very well, we will see what your men have to say about this.' The whole lot of them made as if to withdraw.

'One moment,' Flaccus called.

'Yes, Governor?'

'I may not have been able to help you much, but it would be bad manners if I sent you back into this freezing weather with no refreshment. Won't you stay and have some mulled wine?'

They did not refuse Flaccus's hospitality. Who would turn down a free cup or two of mulled wine before a long, wintry journey? Flaccus came over to Vocula and me, and whispered conspiratorially.

'I didn't think it would be a good idea to let these Gauls talk to the men. I mean, we recruit heavily from these tribes, don't we?'

'We do, Governor,' Vocula said.

'Best not to let the men hear their families are having trouble, I thought, so we'll keep them here in the warmth, and see that they leave as quietly as possible.'

At the time it seemed a diplomatic move, and Vocula and I agreed. However, almost everybody had seen the Gauls' deputation arrive in the camp, and barely anybody saw them leave. By morning, ugly rumours were spreading round the camp, and at morning parade the men were convinced that the Gauls had been murdered in the night. The first I heard of it was when Totavalas woke me up hastily.

'Master, master! Come quickly, the legions are rebelling!'

'What?' I asked, aghast.

'The men think the Gauls have been murdered, and they're demanding to see the ambassadors from the tribes.'

'Get me my armour, and tell one of the slaves to have Achilles ready outside. Go on, there isn't a moment to lose.'

Minutes later, I was galloping Achilles towards the camp. Already I could hear the angry shouts as the men protested. I bellowed up at the guards on the wall to open the gates, and Achilles pawed impatiently at the ground as they swung slowly open. I dug in my heels and entered the melee.

Swarms of men surged in the warren of streets and passages that covered the camp. Some centurions were lashing out with their staffs in an attempt to control the chaos. Others were swamped by the sheer weight of numbers. Achilles knocked a couple of men flying as we hit the crowd, and I prayed that the horse would keep the momentum going.

I shouted at the mob, 'Go to the square, go to the square!' until I was hoarse, and some of the quick-thinking officers joined in with their own cries. The noise was tremendous, as hundreds of sets of armour clattered against each other in the heaving mass. After what seemed like an age, the crowd started to shift, and I could just make out that many men were indeed heading towards the centre of the camp.

Slowly, we shepherded some of the more stubborn ones to join their comrades, as some of the tribunes had followed my lead and clambered on horseback as well. At long last, the legionaries were herded on to the parade square. The centurions and other officers formed a picket line round the mob. Old Tuscus was bleeding a little from his forehead. Many men were still shouting angrily. I caught sight of Flaccus at his bedroom window, his face a mask of horror.

Dropping the reins, I raised both hands in an effort to silence the men. A few stopped shouting.

'Listen to me. Listen!'

Men began to nudge each other and point at me.

'When you've quite finished!' I bawled at them.

Silence at last.

I paused for a moment, looking at the mob in front of me. I shook my head sadly. Then at last I spoke, quietly.

'You call yourselves soldiers of Rome,' I said with disgust. 'Soldiers of Rome do not rebel, soldiers of Rome do not attack their officers. But here we are. Prefect Tuscus,' I called.

'Yes, sir?'

'In all your years of loyal service, have you ever seen anything as shameful as this?'

'Never thought I'd live to see the day, sir.'

Some of the men looked down at their feet, but there were still far too many who stared at me defiantly. I was moments away from losing control of my command.

'I ask myself, why would the famous and respected Rhine legions start a riot?'

I picked a random face from the crowd. 'You, soldier, have you been paid on time?'

'Yes, sir.'

I pointed at another one. 'Are you fed regularly, and treated properly?'

'But, sir . . .'

'Answer the question, man!'

'Yes, sir.'

'Good. And what about you, Gratus? I've watched you teach my son to fight. Why do you now carry your sword against his father?'

The drill-master blushed, and sheathed his sword. 'Forgive me, sir. We are worried for our families.'

'And what have I done to make you fear for your families?'

A man hidden in the centre of the crowd shouted out, 'Because you murdered the ambassadors, that's why!'

'Come out here and say that,' I snapped.

I didn't expect him to, but a tall man shoved his way to the front. I recognized him: Strontius. He was one of the men who had been recruited locally, and delighted in stirring up trouble. But why had he come forward?

'I'll say it again. You murdered the ambassadors. My cousin was one of them.'

'And what if I gave you my word that the ambassadors haven't been harmed? Would you be happy then?'

There was a murmur of agreement, but Strontius stood fast. 'Why should we?'

'Because when a senator gives you his word, that word actually means something. You realize I could have you executed for inciting a rebellion?'

'You can try,' Strontius said, gesturing to the hundreds of armed men behind him.

He was right, I daren't have him executed. All I could do was threaten, for it would be a terrible show of weakness if I didn't consider killing him. I slung myself out of the saddle, and approached the big man, close enough that I could smell the wine on his breath.

'Drinking last night, were we?' I smiled.

He said nothing.

'I will make you an offer.'

'An offer?'

'If I prove that the delegates are alive, you will receive one hundred lashes.'

'And if you can't?'

'Then by all means carry on with your rebellion. Agreed?'

Strontius looked me hard in the eye, and for half a heartbeat I thought he might attack me then and there.

'Agreed.'

I looked around for one of my officers. 'Tribune, you will detail eight men to ride in every direction to look for the ambassadors. Give each man a spare horse to bring back the Gaul who headed the delegation.'

'Right away, sir.'

Vocula caught my eye, and I tried to look at ease as I walked over to him. He leaned down from the saddle, and spoke very softly.

'What if we can't find them?'

Gods, the thought hadn't occurred to me. I was so confident in the knowledge that the Gauls hadn't been killed that I had blithely assumed we would be able to find them without a hitch.

'They must have spent the night near by, and they can't have gone far. It's only an hour or so after dawn. We'll find them.'

'But what if we don't? We'll have a full-scale revolt on our hands.'

'We'll find them,' I said confidently. Silently, I prayed that we would.

The minutes crawled by. There was nothing we could do but wait. I had mounted Achilles once more, partly to look authoritative in front of the men, but also because if things turned nasty I had to get back to the villa quickly and protect my family.

The men were nervous too. When your blood is up, you're armed and your comrades are equally angry, it is easy to be swept away by the tide of events. Now they were having a period of cold reflection. Strontius was popular among the ranks, but as much as they didn't want to see him flogged, they wanted to hear that the delegates were safe. Strontius himself looked resolute, his muscular arms crossed tightly in front of his barrel chest.

Half an hour passed. Some shuffled from one foot to the

other to keep the circulation going. Others chatted, rubbing their hands to keep warm. Most stayed grimly silent. Tuscus was going round to each officer manning the cordon round the crowd, offering words of encouragement. Now there was a cool head in a crisis. I called for the surgeon to attend to his wound. Head wounds always look worse than they are, and Tuscus's was little more than a long scratch, but it all helped to pass the time.

Almost an hour had gone by when we heard the clatter of hooves on the frosty cobbles. The sound came nearer and nearer, and the first rider was met with a disappointed sigh as we saw that he came back alone. A thought occurred to me. What if the group had split up? After all, they had met Governor Flaccus, albeit to no avail. They represented different tribes from the province. Why should they stay together? My only consolation was that the party had come on foot, so it stood to reason that they would leave on foot and my riders would easily catch up with them.

Another rider came in, and another and another. Each returned to the camp when he had covered as much ground as a man might have walked since dawn, perhaps eight miles.

The first angry mutterings were coming out, and they were only getting louder. Vocula was back at my side.

'Where can they have got to?'

I was finding it hard to keep up the confident façade. My insides were churning. I half expected the troops to ignore my deal with Strontius and start rioting, with nothing in their way except a few dozen officers.

'They'll be here, you'll see.'

And at that moment, my prayers were answered. Round the corner came two horsemen. One looked very pleased with himself, the other, a Gaul, was decidedly grumpy. Strontius bowed his head in defeat as the Gaul spoke out to the crowd.

'My friends, you have nothing to fear. We did not get what we came for, but all of us left safely last night to stay in the town.

Governor Flaccus was not able to help our families but there has been no foul play, I promise you.'

'You heard him, men. I am a man of my word. Now return to your quarters. Morning parade in half an hour, I think. Carry on, Tuscus.'

I left the prefect to it, gave a polite nod to the Gaul, and walked Achilles back towards the principia. On my way I passed the building where Flaccus was staying for the winter. The door opened, and the governor himself tottered out.

'Crisis averted, Severus?'

'You have impeccable timing, Governor,' I said scathingly.

'I wanted to come out, you understand. But I didn't think I'd be much use, with this cursed leg of mine.' The old man gave an apologetic smile.

'Actually, I wish you had been there with us, sir.'

'Do you really mean that, Severus?'

'Of course. If I couldn't stop a revolt with words, as a last resort we could have hidden behind you. Then they might have stopped out of pity. Good day, Governor.'

I had a right to be angry, as he was a cowardly old fool. He should have led by example, but instead he had quaked and shivered in his bedroom. And much good that would have done him if the men had broken out in rebellion.

A few minutes later I was still muttering darkly, but seated behind my desk. My mood was not improved by the mountain of work that the clerks had left me that morning. I started making my way through the pile, only to be interrupted.

'Sorry, sir, a message has just come for you.'

'Just add it to the pile, man.'

'The messenger said it was urgent, sir.'

'Very well, then,' I said irritably. 'Read it to me.'

I rubbed at my tired eyes, and leaned back as the clerk began to read.

'"To the Legate Severus. The man I replaced you with in Hispania has forwarded on to me the testimony of a certain Greek clerk named Melander."'

I froze. I already knew who the letter was from, and I didn't like the words 'testimony' and 'Melander' being used in the same sentence. The clerk read on, nervously.

'"This man claims that he has siphoned off one and a half million denarii from the public accounts in your name, and was offering to do the same for your successor."'

'Give that here!' I shouted. I snatched the letter from the clerk and read the rest.

You have left me no choice but to have you tried on the charge of embezzlement. I expect you to continue your duties in Germania until the new year, when I shall send a more worthy man to take your place, and you will come to Rome.
Caesar

'Shall I draft a reply, sir?' the clerk asked.

That brought me down to earth. My right arm shot out. I grabbed the pathetic creature's neck and pinned him against the wall.

'You will do nothing of the sort,' I hissed at him. 'You are going to forget all about this letter, or I will break you into pieces and feed you to the dogs.'

A ghostly pallor on his cheeks, the terrified man nodded frantically.

'Yes, sir. I'll forget it, sir.'

'What have you forgotten?' I asked, squeezing harder.

'E-everything, sir,' he croaked.

I let go and the man sank to his knees, clutching at his throat. He knelt there gasping.

'Now get out.'

XXII

As soon as the clerk was out of the room, I screamed with rage. Grabbing the nearest pile of paperwork, I hurled it at the wall. How dare Galba do this to me! After all I had done to get him his precious throne, he stabs me in the back.

Two guards rushed into my office, swords drawn.

'What's the matter, sir?'

'Nothing's the matter, get out.'

The two men looked around, at the papers strewn over the floor and at me, by now red in the face with rage.

'We thought you were in trouble, sir,' the other man said.

I laughed bitterly.

'Not that kind of trouble. Now leave me alone.'

'Yes, sir. Of course, sir.'

I could still barely believe it. What had I done to deserve this? It is an unspoken agreement that when assigned a province you make a bit of money for yourself. All right, some men went too far. That's how Cicero made his name, bringing down the corrupt Verres. But I wasn't corrupt. I didn't even know how much Melander had made for me in Hispania, or himself for that matter, until Galba told me. One and a half million wasn't much in the great scheme of things. So to charge me with embezzlement meant only one thing: Galba wanted to get rid of me.

Totavalas had been right. I had been too useful to Galba for my own good. I'd joined his conspiracy, helped with Agricola, run the entire Vindex campaign and somehow kept the Rhine legions loyal. That the letter should come today was particularly galling. My legion had been minutes away from full-scale rebellion, and would have gone over to Vitellius in an instant. And why was Galba so insistent that I should come at once? If an official like me is charged with breaking the law, normally the trial would take place at the end of his term of service. I had at the very least another two years of command left, and yet Galba had decided to replace me before my trial had even begun. The more I thought about it, the more I was afraid. And with Galba's record, it wasn't my career I was thinking of but my life.

Moments later I was out into the chilly air, calling the grooms for my horse.

'Your horse, sir? But we've only just put him in the stables.'

'Well, I want him back again. And not tomorrow, boy, now!'

Achilles and I thundered across the open ground between the fort and my villa. The poor creature must have been bewildered, as he was put straight into the stables again when I came home.

'Totavalas!' I called.

'Coming, master,' a voice replied from deep inside the building.

The young man came in from the kitchens, his hands and forearms sprayed in blood. 'Sorry, master, they needed help dispatching a wee lamb for supper.'

'Never mind about the lamb. I need you to go into the town, back to that tavern and find the landlord.'

'You mean old Bel, sir?'

'Be quiet and listen. I want you to give him a message for Fabius Valens, and it's urgent.'

'And the message, sir?'

Ah yes, the message. It had to be carefully worded; Lugubrix's network might well be fast and discreet when the messages were for him, but I didn't want everyone in Gaul knowing what I was about to do. But then if Valens had used it to contact me, it must be fairly safe.

'The message is: "Agreed. In the new year."'

'You don't mean . . .'

'Yes I do. You were right, Galba has betrayed me. I gave him my loyalty, and he flung it in my face.'

'It's always the way, master.'

'Yes, I see that now.' I stood there, thinking deeply.

'I'd best be off, sir.' Totavalas stirred me from my reverie.

'Hmm? Oh yes, you had. Where's my wife?'

'The mistress is in her chamber, master.'

As I strode purposefully towards our bedroom, I imagined the look on Salonina's face when I told her the news. The slap of my sandals on the stone floor echoed along the corridor, and passing open doors I caught slaves trying to look busy as they heard someone approaching. The bedroom door was shut. I didn't think to knock.

Salonina lay on our bed, just lowering her stola back beyond her knees. One of her attendants was with her, an old woman who had been with Salonina since her childhood. Brusquely, I told her to leave us.

'Totavalas told me the legions were rebelling,' Salonina said. 'What happened?'

'I saved Galba's neck, that's what happened. There was a rumour that we had murdered the delegation from the Gauls, and many of the men are from Gallic families. It's all sorted now. But I have some important news.'

'I have something to tell you as well.'

'It can wait,' I said shortly. 'Galba has summoned me to Rome.

He wants to prosecute me for embezzlement. So I'm taking your advice.'

'My advice?' she asked, frowning.

'If Valens is half the scoundrel I think he is, I reckon he will have started his charm offensive on Vitellius, to persuade him to declare himself emperor. Galba has betrayed me, so I shall join Vitellius.'

A grin broke over Salonina's mischievous little face, and it was as though the frost I had endured these last weeks had instantly thawed. She swung her legs over the side of the bed, and held her arms out wide to embrace me. In two quick steps, I took her in my arms and began to kiss her passionately. It was when I broke off and began to kiss her delicate neck and shoulders that she said, 'Don't you want to hear my news?'

'News?' I asked, as my hands began to unfurl the fabric of her dress. 'What news?'

'I'm pregnant.'

I broke off, confused. I looked into her eyes for some sign that she was joking. I mean, we hadn't shared a room for weeks now. She seemed to read my mind.

'Before we argued, you silly soldier.' Her slender hand stroked my cheek. 'You're going to be a father again.'

Overjoyed, I hugged her for all my worth. 'Oh Salonina, I'm so happy. How long have you known?'

'My nurse had just told me, and then you barged in, looking so angry. I wasn't sure it was the best time to share it with you.'

Keeping my hands firmly planted on her shoulders, I leaned back to look my wife in the eyes. 'It was the best time. This is the day where I take the credit I deserve, and give our children a future better than we had ever dreamed.'

It was a cold night, the worst of the winter so far. Snow was falling heavily outside and the slaves holding the torches shivered as they stood, waiting in vain for my guests to leave so that they could huddle in the warmth of the kitchens. It could have been colder, though. There were so many men dining that night that our bodies warmed up my triclinium.

Ostensibly this was a dinner party for the officers under my command, but over the last day or two I had canvassed many of them individually. They had all come through, so that now three men sat as straight as a spear on every couch to accommodate the numbers. The new senior tribune and the one new junior tribune had not yet arrived in Mogontiacum, but the other four junior tribunes were there. Fresh-faced youths who hoped to make a name for themselves in the legions, of sturdy equestrian stock. Tuscus was there, of course, and I had honoured him with a couch to himself. The other ten guests were the senior centurions of each cohort: solid, dependable men who commanded fear and respect among the ranks.

As the last course was cleared away, I called out to Totavalas, who was stewarding for the night. The usual man had come down with a fever. 'No more wine tonight, Totavalas. I want clear heads here.'

Despite the inevitable moans, the domestic slaves took away the cups and pitchers, leaving the officers, Totavalas, two torch-bearers, Salonina and myself in the room.

'If you wouldn't mind leaving us now, my dear, we have things to discuss.'

Salonina smiled, having known what was about to take place long before the dinner had begun. 'Of course.'

She rose gracefully. There was the scraping of chair legs on the flagstone as the men respectfully stood up. She flashed them a smile that must have helped to warm them on that cold night. 'Thank you, gentlemen.' We all watched her glide out of the room, and as I turned to address the men I noticed one of my tribunes watching her a little too long and hard. The man next to him caught my eye, and nudged the other's elbow. The young man's face turned a deep red, and his gaze sank to the floor.

*

'I think you will all agree that my cook surpassed himself tonight, and you have had quite enough of my wine. It is time to talk business. I have spoken with most of you in the last two days, and the reason that you are all here must be clear by now. We must discuss the future of our legion.'

The older heads nodded grimly, while the younger ones exchanged excited glances.

'As you saw on the parade ground that distasteful day, I am a loyal servant of the emperor, and I gave that loyalty because I fervently believed that Galba possessed the wisdom and strength of purpose to save Rome from the tyrant Nero. After all, he had served with distinction here on the Rhine and had governed well in Hispania. His best years were given in the service of Rome and her legions, and I hoped he would treat them well.' Here I paused, and the men looked at me intently.

'It seems my trust was misplaced. His age was taken as a sign of stability and experience, but he is ruled by a cluster of imperial favourites: younger, ambitious men who act out of petty self-interest, and not for the greater good. His march to Rome has been vicious and bloody, and he is fast acquiring a reputation as heinous as Nero's. I received news yesterday that the body of sailors raised by Nero to help defeat Vindex's rebellion petitioned Galba to be confirmed as a legion. At the Milvian Bridge, Galba had them decimated for their audacity to wish to serve the new emperor. I admit now that I was wrong to trust Galba, and to think that he might act in the legions' interest. As your legate, I believe that it is my sacred duty to defend my command from all enemies, whether they are beyond the Rhine or in our beloved city. That is why I have called you here tonight, to decide how to act in the best interests of Rome and of the Fourth Macedonica.'

Tuscus rose stiffly from his couch, and all eyes shifted to watch him. This man had devoted his life to the Fourth, and if any man alive knew what was best for the legion, it was him.

'It is no light matter to abandon your emperor, and I commend you, sir, for your loyalty. I think we all know how easy it would be to ignore our oaths to the emperor and go over to Vitellius in the hope that he will reward us. Of course the rank and file will think differently, but we are their officers. We lead by example in battle, and we should do so outside it as well. It is not for me to offer an opinion, but whatever we decide to do tonight must be decided by us and not by the common soldier, who cares for little besides his own gain.'

I applauded Tuscus loudly, and several of the men followed my lead. 'There speaks a man,' I reminded them, 'who began his life as a common soldier, but learned that honour and respect go hand in hand. Nepos, what do you think?'

Nepos was the first-spear centurion, the most senior in the legion. A stocky man, his cropped brown hair showing the first few greys, he was the natural successor for camp prefect when Tuscus retired.

'I think I speak for the first cohort when I say that we care little for the politics of all this, and only for the glory and honour of the legion. Nero may have been a tyrant in Rome, and he may have had some funny habits, let's say, but he always treated the legions well. There were regular campaigns, regular chances for each man to prove himself on the battlefield and take what he could from the enemy. I think Galba will leave us here to rot. Vitellius, now, he can promise us action.'

'But you're talking about civil war,' a voice interrupted.

There was a sharp intake of breath in the room. Very few would dare to interrupt the first-spear centurion. It was the blushing tribune who had spoken. Superior in class and nominally in rank to any centurion, but with nowhere near the respect, authority or experience; this would be an interesting contest.

'I mean,' the precocious tribune continued, 'if we desert our emperor for Vitellius, what stops him from leading the legions into Italia to fight? Do we want to return to the bloody days of Caesar and Pompey, Augustus and Antony?'

Nepos was struggling to control his contempt. 'With all due respect, sir,' and there was a definite note of aggression in the word 'sir', 'you can quote history all you like. We're living in the here and now, and here and now I say that this legion was ignored and dishonoured by Galba for defending the empire against a Gallic rebellion, and my men would relish a chance to prove themselves in battle.'

There were cries of 'hear, hear' and thumps of agreement from the centurions, while the tribune returned his gaze to the floor.

It was my turn to speak again. 'The problem, then, is how best to act in the interests of the legion without abandoning our honour. Am I right?' More nods. 'I think there is an answer. Tomorrow is the beginning of the new year, the day we renew our oath of allegiance to the emperor. What if the legion refused to swear the oath?'

A centurion from the seventh cohort spoke up. 'You mean rebel, sir?'

'No, just refuse to swear the oath. Not swearing to Vitellius either. If he wants our support, he has to ask for it. I will not allow this legion to offer itself like a whore. Does this course seem honourable to you, Tuscus?'

'Refusing the oath tomorrow does, sir. But we can't swear an oath to Vitellius unless he is acclaimed emperor, otherwise we would just be his private army.'

One of the other tribunes nervously put his hand up. I smiled at the boyish habit, and gestured that he might speak. 'What about the Twenty-Second, and the auxiliaries?'

That made them stop and consider, though I had already thought about the problem long and hard over the last few days.

'We must take the lead, and hope the others will follow. I don't want anyone else hearing of what we plan to do and pre-empting us, or worse, betraying us. Besides, the Twenty-Second have no more love for the emperor than we do. Why should they not follow?'

'And the auxiliaries?' the tribune asked.

Another centurion answered. 'They don't care about politics, just plunder. Why should they oppose us?' There was a murmur of agreement.

'So, we are agreed about what must be done tomorrow?' I asked.

Silence.

'There are no objections?' Some shaking of heads. 'Excellent, then all that remains is method. As the camp prefect says, we the officers must show leadership, but we must also reflect the popular will of the legion. As a recent appointment of Galba's, it is hardly my place to rabble-rouse and convince the legion to mutiny.'

'Clean hands, eh?' I heard one centurion mutter to his neighbour.

'You, Sertorius. Stand up!'

'Me, sir?'

'Yes, you. Stand up.'

I walked slowly over to the man, stretching the awkward silence.

'Do you hope to be promoted one day, Sertorius?'

'One day, sir.'

'Well, that day isn't going to come if you suggest that your legate has no interest in defending the interests of his legion. Galba chose me to command this legion, and what sort of hypocrite do you think I would be if I denounced him just a few months into my command?' I turned to look at the rest of my officers. 'You all know that a legate cannot lead from the front rank. This is why you are all here at my villa. This is my command, but come the swearing of the oath it is you who must lead from the front.'

Turning back to face the unlucky man, I said, quietly: 'I would like an apology, Sertorius. An apology for your insolence and insubordination.'

Those hard grey eyes bored into mine, but my resolve was firm.

'And I would like it now.' My words were as chilled as the land beneath the snow. The centurion knew he had overstepped the mark, and refusal would have meant a court-martial. He clenched his jaw for a moment, and then said, 'I apologize, sir, for my conduct just now.'

'Good,' I said cheerfully, and patted the man on the shoulder, telling him to resume his seat. 'There should be no shortage of ambitious men in your cohorts,' I said to the rest of the centurions. 'Each of you find the more discreet of them, and sound them out before tomorrow. This is where you prove that you are the best officers in the best legion on the Rhine.'

As one, they all sprang to attention and saluted me. I enjoyed the moment, briefly, until I spotted my son Aulus hiding behind my study door. Our eyes met, and he disappeared in an instant.

'The plan is settled, then. I am sure you have much to attend to back in camp.' They laughed gently. 'Totavalas will show you the way out. Until tomorrow.'

Once they had left, I told Totavalas to wake me an hour after dawn, then I made my way to Aulus's room. I gave his door a gentle knock.

'Aulus?'

He was hiding beneath the covers, and completely still.

'I know you're awake. I'm not angry with you, I promise.'

'I didn't mean to listen, Father,' a voice said from the bundle on the bed. 'I was going to the kitchens for some fruit when—'

'It doesn't matter now,' I said, sitting on the corner of the bed. Playfully, I took hold of his bedding and began to slowly tug it. He pulled back.

'How much did you hear?'

The covers came down, and a worried face appeared. 'You're going to break your oath to the emperor.'

'It isn't that simple, Aulus.'

'But you are going to break it, aren't you?'

'Technically, we're just not going to swear a new one,' I began, but then I realized I was saying that more to reassure myself than my son. 'What have I taught you about *pietas*?'

'Like Aeneas?'

'Yes, like Aeneas.'

'To honour and serve the gods, your family and your city. Like Troy, or for us, Rome.'

'Well done. These days, we confuse the emperor and the city. Now I have taught you always to be a true and loyal servant of the emperor. Right?'

'Right, Father.'

'But what if the emperor does not serve the city?'

He thought carefully. 'He isn't being a good emperor?'

'And that is why I helped the emperor to replace Nero, for the good of Rome. But now, the emperor wants me out of the way, because he doesn't like to be reminded that he needed help to become an emperor. He broke his promise to me. Is that the kind of emperor you want to serve?'

'No, Father. So will this other man, Vitellius, will he be a good emperor?'

Not if Valens has his way, I thought. 'I hope so. Now it's time for you to go to sleep. Good night, Aulus.' I kissed him on the forehead, and got up to leave.

I had almost closed the door when Aulus called out: 'Does Mother know what you're going to do tomorrow?'

I chuckled at the irony. I hadn't the heart to tell him that it was all her idea in the first place.

XXIII

The cock crowed to signal the dawn of the new year, and I was awake to hear him. I'd been far too nervous to sleep that night. I had sounded confident in front of my officers, but then I have always had something of a talent for acting. Of course, I realize that actors are the lowest of the low socially, but if you want to make it in politics, go to the theatre now and then. You'll be surprised how much you can learn.

There were some hours left until the swearing of the oath. No symbolic renewal of our loyalty as the sun rose on another year for us. This was the army: we leave such poetic nonsense to the courtiers. We are practical people, and take the oath when it fits in with the busy lives we lead, in other words at midday. That left several hours to wait, and wait. Salonina stirred; now that she was finally awake, I could ease myself out of our embrace. I sat on the side of the bed and contemplated the day ahead. A warm hand slid up my back and rested on my arm. Salonina kissed me on the neck, then rested her chin on my shoulder.

'What are you thinking?' she asked.

'I'm thinking you're going to get me into a lot of trouble one of these days.'

'You're not nervous, are you?'

'Nervous? I'm about to preside over a mutiny, for Hades' sake. I've a right to be nervous, haven't I?' I said irritably.

Her other arm slipped over my chest so that she could reach round into a hug.

'But haven't you been telling me that everything's going perfectly?'

'So far, yes. But once the mutiny has begun, who knows what could happen?'

'You're their legate. Command them.'

'These aren't schoolboys, Salonina. It's thousands of greedy, dangerous men who have just renounced their emperor. Somehow I don't think a snap of my fingers would bring them to heel.'

She shrank back from the tone in my voice.

'You're right, my love, I wasn't thinking. Of course you should be a little afraid.'

I batted her hands away. 'I'm not afraid. It's just not as simple as you make out.' A part of me wondered whether she was just trying to goad me into having more courage. I wouldn't have put it past her.

'Totavalas!' I called.

The slave came hurrying in, and I stood up so that he could dress me. Salonina languished on the bed, looking magnificent. She was right; there were worse ways to relieve my tension, but now was not the time. I was needed in camp. As the young Hibernian was finishing with the buckles on my greaves, I reminded my wife: 'Promise me you'll have the horses ready for you and Aulus if things turn ugly in camp.'

'But they won't . . .' she began.

'Where do you go if they do?'

'We ride for home on the post-horses.'

'You have my seal?'

She rolled her eyes. 'Yes,' she said. 'It's on my dressing table.'

'It's only because I care, darling.'

'But not enough to spend the morning with me, obviously.'

I was beginning to get used again to her girlish ways. I had to keep reminding myself that I had spent years of our marriage on duty, and had missed her as she grew up. Living alone had prolonged her self-centredness. There had been Aulus to care for, but still she had a feline grace and cunning, and the independence that came with it. Not that I would ever have been happy with a thick but faithful old hound for a wife. Life is too short.

'I can give you a kiss goodbye if you like,' I said, playing the game.

'I suppose that will have to do.' She raised herself on to her knees, reached for me, and then I gave her a long, ardent kiss.

The warmth in my heart could have melted the snow that covered my walk to the camp. For all her faults, I did love my wife dearly. I could not have done what I was about to do if she had not been behind me all the way. But looking back on that day, seated here at my desk, friendless and alone, I wonder if it would not have been better if she had simply played the role of a demure and dutiful wife. We might have been spared what was to come.

The guards on duty told me to halt, and asked for the password.

'Aurora,' I called up. The goddess of dawn. Tuscus must have a poetic streak in him somewhere, I thought.

The men were filing back to their billets after morning parade as I walked through the camp. Those nearest the square were already huddled around the braziers, vying for space near the warmth. Their breath wisped up into disparate trails on that freezing morning, but I had a little longer to wait before I could retreat to the warmth of my office. I saw one of the senior centurions on the corner of the parade ground, talking quietly to two legionaries. He spotted me, smiled, and gently nodded. It was beginning.

I made my way around the camp, searching for each centurion who had been a guest the night before. I needed to know how they were doing in sounding out the picked men who would lead the way in the next few hours. Some had not yet had a chance for a private word with them, others had been more successful. Several could already promise me the whole-hearted support of their centuries. One or two had even approached men from the wider cohort. I was nervous about that; if they spoke to the wrong men then the secret would be out. But these were the first-rank centurions, they commanded respect by their very bearing, and they knew their men. Even Sertorius, when I chanced upon him in the mess, was enthusiastic. He had been surly last night, but you can't please everyone. He was one of those officers who resent being junior to younger men, and as I had not even reached the age of thirty yet, I was a particular affront to him. But young or old, this was too good an opportunity for an ambitious man to turn down, and Sertorius had done his bit.

There were only two people left to see. The men threw me smart salutes as I strode towards the meeting place. Some were almost grinning in anticipation, and there was an air of fevered excitement. The stink of horseflesh got stronger and stronger as I neared my last port of call. A groom saw me coming and held open the door for me. Stepping over the dollops of muck and straw, I made my way to Achilles' stall. Nepos and Tuscus were waiting for me.

'Leave us, boy,' Tuscus said to the young groom. 'We are not to be disturbed, you hear?'

'Yes, Prefect.'

The three of us waited in silence as the groom scuttled off. I took a brush from a shelf in the stall and started to give Achilles a good rub-down.

'Things look encouraging, sir,' Nepos began.

'Very encouraging,' Tuscus echoed.

'All the right men have been spoken to. The word is spreading,' Nepos continued. 'No problems at our end. Have you considered, sir, how the governor is going to react to this?'

'Flaccus? He doesn't command any legion, and he's ill at the moment anyway. He won't get involved. But I suppose it would be no bad thing to double the guard on his quarters. Was there anything else?' I asked.

The two men exchanged nervous glances.

'What?'

'You haven't heard, then?' Tuscus said. His tone made it a statement rather than a question.

'Well, obviously I haven't heard, or I wouldn't be asking!'

'The two new tribunes are expected to arrive at any moment, hand-picked by the emperor, probably. They could ruin everything.' Tuscus left the news hanging. 'It's not too late to call the whole thing off, sir.'

I casually resumed brushing Achilles' chestnut coat in long, straight sweeps along his back.

'Or we could delay them until after the ceremony, sir?' Nepos suggested.

'I don't expect any trouble from either of them, Nepos.'

'Sir?'

'The junior tribune will hardly be in a position to argue when he finds out what's going to happen.'

'Surely your second-in-command will have something to say though, sir?' Nepos enquired.

I chuckled. 'I'm sure he will.'

My talk with Tuscus and Nepos had calmed me down a bit. Everything that could be done had been done, and there was little left to do but pray for success. I was worried about Flaccus though; he was a well-meaning, doddering old fool, but who knows what the legion might do now that their officers had been stirring them into rebellion? Unleashed from their oath of loyalty to the emperor, what was to stop them from running riot? Only the officers would be able to keep them at heel, the ones who were encouraging the rebellion in the first place. That was why I had made sure that Salonina and Aulus had horses at the ready. Apart from the treasury, my home was the nearest place that had any valuables. Yes, I commanded the Macedonica, but who's to say that would stop the Twenty-Second or the auxiliaries from Germania, or even my own men? After all, I had only been in command a few months. Was that long enough to instil a sense of loyalty and respect?

The minutes shuffled by. An hour passed, then another. Midday was fast approaching and my insides were beginning to squirm. I didn't dare have any breakfast that day for fear of bringing it straight back up. Instead I sat in my office, quietly shivering. At long last, the clatter of hooves announced new arrivals to the camp.

The muted sounds of greeting and introductions echoed along the corridor and into my office: muffled voices, the stamping of feet to get the blood flowing again, one of the clerks directing the newcomers towards me. There was a knock.

A pale face, surrounded by a shock of blond hair, appeared round the door.

'Legate Severus?'

'You must be Tribune Curtius. Come in out of the cold.'

He held the door open for the man behind him. Grinning, Quintus stepped in and saluted.

'Tribune Vindex reporting for duty, sir.'

'At ease, both of you,' I said. 'No need to stand on ceremony here. I'll keep this brief; it's only half an hour or so until the legion takes the oath of allegiance. First of all, welcome, both of you, to the Fourth Macedonica. I have only been in command a few months myself, but the men and officers alike are used to the high turnover of senior officers and they adapt quickly. You will have to do the same. The camp prefect, a dependable man, Gaius Tuscus, will tell you your duties, have you shown to your quarters and generally help you settle in. I like to think that I am an approachable commander, so feel free to knock on my door at any time. Within reason of course.'

Curtius gave a nervous smile.

'And now if you don't mind, Curtius, I'd like to have a word with my second in command. If you go into the corridor, the door opposite is Prefect Tuscus's. He will sort you out.'

'Of course, sir. Thank you, sir.'

Once the door had closed, I got up and gave Quintus a great bear hug.

'It's been too long, Quintus.'

'It has. I leave you alone for just a few months, and now you're commanding a legion.'

'You're not doing so badly yourself. Your first military posting and you're the senior tribune in one of the Rhine legions. You must have friends in high places.'

'Yes, Lugubrix got your message to me after I relinquished Father's province to one of Galba's men, Blaesus.'

'And how are the rest of your family?'

The smile disappeared from Quintus's face. 'Still in mourning. My two older brothers died very young, Sextus is dead, which leaves just my two sisters and Mother.'

'So you're head of the family now?' I asked.

'For what that's worth. I mean, isn't the name Vindex going to look a bit suspicious to the men?'

'Only a little,' I reassured him. 'You can say he was a distant relation if you like. You should see how many Severi there are in Rome, and none of them closer to me than cousin. I barely know any of them.'

Suddenly a shrill series of blasts announced that it was time for the oath.

'Gods, already?' I murmured. 'Look, there isn't time to explain, but something big is going to take place, Quintus. Whatever happens, keep close to me. Understand?'

Quintus looked puzzled. 'All right, but why can't you tell me what's going on?'

'Not now. But it'll be just like old times,' I said, with a hint of a grin. 'Come on, we should take our places for the oath.'

One of the grooms was waiting for me with Achilles. I hauled myself into the saddle, then led Quintus along the cobbled path towards the parade ground. The Fourth were falling in. Officers were taking up their positions in front of their men. The junior tribunes stood around an old podium that had been brought out for the occasion. I told Quintus to join them, and sought out Tuscus.

'Is that the new senior tribune?' Tuscus asked, glancing at Quintus.

'It is. He's an old friend, and won't be any trouble.'

'Good.' The prefect looked worried, and rightly so. Of the two of us, he had never betrayed his emperor. In a few short minutes, I thought to myself, we would all be rebels. Then the man turned pale, and I don't mean he looked a bit cold, but downright terrified. I turned to see what had scared him. Hordeonius Flaccus had just rounded the corner.

Damn the man. Why did he have to recover, and why did he feel the need to involve himself in army affairs? He and half a dozen guards were heading straight for the podium.

'He's only going to administer the bloody oath, isn't he?' Tuscus said incredulously. 'We could call it off?' He looked at me, almost pleading.

I looked sharply at him. 'Call it off? Never. I'd look just as much a ditherer as Flaccus, or Rufus before him. We've committed ourselves now. Get Nepos, and see to it that a detachment of reliable men surrounds the podium if there's any sign of trouble. You've seen how fractious the men can be. I don't want any harm to come to the old man. It's Galba we're rejecting, not Flaccus.'

There was an excited murmur from the men as they saw Flaccus hobble up the steps and clamber on to the podium. As his guards took their places, the murmur became louder and crosser. The chief augur led a small body of men who carried the two statues of Galba, which stood as proxy for the emperor when the oath was taken. Both statues were conspicuously new, and neither showed the comical nose or the sagging jowls of the emperor, but rather a wise and dignified face. The sculptor had clearly been under strict orders to present an idealistic image of Galba, and had done a good job, but these statues now became the focal point of the legion's resentment and anger.

The noise would not die down, even when Flaccus stamped his staff (or rather his walking stick) on to the wooden boards beneath him.

'The Fourth Macedonica will be silent before they swear the oath,' he bawled shrilly. We officers took up our positions as the augur joined Flaccus on the stage to prompt the governor if he forgot the oath's words. Tuscus was urgently whispering to Nepos, passing on my instructions.

Flaccus began: 'The gods will observe on this auspicious day that we here renew our oath of loyalty and obedience to the empire and our emperor, Servius Sulpicius Galba Caesar. May he protect Rome from all her enemies and bring good fortune and prosperity to all his people.'

Then the old man turned to Nepos and his men, for the oath was sworn one cohort at a time.

'Men of the first cohort, will you give your sacred pledge of loyalty and obedience to the emperor? To defend his empire, to fight all who oppose him, and to lay down your lives for him?'

There was a moment's uncertainty, as though each and

every man under Nepos's command had only just realized the enormity of what they were about to do. Nepos took a pace forward.

'No!' he shouted. Flaccus and the augur looked stunned.

'We will not lay down our lives for an emperor who has treated his legions so shamefully. The Fourth has always acted with honour and loyalty to the empire. Did we not defeat the Gauls in Nero's name? We placed ourselves at the disposal of the Senate and People of Rome when we heard of Nero's death. Now it seems that they were wrong to choose Galba, a man who has ignored our loyalty, rewarded our enemies, and treated the volunteers at the Milvian Bridge without shame or mercy. We of the first cohort demand that the Senate and People of Rome choose again. Are you with me, Macedonica?'

It seemed as though the entire world roared its approval of Nepos's words, and hundreds of men charged straight for the podium. Flaccus stood there, rooted to the spot. Even from ten yards away I could see his weak leg beginning to buckle. The sea of red began to part either side of the podium. They were making for the statues of Galba. The eighth cohort was nearest, and clearly word of my plans had not reached many of their number. Four brave, loyal centurions reached the statues, drew their swords and prepared to defend their emperor. That stopped the first eager mutineers in their tracks. Nepos took the opportunity to climb the podium with some picked men, then forced Flaccus to his knees. The centurion must have realized that the only way to keep Flaccus safe was to arrest him, rather than appear as the governor's defender, like the brave but condemned officers protecting the cold marble likenesses a few feet below him.

Quintus looked dazed. I shouted at him to grab my hand, and heaved him up so that he sat behind me in the saddle. 'Did you plan this?' he shouted over the noise.

'Later,' I shouted back. I tried to force Achilles through the crowd to reach Nepos. Thankfully the men had no intention of attacking me, but just swarmed round my frightened horse as they charged at the statues. I saw the first blow. One legionary had used his shield to batter a centurion to the ground, and another officer retaliated. There was a bellow of rage as he killed one man and wounded another, and he was swiftly knocked out by a blow to the head. The other two centurions were disarmed and became prisoners of the mob. Galba's two statues, robbed of their defenders, were picked up by eager men and smashed against the ground. There was a huge cheer as one of Galba's heads broke clean off and rolled away. Controlling the men was out of the question, but I heard some men shouting that they should join the Twenty-Second, and the call was taken up by the whole legion.

The heaving mass of men began to change direction, awkwardly manoeuvring to head towards the far end of camp, where no doubt Vocula had his men on parade, waiting for Flaccus to oversee Primigenia's swearing of the oath. Yells of victory and delight filled the air, but the square slowly began to empty. Within five minutes, the only men left were Quintus and me, Nepos and his men, Flaccus and Tuscus. There were two corpses: the legionary and the augur, who had panicked and tried to escape, fallen off the podium and broken his neck.

Tuscus spat to ward off evil. 'That doesn't bode well.'

Nepos spoke to me from up on the platform. 'What now, sir?'

'The men know to come back here once Primigenia have joined them?'

'Yes, sir. They won't leave camp. All the officers are with them. Perhaps I should get over there and try to restore some order?'

'I'll lend you Achilles so you stand out better.'

The centurion looked thrilled. 'Thank you, sir.'

'Don't get used to it,' I joked.

Flaccus found his voice. 'Do you know what you've done, man? You've incited the legions to rebel. You're starting a civil war!'

'Galba started it, not me,' I replied. Quintus and I got down to the ground, while Nepos used the podium as a mounting block, and rode away towards Primigenia.

'Besides,' I continued, 'if I hadn't taken control, the legion would have rebelled anyway, after the other legions on the Rhine did, but it would have been bloody. I saved your life, Governor, and the lives of the centurions who were loyal to Galba.'

'You don't expect me to congratulate you, do you?' Flaccus asked.

'I expect you to go back into Mogontiacum, Governor, and to stay there. Galba may have appointed you, and you are still nominally in command of this province. The new emperor will want your loyalty.'

'New emperor? Who?'

'That is for the Senate and People of Rome to decide.'

'You mean for you to decide,' Flaccus sneered.

I allowed myself a small smile. 'Perhaps.'

XXIV

All of a sudden there came a cry of triumph from the other side of the camp. We heard the sound of two legions screaming with one voice. I was uneasy. Of course it was a momentous event, the legions casting aside their loyalty to their emperor, but it was hardly something to celebrate. Why the sounds of victory? My head was teeming with questions, but there was no one to ask. Each man there was as clueless as the next. The first hint of what was to come was the trail of smoke that rose into the sky.

'Sweet Jupiter,' Quintus said.

None of us uttered a word. We just stood there, the implications beginning to sink in.

'See what you've done,' wailed Flaccus. 'The men are rebelling!'

'Tuscus, I thought you told me everything was under control?'

'It was. All the right people knew what had to be done. I can't understand it.'

'Maybe you have some men who think about themselves first and the legion second,' suggested Quintus.

'With respect, sir, Nepos and I know the legion better than any men living. We hand-picked every man.'

'For all our sakes, Tuscus, I hope you're right.'

The column of smoke grew thicker and darker, as if to spite Tuscus's words.

There was nothing we could do until Nepos returned and told us what was happening. The noise of thousands of men – the slap of sandals underfoot, their jubilant shouts – and the smell of burning came nearer and nearer. It was as if time itself had slowed to watch what was happening, and well it might: the smoke enveloped an entire building, which was all ablaze. It was the principia of the Twenty-Second, it had to be. No other building could create such an inferno. In the distance we could see a solitary horseman galloping towards us, down the road that led from Primigenia's side of the fort.

Nepos was wounded, blood seeping from a deep gash in his thigh.

'They've looted Primigenia's treasury, burned the building, and now they're coming this way,' he panted.

There was no time to think, just to do.

'How many men haven't joined the madness?' I asked.

'Two hundred, maybe more.'

Nowhere near enough to contain the riot.

'Then send riders to all the auxiliary troops near by, and have them march here immediately. Tuscus, get over to the forge. Take all the men you need, and see if you can jam the gates, try to stop this chaos from spreading and keep the men in the camp until help arrives.'

'They're coming here next, sir,' Nepos interrupted.

I whipped round. 'For our treasury?'

The centurion nodded curtly.

'Then that's where we will have to make a stand. Get as many men together as you can, and bring them to the principia. You have three minutes, Nepos. Any more and it will be too late. And Nepos!'

'Sir?'

'Send one man to my family, and tell them to ride to safety. The rest of you,' I called to the men on the square, 'will follow me.'

'Madman!' Flaccus screamed. 'You'll kill us all.'

'Shut him up, somebody.'

One of the guards hit him over the head with his sword hilt. The old man tumbled into a waiting pair of arms. That wasn't quite how I'd meant it to happen, but I was glad to be rid of Flaccus's wailing. We ran to the principia, and sent the unconscious governor down the passage and into the treasury itself. There was no safer place in the entire camp. The guards below were brought up into the cold winter air; they would be more use with us outside than alone in the darkness once the looters broke through.

'All of you, go into the principia, stables, anywhere near by and bring things to barricade the roadway. We'll need two barricades at least twenty paces wide, so get moving.' Tables, desks, chairs, anything and everything was used to throw up two barricades ten paces either side of the doorway to the principia. Quintus, pale but determined, was marshalling the legionaries and oversaw the building of the eastward barricade; I took the westward. Nepos, on foot, arrived at the head of perhaps sixty men. They scrambled over Quintus's barricade and automatically split into two groups; one stayed put and the other joined my men.

Nepos looked around. 'Where's the governor?'

'In the treasury. Have you seen Tuscus?'

'I last saw him and a few men by the main gate, driving in bolts to keep the doors shut.'

Good man, I thought. 'Let's hope he can close all of them in time.'

'He should do, though most of the rioters were heading this way, not into the town.'

'Lucky us.'

Nepos smiled briefly. 'Orders, sir?'

'Take command of the east barricade, no killing if you can help it. Quintus and I will hold this flank.'

'Quintus, sir?'

'Tribune Vindex.'

'Good luck then, sir.'

'Go on, man, they could be on us any minute.'

'Legate!' a voice shouted.

'What?'

There was no need to ask what. The noise had been getting louder and louder, and now they were upon us, close enough to hear individual shouts among the sea of voices. I clambered over our makeshift defences to look down on my men. The road was a heaving mass of silver and red, hemmed in by those pushing from behind and by the buildings on either side. I can still remember the noise of hundreds of armoured men in front of us, jostling each other, making a sound like hailstones striking your helmet.

'Listen to me,' I shouted. The first few ranks looked up at me but everyone else was too busy talking to their neighbour.

'By Jupiter, you have listened to me before, and now you will listen to me again!'

The crowd began to quiet.

'Decimus, why do you stand armed before your legate, and you, Pollux, is that gold in your hand, gold stolen from your sister legion?' Silently, I thanked the gods that I had made an effort to learn the names of my men. The men I singled out looked ashamed, and I could see some of that shame spreading throughout the crowd.

'Are we going to bow our heads like children when all that stands between us and the gold is a few men and a pile of wood?'

There could only have been one man who had spoken thus. Strontius, fully recovered from his lashing, dominated those around him.

'They hold back, Strontius, because they still have their sense of loyalty to the empire.'

The big man laughed, as did his friends and supporters in the crowd.

'Loyalty! We are poor, hungry and dangerous, and you are in the way.' He snatched a spear from a man next to him and took aim.

'Throw that spear, Legionary Strontius, and every man in this camp will be crucified.'

That checked his arm. 'Who by?' he sneered.

'By the German auxiliaries who are marching here as we speak, all fifteen thousand of them, along with the rest of the Rhine legions. But if you listen to me, I promise you that every man here will live, and get richer too.'

There were a few shouts of 'How?' from the crowd, and not wanting to give Strontius the dignity of being their spokesman, I addressed them all.

'I still say you are loyal to the empire, and to Rome. Those of you from Primigenia, you won't have heard our brave first-spear centurion Nepos refusing to renew his oath. He has nothing but respect for his men and the empire, and yet he chose not to take his oath to Galba. Galba is old, weak and cruel, a man not fit to be emperor. Macedonica have taken an oath to the Senate and People of Rome, and it is men like Strontius who would make you outlaws, hunted wherever you go. Aulus Vitellius, the man who spared one of your own, is considering whether to challenge Galba's authority. He is a good and generous man; think how generous he would be to the men who made him emperor.'

I left that thought hanging in the air. Most nodded their agreement. Strontius spat on the ground. 'Bollocks. Let's take the gold and run.'

There were many who agreed with him. Too many. There was only one thing I could do to salvage the situation.

'You risk condemning to death innocent men who would rather follow Vitellius than be nailed to a cross. Fight me, Strontius. It's what you want, to even your score with me. Kill me in open combat, and there will be one less man to uphold the barricades. And if I kill you, every other man will live.'

'Now?' he asked.

'Now.'

'Where?'

'In the parade square, for all to see.'

'Then let's get this over with.'

An excited chatter broke out, and thinking of the other barricade and the crowd facing it I called out: 'Spread the word, tell everyone to gather at the parade square.'

I made my precarious way back into the only safe ground in the entire camp. Quintus could hardly decide what to ask first. Nepos was hurrying over.

'Why a duel, Caecina?' my friend asked.

'Strontius and his friends outnumber us. I reckon the idea of crucifixion scared the rest of them, but there were too many who think the way Strontius does to convince them with mere words. If I kill Strontius, what have they lost? A leader, but they keep their lives, rank, pay, everything, and the chance to fight for Vitellius.'

'But why did this man Strontius agree? He could have killed you there and then.'

'I had him whipped for doubting my word.'

'He's also one of the best swordsmen in the legion,' Nepos interrupted, 'and can't resist an audience.'

'And if I die, at least I've given Tuscus time to jam all the gates, and the auxiliaries get closer with every minute we waste here.'

I raised my voice so that everyone between the barricades could hear me. 'Thank you, all of you, for your loyalty today. I am sorry for taking such a risk with your lives. If I die, hopefully

I can buy you some time, and if you hold out long enough the Germans will relieve you. I leave you under the command of Tribune Vindex and Centurion Nepos, but I would have fought with you to the end.'

They did not cheer me. I did not expect them to. They knew how good Strontius was, and I was an unknown quantity as a swordsman. The odds were not good. One of them reported that the men on the eastward side were backing off. The message must have got through and they were heading for the square like everyone else.

'Nepos, do you have the keys to the treasury?'

'Yes, sir,' he said. 'Governor Flaccus shouldn't have come round yet, though.'

'Never mind him. Beneath the legion's eagle is a pair of swords. Would you bring them to me?'

'The ones that are part of the tribute, sir?'

'Yes. I know it's irregular, but humour me this once. Quick as you can, please, I don't want Strontius whipping the men into a frenzy by telling them I've backed out.'

Red in the face after all the steps, Nepos was back promptly. He held the swords reverently, befitting an offering to the legion's gods. Quintus's eyes widened as he recognized the simple hilts and intricate patterns on the blades. He too remembered the good man who had carried the pair of them into battle against this very legion.

'May the gods go with you,' Nepos said, proffering me a hilt.

The men parted in front of me as I strode towards the square. Some tapped their neighbour on the shoulder and pointed, others just watched, silently. The sheer number of them meant that the crowd easily spilled on to the square itself. By the time I came up to Strontius, I was already near the very centre of the space. The last man stepped aside, and there was a circle of clear ground not ten paces across, where one of us would die.

Strontius was confused to see Bormo's sword in my hand.

'Not old enough to use a proper sword?' he mocked.

'This sword was dedicated to the eagle of our legion. I fight for the legion, Strontius. You fight for yourself.'

'Enough talk,' he said, and swung his blade at me.

He nearly took me off guard, but I raised the Celtic sword into a block just in time. There was a clang as iron met iron, and the force of his blow sent tremors down my arm. The first shouts of encouragement from Strontius's friends were lost on me; all I could think about was where that sword would fall next. He attacked again, scything down in a killer blow directed at my head. Unthinkingly I drew Bormo's sword up into the parry, and his weapon slid down and bit into my knuckles.

The pain seared like a hot iron, and for a moment I was back in that terrible room in Vienne, Albanos leering at me, knife in hand. Strontius was too much of a showman not to make the most of the opportunity. He took a few steps back and acknowledged the applause of his supporters. He was toying with me, playing to the crowd.

'You're finished, boy. Hades is waiting for you,' he taunted.

Trying to ignore the pain, I was determined to make the fight less one-sided. He was a big man, but then so was I. I launched a flurry of attacks, scything, sweeping, thrusting at my enemy. My strength surprised him, but he lacked the subtlety to pierce my guard in a counter-attack. The huge man would just beat me into submission, like he had countless others. With every hammer blow I parried I could feel my strength ebbing away, and the blood from my hand made my grip uncertain. Already I could feel the sword begin to slip and slide as I countered each blow.

I am bigger than most men, but strength alone wasn't going to defeat Strontius, so I turned to the one advantage I had left. Speed. My paranoid mother had paid for an old drill-master to train me before I left for my posting in Britannia. I have an idea that had he been watching me that day, the grim bastard might just have managed a smile. I had hoped to weary Strontius with my own strength before letting my footwork dictate the duel. We circled round slowly, and I stole a moment to wipe my bloodied hand on my tunic. Strontius saw this and lunged wildly. I calmly side-stepped so that he struck nothing more than air, then I tried to counter but he saw that he had overreached himself. He dropped to the floor, my blade catching him on the helmet.

I smiled. Strontius had realized why I had chosen my sword. The gladius is an instrument of death, perfect for the melee of battle. But this was a duel, and my Celtic blade was not just a symbol of my devotion to the legion, it also had a longer reach. To land a blow on me, he had to come within the range of my sword, so now it was his turn to circle me slowly, watching for a weakness. My confidence returning, I made a feint at his stomach, let his sword drive mine to the side in the inevitable parry, only for me to follow into a backswing that chopped into Strontius's leg.

The big man bellowed like an ox, but I had no time to savour the moment. Suddenly his left hand smashed into my nose. There was a sickening crack, and blood streamed down my face. Strontius swung again, this time not at my body but at my sword. The force of the blow sent it spinning from my hand and into the watching crowd. I was defenceless, and the men watching saw victory was close at hand. I saw a familiar smile in among the hundreds of faces, and froze for a moment, understanding. Strontius slowly advanced, the crowd held their breath. Madly I dived to the ground, somehow falling to a roll, only to find myself on my back at the edge of the open ring.

No one spoke. They knew what was coming. Strontius stood over me, both hands on the hilt for the killer blow.

'You didn't really think you could beat me, did you?'

Someone pressed something into my flailing hand. Strontius

raised his gladius for the kill. Using the last of my strength, I drove my sword through my enemy's armour and deep into his guts. Strontius's eyes opened wide in shock. A thin stream of blood trickled from the corner of his mouth. His legs gave way, and like a felled tree he crashed to the ground.

XXV

'You're a lucky son of a bitch, aren't you?' Valens said.

I could hardly disagree. Quintus's timing had been perfect. He had followed me into the crowd, hiding the spare sword under his cloak. When Strontius had disarmed me, I flung myself towards where the original sword had landed so that my friend could give me an identical one, with no suspicion of foul play. Thinking back, if I had disarmed Strontius, would I have allowed him to take another sword? Probably not – there was too much at stake – but Quintus's quick thinking gave the illusion that I had miraculously picked up my own weapon.

The men, initially stunned, suddenly picked me up and carried me around in triumph. Simple soldiers like to know their leaders have something special about them, and pride in their commanders helps them to take pride in themselves. Some were happy to see me kill Strontius that day. Maybe my words about Vitellius's future generosity had sunk in at last.

I can still remember the look of surprise on old Tuscus's face when he saw me enthroned on the shoulders of men from Macedonica and Primigenia. He had no idea what was going on. It took us hours to remove the damn bolts that had fixed the gates in place. Meanwhile there was the awkward process of refilling Primigenia's ransacked treasury. Vocula had been taken prisoner by his own men, and was very shaken when we found him tied up in the officers' mess.

'Severus, what the Hades is going on?' he spluttered, once his gag had been removed.

'I'm sorry, I couldn't risk telling you. We've refused to re-new our oath to Galba, and are at the service of the Senate and People of Rome,' I explained, taking my bloodied sword to the ropes that bound him.

He struggled upright and stood awkwardly, trying to coax some feeling back into his limbs. He looked at me. 'You're wounded?'

Now that the immediate crisis was over, I could feel the pain returning, burning like fire. I called for a surgeon, and told Vocula exactly what had happened. Once I had finished, he initially said nothing.

'I suppose we should be grateful we have a command left. If we hadn't, you would be the first to be crucified. You know, I thought you were different. You could have been an outstanding officer, for Rome and the empire. But you're as bad as Valens. I'll say one thing for Nero: if he were still around, ambitious bastards like you wouldn't dare to lift a finger, let alone a sword against him.'

He made as if to leave, but I held out my arm to stop him.

'I lost my finger and sacrificed more for this emperor, only for him to fling my loyalty back in my face. Do not mention Valens and me in the same breath. Galba has brought this on himself, from the very day he ignored those who kept him on his throne. I could have made Rufus emperor in an instant, but I thought Galba was the best man to rule the empire. My conscience is clear.'

Vocula said nothing, and stormed out of the room.

★

It was only once the auxiliaries had arrived, and were overseeing men from the Primigenia as they handed back what they had taken from the now smouldering principia, and while our poor excuse for a surgeon looked at my hand, that I knew it was safe to make sure my family were all right. Irritably dismissing the surgeon, I had Achilles brought to me, and rode out of the one gate we had managed to prise open. Riding hard, I could just make out armed men on the walls. A spasm of fear gripped my heart. Had some of the rioters thought to attack my home and plunder it? Had my family got out in time? By the gods, if they hadn't I would decimate the legion there and then.

Achilles' hooves pounded the frosty turf, and as I came nearer and nearer I saw the men more clearly. Where were the red tunics of the legionaries? All I could see was the occasional glint of the winter sun on metal. Someone must have recognized me or the horse, because the large oak doors swung slowly open as I approached. Looking up at the men on the walls, I saw they were armed with nothing more than kitchen knives.

'What in Jupiter's name is going on here?' I bellowed.

Then my eyes caught sight of a small, wiry man wearing the armour of a legate. What would a legate be doing in my house?

'Are you all right, master?' a young Celtic voice called down from the walls.

'Totavalas?' I said incredulously.

Behind me, the door to the villa itself opened.

'Aulus?'

Salonina stood there, a small dagger in her hand. She dropped it and ran towards me, her chestnut hair streaming behind her. I barely had time to get out of the saddle before we were wrapped in each other's arms.

Salonina, Aulus and I were seated at our kitchen table. As a special honour, Totavalas sat with us.

'Why didn't you ride south as I told you?' I asked my wife.

She reached over the table and clasped my hand tightly. 'We have spent too long apart, my love, and now that we're together again, I wasn't going to leave you in danger while we rode to safety.'

'When the mistress said that she was going to stay put,' Totavalas interrupted, 'I thought it best to try and make this place defendable. The guards had run off to camp when they heard the trouble, you see, and that left just me and the other slaves. So we made the best of it, all grabbing knives, rolling pins, anything we could lay our hands on. I figured if we put as many armed men as possible up on the walls, nice and visible, they might deter a looter or two. Then I thought, begging your pardon, that if they saw an officer on the walls, well, it could only help us. So I went and borrowed your spare armour, master, and mighty big it was on me too. Thank the gods it never came to a scrap, we'd not have lasted long, that's for sure.'

'Totavalas and the slaves were so brave, darling. All they had for armour were a few pots and pans, and they would have risked their lives to defend us,' Salonina told me.

'I wanted to fight too,' Aulus said.

'Begging your pardon, Master Aulus, but your father would have had my guts pulled out if we let anything happen to you. That's why I told you and your mother to lock yourselves safely indoors, with a dagger each if things came to the worst.'

'Well, Totavalas, it sounds as though you're a better soldier than you are a body slave,' I began.

'You could be a little more grateful than that,' Salonina chided me.

I held up my hand for silence, then continued. 'You have shown bravery and loyalty far beyond what we could have expected of you. Would you stand up?'

The slave stood up, looking confused, and even more so when I took a delicate dagger from the table. Then I stood, and held the blade to his neck. His eyes looked questioningly into mine.

A quick flick of my wrist, and there was the noise of something breaking on the floor. I had cut the cord which held our tablet of ownership.

'You are now a freedman. Thank you, Totavalas.' I embraced him, as a grateful husband and father.

'Didn't you hear me? I said you're a lucky son of a bitch.'

I nodded my agreement, and watched the water splash off my sandals as I walked. Everyone in Colonia with any sense was indoors on that filthy evening a few days later as Valens and I strolled along the forum. It was early evening and the market stalls had long been closed or wheeled back home. We had the place to ourselves, aside from the miserable beggars on street corners, and the stray dogs that roam all cities hunting for scraps.

I had been very lucky in some things. A family that loved me, and I loved back. Salonina was pregnant, and my son was promised to the daughter of my best friend, a man who would certainly go on to be one of the greatest generals of our time. Totavalas had been an incredible find, and I was pleased when he decided to stay on with the family. Of course he had nowhere else to go until he earned enough money to make himself independent. He was here in Colonia with me. That agile mind of his would surely come in useful. My happy thoughts were marred by the brooding presence of the man walking alongside me. Valens, the schemer, the plotter.

Vocula's words had hurt me. I promised myself I would never become like Valens. All he cared for was himself. I had a higher loyalty, one that I had tried to instil in my son. *Pietas*. Honour the gods, the family and Rome.

'I was with Vitellius that night,' Valens continued.

'Night? Which night?' I said, coming out of my reverie.

'New year's day. Vitellius, me, one or two others. Vitellius has a wonderful cook. He needs to be good, to keep the big man happy.' He chuckled. 'Your messenger burst in when Vitellius had his fat face buried in some chicken. Nice touch, sending your standard bearer to the provincial capital to offer him the loyalty of his legion.'

'Thank you.'

'Was it also you who told the messenger to acclaim him emperor?' he asked.

'The aquilifer speaks for the legion, not me,' I said, cautiously.

'I must admit, you stole a march on me. Of course I had my men salute him as emperor the next day, but you stuck your neck out for him. He won't forget that.'

'Nor will you, it seems.' I didn't like where this conversation was going. This was the man, remember, who murdered an imperial governor for not being as ambitious as he was.

'You have one legion, and I guess Primigenia support you. I have mine, and there are more legions in Lower Germania than your province. We both have Vitellius's gratitude. Let us see where it takes us.'

We walked on in silence for the last part of the journey. The governor's palace loomed before us, flickering torches illuminating the faces of the guards stationed outside. They stood, motionless. Raindrops would fall on the curve of the helmet above the neck, then run off to drip constantly on to their shoulders and back, but they bore the irritation well.

'Legates Valens and Severus to see the governor,' I announced. The guards stood even straighter to attention, if that was possible, and we were allowed in. We were led by a slave through a long colonnade, flanked on either side by beautifully manicured gardens. It was a comfort to find luxuries like these on the banks of the Rhine, with barbarian tribesmen only a few miles away. It was a reminder of what Romans could achieve when they put their minds to it. Not gardens, I mean, but you could see the benefits of civilization and Roman rule from Britannia to Parthia, from the cold wastes of Germania to the searing deserts of Libya. But all of this is nothing without the army to defend it. Vitellius was a man the legions could follow. Gods, that line looks strange now that I read it back. But all those years ago it seemed true. All of Germania, the veteran legions of the West, had declared for Vitellius. Surely nothing could stop him now?

The slave showed us into a huge atrium, seemingly made all the bigger by the lack of furniture and art that you would expect a wealthy senator to display to his guests. We stood in silence for a time. I had nothing to say to Valens. But there was another question the man wanted to ask.

'What I still don't understand,' he said softly, 'is why you decided to join me in the first place.'

'I did not join you, Valens. I came to the conclusion that Galba was not the emperor I hoped he would be. The legions weren't happy either, so I made my choice for the good of the empire, not for myself.'

'Bollocks. You were Galba's blue-eyed boy, why would you betray him?'

'Did it not occur to you that Galba might want to get rid of me once he was in Rome?'

'So he shafted you like he did me, eh? Two of a kind, we are. Vitellius is weak; together we will rule our future emperor.'

'We are not alike,' I told him. 'Do you want to know why Galba ignored you?'

'Why?'

'Because I told him to,' I said venomously. 'Because you are a liar, a schemer and a murderer. We all have ambitions, Valens. Yes, I admit that when Galba first brought me into his conspiracy I was excited. Nero was rotting the empire from the top downwards, and Galba promised change for the better, and a career for me. But if you had gone through what I have these past months, you would not relish what we are about to do. Thousands of men have given their lives because of the ambition of men like you, and your scheming has made war inevitable. All I have done is choose which side is the right one for the good of the empire.'

While I spoke, Valens's face had gone redder and redder, his knuckles almost white. Before he could curse me, we heard a door open, and another slave gestured for us to enter. The two of us walked towards the door.

Valens whispered, 'So we are enemies, then?'

'You are no friend of mine, if that's what you mean,' I answered.

'So be it.'

'Severus, Valens, you're just in time. Slave, bring out some more wine. I want to be in my cups before suppertime.'

The huge Vitellius waddled over, took a moment to change his goblet to his left hand, and then took my right in his fleshy grip. 'Severus, I want to thank you for the confidence that you have shown in me.'

'The confidence of my legion, Caesar, more importantly than mine,' I replied modestly.

'Quite so, quite so. But please don't call me that. I am not a Caesar. Gods, my grandfather was Augustus's steward, only just a knight.'

'Germanicus, then?' Valens suggested. 'He made his name on the Rhine, and could have been Caesar if he wished.'

'Germanicus, eh? I like it. But we can attend to those matters later. First we must celebrate, feast and drink, preferably all at once!' Vitellius laughed boisterously, even spilling some wine on the floor.

'If the gods are willing,' he continued, 'I will be emperor. And as emperor, I will need two consuls.'

He drank heavily from his goblet, but still kept his clever eyes on both of us, watching our reaction. Vitellius may not have been a subtle man, but gods he could be generous! Me, consul?

Less than a year ago I had been sailing for Hispania, just twenty-nine years old, on the first step of my military career. Now this man was dangling in front of us the highest honour in the empire. Salonina would be wild with delight. The slave brought two more goblets on a silver tray. Valens and I picked them up. Forgetting our differences for a brief moment, we raised them in salute.

'To Aulus Vitellius Germanicus,' we toasted.

Vitellius smiled, and proposed his own toast: 'To the men who will give me an empire, and who will receive their just rewards.'

Timeline

AD 14 – Death of Augustus. Imperator, Princeps and Pater Patriae, Augustus cloaks himself in republican imagery while establishing the dynasty that will rule Rome. He is succeeded by his stepson, Tiberius.

AD 37 – Death of Tiberius. Vilified for the rise of treason trials and unleashing the ambitious Sejanus upon Rome, he retreats to Capri, bitter that the throne he had coveted for so long has given him no enjoyment. Chooses Caligula as his heir, allegedly so that his own reign will be remembered favourably in comparison.

AD 41 – Caligula's reign is short and savage. He declares himself a god, is thought to have had an incestuous relationship with his sisters and displays a flagrant disregard for the Senate. He is assassinated by a group of officers. There are few members of the Julio-Claudian dynasty left, but the Praetorian Guard find Caligula's uncle, the limping, twitching and stammering Claudius, and declare him emperor.

AD 54 – Death of Claudius. He is succeeded by his stepson Lucius Domitius Ahenobarus, who on his adoption as Claudius's son takes the name Nero. He ascends the throne aged seventeen. Britannicus, Claudius's only son, dies a few months later in mysterious circumstances.

AD 58 – Nero's mother, Agrippina, comes to regret helping her son to the throne. Over the course of three years he strips her of her power and honours, expels her from the imperial palace, and finally has her murdered.

AD 60–1 – Boudicca rebels against Rome. Finally defeated at the Battle of Watling Street by Suetonius Paulinus.

AD 64 – Nero 'fiddled while Rome burned'. The Great Fire of Rome: Nero blames and persecutes the Christians, then builds a new Golden Palace on the area cleared by the fire.

AD 65 – Gaius Calpurnius Piso leads a conspiracy to overthrow the emperor, because of his lack of respect for the Senate and his increasingly despotic rule. The conspiracy is betrayed and the plotters are executed, including Nero's old tutor, the philosopher Seneca.

AD 67 – Nero orders his most successful general, Domitius Corbulo, to commit suicide.

AD 68 – Aulus Caecina Severus is posted to southern Spain as the new quaestor.

Historical Note

I always make a point of reading the historical note, even the reams in the *Flashman Papers* that detail the lives of exiled maharajahs and tomahawk-toting tribesmen. But I don't think I've ever seen a hat tip to Wikipedia, and probably for good reason. I must admit that before writing this book, the 'Year of the Four Emperors' was little more than a phrase I had chanced upon in my studies. My tutorials in Roman history had focused on the period from Hannibal to Claudius, and then there had been a centuries-wide gap until the fall of the Western Roman Empire. I knew that I was going to write a Roman novel; the question was when to set it. This is where five minutes on Wikipedia gave me a story worth writing. Strictly speaking, this period should be known as the Eighteen Months of the Five Emperors, though I can see why the name didn't catch on. Imagine my surprise on finding such a wonderful central figure in Aulus Caecina Alienus, a soldier and politician intricately involved in the chaos of AD 68–9.

Like every aspiring historical novelist, I am sure, I set out with the intention to remain as close to the facts as I possibly could. The trouble is that we know next to nothing about Caecina before his betrayal of Nero for Galba. We know that he had been born in Vicenza, and that Tacitus calls him 'young, good-looking, tall and upstanding, as well as possessing inordinate ambition and some skill in words'. We also know that Galba had recruited him to his conspiracy once he had arrived as the new quaestor in southern Spain. When searching for what sort of background he came from, I wasn't able to find any other members of the Caecina Alieni tribe, but a few from the Caecina Severi. The fact that Alienus can be translated as 'the stranger' was too good an opportunity to waste. There had been a precedent for bestowing illustrious Romans with a new cognomen to honour their achievements, hence Coriolanus and Africanus. Given the fate of Caecina at the end of this period, why shouldn't a cognomen be used to shame a Roman? The other liberty I have taken with Caecina's background is to have given him a role in Boudicca's Revolt. It was customary for young men from the senatorial order to serve as tribunes for the first years of adulthood. For reasons of plot I had decided to make Caecina a close friend of Julius Agricola; so why not have them serving together in Britain, given they were the right age to have taken part in the campaign?

The Vindex Rebellion has also been left as unchanged as possible. Julius Vindex, a Romano-Gaul, did indeed write letters to his neighbouring governors. Most of them would probably have reported Vindex to Nero for fear of being accused of treason. Only Galba was brave enough to raise his head above the parapet. Again for reasons of plot, I added the father of the historian Tacitus to the early stages of the conspiracy, though we know very little about the historian's family background. As far as we know, Caecina most likely stayed in Spain for the spring and summer, diverting funds from his province to Galba's campaign, and was rewarded with the command of a legion several years before the usual age for the post of legate. However, placing Caecina in the Vindex Rebellion allowed me to demonstrate Caecina's talent for command and politics long before his decision to back Vitellius, and to show what it must have been like for a Roman to lead a barbarian army against his own kind.

The rest, as they say, is history. Or as close as I can make it. The dazzling Salonina, the scheming Valens, the indulgent Vitellius: all are historical characters who together engineered a civil war that would claim thousands of lives and establish a new ruling dynasty. I am indebted to the likes of Gywn Morgan for his book *69 AD: The Year of Four Emperors*, to Kenneth Wellesley for his work on the same subject, and to two St John's graduates, Philip Matyszak for his sharp and informative *Legionary: The Roman Soldier's Manual* and Adrian Goldsworthy for *Roman Warfare*. More importantly, I should be grateful that the works of the historians Tacitus, Suetonius and Plutarch have survived to this day; and more importantly still, that my parents gave me *Asterix & Obelix* when I was a boy, which gave me the Roman bug!

Henry Venmore-Rowland, 2011